BLIZZARD ON THE MOUNTAIN

OLIVIA MICHAELS

 Created with Vellum

ONE

September, one year ago

"ANY SIGN OF THE UNFRIENDLY?" Waylon "Ram" Ramson asked his brothers already on the scene of their current mission. He drove the speed limit—a true test of his patience—wary of speed traps. Waylon passed a semi while watching for one of those damn-ugly Tesla trucks that looked like something straight out of a video game, license plate reading W1NN1N.

"Negative outside the site, over." Ben's calm voice came through the radio.

"Negative at the entrance, over," Shane reported.

"Happy's a go," added Charlene King, referring to their principal, Felice, by her code name. Charlie was not part of Mountain Division, but worked with Shane at Watchdog. She agreed to help them today, to help keep Felice calm and focused. Plus, the former Swick had a special talent they needed in order to ensure Felice would be safe in the future.

Waylon glanced at Elias riding shotgun. "So, tonight? Cocks and Strippers?"

"You know it," Elias grinned.

Waylon smiled as he took the next exit and turned left. They were overdue for a night out at Cocktails and Chicken Strips and he was in the mood for some line dancing, flirting, and maybe a little more if he was lucky. And if he wasn't lucky, Elias was the best wingman. Whenever Waylon felt his confidence flagging, Lion was there to talk him up to whatever hottie he'd targeted.

Waylon put aside his thoughts and focused on the mission. They were almost there, and with no sign of Preston, he assumed the man was too cowardly to confront them. Waylon didn't understand men who took their insecurities out on people who were weaker than themselves. Why tear someone down to build yourself up? Especially your wife, the person you should love and cherish the most.

Even if she doesn't love you back.

Waylon ignored the old memory threatening to surface.

They turned left onto a brick-paved road and passed the sign for the gated community, The Reserve.

Shane's voice came back through the radio. "Elk to Moose, visual on Ram and Lion. Elk to Ram and Lion, target not sighted, over."

"Roger that," Waylon responded.

As they wound through the affluent neighborhood, Elias asked, "How much trouble do you think Preston would cause if he shows up?"

Waylon smirked. His brother had read his mind for the millionth time. "At most, sic his lawyer on us. He won't throw a punch."

"I disagree. I think you're underestimating him."

Waylon glanced at Elias. "Nuh-uh. He's just a punk."

"A punk with a concealed carry."

Waylon shrugged.

"Friendly wager?" Elias asked.

Wow. Elias considered old Presto a threat. 'Friendly wagers' went back to their military days. They'd make a friendly wager before a particularly gnarly mission as a superstitious ward against SNAFUs. It almost always worked.

Almost.

"Yeah, I'll take you up on that," Waylon said. "When I win," he grinned, "I get your truck for a week, starting tonight." Elias' 1973 Ford F100 Flareside was his pride and joy, and the front bench allowed for some killer makeout sessions.

Elias eyed him. "Okay, but if I win, you're taking the bus everywhere for a week."

"Damn, that's harsh." Waylon chuckled. "But since I'll win, deal." They fist-bumped as they pulled up to the McMansion.

From what Waylon had read in the SITREP, Felice had fallen hard for Preston, never suspecting that the man who wined and dined her and bought her a huge rock to impress her was a cold-hearted sociopath who gave her nothing but his fists after they were married. Waylon understood too well why it took Felice years and several tries to leave her abusive husband. That's when a man became the most dangerous, with his intimidation and sick possessiveness. Women sometimes died trying to leave monsters like Preston when they followed through with their threats.

Not today, Satan, Waylon thought.

Waylon backed the moving truck into the driveway. He'd used his own name on the rental to avoid suspicion if Preston started sniffing around. Ben appeared beside his window. For such a huge guy, Ben moved with surprising stealth, reminding Waylon of their other friend, Bear.

Waylon and Elias got out of the truck. "She ready for this?" Elias asked as they walked toward the front door.

Ben nodded. "Charlie took care of everything."

"Excellent."

Inside, they saw a few moving boxes in the entryway—Preston's things, no doubt, courtesy of Charlie. She'd even swapped the locks, and Ben planned to personally serve Preston the divorce papers, complete with an emergency restraining order that'd relieve him of his guns. If it were up to Waylon, he wouldn't even do old Presto the courtesy of removing his things to a storage unit. Felice deserved everything in the house, even if she didn't want her soon-to-be ex's clothes and knickknacks.

She should throw a celebration party with a bonfire fueled by his shit.

Ben called, "Charlemagne, all clear."

Charlie appeared in a doorway. She carried a plastic evidence bag in her gloved hands. Felice stood in the shadows behind her. Next to Felice was a beautiful German Shepherd whose attention was fully focused on Charlie—one of the dogs from Watchdog. The tall bodyguard turned and gave Felice a reassuring smile then nodded for her to follow as she gave a hand signal to the dog. When Felice stepped into the light streaming in from a tall window, Waylon clenched his jaw. He caught Elias' anger when the man stiffened beside him. Any decent man would.

Appalling.

The right side of Felice's face looked like it was still in dappled shadow—thanks to the purple bruises. Her eyelid was swollen half-shut and her bottom lip was split—more testaments to Preston's abuse.

She covered the side of her face, unwarranted embarrassment in her eyes.

Oh, darlin'. He deserves to die just for that.

"Thank you so much for your help." Felice spoke slowly through her broken, swollen lips, and her muffled voice hurt Waylon's heart.

The men brushed off her thanks, knowing she didn't owe them anything.

Waylon picked up a moving box. "Anything with red stickers going, right?"

Charlie pointed back toward the hallway. "Yeah, just a few pieces of furniture through there. But this"—she held up the evidence bag —"is going straight to the detective."

"I should keep it," Felice whispered. "Just in case."

Charlie placed a comforting arm around her. "This and the footage will be enough to keep him away from you for good."

Waylon and Elias exchanged a look. They knew justice wasn't always so simple, especially against men like Preston who had the money to hire the best lawyers and buy his way out of the justice system like so many others. Waylon swallowed the truth—Felice needed support, not discouragement.

"We've got your back in the meantime," he said, giving Charlie a nod. "Nice work."

Charlie shrugged, but Ben added softly, "Not everyone can break into a safe like that." A pleased pink bloomed across her cheeks as Ben praised her special talent.

"Let's get on the road while we're still in the clear," she told Felice as she grabbed their coats off a chair. "We can head to the safehouse at Watchdog right after talking to the detective."

Felice looked at everyone one by one. "Thank you again." She took a pair of oversized sunglasses out of her coat pocket and put them on before walking out the door. Waylon wondered how many times she'd used them before to hide the damage that she didn't deserve and wasn't her fault.

With everyone on high alert, they left the house. Felice's hands trembled as she clutched her purse, her eyes darting anxiously as she stepped outside, Charlie on one side and the German Shepherd on Felice's other, flanking her. Waylon tossed Preston's things into the truck, smirking as something fragile shattered on impact.

When Charlie and Felice got to Charlie's SUV, Charlie opened the passenger side door for Felice, her head on a swivel, always alert. The dog too, seemed poised for danger and hesitated jumping into the SUV where Charlie crated her. Watching their wariness, Waylon felt a flicker of doubt about the wager he'd made with Elias. He exhaled as Charlie's SUV pulled away, taking Felice to safety.

Ben stood behind him, holding another box. "Principal's safe, Ram. Charlie'll see to it." He dropped the box into the truck with a heavy thud, followed by another satisfying crunch as something broke inside.

Waylon shrugged. "I'm not worried, Moose," he lied. "Go talk to Lion if you want to reassure someone."

The truth was, Waylon should have felt calmer with Felice out of harm's way, but the hairs on the back of his neck prickled now.

Stop. We made the wager. Nothing's gonna go south.

Ben only smiled and turned back to the house.

As they packed the last of Preston's belongings, Waylon hefted a garish bronze lamp shaped like a woman's naked torso, her arms holding up a white glass sphere where her head was supposed to be. "This thing's uglier than the lamp from *A Christmas Story*. But the worst part is the shiny tits. How many times a day do you think old Presto rubbed them to wear off the patina?"

Elias grimaced. "Moving on, please."

Then came the crackle over Ben's radio, Shane's voice tense. "Incoming. Following, over."

Waylon tensed. "Well, shit. Guessing a neighbor squealed."

"Get ready," Elias said.

Ben took an envelope out of his jacket. "I've got to serve him anyway."

A moment later, Preston's Douchemobile rounded a corner doing about forty, then screeched to a stop, blocking the driveway as Shane's SUV rolled up behind. The driver's door opened and Preston Rudolph got out. Oozing arrogance, Preston strode up the drive. He pulled the side of his jacket back, revealing a shoulder holster. Waylon and his brothers fell into a shoulder-to-shoulder stance as Shane waited behind him, arms crossed.

Preston sneered. "Which one of you bastards is sleeping with the bitch? Or is it all of you?" He gestured at the moving truck. "I'm not letting you take her shit. I bought her everything she owns."

Waylon smirked. "Nah, that's your junk. And dude, you have shitty taste."

Ben stepped forward, envelope in hand. "I'm not going to bother addressing your absurd insults against Felice." He handed over the envelope. "Consider yourself served. Divorce papers and a protection order, effective immediately." Ben nodded at Preston's gun. "Colorado law requires you to turn in your firearms. I'm an FFL, so we can do this easy and I can take them now—or you can visit the sheriff."

Preston's face darkened with fury. "Fuck you. I'm not handing over anything. And she's not leaving with a single dime of mine." He tossed the papers to the ground like a toddler denied screen time and called out, "Felice! Get your sorry ass out here, now!"

"She's gone, Preston. You're not going to see her again," Waylon said, voice calm.

Preston's gaze flicked back and forth, trying to gauge Waylon. "You the one sleeping with her? Where the hell is she?"

"She's somewhere safe until you get the hell out of here."

Preston puffed up his chest, a hand twitching toward his gun, but he hesitated. "No. This is my house, my things. I have every right to be here. I'm calling the cops."

"Already did," Shane called from behind him, holding up his phone with a smirk. "Should be rolling up any second now."

The asshole turned on Shane and took a step closer, but Ben's voice stopped him cold. "You've been served, Preston, and you're breaking the law. Hand over your firearm and leave. Now."

He spun back around and glared at Ben. "Good. I'm on the city council," he sneered.

Waylon chuckled. "La-de-fucking-da. I'm sure they'll be more interested in what we found in your office safe."

Preston's face paled, though he managed a shaky scoff. "Bluffing."

"Are we?" Waylon's voice held steady. "We cracked it wide open."

Preston stiffened as the rest of the color drained from his face. "You broke into my house? Into my *safe*? I'll have you all arrested."

"Yeah, I don't really think so," Waylon replied, keeping a careful eye on Preston's hand, which had gone twitchy. "The false ledger?

The one showing how you've been using your council position to accept bribes from construction companies? There's enough in that safe to keep the DA busy for months."

"Bullshit! That's all lies—"

Ben's voice cut in, calm but firm. "There's more. Felice got you on video. She recorded your confession—then you hit her. That was for the last time."

A cruiser pulled up behind Shane's SUV, lights flashing, and two officers stepped out. Waylon recognized them immediately—Officer Sylvie Hoff, who was married to Watchdog's kennel master, and her partner, Officer Carla DeVivo. Shane nodded his greeting and they acknowledged him while focusing on Preston.

"Mr. Rudolph," Officer Hoff called, her voice steady, almost friendly. "Can we have a word?"

Preston was a pro at puffing out his chest. He pointed at Waylon, Elias, and Ben. "I want these men arrested for breaking and entering, theft—just look in that truck! Oh, and kidnapping. They took my wife!"

Carla raised an unimpressed eyebrow. "Is that so?"

"Kidnapping, wow," Sylvie said, exchanging a glance with Carla.

"Yes!" Preston insisted, his tone confident as if expecting the officers to side with him. "I want them all arrested."

Sylvie addressed Ben. "Felice is safe."

He nodded. "Good."

Preston's agitation grew, his gaze darting between Sylvie and Ben. "She sure as hell is not safe! They're all lying! These assholes *kidnapped* her."

"That's enough, Mr. Rudolph," Carla said, unfazed. "We know she's not a victim of kidnapping. However, she appears to be a victim of domestic abuse."

Preston let out a laugh, dry and bitter. "Domestic abuse? That's slander. I'll have your badges."

Sylvie's tone turned icy. "Your soon-to-be-ex-wife gave us a statement an hour ago, attesting to your abuse and she's pressing charges. She also provided evidence of your involvement in bribery."

The wild look in Preston's eye sent a chill down Waylon's spine. "Officers, he's been served and is refusing to turn over his firearm. Left shoulder holster," he informed them.

Carla and Sylvie nodded in acknowledgment, their posture alert. "Preston, put your hands up against the truck—"

"You can't just take my life apart!" In a flash, he reached behind his back and pulled a second gun. But before he could aim, Waylon's hand shot out, gripping Preston's wrist and twisting it with a swift, practiced move. The gun dropped to the driveway with a loud clatter as Waylon pinned Preston's arm and slammed him against the truck.

"Congratulations, you just added aggravated assault on a police officer to your list," Sylvie said as she stepped forward and removed the weapon from Preston's jacket while Carla read him his rights. Preston went slack, the fight finally draining from him.

"So," Elias said with a smirk, watching the officers haul Preston to the cruiser, "about that wager..."

AND THAT'S how Waylon found himself riding the bus to his paramedic job in Longmont.

It was killing him.

Waylon loved his rides—the Camaro, the Dodge Ram (of course he owned a Dodge *Ram*), the Jeep—and he loved adrenaline. Not only did he have to take a bus, but he had to take the one with the most stops along the way, slowing him down even further. If there was one thing that Ram hated, it was anything slow.

Worse, the bus was getting crowded and he wasn't too fond of that, either.

He'd just given the seat he'd snagged toward the back of the bus to a woman with a cane—feeling annoyed at all the people she'd walked past who didn't have the common manners or decency to give up theirs—when he spotted another woman standing in the crowd ahead of him. She was laughing hysterically. Waylon looked around to see who or what could have set her off and saw nothing but people staring at their phones or gazing listlessly out the windows at the gray clouds and drizzle.

So he studied her instead, which was pretty easy since she was gorgeous. Long, dark hair cascaded over her shoulders. She was slightly plump with the most tempting curves. What really caught and held his attention was the sparkle in her eyes and her easy laugh. But just what was she laughing at? When she ran her hand through her hair and tucked a lock of it behind her ear, he got his answer when he noticed the earbud.

Maybe she's listening to a funny podcast.

He wanted to be in on the hilarity—God knew he needed something to laugh at, but didn't everyone? A quick glance around the bus showed him tired faces, boredom, listlessness. Everything looked drab and washed out, and she was a bright spot of color with her laughter and flashing eyes. She was totally unselfconscious about who might be watching her, which was charming on one hand, and on the other, he couldn't help but worry that she was a little too unselfconscious, opening herself up to all sorts of trouble from pickpockets or anyone who might want to...

...Stare at her like you're doing right now? he asked himself. *Yeah, stop perving on the pretty lady already, before you creep her out.*

He started to look away just as she turned her head. Their eyes met one second before he could look away, and then she smiled right at him and he was hooked.

The bus came to another stop and a flurry of people crossed between them. That should have been the end of it, a moment shared and then back to being two passengers on a bus. But Waylon couldn't help looking back again and when he did, she was smiling at him—actually leaning a bit to the side to see around a tall man standing directly behind her. She laughed and Waylon chuckled. Her smile was infectious.

He tilted his head and pointed to his ear as he mouthed *What are you listening to?* Her eyebrows lifted just as the bus stopped again. In the space between people clearing out and others coming in to take their place, she pulled out an earbud and tossed it down the aisle just ahead of the next group of riders cramming themselves in.

Waylon grinned and put in the earbud, not sure what to expect, maybe some stand-up comedian.

"...found myself standing in front of an actual *penis museum!*" a woman exclaimed into his ear.

"Whoa!" He damn near ripped the earbud back out. Waylon was too stunned to catch where the hell the podcaster said this penis museum was so that he could avoid the place like the plague.

His shock was worth seeing the gorgeous woman howl at his reaction, much to the annoyance of the people around her.

You did that on purpose he mouthed, since there was no chance she'd be able to hear him, and that just sent her into more hysterics as she nodded vigorously. She put her hand out as her eyebrows rose and she mouthed *done?*

He shook his head. *Oh hell no. Challenge accepted.* Which just made her laugh again as she gave him a thumbs-up.

As Waylon listened, he realized it was a podcast about the misadventures of a woman traveling alone, and the stories she told were hysterical. He couldn't help but laugh just as loudly as the woman on the bus. Then the podcaster launched into a story about the next place she visited, a punk rock museum in a former public toilet—which, he had to admit, actually sounded pretty cool. Whenever the podcaster said something particularly hilarious, he glanced at the woman ahead of him to catch her response. Seeing her laugh just made the podcast that much funnier, until he was laughing right along with her.

Damn, she was magnificent when she laughed.

The bus stopped and more people crowded on. Seriously, was this the only bus in town? The new passengers prevented him from watching his new friend laugh, dammit. He couldn't see her now. As soon as he possibly could, he would make his way up to her, ask her name, see if she wanted to go for coffee.

No you won't.

Waylon squeezed his eyes shut and clenched his jaw. His heart ached as he remembered exactly why he wouldn't ask her out. Her or any other woman he found attractive beyond a night of dancing at Cocks and Strippers and maybe a hookup after.

She'll want her earbud back though, a hopeful little voice in his head told him.

So I'll give it to her, then get straight off the bus. I'm only a couple stops away from the hospital. I'll walk the rest of the way. Forget all about her, which is best for the both of us.

The bus lurched forward, the podcaster started talking about a boat trip to see puffins, and a moment later the podcast fuzzed out and went silent.

Did she turn it off? Were there too many people between them, blocking the signal? Not caring if it was rude, Waylon started pushing his way through the crowd to find her.

Don't, don't, don't!

Ignoring the scolding voice, he pushed on. But when he got to where she'd been standing, she was gone.

Maybe someone gave her their seat.

Waylon looked around the bus but there was no sign of her long, dark hair or her beautiful, sparkling eyes.

Leading Waylon to one conclusion—she'd gotten off at the previous stop without bothering to get her earbud back.

So, her better instincts finally kicked in. Good for her.

The bus slowed for the next stop and for a moment he was tempted to still exit, and instead of walking another block to the hospital, backtracking to see if he could find her.

Stop it, asshole! Don't you remember? Pathetic.

He gritted his teeth as he let the stop go by.

The next stop was his. When he stepped out of the bus in front of the hospital, he started to toss the earbud into a trash bin on the way in.

Wait. If she rides the bus the next day, it's only polite to return it if I see her, he rationalized to himself.

Waylon slipped the earbud into his coat pocket instead.

But she wasn't on the bus the next day, or the day after. He didn't see her the entire week. Or the next, when he talked himself into taking the bus again, even though the terms of the wager had ended *and* it was his day off.

He realized what he was doing. He told himself he was pathetic and gave up. Waylon went back to his Friday and Saturday nights at Cocks and Strippers. Back to using Elias as his wingman. Back to one-nighters. Easy fun, no deep connections.

He didn't throw away the earbud though. He kept it in his pocket, played with it like a worry stone every time he wore that coat.

Then he forgot about it when he put the coat away for the summer.

TWO

Early April

"AND THAT'S the last of it," Nurse Bea told Frankie as she switched off the pump. She blinked rapidly. "Sorry, I always get a little teary at this part."

Frankie's heart clenched. She'd grown close to Bea during this round of chemo and was sad to see her leave. Not only that—Bea was going all the way to Puerto Rico, with plans to stay at least a month after her fourteen-week assignment was over.

"I'm just glad you're still here for it," Frankie said as she blinked back her own tears. Then she mock-frowned. "Not sure I can forgive you for taking off. I'm running low on friends these days."

"I am so sorry about that." They were both quiet for a moment. Then Bea brightened. "Are you planning on trying that friend app I told you about?"

"Oh, shoot. Run it by me again." Frankie tapped the side of her head. "Chemo brain."

Bea smiled. "Of course. I'll write it down for you, too." Bea grabbed a pen and a scrap of paper out of her scrubs pocket. "It's BeMyNeighborCO," she said as she wrote it down. She handed Frankie the slip of paper.

Frankie pulled her into a hug and Bea squeezed her gently. "You're going to make it," Bea said. "I just know it. Now go ring the bell."

The bell. It was tradition for patients to ring the bell in the cancer center after they received their last chemo treatment. Frankie had heard it ringing twice since she'd started her infusions. Each time, she smiled and clapped for the lucky soul who'd come out the other side of hell. Hoping one day, she'd ring it, too.

She knew all too well that not everyone made it.

Shaking the dark thoughts out of her head, Frankie waited until Bea removed the needle from her port, then stood with Bea's help and crossed the room to the bell. As soon as she rang it, both staff and patients clapped and cheered for her this time. Frankie blinked back tears as she smiled. She heard someone behind her clear his throat and she turned.

Dr. Derek Sloane stood right behind her holding a dozen red silk roses.

Oh, great. How long has he been hovering over me?

Frankie didn't want to be rude or appear ungrateful in front of so many people—which is why she suspected Dr. Sloane had decided to give her the roses right then with all eyes on her. It didn't matter he was a doctor, the guy was a creep, that's all there was to it. She couldn't put her finger on why he made her skin crawl the minute she met him, but that didn't mean she had to tolerate him or his unappreciated attention.

He thrust the bouquet at her and opened his mouth to say something, when Bea swept in and grabbed the bouquet with a smile.

"How nice, Dr. D!" she said. "I'll carry them for Frankie down to the car." She shoved them under her armpit and gripped the handles of a wheelchair.

As the doctor's expression turned confused, then angry, Frankie plopped herself into the mandatory (and much-appreciated) wheelchair and Bea practically jogged her out the door and into the hall. Frankie felt like shit, but that wasn't stopping her from laughing.

The glass doors at the entrance whooshed open and Bea pushed her through. "Would you like the honors of dumping these in the garbage can, or shall I?" Bea asked her.

"Go right ahead." Then Frankie turned to look up at Bea. "Or am I being a bitch?"

"Oh, honey, no." Bea shoved the flowers into the can beside the door. "His behavior is totally inappropriate, but of *course* he's never disciplined for it." She rolled her eyes. "Makes me glad I'm moving on to my next assignment."

"Not me," Frankie said. "I'm going to miss you." She reached into her purse and pulled out a thank you card.

"Thank you. For everything," Frankie said as she gave it to Bea.

"Oh! It was my pleasure, Frankie." She pressed the card against her chest. "I promise, I'll keep in touch."

Frankie's smile masked her doubts. She'd heard that promise before.

Of course Bea saw through it. "I *will*," she assured her. "Especially since Dan—"

Frankie put her hand up and squeezed her eyes shut. "Please, no," she said, cutting Bea off. "I don't want to talk about it."

"I'm sorry." Bea rested her hand on Frankie's shoulder. "But if you ever do want to talk."

Frankie's ride share pulled up just then, thank God. She stood and hugged Bea one last time, and they made the obligatory patient/nurse joke—*you're wonderful and I hope I never have to see you again.* Frankie greeted the driver, got into the back seat, and closed her eyes.

When she got home, she woke her computer and glanced at her mom's latest email. She closed it halfway into the first sentence. Frankie picked up her phone and looked at the icon for the friend-finding app she'd downloaded that morning, BeMyNeighborCO.

Her finger hovered over the button before she tapped on it. She created a profile, read it over and deleted it, retyped it, then hit save before she could talk herself out of deleting it again. She wiped away a tear.

Frankie took a deep breath and thought, *The rest of my life starts now. Don't waste it.*

Then she cleared off her desk, moving everything over to a couple of chairs.

Frankie opened her desk drawer, took out a big sheet of rolled-up butcher's paper, and smoothed it out across her desk. She'd drawn a rough map of the world as if seen through a fisheye lens, with Colorado's rectangle huge and in the center. A tiny New Zealand was at the far left edge and a tiny Japan at the far right. She'd drawn a series of concentric circles out from the star that marked her rental house at the dead center of the paper. Words ran along the circles. The closest one read *Hike with my soulmate in the Rocky Mountains.*

Frankie tapped it and said, "Monday."

The next circle out was *Fancy dinner for two in Denver.* "Tuesday."

The next one read *Crazy-scary zipline with crazy-scary D!* She started to tap that one and say Wednesday but hesitated. She read some of the others. *Hang gliding—naked. Camp under the northern lights and count our blessings. Crazy stuff in Vegas that stays in Vegas. Snorkel with sharks and swim with mantas in Hawaii. Eat a hot dog in Fiji* - she smiled wistfully at that one and wiped away another tear. *Kayak in a cave full of glowworms in New Zealand. Dress like geishas in Kyoto.* Her finger trailed out from the center to the far edge of the paper. The far edge of the world.

The map blurred. Frankie dashed off to the bathroom to empty her stomach into the toilet.

She lay down on the cool tile of the bathroom floor, exhausted.

"Maybe I'll start with an epic session of staying in bed today."

MID-SEPTEMBER

FRANKIE STARED at the strange notification on her phone from some app called BeMyNeighborCO. The heading read: *You have a match!*

Right before she removed the app from her phone, she remembered.

Oh yeah.

Not only had she forgotten about signing up and creating a profile back in April, but the entire app had slipped her mind.

Stupid brain fog.

Frankie had only started feeling human again over the past couple of weeks. Before that, she'd been fuzzy and beyond absent-minded. It still wasn't entirely gone, but at least now she wasn't searching every room in her house for her phone while holding it.

Frankie sat down at her desk and read the notification again. *You have a match!* She sighed and wondered if she should bother clicking on it.

Is it weird to reach out to a perfect stranger just for friendship?

Frankie had friends already. There was the proof of it right there on the wall.

Or at least it *had* been proof, once.

She smiled wistfully at the framed photograph. Dressed up like a flapper and surrounded by eight other college-aged women, everyone holding up martini glasses in front of a bar in Missoula, Montana. The same martini glass sat on the corner of her desk, right under the photo. She'd stolen it from the hidden speakeasy she'd talked everyone into finding that night. The glass held a sand dollar and a couple of shells.

She picked up the glass and absently ran her finger around the rim as she looked at another photograph of the same group at the beach. They'd called her crazy that Saturday morning a couple weeks before finals, when she went around knocking on their doors at the crack of dawn. But, she still convinced them all to drive straight to the beach in Washington just to watch the sunset together before school ended and they'd all go their separate ways.

Frankie took the sand dollar out of the martini glass and studied it.

Funny how I was the only one to leave Montana after graduation.

She'd taken a job in Santa Fe for a while. Then, she moved to Arizona. Then all the way out to Wisconsin (never again—too cold and wet). Now, she was in Colorado. She was always the one to fly back home to see her friends, but she never minded. Frankie loved airports, loved flying, loved everything that had to do with travel.

Then after one brutal phone call, everything changed. She hadn't traveled out of state in almost a year.

She called her friends in tears and they promised to help her through. And they did at first, thank goodness. They all tried to outdo each other, honestly, with their gifts and their visits in the weeks after. Until things got really bad. Suddenly everyone's schedule filled up.

Now, months later, her friends barely texted.

Frankie returned her attention to the app, and the friend match. She clicked on the notification to open it, just out of curiosity more than anything. It was from someone named XMarkstheSpot. Well, their name wasn't actually XMarkstheSpot of course, that was just their username. Frankie's was...

"What did I name myself? Oh yeah. WereWwoofer."

A message from XMarkstheSpot popped up on her screen. It read:

> Hey, neighbor! I'm new to the area and I'm looking for someone who likes camping, mountain climbing, good conversation, and fine dining. Judging from your profile, that looks like you, too.

"Check, check, check and one more check for good measure." Frankie smiled.

This might not have been a bad idea at all.

She kept reading:

> I'd like to talk online first. Hope you
> understand. And I hope we're a match! –X

"I do understand, X." Frankie wasn't about to meet a total stranger in person—her brain fog wasn't *that* bad. She was glad X was being careful, too. There was a little green circle beside X's name. Frankie assumed that meant she was online. Frankie clicked on it and a dialogue box popped up.

> Hi? XMtS?

She only waited a few seconds before she got a response.

> LOL Just X will do. Hi WereWwoofer! Hey,
> I'm glad you answered.

Frankie grinned and felt the warm bloom of a new friendship in her chest.

> Me too. I actually forgot I'd installed this
> app, lol

Great, now I sound like an idiot.

> LOL! Well, I'm glad you remembered. I
> could use a friend. It's kinda lonely when
> you don't know anyone.

Whew. Maybe I don't sound like an idiot. Or X is just a nice person. Score!

> Yeah, I totally agree. I'm fairly new to
> Colorado, too.

Aw!!! No friends either yet? That sucks!

Frankie wasn't *completely* friendless here, and she'd been in Colorado for just over a year, but she leaned into what X was saying.

Well, no one I can have adventures with, know what I mean?

Yeah, I do! I was hoping to find someone who felt the same way, and here I lucked out right off the bat. :-)

"Aw!" X sounded awesome already. Maybe she'd be the kind of friend who was up for anything. Someone fun, someone who...

"Oh, Jesus!"

...just sent her a dick pic.

Frankie slammed her phone face down on the desk out of shock and sat there for a moment. "I specifically signed up for just women friends!"

She snickered.

"Someone sent me a dick pic."

Then she erupted in giggles.

"An actual dick pic. Whelp, I guess X isn't a woman."

She tried to stop giggling. She clapped her hand over her mouth but her laughter bubbled through her fingers.

"I *should* be appalled. But then again, it's not much of a dick."

She flipped her phone over and there it was in all its stumpy glory.

Frankie couldn't stop laughing. She took a screenshot and shrank the app so she could call one of her friends and tell her about it before forwarding it. And then stopped when she remembered.

"Yeah, right. Brain fog. The whole reason I was on this stupid app is because I don't have a friend I feel like I can call anymore." And she couldn't exactly show it to the one person she did have in town.

Her laughter evaporated. She blew out a breath as she set her phone down. She was tempted to complain to the site, but why bother? Frankie wasn't going to answer this guy, and she obviously wasn't going to use BeMyNeighborCO again.

Except that she didn't want the same thing to happen to another woman who might not laugh at a teeny weenie like Frankie did. She picked her phone back up and woke it. The Vienna sausage popped up on the screen.

"And you're blocked and reported. Good deed done."

She deleted the app. So much for that.

"What did I used to do before my life went to hell?" Frankie pursed her lips. "I don't think I spent *all* my time talking to myself."

Then she remembered. *Right. I used to go to the rec center.*

Where Stephanie works.

Frankie bit her lip. Crazy how everything had been stolen from her. How could she forget about *Steve*?

"Well. Time to get it all back."

Her heart clenched. That would be impossible—she couldn't have *everything* back, not anymore. Frankie blinked back sudden tears.

"At least I can see how much is left. Steve will be surprised to see me."

Frankie stood up. She found her purse and then her keys inside her purse—a banner day—and went out to her car.

She was halfway to the rec center when she remembered her gym bag sitting on a bench beside the front door.

Shit.

Half an hour later, she stood at the entrance and stared up at the *Welcome New Members!* banner over the door.

Members. She snickered, remembering the dick pic.

She wasn't a new member (ha-ha), but when the heck was the last time she'd been there? A year? Over a year?

Hell if I know. Her life had been put on hold for so long, she'd lost track.

She'd hoisted her gym bag up on her shoulder, which was a lot skinnier now and more apt to let things slip right off again, and walked up to the automatic glass doors. Cool air whooshed out at her, bringing the familiar smells of exercise mats, guys' obnoxious body spray, tennis balls, a faint wisp of chlorine, and no hint of sanitizers or bland food whatsoever.

Smells like plain old life in there.

I've missed it.

The Colorado sun was brutal that day and it took her a few blinks to get her eyes to adjust to the darker interior. When they did, the first person she saw behind the receptionist's desk was gorgeous, funny, uplifting, snarky Stephanie. In her seventies and full of energy, Frankie wanted to be her when she grew up.

Not that Stephanie had necessarily grown up herself.

When Stephanie looked up and saw her, it took her a few seconds to recognize Frankie. But when she did, the most beautiful smile bloomed on Stephanie's face.

God, I've missed you, too. I just didn't know it.

Frankie saw the same emotion reflected right back at her in Stephanie's smile.

"Hey, Steve." It was their little joke, calling each other by their guy names.

"Been a while, Frank," Stephanie said as she stood up and circled the desk. "When you cancelled your membership, I wondered what happened. Wasn't sure you were ever coming back."

"Wasn't sure I was coming back either. But here I am."

The hug Stephanie gave her threatened to make Frankie cry.

"Welcome, stranger," Stephanie said. "I've missed you to hell and back."

"That's funny. I've been to hell and back and I didn't see you there."

Stephanie held Frankie at arm's length and looked her up and down. "Not *my* fault. I'm very mad at you."

"Why?"

"You didn't tell me about the cancer." Stephanie's eyes misted over. "I would have helped."

Frankie didn't have to wonder how Stephanie knew. Her body had changed so much since the last time she'd been to for a yoga class or a workout. She could have cried, thinking about the muscle she'd lost. But she didn't want Stephanie's pity.

"Eh. It was boring. Zero stars, would not recommend."

Stephanie pursed her lips. "You did have help though, didn't you? It was a big thing you went through, looks like."

"And I'm through it." Frankie shut down that line of questioning. It would only make Stephanie feel worse about not knowing and helping. "So. Do I need to renew my membership?"

Steph paused, studying her, and Frankie hoped she wouldn't pry any further. To her relief, she turned, went back behind her desk, and sat down. "Nope. I'll just reactivate you. Once a member, always a member."

Frankie's mind went right back to the dick pic. She smothered a giggle.

Stephanie typed something into her computer that reactivated Frankie's membership. Then she propped her elbows on the deck, laced her fingers together, and dropped her chin on them. "All right, tell me what's so funny, Frank. I could use a good laugh."

Frankie rolled her eyes.

"Oh, it's stupid."

"Stupid's fun. I'm all ears, Frank."

"Okay, fine. I downloaded an app a couple months ago, then forgot all about it. BeMyNeighborCO. It's for finding local people to hang out with. Ever heard of it?"

"Nope." She raised an eyebrow. "People to hang out with?"

"Not like *that*. It's not a dating app."

Steph grinned. "My mistake."

"Well like I said, I signed up, forgot all about it, and then I got a match this morning. So I clicked on the notification to open it, just out of curiosity more than anything." Frankie told her about the dick pic.

Stephanie howled "You are kidding me!"

"Nope!"

"Lemme see it!" Steph held out her hand.

"Oh, God no!"

"Come on."

Frankie laughed. "Fine." She unlocked her phone and scrolled through her screenshots. She frowned. "Hang on. It should be the first one but I can't find it. I must have accidentally deleted it when I blocked the jerk and reported him. I deleted the app, too."

"Good deed done," Stephanie said. "I'm sure you'll be rewarded." Once she got her laughter back under control, Stephanie keyed something else into the computer. She looked back up at Frankie and tilted her head, lips pursed again.

Oh no. She's studying me for real. That can't be good.

"You know, it's funny that you were looking for a friend to have adventures with, because I just so happen to need some help with that."

"You need an adventure buddy?" Frankie perked up. Steve was a ton of fun.

"Well, not *me*, exactly. But I need one for the Adventure Buddies Club. It's...a new thing we're doing."

"Okay, what is it?"

Stephanie smiled. "It's exactly what it sounds like. Buddies meet every Saturday morning and we go out together to have adventures. I'm one person short, or else it's a no-go."

"One person short?"

Steph nodded. "Buddies are paired up together and I ended up with an odd number."

Frankie's stomach dropped. Was she trying to set her up with someone? "And you want me to fill out the roster."

"Correct. What do you say? It starts...oh, let's see. Saturday, October first."

"I...don't think—"

"Please?" Stephanie gave her big puppy-dog eyes.

"You don't fight fair."

"Nope. Never have, never will."

Frankie blew out a breath. "How...vigorous is it?"

"Not very, to start. Gotta test out the group's physical tolerance. First outing is a simple getting-to-know-you hike." Stephanie gave her the charming grin Frankie absolutely could not resist. "What do you say, Frank?"

"Fine, fine, I'm in." She pointed at Stephanie. "But only because you're a big old brute, coercing me into this."

"Aw, you say the sweetest things." Stephanie winked. "You'll love it. Trust me."

"So long as it's a 'just friends' thing." She giggled.

"Of course it is. Consider it your reward for your good deed."

THREE

One Week Later

"WAYLON!" Stephanie West, Receptionist Extraordinaire, waved Waylon over to her desk the minute he stepped inside the rec center. Waylon's friend, Gabe, stood beside the desk, giving Waylon a look that said *Good luck and beware, brother.*

Oh boy. With Stephanie, that look could mean anything.

"Yes, Steph?" Waylon asked when he got to the desk. "What can I do for you?"

"I've started a club," Stephanie told him, beaming.

"A club." Waylon looked at Gabe, hoping for some insight, since he was one of the rec center managers. He counted off on his fingers as he said, "Steph, I thought you already had a book club, a yoga club," he decided to yank her chain, "a cougar club..."

"Hey now." She ran her hand down her silver-white hair, "you guys are the ones who refuse to let me join your little animal-nickname club. I still want to be Cougar."

"Never, Steph," Gabe said.

She pursed her lips. "You are not my favorite boss anymore, T-Wolf." She turned her attention back to Waylon. "Anyway, I've started a new club."

"Okay, I'll bite. What kind of club?"

"An Adventure Buddies Club! We meet every Saturday in October. It's for rec center members who maybe wanna go do activities and don't have a buddy to go along with them, thus the name." She pointed at Waylon. "And *you're* signed up."

"Wait, what?" He looked at Gabe to see if this was some kind of joke, but going by his brother's expression, this was news to him. "I *have* buddies. There's one of them now." He pointed at Gabe, who did him the courtesy of nodding. "If I wanted to go hiking and asked him, he'd come with me."

"That's true, I would," Gabe confirmed.

"So I don't need to be in a, what'd you call it? Activity Bros Club?"

"Adventure Buddies Club! Sheesh. I know you have friends, but it starts this Saturday and I'm one person shy and I haven't had any takers. So, tag, you're it." Stephanie picked up a pen and wrote Waylon's name on a sign-up sheet. "I've got you paired up with Frank."

"Who's Frank?" Gabe asked.

"I don't think Frank's been into the rec center since before you started here, Boss."

Waylon shifted his gym bag on his shoulder. "Why do I need to be paired up for a club?"

"Waylon, I'm surprised you don't get it. It's baked into the name, don'cha see? You go to Cocktails and Chicken Strips with a wingman, right?"

He rolled his eyes. "Not anymore." Not since Elias met and married Wren Stapleton.

"Everyone needs someone watching their back or it's not as fun, is it? The Adventure Buddies Club is about having fun and having a Buddy to watch your back. And since I'd hate to disappoint Frank after being gone so long, I've signed you up. Problem solved."

"Why me? Why do *I* have to do this?"

"Because you don't want to let down an old lady, do you?" Steph stuck out her bottom lip into the biggest pout ever and fluttered her eyelids at him.

Waylon crossed his arms. "You have never once in your life thought of or called yourself an old lady, Stephanie."

"No, but I *will* do whatever it takes to get my way. Just ask Gabe."

"She's a monster."

"*Thank* you. You're my favorite boss again." Stephanie beamed at Gabe. "Now, what do you say, Way?" She grinned at her own rhyme. "Are you on the bus, Gus? Is it a new plan, Stan?"

"*Stop*." Waylon looked at the ceiling then back at Stephanie.

She's going to be insufferable if I say no.

"Fine."

"Yes!" Stephanie fist-pumped the air.

"But only one time. This Saturday, and then that's it. I'm not doing this every week."

She narrowed her eyes. "So then you're gonna leave Frank high and dry for the rest of October? Not cool. Actually, worse than not cool."

Dammit. He hated the way Stephanie was appraising him.

She's thinking of ways to make my life about as fun as jock itch if I don't agree to help.

"Okay. But, you have to promise me that you'll keep looking for a replacement, and the minute someone else signs up, I'm out, free and clear."

"Hmm." She continued to study him like he was a frog pinned to a board and she had a dissecting kit. Then she smiled. "Okay. Deal."

Waylon didn't trust that smile one bit. "You *have* to look for a replacement."

"Okay."

"*Actively* look. You can't hide the sign-up sheet."

"Right."

"And you need to tell people—out loud—that you need one more person."

"Yup." Stephanie popped the P.

"And the second you find someone else, I'm out, no exceptions."

"Got it. No exceptions." She grinned in a way that murdered his trust.

"Do I have your word?"

"Sure do." Her grin got wider.

"Shake on it."

"Want me to spit on my palm first?"

Waylon flinched. "Please, no."

Stephanie stretched out her thankfully dry hand. "Deal."

Waylon shook her hand. "Deal."

He spent the next three days dreading Saturday morning. But a promise was a promise, and now Waylon was standing in the rec center bright and early when he should have been home nursing the hangover he'd worked hard to build Friday night at Cocks and Strippers. At least he hadn't gone home with anyone, not that he'd had the opportunity. He danced with a couple of women but neither seemed interested in anything more than a dance.

"Adventure Buddies," he scoffed under his breath. "I don't need this."

But he kind of did now. Last night was proof he needed a wingman.

And now Elias has Wren.

Bear and T-Wolf were married too, so if they went they'd bring Ellie and Rochelle along. Hanging out with three couples was not conducive to picking up hotties.

Of his single friends, Shane was out. And Ben? Well, the meat market was never really Moose's scene. He tended to be the designated driver and the one who talked his brothers out of making bad choices a time or two. Waylon had no one to talk him out of his bad choices except himself, and where was the fun in that?

I wonder if this Frank guy is single. Yeah, probably, or he'd be out with his wife or girlfriend on a Saturday, right?

Wait a minute.

Stephanie knew he'd lost his wingman. Maybe Frank needed a wingman, too.

That's why she signed me up. Sneaky woman!

And speak of the devil, there she was, popping out of a doorway and smiling like a kid with a new puppy.

"Come on back," Stephanie said as she cocked her arm and waved him down the hall. "We're all waiting for you, slowpoke. Frank's feeling like the odd man out." She turned and disappeared back into the room.

Waylon made his way down the hall, feeling like he was nine years old again, starting at a new school and hoping to make friends. He shook off the ridiculous feeling. Then again, he'd met his brothers at the age of five, when his family moved to Colorado. They'd recognized a kindred spirit and brought him right into the pack. Maybe this would go the same way.

Either Frank would make a great wingman or Waylon would tell Steph to find someone else, double-time.

He stopped in the doorway and looked in. The room was full of people talking to each other in pairs. A couple of women by the window, another pair sitting down and chatting like they were old friends. Two sets of men rounded out the group, leaving one person standing alone.

A woman.

What the hell?

Waylon definitely did not need a wing*woman*.

She stared at her shoes as Waylon studied her. The word pixie came to mind. She had a slim build hiding under clothes that looked a couple sizes too big. She wore a tight beanie and not a strand of hair escaped it, so it must have been short.

Waylon turned to Stephanie, standing just inside the room. "Uh, Steph? Where's Frank?"

He hoped she'd tell him that she'd changed her mind about having a Buddy and the pixie-woman was Stephanie's partner for the day, and that Frank was off taking a leak.

"What? Are you blind? Frank's right over there." She pointed at the woman. "Hey, Frankie!"

Her head shot up when Stephanie said her name. Her eyes, touched with sadness, looked almost too big for her thin face.

Waylon liked his women curvy, with long hair he could play with —tug on during sex. And he liked them cheerful and drama-free— there for a good time, not a long time.

Whatever joke Stephanie was playing, Frankie was a great, big nope. The sad-eyed pixie wasn't his type, even if those big eyes were the most beautiful he'd ever seen.

But as they studied each other, the corner of Frankie's mouth quirked up and those gorgeous eyes quickly lost their melancholy look as they took him in. They widened even further, obviously liking what they saw as she started walking toward him. Her gaze stirred something inside him that wanted to cross the room to get to her before she got away. He felt his heart race and almost took a step towards her.

Almost.

What am I thinking? Waylon shook himself out of the spell her eyes cast.

She looks too eager, he told himself. He did not relish spending the day with this wisp of a woman who would probably 'accidentally' fall into his arms every ten feet and ask him if he'd accepted veganism into his heart yet.

Waylon frowned at her, then watched as the eagerness in her eyes dimmed. He immediately regretted it.

There had to be some way of getting out of this. He turned fully toward Frank, hoping maybe he could still talk both her and Steph into being partners, and he could get back to his life.

But as soon as he turned, Frank took one look at his shirt and pulled a face.

Quite a face, actually. Like she'd just picked a fuzzy up off the floor and realized it was a spider squirming in her fingers instead.

What's that about?

Had he spilled something disgusting on his shirt? He looked down and saw nothing wrong with it. It was one of his favorites; the "Run for 911" race shirt he'd worn for a 5K benefitting the ER—a shirt that Waylon thought made his pecs look particularly good.

The pixie stopped in front of them and looked at Stephanie. "Steve. You didn't."

Steve?

Stephanie shrugged nonchalantly. "I had no choice, Frank. We were short one person, so," she gestured at Waylon. "There you go." Then she introduced them. "Waylon Ramson, meet Francesca—Frankie to her friends—Whitmore. Frankie Whitmore, meet Waylon —Ram to his friends—Ramson."

"Ram, huh?" Frankie inspected him again as she sucked in her lower lip and Waylon pretended that it didn't send a jolt straight to his crotch.

What the hell was that?

"I don't need a Buddy," Frankie told Stephanie. "Especially not this one." She dismissed him with a wave.

Whoa, wait a minute. What's wrong with having me *for a buddy?*

"Nope. You have to have a buddy, Frankie. Thems the rules."

"*You* don't have a buddy," she pointed out.

"Told you, that's because I'm in charge," Stephanie said. "I don't need one."

"Yes you do. I'll be your buddy, and we'll send Mr. ER Guy back home where he belongs." Frankie brushed her palms together— smack-smack—like she'd just finished doing a distasteful job. "Done."

"Hey, now, wait a damn minute," Waylon said. "What's wrong with me? I'd make a perfectly good Adventure Buddy."

Frankie crossed her arms. "Maybe for someone else, but not for me. And Steve should've known better." She eyed Stephanie, and Waylon witnessed something he never thought he'd see.

Stephanie flinched and looked away.

Frankie reacted immediately. Her frown disappeared, replaced by absolute dismay. "Steve, I'm sorry. I didn't mean to come across so harshly."

Stephanie shrugged while she looked at the floor, obviously crushed. "No worries. You don't want to be an adventure buddy, Waylon *really* doesn't want to be an adventure buddy—"

"Wait, I—" they both said simultaneously, then looked at each other.

Frankie touched Steph's arm. "I'm sorry. I know you're excited about the Adventure Buddy Club. I am, too." She gave Waylon a soft smile. "I think I can work with him."

Waylon hated to see Stephanie upset—that's how he rationalized his next words.

"Yeah, and I think I can work with her."

He tried to pretend his change of heart had nothing to do with that soft smile Frankie gave him. A smile that reached all the way to her big blue eyes and took some of the sting out of her snarky "ER guy" comment.

Stephanie's head snapped up as she clapped her hands and smiled wide.

"Excellent! I know you two are going to make great buddies. Now, let's shake some tailfeathers and go on an adventure." She clapped her hands over her head to get everyone's attention. "Now that we're all present and accounted for, please sign one of the release forms on the table over there. Then follow me if you want to have fun!"

As Stephanie strutted out of the room, Waylon and Frankie shared another look.

One that said they both realized they'd just been played like a pair of violins.

THE REC CENTER bus made a left off of Peak to Peak Highway onto Overland and said goodbye to paved road. From here, it was well-graded dirt and gravel all the way to the Ceran St. Vrain trail. Waylon had wanted to drive up by himself in his truck, but Stephanie wasn't having it.

"On the bus or you're out of the club, and I'm not letting you out of the club," she'd shouted to him from the driver's seat after all the other Buddies turned over their release forms and boarded. Including his so-called Buddy, Frankie. Waylon got on and took the last seat beside her. She barely acknowledged him except to move her pack closer to her window to make room for his.

Waylon sat with his arms crossed, sneaking glances at his "Buddy" who was pointedly staring out the window. Her posture was stiff inside her oversized jacket, and the tight beanie covering her head made her look even more self-contained, like she didn't need anyone at all, especially not him.

Not that Waylon cared what Frankie thought of him. Nope, not at all.

Not even when her face lit up as she first caught sight of him. Definitely not when the sadness lifted from her eyes. And especially not when her attitude turned on a dime and she didn't want anything to do with him.

Waylon knew *his* reasons for not wanting to be partnered up with her. Good, sound reasons. They didn't even have to do with Frankie specifically—he would've resented any woman Stephanie chose for him. He didn't want or need a matchmaker setting him up on a blind date.

So why does Frankie think I'd *be such a bad partner?* The thought niggled at him. Obviously, she'd been game for this match-up. Hell, maybe she'd even asked Stephanie—oh, wait, *Steve*—to find her a man.

And I don't measure up. He fought back the next thought, but it clawed its way through. *Wouldn't be the first time.*

Waylon leaned forward slightly, trying to catch Frankie's eye, but she kept her face angled toward the passing trees.

He cleared his throat.

Frankie turned her head away from the window. She looked vaguely hopeful again. He felt a small thrill of victory. At least she wasn't ignoring him anymore.

"Yes?"

But now that he had those damningly beautiful eyes on him, his mind went blank, so he just blurted out, "What is it?"

She tilted her head. "What is what?"

"What is your problem with me?"

Boom. The hope in Frankie's eyes disappeared as they widened in surprise. "*My* problem with *you?*"

"Yeah. You gave me the stink eye back at the rec center"—he tried to forget the first look she'd given him, the one that woke his entire body up—"as soon as you got a good look at me. I don't see what's so terrible about me being your Adventure Buddy. I'm dependable, good in a crisis—"

"And modest, too," she said flatly.

Waylon chuckled despite himself. "Okay, fair. But seriously, what's your deal with me? Do I remind you of someone? An ex maybe?"

The faintest glimmer returned to her eyes as she studied him for a moment. "You don't remind me of an ex, no." The glimmer disappeared. "But you're one to talk about who gave who the stink eye. You gave me one first, *buddy*."

"I...didn't..." he lied. "I mean, I didn't, mean to, um..."

But too late, Frankie's jaw tightened and she turned back to the window as her arms wrapped protectively around her torso. Whatever tiny crack he'd made in her armor had been sealed up tight again, and it was his own damn fault for lying, just not for the reasons she assumed.

Great. Just great.

Dammit, Stephanie.

Waylon checked his watch. At least Steph was making good time. She drove with the confidence of someone who firmly believed speed limits were suggestions. If she drove like the little old lady she almost never claimed to be, this awkward ride would've felt like an eternity.

Okay, a longer eternity than it already is.

With Frankie glued to the window, he hoped Stephanie hiked the way she drove, and that this stupid day would be over that much faster.

FOUR

Great. Just great. The first hot guy my body's responded to in a year and I repulse him.

Frankie glanced at Waylon out of the corner of her eye.

My reward for my good deed. Some reward. Why do I get stuck with all the jerks?

When Waylon cleared his throat on the bus to get her attention, she thought for one stupid moment that he might be apologizing, or maybe striking up a conversation with her like she was a normal human being, which would have at least made the day tolerable.

Maybe even fun.

But no. Her hot, full-of-himself 'Buddy' wanted nothing to do with her beyond wondering what she had against him. After the cold look he'd given Frankie when he'd gotten a better look at her, no way was she going to give Waylon the satisfaction of telling him the other reason why she didn't want to waste a perfectly lovely autumn day paired up with him on a hike.

Stephanie set me up with him because she feels sorry for me.

Frankie batted the thought away. She didn't want pity. Now that she was done with her cancer treatments, she wanted normal again.

More than that, she wanted the adventures she'd promised herself once she got better. The last thing she needed was someone humoring her—or worse, trying to hold her back. And Mister Whatever-Hospital-Related-Job would undoubtedly do just that once he realized she'd been a cancer patient. He'd be over-the-top protective, reminding her of what she couldn't do.

She pulled her beanie down lower and sank into the coat that had been a little tight on her last fall. She wondered again, *How could I have let Stephanie guilt me into this?*

The bus pulled into a parking lot at the Ceran St Vrain trailhead. Outside the bus, the gorgeous day waited for them. A few aspens were starting to turn, leaves like golden coins flickering and flashing in a cool breeze. In a couple weeks, the trail would be lined with solid-yellow trees against dark evergreens—and packed with leaf-peepers.

Waylon grabbed his pack and scooted off the seat without a word to Frankie, getting out ahead of the other Buddies. Frankie picked up her daypack and let the people behind her exit until only she and Stephanie were left. She tried not to glare at Steph, who was already squinting out the window at Waylon.

"Are you sure I can't be *your* Buddy?"

"Nope," Stephanie answered, her eyes still on Waylon. "Once we hit the trail, you guys will be fine."

Frankie sighed. "I don't think so. He really doesn't like me."

Stephanie turned and smiled at Frankie. "Don't be so sure."

"Pfft. We have nothing in common."

"Eh, I'm pretty sure you'll find something in common today."

"I doubt it."

Stephanie rolled her eyes. "Go on, scoot, Ms. Pessimism." She shooed her off the bus then stood up and followed.

Waylon stood off to the side. The other Buddies were all getting along great. Frankie envied them. She reluctantly joined Waylon, who at least didn't scowl or walk away this time.

"All right, every...buddy." Stephanie smirked at her own pun.

"Today's hike is an easy one to get us warmed up. It's a bit low on adventure but high on getting to know your Buddy. Hopefully, it won't be too boring. Follow me." She turned and headed for the trailhead as everyone followed her two-by-two.

Like she's a modern-day Noah. Frankie couldn't help grinning. Out of the corner of her eye, she watched Waylon glance at her, then back up to Stephanie. The corner of his mouth quirked up for a fraction of a second—*maybe he sees it that way, too?* she wondered—before he went back to scowling.

Well, at least the sun came out for a second before going back behind the scowly clouds. She wondered what he'd look like smiling for real.

Probably gorgeous. No. He's already gorgeous. More *gorgeous.*

"Ugh," she breathed. That earned her another scowl.

Guess I'll never know.

Frankie and Waylon fell in at the end of the line. She was disheartened at first when Stephanie said it might get boring. She definitely was not going to get to know Waylon better. It had been a long time since she'd gone hiking in the mountains and she already felt her heart pounding in the thinner air. She was so out of shape. The upside was that maybe she'd get kicked out of the group by default if she couldn't keep up. But that was the only upside.

She gritted her teeth as she thought, *I've lost so much. This is the least of it.*

Stop thinking that way. Look at what you do have. A good life. A beautiful day in the mountains. Another chance. She glanced at Waylon. *And admit it—something nice to look at.*

Maybe it was a blessing that they weren't talking. Frankie was already getting out of breath and they'd been walking what, fifteen minutes? Talking would have made it worse. She promised herself that she would hit the rec center every day next week before Saturday's adventure.

They continued on silently until they got to a rough wooden bridge spanning the river. Waylon walked down the middle while

Frankie grabbed the guard rail, wondering just how long this trek was going to be. They made it halfway across the bridge before she said, "This whole thing is a mistake. I'll tell Steve I'm done after this hike and she can find you a new partner."

Waylon frowned. "What do you mean find *me* a new partner? Steph's already on the lookout for someone else for you."

Ouch. That hurt. And it took her by surprise. She hadn't caught Waylon asking Stephanie for a replacement this morning.

He didn't even want to give me a single day.

She was so upset she almost missed what he said next.

"That was our agreement when she roped me in. I thought I was getting paired up with some guy named Frank. She obviously knew I'd back out of a blind date."

"Huh?" Frankie blinked at him. "What do you mean a blind date?"

"That's what this is, isn't it? You needed a 'Buddy'—"

Frankie stopped in her tracks. "Hang on. I didn't need a Buddy, *you* needed a Buddy."

Waylon had kept on walking, but now he stopped and turned. "Me?"

"Yeah you. Steve told me she was one person short and talked me into joining." She crossed her arms and debated marching right back to the bus.

The rest of the Buddies crossed the bridge and disappeared around a bend as Waylon walked back to her. "Hang on. When was that?"

"A little over two weeks ago."

Waylon shook his head slowly. "She told me only a couple *days* ago that she needed an extra—for Frank, specifically. I told her I'd only do it if she promised to actively find someone else to take my place."

"Oh." Frankie hated the way her chest loosened when she realized Waylon had wanted out before he'd even met her. It wasn't personal.

"So...you're telling me that Stephanie set you up, too?" Waylon asked.

"Of course she set me up." Sudden anger flared inside her chest. "Wait. Do you think I asked her to do this? To force some total stranger to spend the day with me? For the record, I thought *you* were going to be a woman."

"That's not what I said."

Frankie started walking again, sliding her hand along the top of the wooden railing. "How dare you think I'd be desperate enough to coerce—"

Something sharp poked her arm between her wrist and the cuff of her jacket.

"Ow!" She stopped and examined her arm. A long splinter had pierced her and lodged itself sideways under her skin.

"Oh, shit." Her heart sped up as she stared at it and her brain screamed *Infection!*

How many germs were on the damn thing? Puncture wounds were the worst. God, how could she be so careless? Panicked, she started tearing at her skin, trying to rip the splinter out of the wound before it was too late.

FIVE

One minute, Frankie was chewing out Waylon—unfairly, he felt—and the next she was clawing at her arm and making panicked sounds.

"What? Did something bite you? Bee sting? Shit, are you allergic?" He shrugged off his pack, ready to find and break the ampule of epinephrine and draw it up to give her a shot, as he studied her for signs of anaphylaxis.

Frankie shook her head violently. "No, no, it's a really bad splinter," she said in a shaky voice.

Waylon relaxed. *Is that all? Not much of an adventurer, is she?* Then again, Frankie hadn't signed up for the Adventure Buddy Club on her own. Steph had fooled her, too.

"Here, let me see." Waylon reached for Frankie's arm and she flinched as she took a couple steps back, her hand covering her wound. He thought she was just being stubborn until he saw the whites surrounding her irises and realized she'd flinched out of fear. He'd seen that look a million times from patients.

He softened immediately. "Hey, whoa now. You're okay," he said gently, offering her a reassuring smile. "I'm not going to hurt you. We're Buddies, remember?"

Frankie's breathing slowed. She nodded and smiled reflexively. "Sorry. You probably think I'm some crazy germaphobe."

"You don't need apologize." He reached out tentatively. "Can I see your arm? Because you were right about Mr. ER Guy. I'm a paramedic."

"Figured." She swallowed hard, still clutching her arm as she took another step back.

But now it was starting to make sense to Waylon—the way Frankie's lip curled when she got a good look at his shirt. Maybe it wasn't him specifically she didn't like. Maybe she wasn't too crazy about medical personnel in general.

"My shirt gave it away, huh?" He grinned.

She nodded.

"Let me get my first aid kit." He set his backpack on the bridge and unzipped the top, then pulled out a red bag with a white cross on it. He unzipped it, took out a small bottle of hand sanitizer, flipped the cap open, and squirted it into his palm.

Frankie took one look at the bottle and went pale. She backed up against the railing and looked like she was considering jumping into the river.

"Well, now I know for sure you aren't a germaphobe or you'd be all over this stuff," Waylon joked, trying to get her to relax.

She covered her nose and looked away, wrapping her other arm tightly around her torso. "I'm... sensitive to the smell of some hand sanitizers. That happens to be one of them."

"This?" He turned it and looked at the label, as if he didn't know it was one of the sanitizers he'd swiped from the hospital, a brand you couldn't buy in a grocery store.

That's when it hit Waylon like a punch to the gut. How could he have been so blind?

She was overly worried about a splinter—no, a puncture wound by something that God knows how many people ran their dirty hands over. She obviously didn't like hospital personnel. And not only did she not like the smell of the hospital sanitizer, she had a visceral reaction to it.

Add to that she was thin, too thin. Her hair had to be cropped short under that beanie, and she got winded way too quickly for someone her age. The signs were all there—signs he'd been too self-absorbed to notice.

Frankie had spent some serious time in a hospital, and not that long ago, he'd wager. He was good at treating acute trauma, broken bones and heart attacks. He wasn't used to dealing with chronic diseases, but that was no excuse for missing the most obvious thing in the world.

Frankie had been a cancer patient. Maybe she still was.

And she wanted off the battlefield, not to be reminded of it.

But that's all Waylon seemed to be. Without ever meaning to, he was a walking, smart-talking reminder of everything she wanted to put behind her. No wonder Frankie wanted nothing to do with him. And if Stephanie knew how she felt and still set her up with him? Yeah, she had more reason to be hostile than he did.

At least outwardly.

"I won't use this one, then," he said softly.

When he snapped the cap shut, she dropped her hand. She looked surprised that he was humoring her—until she caught the sincere look in her eyes. Frankie blinked, then nodded. "Thank you. I appreciate that. Buddy."

When she smiled, not only did her eyes brighten, the whole day got brighter. Waylon couldn't help but stare a moment longer than was polite. Then he snapped himself out of it and finished putting away the sanitizer. He opened his water bottle and poured some into his hands, rubbing them together to rinse off the sanitizer. He wiped his hands on his cargos.

"Better?" He held his hand up, palm out.

Frankie hesitated. She leaned forward, one foot still back, like a skittish woodland creature ready to bolt into the underbrush, and sniffed. She nodded and said, "Better." He dropped his hand and her shoulders relaxed. "I'm not sensitive to *all* sanitizers," she added quietly. "Just... certain brands, I guess."

"Good to know," Waylon said. "Do you have any that you like, that I can use?"

She giggled—a beautiful sound to Waylon's ears. "I do, but I doubt you want to smell like a field of flowers."

"Try me."

"Okay, it's your pride on the line." She reached into an outer pocket on her bag and pulled out a blue plastic bottle. She popped the lid and the crisp air filled with the smell of lavender.

"What a coincidence. It's the same stuff I always use after my mani-pedis," he joked.

This got him an actual laugh. Frankie giggling was cute, but her laugh was on another level—warm and sweet, and so welcoming that he laughed too. For a weird moment, he felt like he already knew her and—God help him—liked her.

Waylon held out his hand to take the bottle. After a long moment, Frankie gave it to him. He held up his other palm and she gave him the lightest high-five, like it was a truce.

And maybe it was.

"Now, let me see your arm."

This time, Frankie rolled up her sleeve and extended her arm willingly. "It's fine," she said, color blooming on her cheeks. "I was just being stupid."

Not if your immune system is compromised. He almost said it out loud but stopped himself. He was still making assumptions. And even if he was right, Waylon had already upset her enough. Most cancer patients he'd met were hyper-aware of cuts, colds, and anything that could risk infection. Immune systems worn down by chemo made every little thing a potential danger.

"You weren't being stupid. Not at all."

That got him another smile. He took her arm, trying not to focus on the soft warmth of her skin beneath his touch, and examined the wound. It wasn't as bad as he'd thought, given the blood smeared across her arm where Frankie had dug in, trying to tear the splinter out. She'd broken some capillaries and that made it look worse than it really was.

Frankie examined it with him. "I freaked out and made it worse."

"It's not that bad. Can I pull the splinter out and patch it up for you? I've got bandages." He had a thought and smiled. "I might even have a Snoopy one."

Her eyes widened. "How did you know I love Snoopy?"

"I saw the Snoopy pen you used when you signed the release form this morning."

Frankie looked surprised. "I can't believe you noticed something that small."

Waylon shrugged. "Sometimes I'm better at noticing the smaller things than the bigger ones."

She tilted her head, studying him. Waylon instantly regretted his words. Of course she'd read right into what he meant. She hadn't mentioned cancer—she obviously didn't want to. She couldn't even stand being paired with a paramedic, for crying out loud.

"Well," she said, breaking the uncomfortable silence, "are you going to fix me up so I can have my Snoopy bandage?"

Waylon gave a quick shake of his head, clearing his thoughts. "Yeah, right. Sorry. Hang on."

He reluctantly let go of her arm and dug into his kit, on the hunt for his tweezers and an alcohol swab. He took her arm again and carefully wiped off the blood. Frankie seemed much calmer now as she watched him clean her scratched-up skin.

"Sorry, this might hurt a little," he said as he readied the tweezers.

Frankie chuckled ruefully. "No worries. I have a pretty high pain tolerance. Do your worst."

Waylon glanced up at her, catching the mischievous twinkle in her eye. Like her laugh, it felt oddly familiar, like a memory he couldn't quite place. Then it was gone.

To her credit, Frankie didn't even flinch when the tweezers grabbed the splinter and he pulled it out. The splinter was long, at least half an inch, but the wound was shallow, the splinter having gone in across her skin instead of straight into the meat of her arm.

Waylon wasn't kidding about the Snoopy bandages. He was a Snoopy fan himself, and he always carried cartoon bandages for his younger patients in the field. If a kid was scared, he'd spill the bandages out on a nearby surface without a word and ask, *"Which one do you like best?"* The question usually distracted them. Once the kid picked their favorite, he'd grin and say, *"Yeah, that's my favorite one, too."* Then he'd ask them to tell him about the cartoon characters as he worked, and before long, the kid would be chattering away, too caught up to notice what Waylon was doing.

And of course, he used the bandage they'd chosen—a small prize for their bravery.

Grinning at the thought, he decided to try the same trick with Frankie.

"Which Snoopy is your favorite?"

"Oh, that's easy. Snoopy pretending to be an ace World War I pilot."

"Huh. Yeah, me too," Waylon said, meaning it.

Frankie raised an eyebrow. "Really? I'd have figured you for a Joe Cool kind of guy."

"Nope. Ace pilot all the way," Waylon said, grinning. "I loved the Halloween special when I was growing up."

"Right? That's my favorite part of the whole cartoon," Frankie said, her eyes lighting up. "Snoopy's imagination completely takes over, and he's totally in his own world. I didn't get it as a kid, though. I thought he really *was* wandering through some French countryside, looking at signs and running past crumbling buildings. Especially when he sneaked into the party the Peanuts gang was having—I thought they'd found some old, haunted farmhouse to throw their party in, which was perfect."

Waylon chuckled. "Yeah, but it was probably just one of their suburban houses."

"Exactly, but Snoopy's imagination changed it completely. Pretty cool," Frankie said with a shrug.

Waylon nodded as he peeled the backing off the bandage. "Well, let's see. I think I've got one Snoopy pilot left." He rummaged through his supplies, letting out a small sigh of relief when he found not one but two. "Hey, look at that." He pulled them out and held them up for her approval.

Frankie's face lit up with another hundred-watt smile. "Yeah, perfect."

Carefully, Waylon placed a gauze square across the area she'd scratched up. He taped the Snoopy bandages over the gauze, covering it. Frankie inspected his work, nodding once, tiny smile as she ran a finger over Snoopy.

"Perfect."

She looked down the path where the others had gone. "Think we can catch up with them?"

He followed her gaze. "They're probably way up ahead by now."

"We can catch them," she said brightly, eyes twinkling.

He thought about how winded she'd gotten just walking to the bridge. "Naw, we should probably take it easy."

Frankie stiffened beside him. All the light that had crept back into her eyes stole away again.

"I'm fine. It was just a splinter."

"Are you sure you aren't winded? We could wait here, or go back—"

Frankie sighed and closed her eyes, looking pained. "No offense, but *this* is why I didn't want to be paired up with you. I've had enough of medical personnel telling me what I can and can't do." She grabbed her pack and sprinted off the bridge.

Ah, so he was right. She had spent time in a hospital.

"Wait up." Waylon slung his pack across his shoulder, not bothering with the other strap. He had to give her credit; when Frankie wanted to move, she *moved*. He had to run to reach her.

"See? I'm just fine," she panted when he caught up with her. She slowed to a walk. "I can...do this."

"Didn't say you couldn't."

Frankie stopped walking. "Yes, actually you did."

Shit. Yup, he did, in so many words, didn't he?

She's not my patient.

Waylon grinned. Elias had said the very same thing after he'd treated Wren when she'd escaped a burning building. Only, for Elias, it was an excuse to ask her out. The last thing Waylon wanted was to take Frankie anywhere.

Frankie cocked her head. "What's that grin about?"

Before Waylon could respond, they both froze at the sound of rustling bushes under the think cover of pine trees. Frankie glanced toward the noise. "Swear to God, if that's Stephanie sneaking up on us—"

She didn't get a chance to finish. It wasn't Stephanie, or anyone else from the Adventure Buddy Club, or even a stray hiker.

They both froze as a massive nose appeared through the bushes, followed by a head adorned with the largest rack of antlers Waylon had ever seen. The moose emerged fully, towering over the trail.

"Oh, shit," they said in unison.

"Okay," Waylon began, his voice low and steady. "I don't want you to panic."

"I grew up in Montana," Frankie said, keeping her voice calm but firm. "I've seen moose before."

Waylon raised an eyebrow. The moose, now fully in the middle of the path, snorted and turned its head toward them, massive ears swiveling to catch every sound. Waylon searched the underbrush, scanning for movement. It was late September, the beginning of mating season when bull moose were notoriously unpredictable.

"Okay," he murmured, keeping his voice even. "I don't see any others. On the count of three, we're going to slowly turn and head back to the bridge—"

"Oops, nope. We're not," Frankie cut him off, glancing over her shoulder. Another moose emerged behind them, blocking their escape route.

"Oh, double shit," Waylon muttered, his stomach sinking. "I think we're in the middle of a herd."

"Moose don't herd, deer and elk do. I thought you said you knew moose."

"I do, but I don't think right now is the time to argue that."

The first bull snorted again, shaking its head. The moose behind them stopped when it caught sight of the bull on the path. A tension filled the air so thick Waylon felt it fill his chest with every breath.

"Uh," Frankie whispered, her voice tinged with both awe and worry. "I think we're in the middle of a standoff. Let's slowly back into the underbrush on the other side of the trail—"

"No time for that!" Waylon swept her up into his arms just as the bull in front charged right at them, aimed toward his opponent. He carried Frankie, dashing out of the way and into the trees just before a deafening crack filled the air. The two bulls collided, their antlers crashing together with bone-rattling force. Deep bellows echoed through the forest as the animals locked horns, muscles bulging, each trying to overpower the other.

Frankie slapped a hand over her mouth. Waylon glanced at Frankie, expecting to see fear and ready to reassure her, but instead she radiated excitement. Her eyes were glued to the battling moose, wide with wonder. Her body shook—not with fear, but with suppressed laughter.

"This is so cool," she whispered, barely containing herself.

Waylon stared at her in disbelief. Frankie was having the time of her life, entranced by the spectacle in front of them. Waylon shook his head, adrenaline still coursing through his veins. He told himself it was from their escape, and not from watching the feather-light pixie in his arms.

Too soon, she looked at him and said, "You can put me down, you don't need to carry me."

His first instinct was to tell her *yes, actually I do need to carry you so I can feel you every time you shake with laughter,* but he didn't think that would go over very well.

Besides, the voice of reason in his head told him, *aren't you forgetting how you didn't want to be paired up with a woman who would 'accidentally' fall into your arms? And here you are picking her up on your own.*

Waylon let Frankie slip down out of his arms. He missed her slight weight immediately. He reminded himself that he preferred bigger ladies with nice curves.

She's not for you. No woman is, not for long.

They eased farther back into the trees, moving slowly and quietly as the bulls squared off again. Waylon pointed in the direction the rest of the Adventure Buddies had gone.

"Let's keep moving," he whispered. "Just in case one of them decides to chase the other into the trees. I'd rather not become a speed bump for an angry moose."

Frankie grinned but kept her eyes glued to the fight. Waylon had to admit, it was pretty amazing. He'd never seen anything like this before. The only moose he'd ever spotted were lone wanderers, and never this close.

The two moose circled each other, their bugles echoing through the forest like prehistoric trumpets, primal and powerful. When their antlers clashed, the sound reverberated like boulders colliding. Sure enough, one moose turned as the other charged. The retreating bulls thundered off the path right where he and Frankie stood moments ago. They crashed through the woods, snapping branches and trampling saplings and undergrowth as they went. In moments, they vanished, leaving the trail eerily quiet in their wake.

It was like the forest had swallowed them whole.

"Was that real?" Frankie whispered.

"I was kind of wondering the same thing," Waylon admitted, still half-expecting the moose to reappear. "But I don't think our imaginations could've broken trees like that."

Waylon looked down to find the pixie beaming up at him, her smile full and unguarded. His breath hitched.

Damn.

"I bet Snoopy's imagination could," she said.

He snorted. "I think you're right."

The sound of approaching footsteps reached them.

"Waylon? Frank?" Stephanie called out, full of worry. "Are you guys okay?"

"We're fine, Steve!"

"We're alright!" Waylon called back at the same time. He and Frankie stepped back onto the trail to find the rest of the group rushing toward them, Stephanie leading the charge.

Stephanie clutched her chest dramatically. "Oh my goodness. Did we hear a moose?"

"You heard two of them," Waylon replied. "A couple big bulls decided to have a fight, and lucky us, they picked right where we were standing."

"Front-row seats," Frankie added, shaking her head. "That was wild."

The other Adventure Buddies continued back along the path, murmuring in awe as they examined the shattered saplings and trampled underbrush where the moose had retreated. Stephanie grinned knowingly at Waylon and Frankie.

"See?" she said, smirking. "This is why Adventure Buddies need to be paired up."

"Oh, so you were planning for a couple of moose to charge us?" Frankie asked.

Stephanie shrugged, utterly unapologetic. "Well, it was turning into a boring walk. Had to spice it up somehow. You make a good team, by the way." She winked and sauntered past them to join the rest of the group.

Frankie shook her head, her expression torn between disbelief and admiration. "You know, if anyone could conjure up a couple of moose, it'd be Stephanie."

Waylon chuckled. "Can't argue with that."

Frankie gave him a sideways glance. "Wait a second—are we actually agreeing on something besides Snoopy?"

"Sure sounds like it."

Frankie grinned again, and Waylon couldn't help but grin back.

SIX

So maybe Mr. Medic's not so bad after all.

They were back on the bus after the hike, a pretty uneventful one after the Battle of the Moose—but then again, how could you top that? The deer, rabbits, squirrels and chipmunks were pretty cute though, and the homemade cookies Stephanie brought along couldn't be beat. Waylon's scowl was gone and Frankie's suspicions had been correct—he was even more gorgeous when he smiled. And that laugh, when she finally pulled one out of him, felt almost familiar. *Welcoming* was the word in her head describing it, which was so odd. Welcoming her to *what* exactly?

Too bad he pities you.

Ever since her freakout over the splinter, Waylon watched her like she might fall over and break if the wind blew too hard. Frankie wasn't sure if that was better or worse than the look of disgust he'd given her at first. She was probably lucky he didn't look at her like she was crazy. Her medical team had drilled it into her head to watch for infection from any cut or scratch but she'd never reacted that way. She thought after her treatment ended, she could go back to her 'normal' life. What was this, PTSD?

You're never gonna make it down the block, let alone to Iceland if you're going to jump at every little issue.

The van hummed steadily as it wound its way back toward town, the voices of the Adventure Buddies blending into a comfortable murmur. Frankie sat by the window again, stealing glances at Waylon from the corner of her eye.

He sat a little sideways in his seat, one arm draped casually over the back of the bench. The sunlight streaming through the window illuminated his profile. He had the most annoyingly perfect jawline covered in dark scruff. Her fingertips prickled at the thought of running her fingers over it.

He caught her looking and raised an eyebrow, flashing her a grin that was unfairly charming before looking away again.

Frankie sighed. "Hey," she said, leaning slightly toward him. Her voice was low, so as not to draw the attention of the others. "Can we talk?"

Waylon straightened, clearly surprised by her serious tone. "Okay," he said, turning to face her fully. "What's up?"

Frankie hesitated, her fingers fiddling with the zipper on her jacket. "Look, I know you mean well. And I appreciate that you helped me back there with the splinter. But..." She trailed off, searching for the right words.

"But?" Waylon prompted, his tone careful.

"But I don't need a babysitter," Frankie said, her voice firm but not harsh. "I'm not fragile, and I don't want you looking at me like I'm about to crumble."

Waylon's eyebrows shot up. "I'm not—" He paused, clearly rethinking whatever he was about to say. "Okay, maybe I am a little. But it's not because I think you're fragile."

That took her by surprise.

"Then why?" she asked. "You didn't look at me like that until you figured out I'm... Well, you know."

Waylon's mouth opened, then closed again as he leaned back against the seat. He rubbed the back of his neck, his gaze flicking to

Stephanie before returning to her.

"You're right. I put two and two together, much later than I should have." He studied her face, his gaze drifting to the beanie. "You have cancer."

Even though she was sure he didn't mean to hurt her, the words felt like a slap.

"Had. I *had* cancer. I'm not a patient anymore. I'm post-treatment. My last dose of chemo was months ago, and my follow-up tests show no signs of it." She realized she was being defensive when she heard her mother's voice chastising her.

Very unladylike, Francesca.

Frankie softened her tone. "I don't want to be treated differently from anyone else. I'm here to live my life, not have people tiptoeing around me like I'm made of glass." She took a deep breath. "If you're going to do that, this won't work." As soon as she said the words, she regretted them. "I mean, as long as you stay with the group. I know Steve's looking for your replacement." She shrugged. "She may find one by next Saturday and it won't matter."

Waylon looked surprised as he studied her. "So, you're not quitting after today?"

He thinks you can't cut it.

"Maybe I should."

Waylon's eyes widened, hurt flashing through them and disappearing so quickly Frankie thought maybe she imagined it. The scowl came back.

"Whatever," he said as he shrugged, then crossed his arms and stared forward.

That hurt, too. Then hurt turned to anger.

"You know what? I'm not quitting. I enjoyed today, believe it or not. And I need to build my endurance back up."

He gave her the side-eye, one brow raised.

"You don't think I can?"

"Didn't say that."

"You didn't have to." Frankie crossed her arms. "Nope, I'm

coming back next week. Besides, I don't want to hurt Steve's feelings."

"*Steve's* feelings." He shook his head then turned to look her in the eye. "Well, I don't want to hurt *her* feelings, either. And I promised that I'd do this until she found a replacement. So, I'm stuck no matter what."

Stuck, huh? So much for thinking he's not so bad. "Fine. I guess we'll see if we survive another adventure next week."

"I guess we will."

"Great."

"Great. Fantastic."

They rode in silence the rest of the way.

About a block away from the rec center, Stephanie's voice rang out. "All right, listen up, everyone. We're not taking the bus next week because the rec center needs it, which is fine, since we can't drive directly to our next adventure anyway."

Whew. At least I won't have to endure the silent treatment again.

"So here's the plan," Stephanie continued. "We'll meet up in Idaho Springs. If you've been up there before, you know parking is practically non-existent this time of year. So, in the spirit of Buddy-hood, as well as keeping things green, I want each of you to decide which Buddy is driving and ride up together."

Frankie's eyes widened as her stomach sank. Glancing at Waylon, he looked about as happy as she felt.

Before she could open her mouth, he said. "There is no discussion. I'm driving."

"Fine."

"You aren't going to argue?"

"Nope." She pulled out a small spiral-bound notebook, jotted down her address, tore out the page, and thrust it at him.

Stephanie pulled into the rec center parking lot. "Don't forget to hydrate and stretch. Next week's going to be a lot more challenging. Wear long pants and long-sleeved shirts, shoes with good grips, and," she paused, "Bring a swimsuit. I've got a nice treat planned for after."

A swimsuit? Frankie swallowed hard, trying not to throw up. *This just keeps getting worse.* She sank down into her coat while everyone else talked excitedly. Except of course for Waylon. He looked like Stephanie just announced they'd be diving into a pit of snakes and broken glass.

Great. One more thing we see eye to eye on.

The second the bus came to a stop, Waylon shot out the door without looking back.

STOP WORRYING. *It shouldn't matter.* Frankie thought as she parked at the rec center on Monday morning. This was her first time back since Saturday, and she dreaded seeing Waylon there. What if he worked out before going to the hospital, or it was his day off and he was a gym rat? She wouldn't be surprised—Waylon was in amazing shape. Fighting fit.

An image of Waylon in his pec-hugging race shirt popped unwanted into her head.

But now that the vision is here, there's no reason why I can't enjoy it for a second.

Grinning to herself, Frankie slung her gym bag over one shoulder and headed into the rec center.

"Hey, Frank! Whatcha doing here? It's not Saturday yet," Stephanie called from her desk.

"What? I'm not allowed to come in otherwise, Steve?" Frankie shouted back as she walked toward the receptionist area. Stephanie wasn't alone. Two very good-looking men stood beside the counter, watching Frankie as she approached—a gorgeous blond and a handsome brunette.

Not as attractive as Waylon, she thought like a reflex.

Hush! He doesn't like you. And you don't like him, remember?

The dark-haired man stepped forward. "So you're the notorious

Frank." He held out his hand to shake. "I'm Gabe, one of the managers here. Good to meet you."

"Notorious?" Frankie looked at Stephanie as she shook Gabe's hand. "What has Steve been telling you?"

Stephanie placed her hand over her heart. "All I said was that you used to be a regular here and that you were kind enough to be Waylon's partner."

Frankie snorted. "Well, someone has to do it, I guess."

The blond laughed. His bright blue eyes twinkled as he shook his head. "My sympathies."

"Oh, you've met him?" Frankie asked, surprised. *Shoot, maybe he is a gym rat.* She fought to keep from looking around, as if Waylon might jump out from behind a pillar.

"You could say that." The blond held out his hand. "I'm Elias. Good to meet you, Frank."

Stephanie frowned. "Hey, I'm the only who gets to call her that, right Frank?"

"Whatever you say, Steve." She turned her attention back to Elias. "I guess I'm Frankie to you."

Elias chuckled. "Stephanie's orders."

Stephanie gave Elias a stern look with very little malice in it, then asked Frankie, "You here to work out on your own or are you in a class?"

"Oh. Well, I...didn't think about it."

Gabe squinted. "Sorry." He pointed at one of the speakers in the ceiling. "I have trouble hearing when the music's loud. Did you say you want to be in a class?"

Did she want to be in one? "I haven't signed up for anything today."

"Oh, would you look at that," Stephanie said as she read something on her monitor. "There's one opening left in the next Jazzercise class. Starts in about ten minutes. You in, Frank?"

"Do I have to partner up with anyone?" She winked at Elias.

He chuckled again and said, "Actually, my wife is in that class." He shoulder-checked Gabe. "His, too."

Frankie's eyebrows rose. "I'd like to meet them," she said before a little voice in her head could stop her—the voice that told her not to get close, that people were undependable.

"Wren and Rochelle," Elias said. "They're..." he looked around, "somewhere..."

Gabe watched Elias. "If you're wondering where they are, they're in the bathroom." He looked at Frankie. "My wife's name is Rochelle and his is Wren."

"Thank you." Frankie nodded, a little confused as to why Gabe repeated their names. *He really must be hard of hearing.*

"Here they come." Elias pointed down the hall at two women walking toward them, laughing about something. They looked friendly. Would they like her?

I never used to be this insecure, Frankie thought. *But that was in the Before Times.*

Before the diagnosis. Before they removed a part of her body that had viciously turned on her. Before she found out who her friends were, and who they were not.

She smiled at the women, feeling shy and suddenly self-conscious. The women returned her smile. Then, they gave each other a quick look that said they knew something Frankie didn't, which added to her insecurity.

"Hi there," the taller of the two said when they reached her. Elias put his arm around her, which told Frankie this was Wren. Gabe lifted his hands and he signed something to Rochelle, who grinned and signed something back.

"Ladies," Stephanie said, "This is my dear friend, Frank*ie*," she emphasized the last syllable of her name, "and she'll be joining you at Jazzercise."

"Awesome!" Rochelle said, giving Wren another knowing look before she and Wren introduced themselves.

"Better get a move on." Stephanie made shooing motions. "You're gonna be late otherwise."

SEVEN

The Jazzercise class was held in a bright, mirrored room filled with energetic music and even more energetic participants. Frankie lingered near the back while Rochelle and Wren greeted their classmates like old friends. Then they came back and stood on either side of Frankie as the rest of the class got into lines and faced the instructor in front.

"First class?" Rochelle asked Frankie.

Frankie nodded. "Yeah, but it looks like fun."

Wren leaned in. "Oh, it is. Especially when you screw up as much as I do."

Frankie chuckled. "Good to know. I'm pretty sure I'll spend the whole time tripping over my own feet."

"Then you'll fit right in," Wren said, her eyes sparkling.

"If you don't want to do a move, just jog in place to keep your heartrate up. Trust us," Rochelle added with a laugh. "That's half the class."

The instructor, a bubbly woman with seemingly boundless energy, called the class to order, and the music kicked up a notch.

The movements were fast-paced, but not overly complicated, and Frankie quickly found herself caught up in the rhythm.

True to their word, Rochelle and Wren came close to knocking her over a couple of times, and she darn-near returned the favor. The instructor was going way too fast for a beginners' class. Frankie found herself jogging in place more than once, just to catch her breath. And true to what Wren and Rochelle told her, most of the class ended up jogging, too. By the time the cooldown began, Frankie was sweaty but exhilarated.

I did it! I got through the entire class without stopping.

"You did great," Wren said, handing her a towel.

Frankie wiped her face, shaking her head. "You sure? I feel like when I wasn't jogging in place I flailed through the rest of it."

"Just like we did," Rochelle said, grinning.

Wren rolled her eyes. "Flailed, jazzed—it's all the same."

Frankie laughed, her heart feeling lighter than it had for months. She enjoyed their company much more than she'd expected.

She also expected them to tell her it was nice meeting her, then walk out together. But as the class filtered out, Wren and Rochelle lingered, clearly waiting for her as she caught her breath.

"Coming back next class?" Rochelle asked.

"Yeah, definitely," Frankie said as she ran her hand through her short, dark hair, hoping it didn't look too crazy. She'd always kept her hair long—easier to maintain and just throw into a ponytail when she needed it out of the way. It was still growing back in, but now it had a funky curl to it that had a mind of its own. The rosemary oil she used that was supposed to make it grow back in faster unfortunately didn't act like a styling product.

"You look great," Wren said, as if reading her mind. "Very cute style."

Frankie almost told her what a pain it was, but smiled and thanked her instead.

"Are you heading home now, or maybe back to work?" Rochelle asked.

"Not yet. I work from home, so I got up early and finished everything so that I could spend a couple hours here. I was hoping to hit the weight room and the machines. I need some toning."

"Us, too," Wren said, glancing at Rochelle, who raised her eyebrows but then smiled quickly. "We can spot each other."

"Sounds good," Frankie said. As they walked down the hall to the weight room, she wondered again about the looks they kept giving each other. "But do you guys need to be anywhere? Am I keeping you from anything?"

"No, not at all," Rochelle said as opened the weight room door for the others. Frankie picked up a set of hand weights and sat on a bench while Wren used a leg curl machine beside her. "I'm a translator and Wren is a photographer." Rochelle added as she grabbed the handles on a cable machine beside Wren to work her arms. "We kind of set our own hours, too."

"So, what do you do from home?" Wren asked Frankie. The room wasn't too crowded and the music was muted, making it easier to talk.

"I'm a grant writer at the moment."

"At the moment?"

She nodded as she curled her arm, the hand weight reminding her biceps that they needed some serious work. Thankfully, her fingers didn't feel numb or tingly like they sometimes did post-chemo. "I'm not up to wwoofing quite yet."

"Wolfing?" Wren tilted her head and gave Frankie a playful smile. "You're a werewolf?" she teased.

Frankie laughed. "Not wolfing, wwoofing, like what a dog does, but with two w's. It stands for World Wide Opportunities on Organic Farms. W-W-O-O-F."

Rochelle nodded vigorously through Frankie's explanation. "My sister and I wwoofed with our parents for a few weeks when we were kids," she said. "I loved it, but they thought working in an orchard wasn't worth the room and board."

"Where were you?"

"Greece. It was beautiful."

Frankie smiled and sighed. "No wonder you loved it. Greece is on my wwoofing bucket list, along with a ton of other places." She did another biceps curl. "I grew up on a ranch in Montana. Loved it." She shook her head, not wanting to get into her past. "So far, I've only been on farms in the U.S. I'm kinda stuck here for now, so I'm writing grant proposals for the organization until I can get back out there. In the meantime, I'm doing everything I can to get back into shape." She paused. "Both physically and mentally."

Wren nodded slowly. "How's Adventure Buddies going?"

Frankie blinked, caught off guard. "It's...fine, I guess. We only had our first adventure last Saturday."

"Gabe told me about that," Rochelle said. "Steph told him you and Waylon dodged a couple of moose."

Frankie laughed. "Yeah, almost literally. It made the day interesting, that's for sure."

"What's your next adventure?" Rochelle asked.

"No idea. Stephanie's keeping it under wraps." Frankie grimaced, remembering that she needed to bring a swimsuit.

Rochelle let go of the cables and frowned. "Are you okay? Was the moose too much adventure?"

"No, not at all." Frankie set the weights down on the bench beside her. "Actually, I'm hoping Stephanie ups the ante. I want to challenge myself. There are so many things I want to do, besides wwoofing."

"Like what?" Wren asked. She lifted her hair to wipe the back of her neck.

"Oh, I have a list. Go do crazy things in Vegas, see the puffins and the northern lights in Iceland." She hesitated, wondering if she could tell them what else she wanted to see there, and decided not to. "Swim with mantas—"

"Mantas?" Wren grinned.

"Yeah, in Hawaii." She laughed, even as a bittersweet pang hit her heart. "And while I'm there, I need to go hang gliding naked in the moonlight just to see if I can get away with it."

Wren practically sprang off the leg machine. "Oh my God, take me with you! Wait, you've gotta take my friend, Barbie, too. She would die. No, she would kill me if I went without her."

Rochelle covered her mouth, laughing. "You guys hang gliding naked would be hilarious."

"Yeah, absolutely you could come with me," Frankie said, delighted.

"Oh, while we're at it, we should all go to Frozen Dead Guy Days," Rochelle said, her eyes wide.

Frankie cocked her head. "Wait, what? Frozen Dead Guy Days?" Wren looked just as confused.

"Yeah! Gabe was telling me about it. It's this crazy weekend in March where they honor this old guy named Grandpa Bredo who had himself cryogenically frozen in Norway, then his family brought him here and he ended up in a Tuff Shed up in Nederland."

Frankie's jaw dropped. "You are shitting me right now."

"Nope! It's a thing," Rochelle said. "It used to be up in Nederland—"

"Because they're nuts up there," Wren interjected.

"—then they moved both Grandpa and the festival to The Stanley Hotel in Estes Park. But the important thing is, they still do the team coffin races."

"Coffin races? Are you serious?" Wren said. At the same time Frankie said, "Oh! We could put a team together!" Her eyes went wide. "I mean, that's kind of presumptuous of me—"

"No, that's perfect!" Rochelle said while Wren shouted, "Yes!"

Frankie grinned ear to ear. *I have new friends!* "Okay, we are doing this. It's in March?"

"Yup!" Rochelle said. "And we have to bring the guys along for the Blue Ball."

Wren snorted.

"It's a dance at the Stanley Hotel, where everyone dresses up like a frozen zombie," Rochelle said. She looked at Frankie. "I would love to see how Waylon would dress. You guys could coordinate."

Frankie opened and closed her mouth. The idea of dancing with Waylon sent her into a sudden panic. "I...don't think that's going to happen."

As soon as the words came out of her mouth, she watched Wren and Rochelle look her up and down as their enthusiasm faded.

They think I said that because I'm not going to live that long.

"No, it's not... I mean, I want to travel the world so maybe I won't be here. I want to see everything, do everything. Life is so short."

She paused, as a bittersweet sadness filled her heart. "Not everyone gets a second chance. I don't want to waste mine."

Wren sat down on the bench beside Frankie. "Cancer?" she asked quietly.

Frankie nodded. Of course they knew. "My hair—or the lack of it —gave it away, didn't it?" she joked.

Wren shrugged. "Well, that and Waylon might have said something to Elias."

"Waylon was talking about me?" Frankie felt her face grow warm and the back of her neck prickle. She told herself the heat rushing to her face was from anger.

"Elias and Waylon are best friends. They talk about everything." Wren covered her heart with her right hand. "It wasn't anything bad, I promise."

Frankie scoffed. "It probably wasn't anything good, either." She could only imagine Waylon rolling his eyes as he talked about her freakout with the splinter.

"Eh." Wren smiled and shrugged. "I wouldn't say that. It sounded like he was impressed."

Frankie reared back. "He was...what now?"

Wren laughed. "Impressed by the way you handled the moose. He said anyone else would have freaked out and probably gotten you both trampled."

"Oh." She felt her face grow even warmer and imagined it was bright red.

"What were you expecting he'd say?" Rochelle asked.

"That I'm a total wimp." She shook her head.

Rochelle laughed. "Wimps don't face down a couple of moose."

"It's not like I did it on purpose." Frankie grinned. "But I did love the way it got my heart going. I used to be such an adrenaline junkie. It was fun to feel that again."

Wren bumped her shoulder against Frankie's. "Waylon's the biggest adrenaline junkie I know. Steph knew what she was doing when she paired you guys up."

If only that were true.

Still, Frankie couldn't stop the small smile tugging at her lips. She felt a flicker of disbelief that Waylon had been impressed by her handling of the moose situation.

The weight room door opened, and Frankie heard two men laughing. She turned just as Elias strode in.

Followed by Waylon.

EIGHT

If Frankie thought he looked good in a tight racing shirt and cargos, his workout clothes put them to shame. Every arm muscle was perfectly defined along with his six-pack. His bare calves, visible below his cut-off sweats, looked sculpted from marble. And those sweats were stretched tight over powerful thighs, not to mention the bulge...

Cheeks heating, Frankie quickly raised her eyes back to his face and his dark, slightly disheveled hair. Yup, Waylon flat-out had the most gorgeous body she'd ever seen.

But that wasn't what made Frankie's heart skip a beat. Well, okay, not the *only* thing. Instead of his usual scowl, Waylon was still smiling from whatever he and Elias had been laughing about, totally unguarded in that moment.

Until he spotted Frankie. His eyes widened in a look of surprise as he took in the scene—Frankie hanging out with his friends' wives. He stared at her for a moment. Frankie realized this was the first time he'd seen her without her beanie and her coat. Her hand automatically went to her short hair, still slightly damp from the Jazzercise class. She was thankful for her oversized workout shirt. He didn't need to see her body.

Waylon's smile faded. Then he gave Elias a look that clearly said he wasn't happy and it was somehow Elias' fault.

Ugh! Frankie's first impulse to cover up as much of her body as she could came straight from her mother.

Then she had a second, unexpected thought. Maybe it was because she'd kept up just fine at Jazzercise. Maybe it was being in the presence of two awesome women who never once tried to stop her or treat her differently. Who only wanted to get to know *her*, Frankie, and not Frankie-with-cancer.

Why do I care if Waylon doesn't like what he sees? Just because he's a freaking Adonis doesn't mean I have to be self-conscious. My body is strong enough to have survived cancer. That's all that matters.

Frankie squared her shoulders and met Waylon's gaze head-on, daring him to say something, anything.

Instead, he tilted his head.

And gave her the smallest of smiles.

Her heart skipped a couple more beats—from shock, she told herself.

"Hey, babe," Elias called to Wren, who lit up at his arrival. He turned his attention to Frankie. "I didn't realize you were sticking around after class."

Waylon gave him a look that said Elias wasn't kidding anyone.

To Frankie's surprise, Wren grabbed her hand as she stood, tugging Frankie up with her.

"Heck yeah, she can't leave until we're done interrogating her," Wren said with a laugh.

Grinning, Elias rolled his eyes. "And, so it begins. I take it she's pack now." He gestured at their hands.

"Pack?" Frankie raised an eyebrow. "What does that mean?"

Whatever it meant, it turned Waylon's face red. He clenched his jaw as he looked down and studied the floor like it held the answers to the mysteries of the universe.

Wren squeezed Frankie's hand before letting go. "Waylon hasn't told you his nickname yet?" Her eyes sparkled with mischief.

Waylon's head shot back up. He looked horrified.

"He has a nickname?" Frankie asked, her grin growing into a wide smile as she raised both eyebrows.

"They all do," Rochelle said. "Animal nicknames, ever since they were kids. Gabe is Timberwolf." She pointed at Elias. "That guy is Lion."

"Don't you think he looks like one?" Wren chimed in, and Frankie had to agree—with his intense blue eyes, broad face, and blond hair, Lion was the perfect nickname for Elias.

"So, what's yours?" Frankie asked at the same time Waylon said, "You don't need to know my—"

"It's Ram," Elias interrupted, speaking over them both as he clapped a hand on Waylon's shoulder.

"Ram, huh?" Frankie's lips twitched as she fought back a stupid joke in her head.

Fought and failed.

"So is that your name or is that what you do in—"

"It's short for *Ramson*," Waylon practically growled. But it was too late; everyone else was already laughing. If his face was red before, it was positively glowing crimson now.

"She's pack! She's pack!" Wren shouted as she flung an arm around Frankie's shoulders. "Sorry, we must sound insane." She laughed.

"Pfft, the good kind of insane. What about the women? Do we get nicknames, too?" Frankie only realized she'd said 'we' after it was out of her mouth. It felt good.

Pack. She wasn't sure she'd earned it yet, but the idea of belonging made her heart ache in the best way.

Especially when no one corrected her.

"Nope," Rochelle said. "Just ask Stephanie. She's been trying to get them to call her Cougar for months."

Frankie snorted. "Yeah, Steve would."

Rochelle's phone buzzed in her bag. "Hang on." She pulled it out and frowned. "It's Sandra." She took the call. "Hey, what's up, Luggage?"

Before Frankie could ask, Wren leaned in and told her, "Speaking of nicknames, that's her sister's. They traveled a lot as kids."

Frankie grinned. "Cute."

Rochelle frowned. Her eyes rolled. "Yeah, yeah, I can. But you've *got* to get a spare one. Yeah, I'm sure he'd love to." She rolled her eyes again. "Okay, see you in a few."

Rochelle shook her head as she disconnected. "Sorry, Sandra's got a flat at school and the used car she just bought doesn't have a spare. I'm going to go pick her up, and send Gabe to find her a tire and a *spare.*"

"Oh, crap," Wren said. "Tell her hi for me, and that she definitely needs a spare before we go on our next shoot. I need the best intern I've ever had."

Rochelle tilted her head. "I thought she was the only intern you've ever had."

Wren shrugged. "Well, yeah, but she's still the best."

"Will do. Sorry about Pickleball."

"Sandra's more important than a Pickleball game. Go." Wren hugged Rochelle before she left. Then she turned to Frankie.

"So, ever play Pickleball?"

"No, actually."

"Wanna *learn* to play Pickleball?" Wren grinned. "We've got the rec's court reserved but we need four people, so tag, you're it," she said as she tapped Frankie on the upper arm.

Frankie couldn't help but glance at Waylon, only to find him looking at her, his expression unreadable.

"Great idea," Elias said. "We were gonna play guys against girls, but since you guys are already Adventure Buddies, you could team up."

Frankie and Waylon both realized the insinuation—Buddies versus married couple—at the same time.

Waylon cleared his throat. "That's okay, let's stick with the plan. Guys against gals."

Frankie gave him a relieved smile, even as she felt her heart tug. She shook it off and told herself that this way, she'd get to look right at him and his stupidly perfect body without being accused of ogling.

———

"YOU WERE TOTALLY OGLING WAYLON," Wren said when they were back in the women's locker room.

"Pfft. I was not."

Yes, I was.

Pickleball turned out to be a lot of fun—much more fun than she'd expected, once Wren explained the rules and the game got going. Waylon looked incredibly tense before the first serve. Frankie figured he just took his sports very seriously. She stopped focusing on him after about three seconds when Elias sent the ball to Frankie's side. She had to decide quickly if it was going to land in bounds or hit the outer 'kitchen.' She took a chance, swung, and sent it flying straight at Waylon. He returned with a heavy hit and the ball flew right between Frankie and Wren, scoring the first point for the guys. After that, he loosened up—probably because he and Elias were winning right off the bat. He kept a sharp eye on Frankie. She figured he was studying her playing style, looking for her weaknesses— mainly, her backhand.

Though he did something she truly appreciated—well, besides giving her a tantalizing peek at his abs every time he jumped and his shirt rode up—he didn't pull any of his serves or swings. Even after she called for a break to catch her breath, he still played hard.

By the end of the match, Frankie was ready to collapse. She was hot and sweaty under her oversized shirt. But no way would she wear anything that showed off her body. Wren had asked if she was okay, and she nodded and told her she'd catch up with her in the locker room. She sat down on a bench at the back of the court and put her head down.

She was surprised when Waylon sat next to her.

She lifted her head. Elias was gone, too. It was just the two of them. That shouldn't have made her heart jackhammer, but it did. Last Saturday, Waylon couldn't get away from her fast enough, and now he was waiting for her. Maybe he was angry at her.

"Just so you know," she started before he could say anything, "I didn't home in on your friends. Steve introduced us earlier."

"Of course she did." Waylon didn't look mad. If anything, he looked amused. "Though, I have a feeling Wren and Rochelle would have figured out some other way to meet my Adventure Buddy."

"Really?"

"Oh yeah. Nothing stops Wren." He paused. "She's a lot like you that way. Nothing stops you, does it?"

She felt heat creeping into her cheeks. "What do you mean?"

"The way you played today. You were determined to keep up."

She shrugged. "It was fun, that's all."

Waylon looked deeply into her eyes. Then he shook his head and stood up. He offered her his hand to pull her up and she took it. His palm was dry and calloused and its warmth shouldn't have felt as good as it did. Neither should she have still felt his palm against hers after he let go.

Now she was in the women's locker room defending herself from Wren.

"I was not ogling him."

Wren chuckled at Frankie's denial. "You were. It's okay—Waylon's easy to look at."

Frankie felt her face heat for the hundredth time. She took her boots out of her duffel, an old broken-in pair of Ropers that were scuffed and distressed for real from riding.

"Has he mentioned that he has a thing for cowgirls?"

And, she dropped them.

Thankfully, Wren changed the subject, asking her more questions about wwoofing. Frankie was pretty sure she had her blush under control when they walked out of the locker room.

Which was a good thing, since Waylon was watching for them.

He took one long look at her boots, then quickly directed his attention at Elias.

Her lips twitched as she squashed down a smile. *No way. No way does he have one iota of interest in me.*

Just like I'm not interested in him.

"Ready to go, babe?" Elias asked Wren.

She nodded. "Rochelle texted that she's already there."

"Where are you guys going?" Frankie asked.

"We're heading to Bear and Ellie's," Wren said. "Bear is—"

Frankie held her hand up. "Don't tell me. Could he be...one of the pack?"

"Wow, you catch on quick!" She laughed. "Yeah, Bear is one of their old friends, and his wife Ellie is pregnant. We're helping them out with some chores from Ellie's honey-do list."

"Oh, that's so sweet."

"You should come with us, too. It'll be fun."

Frankie's stomach did a little flip as she felt Waylon's expectant gaze on her. She was tempted—okay, more than tempted—but she couldn't.

"Sorry," Frankie said quickly, trying to sound casual, "but I have a date."

She didn't miss the way Waylon's shoulders tensed slightly, his expression shifting from neutral to something harder to read.

Then he smiled. "No problem," he said.

"Do you?" Wren sounded intrigued, yet she looked disappointed. She took out her phone. "Give me your number and we'll set something up another time?"

Frankie's heart lifted. "Sure, that'd be great." She dug her phone out of her gym bag. The battery was almost drained. *I must have forgotten to put it on the charger again. Chemo brain.*

"Or you could just drop into Riversong pretty much any given day," Wren added as she glanced at Elias and Waylon, as if daring them to stop her.

"Riversong?"

"Sorry, that's a coffee shop in Lyons."

Frankie brightened. "Oh, yeah, I think I know the one. Cute place."

"It's where Rochelle does most of her work. Our friend April is part-owner with her family."

As Wren exchanged numbers with her, Frankie was acutely aware of the way Waylon seemed to be deliberately not looking at her now. She wondered what he was thinking.

"Well, I'll see you guys."

"I'll pick you up on Saturday morning," Waylon said.

"Absolutely. See ya, Buddy." She tagged him on the arm and turned away.

As Frankie left the rec center and headed home, she couldn't shake the image of Waylon's expression when she'd mentioned her plans. She tried not to over-analyze it as she got ready for her date, anticipating a longer-than-usual conversation—but not a bad one. She wouldn't even have to sugar-coat anything this time.

Dan will be so proud of me.

FOR THE REST of the week, Frankie set aside time every day after she finished her grant writing to go work out at the rec center. By the time Saturday morning rolled around, Frankie felt a little more like her old self from the BC days—Before Cancer. The soreness in her arms and legs after a week of workouts was the good kind of ache—the kind that reminded her she was making progress. Her stamina improved as well, along with her mood. Even though she didn't run into Wren and Rochelle again, Gabe always had a smile for her, and of course Steve was Steve and never failed to make her laugh.

I've got new friends she told her naked reflection in the full-length mirror as she studied her body. The bathroom scale told her she was gaining weight and the mirror confirmed it. She was far from her curvy BC self, but her ribs didn't show quite as much and her hips were beginning to flare out again. She turned and looked over her shoulder to confirm that her butt was returning, which made her smile. Feeling a little more optimistic, she pulled her swimsuit from the bottom of a dresser drawer and pulled it on.

When she looked in the mirror again, the first thing that caught her eye was the port just under her skin on the left side of her chest, right above the place she avoided looking at.

The place where her breasts used to be. The flatness there. And under the swimsuit, the scars.

Accentuate the positive her mother always said, which, she hated to admit, was good advice.

Hard to do that with a swimsuit though. Frankie sighed as she took off the swimsuit and put it into her pack. She got dressed without looking in the mirror again.

Her mother also said Frankie needed to 'do something about the disfigurement soon or you'll live to regret it' at every passing opportunity—opportunities that Frankie limited as much as possible. Not all of her mother's advice was helpful. She didn't seem—or want—to understand that boob reconstruction *hurt*. It meant painful expanders. It meant more surgery, more hospital stays. It meant coming home with drainage tubes. It meant putting her life back on hold for another two months, and that was if everything went well.

And shouldn't a man love her no matter if she had boobs or not?

Sure, she could tell herself that all day long, then look at social media for five seconds and know it wasn't true.

And damn if her thoughts didn't snap right back to Waylon and their first adventure. The way he'd scowled the moment he'd gotten a good look at her when he walked into the room.

But he was gentle as he dressed her wound. Funny, too. Hell, a Snoopy fan, to boot.

And the way he'd swooped her up into his arms to get her out of harm's way. She hated to admit it, but that was a huge turn-on.

"He would have done that for anyone," she said out loud. She still found herself grabbing a now-oversized swim shirt out of the bottom of her drawer and setting it next to her bag, debating on taking it with her. Frankie barely had her shoes on when the doorbell rang. Her stomach flipped. She glanced at the clock.

Of course he's early.

She grabbed her phone and slung her pack over her shoulder, just in case he demanded they get in his truck immediately, the sooner to get the day over.

"Hang on," she shouted as she headed to the door, annoyed that she wouldn't have time for one more cup of coffee.

Unless she invited him in for a mug.

Like he'd want to come in.

But she really wanted that coffee.

"I wasn't expecting you to be so early," Frankie said as she opened the door, hoping that Waylon would want coffee, but expecting him to fight her.

Her breath caught at the sight of a dozen roses.

NINE

The morning air was crisp. The trail curved sharply, leading the Adventure Buddies into a dense cluster of trees, their footsteps crunching against fallen leaves. Waylon kept his gaze forward, determined not to let Frankie get under his skin again, but damn if she wasn't making it hard. He'd done his best to start things on a positive note, from the moment he picked her up. He'd even given her a peace offering. Now, they were arguing, and Waylon couldn't even remember how it started.

"I'm just saying," Frankie said, her tone defiant, "not everything has to be about competition or vanity. Some people hike just because they love it."

Waylon snorted. "Sure, but they aren't the same ones who carry their tiny dogs in backpacks and post inspirational quotes under pictures of sunrises."

Frankie stopped mid-stride, her glare sharp enough to cut through bark. "Wow. Way to dismiss anyone who doesn't live up to your macho mountain-man standards."

He turned to face her, crossing his arms. "It's not about standards. It's about reality. The wilderness doesn't care about your feelings.

Either you're prepared, or you're screwed. People who romanticize it are the ones who end up needing a rescue team."

Frankie stepped closer and jabbed her finger into his chest. "You think I don't get that? You think I don't know what it's like to be unprepared for something life throws at you?"

Her voice cracked slightly, but her fire didn't dim. It hit him like a blow—raw, honest, and completely unexpected.

"What the hell is your problem?" he growled, feeling his own pulse quicken.

"My problem," she said, closing the gap between them, "is you standing there like some know-it-all, talking down to me like I'm an idiot."

"I'm not—"

"Yeah, you are!"

Her cheeks were flushed, her eyes blazing, and before Waylon could stop himself, he grabbed her arm and dragged her off the trail.

"What are you doing?" she hissed, stumbling slightly as he pulled her behind a thick tree trunk away from the other Adventure Buddies, half-thinking he didn't want to broadcast their fight, half-wanting to be alone with her to savor her anger, her enthusiasm. His body told him in no uncertain terms that it wanted her pressed close against his chest, his lips on hers as his cock hardened.

No way that's happening.

Once he got her alone, he stared at her, caught between frustration and something he couldn't name. Her energy was intoxicating, her fury pulled him in.

Before he could find the words, Frankie dropped to her knees in a move so abrupt it left him speechless.

"What the—"

She stared up at him, her eyes blazing with fury. Then her fingers brushed against his belt buckle, and the world tilted.

"What? What are you doing? Why are you on your...oh..."

His breath caught as she moved so fast he barely registered her hands on him. His pants were suddenly down, and her mouth—hot, soft, demanding—was on his cock.

"Oh, God." The words slipped out as a half-moan. How did she move so fast? That thought got obliterated as pleasure slammed into him, white-hot and overwhelming when she sucked him in hard, her tongue teasing his shaft, circling the tip, and she moaned.

"What is this? A grudge blowjob?" He tried to pull away, even as he laughed at the absurdity of the moment, but she wouldn't let him. Her lips tightened around his cock, and God help him, she actually growled like a wild animal guarding her meal. The sound sent a jolt of lust straight through him, and before he could stop himself, his hands tangled in her short curls, his hips thrusting. He fucked her sassy mouth. Her gorgeous lips, her magic tongue, all his now, all he wanted. Everything.

How? How could it feel this good?

"Frankie..." His voice cracked as she moved with him, taking him deeper. The woman who hated him—he was sure of it, or had been up until this moment—repositioned until she took his entire cock inside her mouth, all the way to the back of her throat. She was incredible, all fire and velvet.

Her gaze locked on his, no longer furious but lit with something else. Laughter? Challenge? His heart leaped in his chest as a strange feeling of familiarity and warmth flooded him. But of course she was familiar; he'd spent his Saturdays with her.

What a weird thought to have.

Before he could wonder anymore, her head bobbed faster and he groaned.

"Ah, Frankie, yeah, just like that. God, that feels amazing. So damn good, baby. Oh, fuck, *fuck*...can't hold back..."

His body shuddered, pleasure ripping through him as the world blurred. For a fleeting second, he thought he'd never felt this good, this complete.

Then he blinked, and it was gone.

"No, no, *no*," he groaned, waking up as he ground his cock against his wadded-up bed sheets and blankets, jetting all over them. Waylon grabbed his cock and stroked himself through the last of his powerful orgasm. When he got his breath under control, he growled at the mess he'd made.

"What the hell was that?"

The answer was obvious—and infuriating.

Frankie.

Waylon scrubbed a hand over his face, sweat slick on his skin. *What am I, a teenager?*

Except even as a teenager, he'd never come that hard. His still-hard cock throbbed in time with his heart banging against his chest. It wanted more. He hadn't come in his sleep for at least a decade. Then again, he hadn't had a long dry spell like this one, either. That explained it.

"But why her, you idiot?" he asked his cock. It twitched at the mere thought of Frankie, at remembering her in his dream. God, it was so vivid that if Waylon didn't know any better, he would've sworn the mischievous little pixie had sneaked into his room, played with him mercilessly, then vanished the moment he started to come.

"Dude, you're not supposed to like her."

Especially ever since she left the rec center. The way she'd casually tagged him on the arm and turned away. Just walked off like she hadn't zapped him with an emotional cattle prod straight to the heart.

Sorry, but I have a date.

He'd felt a surge of heat and cold shoot through his entire body at once, like he'd been electrocuted by a lightning bolt made of icicles.

A date?

Date? As in dating? A guy?

Oh, shit. Am I jealous?

I'm jealous.

Shit.

All he could do was tell her *No problem.*

And let her go.

That's the important thing, isn't it? I let her go.

A traitorous vision of her eyes flashed through his mind. Not angry, only warm, laughing eyes. Beautiful beyond belief. That weird feeling of familiarity returned, as if she reminded him of someone. He ached to know who. He also tried to remember what 'peace offering' he'd given her in the dream. Something small and ordinary but important somehow that he'd pulled out of his pocket. He felt like if he could just remember what it was, he'd know who she reminded him of.

Sighing in frustration and a strange feeling of loss, Waylon got out of bed, tore off the sheets, and dropped them into the laundry hamper. Then he plodded into the bathroom. He was already naked, so after taking a piss, he went straight into the shower. His cock woke back up as warm water hit it. Snippets of the dream came rushing back, taunting him. The way her mouth felt, her lips stroking his cock, her heat, her sexy moans.

But it wasn't really her. It was just a dream.

Didn't matter to his cock.

Waylon tried to concentrate on other parts of the dream, hoping to settle his dick down. He snorted when he remembered their argument—he couldn't see Frankie caring one way or another about influencers hiking only for the selfies, or himself caring enough to fight about it. That must have come from his first impression of her, thinking she was some sort of vegan.

You think I don't know what it's like to be unprepared for something life throws at you?

Now that was more like the real Frankie. Waylon felt his face turn hot, as if she'd really said those words to him, like he didn't understand or care what she'd been through.

"Just a dream, dude."

And he went straight back to the vision of Frankie sucking him off, her eyes on fire with lust. His cock jumped.

It was one thing to have a wet dream about someone who wasn't interested in you. That was beyond his control. It was another thing to actively jerk off to a fantasy about them. No way Frankie would ever know, but it still felt like a violation.

Something a stalker would do.

That unwanted thought shut his cock down faster than a bucket of ice water as shame flooded him. Waylon quickly finished his shower and got dressed.

"Fuck, I'm running late." He'd never get to her house on time, and that bothered him. It was rude.

He grabbed his pack and a protein bar and went out to his truck. He checked the address again, even though he had it memorized the moment he read the scrap of paper she'd given him. As soon as he'd gotten home, he'd looked it up on the street view of an online map. Her rental house was tiny but in good shape and the neighborhood looked like a safe one. He'd almost asked Shane to double check its safety since Watchdog had the resources beyond an online real estate report. Waylon had told himself there was nothing wrong with making sure a woman living on her own was safe, especially a little pixie-sized woman with no family in town.

He'd picked up the phone to call Shane but stopped himself just before he hit the call button. That was going too far he told himself. *Back the fuck off.*

As he drove to her place, Waylon remembered his surprise at seeing Frankie in the weight room and clenched his jaw. Elias had totally set him up. He didn't appreciate that one bit, firstly because Elias had been asking him about Frankie non-stop between call outs at work, not taking Waylon at his word that there was absolutely no chance he'd be dating his Adventure Buddy.

"JUST PERFORMING MY WINGMAN DUTIES," Elias had said

in the back of the rig after they'd taken a patient to the emergency room on Monday.

Waylon scoffed. "That's only appreciated at Cocks and Strippers, brother. Not with someone I have to spend time with every single weekend for the next month or so."

"I can't think of a better time to be a wingman," Elias countered.

Waylon ignored that, pretending to be absorbed with charting on his tablet—as if anyone ever loved that part of healthcare. And his thoughts kept drifting back to how light Frankie had felt in his arms, like he was cradling thistledown.

"Stop ignoring me," Elias said.

Waylon set the tablet aside. "The only reason she's sticking with the club is for Stephanie's sake. Same with me."

"You sure about that?"

"Positive. Frankie outright told me." And it shouldn't have mattered to Waylon, but when she'd made her reasons clear on the way back to the rec center, he'd felt an unfamiliar pang of loss, one that sent him practically running off the bus.

"Eh, people change their minds all the time," Elias said with a nonchalant smile.

"Not in this case, brother. I say this with all due respect, but lay off. There's nothing there now and there won't be when this is over."

THE OTHER, perhaps bigger reason Waylon didn't appreciate being blindsided at the rec center was because that meant Frankie was also blindsided. He could tell the moment she looked up at him when he walked in—the shock in her eyes, the way her hand went straight to her hair. She was obviously self-conscious of it, though Waylon had no idea why. She had dark, glossy hair, short of course, because it was growing back out. He could only imagine how beautiful it would be once it cascaded over her shoulders in waves. Hell, it was cute now, the way it stood up in some places and curled in others.

Pixie.

He'd turned to see if Elias was in the least bit sorry he'd put Frankie on the spot like that, and it was apparent the asshole didn't regret it in the least. Hell, he was gloating. Waylon gave his brother the stink eye, then looked back at Frankie to reassure her he hadn't meant for this to happen.

Too late—she was glaring at him with those incredible eyes, issuing a challenge. Didn't matter how tiny she was, her eyes held all the fierceness of the bravest warrior. If he were back on the battle-field, he'd think twice before fighting a soldier who looked at him like that. He'd undoubtedly lose the fight. God, he admired her at that moment; no wonder she'd beat cancer. He couldn't help smiling.

And when Wren had grabbed Frankie's hand and pulled her up, he felt his heart thud against his chest. Frankie wasn't friendless in Colorado anymore. She'd been swept into the pack as fast as Wren had been, thanks in part to Waylon pushing Elias into admitting his feelings for her.

Shit. If Elias thought this Adventure Buddy situation was even remotely like his with Wren, he was completely wrong. Elias and Wren had been love at first sight—something Waylon didn't believe in.

Not anymore. Not for a long, long time.

Hard to keep that in mind as they played Pickleball. He loved watching her in action. She wasn't about to let anything or anyone stop her as she sent the ball flying back at him time after time. He found himself thinking, *if only we'd met before. The adventures we would've had.*

He couldn't help his heart speeding up when Wren invited her to Bear and Ellie's. He could spend a little more time with her without freaking her out. Just a group of friends getting together, not a date.

I don't deserve to date.

Especially not when Frankie was already dating someone else.

He turned the corner onto Frankie's street.

Whoa. Nice Corvette parked in front of her house.

Waylon grinned. "Maybe I'll let her drive us after all."

He pulled up behind it and looked at her porch.

Where he saw Frankie's boyfriend. And Frankie herself, holding a dozen roses.

TEN

Frankie couldn't believe Waylon had brought her roses.

She smiled, surprised, before a split-second later she realized that the man holding them wasn't Waylon.

It was Dr. Derek Sloane.

She froze.

He didn't pick up on her reaction, or if he did, he didn't care. Instead, he smiled back, looking like a shy little boy behind his glasses. His dishwater-blond hair, normally slicked back, was tousled. He was wearing jeans that looked like they'd been pressed, and a quarter-zip sweater. He looked harmless, even charming with the roses.

Yet, he still creeped her the hell out.

"Dr. Sloane. It's...I... What a surprise," she stammered, having no idea what else to say and hating how she automatically smiled.

How does he know where I live?

"Derek," he said in an 'aw, shucks' tone of voice that was ever so slightly nasal. "Call me Derek. And I'll call you Francesca." His voice broke a little on her name. He looked at the roses as if he just remembered he was holding them. "These are for you. You're far enough out from chemo, you can have real ones now." He held them out expectantly.

Frankie watched her hand lift to take them. Her fingers brushed against his, cold and clammy. Her stomach churned. "Thank you. They're lovely."

Why did you do that? Give them back to him and tell him to leave, you aren't interested.

Instead, she clutched the roses like a shield.

Derek smiled as color rose in his cheeks. "I wasn't sure if roses were your thing after last time, but I thought I'd take a chance again."

Her breath hitched. *Last time?* Did he mean the silk bouquet he tried to give her at the cancer center?

He cleared his throat, and the aw-shucks voice came out full force. "You didn't have to throw the last bouquet away, you know. If you didn't like them," he added with a small laugh, "I would've kept them and gotten you different ones."

Frankie's eyes widened as her chest tightened. *Oh, God, he did mean the silk roses.* What did he do, go through the trash can outside the hospital?

"I... Bea was the one who threw them away." Great, now she was ratting out Bea, though she was still safely away in Puerto Rico, or at least that's what Frankie supposed. She wasn't coming back to work at the cancer center at any rate, thank goodness.

Derek's eyes went frosty even though his smile remained. "She was always overprotective. It's good she's moved on." He tilted his head slightly. "You...aren't still in contact with her, are you?"

"N-no. She hasn't... we haven't..."

"Good." The frost left his eyes and the little boy act returned. "So, hey, I was hoping I could take you to breakfast this morning." He gestured to a Corvette parked in front of the house. "I'll let you pick where, but I have some suggestions. We could even go all the way down to Denver. How does that sound?"

Horrifying. Trapped in a car with Dr. Sloane—Derek—for an

hour, then breakfast, then God knew what. He'd have her miles away from home, in a city she didn't know well.

He's a doctor! She could practically hear her mother's voice in her head. *He's interested in you. What are you waiting for? You won't get another chance so stop being a little fool.*

Ugh! Shut up!

Derek's smile faded at the edges. Was her face giving away her loathing? She schooled it back into something passing for pleasant. "Well, actually," she lifted her shoulder, indicating the backpack strap, "I made plans this morning."

"Really?"

Isn't it obvious, or are you just ignoring me? she wanted to shout. *Now get off my lawn! I mean, porch.*

"You...could change your plans." He looked down, fake-bashful. "I'm sure whoever you're meeting wouldn't mind waiting a little while. Just an hour for breakfast?"

He's ignoring me.

"I really can't," she countered, then regretted it, apprehensive of how he might react. Her mother's voice in her head reiterated she was being a fool, it was broad daylight, and they were on her front porch in front of God and everybody for heaven's sakes, and may I remind you—*doctor.*

The sound of an approaching truck trickled in under her mother's berating.

Please be Waylon. She smirked at the words that a week ago, she never thought she'd say.

Derek glanced back up and caught the smirk. He frowned.

Shit, he thinks I'm what? Making fun of him?

A truck turned the corner and pulled smoothly to the curb behind Derek's Corvette. Behind the windshield, Frankie made eye contact with Waylon, wearing his usual scowl. No, not his usual one —this one put the others to shame. Still, her shoulders sagged with relief.

Derek clocked her reaction. Curious, he looked over his shoulder at what caused it. He froze.

Shit.

Derek looked back at her, features blank.

"That's my ride," Frankie chirped, a defensive smile on her face. "I've gotta go." She tucked her phone under her opposite armpit and stepped out onto the porch, doorknob in hand. She turned, reached around the doorframe, and punched in the away code on the burglar alarm at the last second—as a disturbing image of Derek inside her house while she was gone flashed across her brain—and slammed the door.

Derek didn't move. He stood like a stone between her and Waylon's truck, his gaze practically gripping her, holding her in place. She slid her phone out from under her arm and held it in a death grip.

Frankie heard the truck door open, then Waylon stepped out of his truck. Derek looked over his shoulder at him. When he looked back at Frankie, his smile returned, along with the frost in his eyes. "Seems I came at a bad time."

"Seems you did."

Derek took a step backward. "Maybe later, Francesca." It wasn't a question.

Maybe never.

Before she could tell him no way, he turned and walked briskly back to his car. He stared at Waylon all the way back to the Corvette. Frankie waited until Derek started the engine and pulled away—more like peeled out like an asshole with something to prove—before sprinting to Waylon's truck.

Roses still in hand, dammit.

ELEVEN

Waylon squeezed the steering wheel as he watched the scene unfolding on Frankie's porch. Frankie stood in the doorway holding a huge bouquet of roses and talking to some guy who was obviously not just a delivery boy.

This guy must have been the date she was talking about. And he'd brought her roses first thing in the morning. That was more of a boyfriend move than a friend with benefits. But if Frankie were in a serious relationship, Stephanie would have paired her with another woman. She wouldn't have set Waylon up with her, because there was no doubt in his mind that Steph was playing matchmaker.

Frankie's gaze went straight to Waylon as he parked. She looked upset—at him for showing up while her boyfriend was there? Probably. When the guy turned, Waylon was sure of it. The way he looked at Waylon told him this was more than just friends with benefits. That look said, *back off, she's mine.*

If this is turning serious between them, I should just drive away. Consider the Adventure Buddy thing over. He hated the way his heart clenched at the thought.

No. Be an adult. Turn off the truck, go up and introduce yourself as just a friend.

Then he could drive away.

Waylon killed the engine and grabbed his door handle, ready to make nice, when the guy looked back at Frankie. She stepped onto the porch and pulled the door shut behind her with a slam. She had her pack over her shoulder and looked ready to go. Smiling, she said something to him as she pointed her chin toward Waylon.

The guy stood there without moving, his body language reading as possessive. Waylon wondered if the roses were a romantic gesture or an apology—but either way, it set warning bells off in Waylon's head. He opened his door and stepped out of his truck.

The guy gave him another look before saying something to Frankie. He stepped back, turned, then walked down the porch steps and headed toward the Corvette. His stride was brisk and tight, shoulders hunched like he was barely containing his anger. Waylon narrowed his eyes as the guy glared at him the entire way to the car, his eyes icy.

Waylon's jaw clenched. *Yeah, buddy, keep walking.*

The Corvette tore out with a screech. Frankie watched it from the porch. As Waylon started toward her, she surprised him by bolting toward his truck, phone in one hand, roses in the other.

Waylon frowned. *She's bringing them?*

Frankie's expression stopped him cold. She looked upset, her lips pressed into a tight line and her cheeks flushed, either from anger or embarrassment. The way she flung open the passenger door, let her pack slide off her shoulder to the floor, and tossed the roses onto the dashboard like they were trash? Definitely anger.

Waylon got back into the truck. "Hey." He twisted in his seat to face her. "You okay?"

"Fine." Frankie smiled as she waved a dismissive hand. "Let's just go." She set her phone on top of her pack and pulled her seatbelt across her waist. She tucked the shoulder strap under her right arm, not letting it cross her chest.

Fine? As if Waylon would buy her act for a second. He leaned toward her, his voice low and steady. "Frankie, who was that?"

She sighed heavily, her head falling back against the seat. "Oh, that was just Derek. He hadn't gotten the hint that I never want to see him again."

Waylon's teeth ground together. His protective instincts roared to life. All he wanted was to tear away from the curb, hunt down Derek, and give him a lesson on respecting boundaries. But he tamped down the urge—for now. Frankie needed him calm, not going off after the asshole with her in the truck.

"My friends and I... We can do something about that," he said, his voice sharper than he intended. "It wouldn't be the first time."

That was an understatement.

Frankie turned to him, her lips quirking up in a tired smile. "No, no. It's fine. I think you driving up when you did sent a message. Thanks for that, Buddy."

The way she said "Buddy" made it clear the conversation was over, but Waylon's mind was racing. The Corvette wouldn't be difficult to track down, especially since Waylon had memorized the license plate at a glance. This time, he'd have a real reason to ask Shane to help him out. It wouldn't hurt to know where this guy lived, what he did for a living, if he was into anything shady.

If he had a pattern of abuse.

"Waylon." Frankie placed her hand on his upper arm. "Seriously, it was not a big deal. Besides," she grinned, "you did a great job of scaring him away. He thinks we're dating. He won't be back around."

Waylon didn't trust her smile so he looked deeply into her eyes. They went a little unfocused. Or maybe that was him. Frankie was seriously beautiful. Especially when the fierceness rose in her eyes.

Damn.

He shook his head a little to clear it. He focused on the bridge of her nose so he wouldn't fall back in.

"I mean it, Frankie. If he's bothering you. If he's hurt you. We can do something about it."

Her eyes widened. She laughed nervously.

Oh fuck. Now I've gone and scared her. Of course I have. It's what I do best.

"I'm sorry," he said quickly and looked away.

She squeezed his arm. "Hey, I appreciate you looking out for me, I do. But no, he's never hurt me. He's just...awkward, that's all."

Waylon looked at her again. He could feel the heat of her hand through his flannel. "I didn't mean to scare you, Frankie. I'm sorry."

"Pfft. You didn't." She gave him a genuine smile, twin to the one on her face the first time she laid eyes on him. "You're my Adventure Buddy. You've defended me from deadly splinters and mooses gone wild. You've got my back."

You've got my back. Her words reverberated in his chest as she sat there grinning, eyes full of glee.

He felt the corner of his mouth turn up. "Mooses?"

"Yes." She nodded definitively. "Mooses."

He cracked a full-on smile as the tension in the air eased. Frankie wasn't afraid of him. There wasn't a trace of fear in her eyes—and he didn't think those eyes were capable of lying.

She took her hand off his arm and he missed her touch immediately. "So, we'd better get going if we're gonna get to our next adventure on time. I don't think Steve appreciates tardiness."

Waylon snorted. "You make her sound like an old school marm."

Frankie covered her mouth as she laughed. "That's the last thing she'd be. God, don't ever let her hear you say that."

"Good advice." He started the truck, then pulled away from the curb. "You know, if you don't want those," he raised his chin at the roses on the dash, "we can find a Dumpster to toss them in."

"Oh." She sounded surprised. "Yeah, I don't. I'm not even sure why I brought them. I was in a hurry, I guess."

Uneasiness crept back into Waylon's chest.

Let it go.

Another thought rose.

If Derek's out of the picture...that means Frankie's single.

The unsettling thought sent a small burst of satisfaction through him, quickly followed by guilt.

Why the hell do you care if she's single? You are never, ever going to ask her out.

Adventure Buddies. Emphasis on *Buddy.*

Waylon tightened his grip on the wheel, forcing his focus back to the road. They drove in silence through her neighborhood then turned onto a main road heading for Idaho Springs.

"Before we get onto I-70, do you mind not tucking that seatbelt strap under your arm?"

Instead of letting it cross her body, she reached for her pack on the cab floor, picked it up, and unzipped a side pocket. She pulled out a square of padded cloth, untucked the shoulder belt from under her arm, and put the cloth between her chest and where the belt crossed.

Oh, right. She must still have her chemo port in. He'd seen a port pillow before. Frankie was using it to keep the strap from irritating her port site.

He noticed her cheeks redden and wondered why.

Frankie broke the silence a few miles down the road. "So, what do you think Steve's got planned for us today?"

"No idea about the first part, but I'm pretty sure I know why we're bringing swimming suits."

"You do?" Her curious tone was laced with unease.

"Don't worry, I don't think we're gonna be jumping into any freezing cold mountain lakes."

"No? Then what?"

"Oh, right, you're still pretty new to town. We're going to Idaho *Springs.* Does that give you a clue?"

"Hmm..." She tapped her chin. "Could it be...hot springs?" The sarcasm in her voice reminded him of Wren. *No wonder they hit it off right away.*

"Wow, give her a cookie."

"Yup-yup-yup, I'm a bright one. Uh-huh."

They both laughed. Then Waylon remembered—the more

nervous Wren was, the more she cracked jokes. Was Frankie the same way?

"Wren says you're a Wwoofer," Waylon said, changing the subject to something he thought would put her at ease.

"I am." Her voice sounded instantly brighter. "I love the work, and it lets me travel on the cheap. They provide room and board, and in return I get to do something fun like help plant a garden, or tend an orchard." She paused. "Or rope some cattle."

Waylon inhaled sharply, remembering Frankie's broken-in cowboy boots. Those weren't just for dancing, they'd seen actual work. Wren had also mentioned that Frankie grew up on a ranch—knowing exactly how he felt about cowgirls. He suddenly had the clearest image of Frankie riding horseback through a meadow, her long, dark hair flying behind her. And damn if that enjoyable image didn't tickle something in the back of his mind.

Not to mention his cock.

It's just because of the dream.

And because of the way she'd paused...oh, shit, what did Wren tell *her*?

"Cattle, huh?" Waylon adjusted his grip on the steering wheel, hating the crack in his voice. He coughed to cover it, shifting his gaze to the road ahead.

"You think I can't rope cattle?" Frankie shot him a side-eye, her lips curving into a smile like a baited hook. She leaned back in her seat, folding her arms across her chest, her confidence unmistakable.

"I'm sure you can. Wren mentioned you grew up on a ranch. In Montana, right?" Waylon tried to sound casual, but the image of Frankie on horseback popped back into his head, unbidden.

"Right." Her voice softened, and her gaze drifted to the passing trees outside the window. "I was supposed to take a spot on a ranch east of here, but then I got sick." She sighed and ran a hand through her short hair, her fingers ruffling the dark waves absently. "Last year, I thought I'd be wwoofing in another country by now, but I got sideswiped."

Waylon's stomach sank at her words, the weight behind them felt like a rock in his gut. "Where...do you think you'll go next?"

She shrugged, glancing at him briefly. "I'm not quite ready to leave the country just yet. Not until I'm cleared." She leaned forward to adjust her pack on the floor, her voice brightening. "So, instead of being disappointed that I can't leave yet, I thought I'd leave it up to fate. Make it interesting."

"How so?" He raised an eyebrow, stealing a glance at her as she settled back in her seat.

"Well." She grinned, her eyes lighting up. "I thought it would be fun to save a bunch of quarters, the ones with different states and parks on the back. I'd put them all into a bag, then reach in, grab one, and that would be the place I'd go."

Waylon grinned, shaking his head slightly. "Really? That's cool. Except what if you choose a place you don't want to go?"

She turned to him, her brows arching like he'd said something absurd. "There is no place I don't want to go."

"Come on. What if it's boring?"

"There is no boring." Frankie leaned toward him slightly, gesturing with her hands for emphasis. "I can figure out how to have a good time anywhere."

"Anywhere?" He gave her a skeptical look, tilting his head.

"Yup." She nodded decisively, her tone leaving no room for argument.

Waylon smirked. "Okay. What if you pulled Kansas?"

"Easy." Frankie shifted in her seat, sitting up straighter as if accepting a challenge. "I'd go to the Oz Museum and the Cathedral of the Plains. Next?"

He chuckled. "Ha. Well, okay. New Jersey."

"Jersey Shore, just like the reality show, duh! Gym, tan, laundry." She said it with such exaggerated enthusiasm that Waylon burst out laughing.

"I think you're probably the only person I know who could make gym, tan, laundry interesting." He shook his head, his grin lingering.

"Okay, different tact. Where do you want to go the most? What quarter would you be thrilled to pick out?"

He half-expected her to dodge the question, but she answered without hesitation.

"Easy. Hawaii. The U.S. Virgin Islands wouldn't suck, either." That smile got him—hook, line, and sinker—daring him to ask her why.

"What's in Hawaii or the Virgin Islands that has you smiling like that? Cabana boys?"

She scoffed, swatting the air between them. "Nope. I want to swim with either manta rays or sharks."

Waylon couldn't help his surprised laugh. "Of course you do." He thought of how she'd watched the moose fight without a trace of fear.

"What? People do it all the time. If a shark bothers you, you just punch it in the nose."

"Right, and then you beat it with your bloody stump."

Frankie laughed as her hand darted out to push his shoulder playfully. The light, easy contact sent a surprising warmth through him.

"You really are fearless, aren't you?" Waylon said, half in awe.

Frankie's laughter quieted, but her smile remained. She looked out the window for a moment before meeting his gaze. "No. I'm not. I'm full of fear. I just don't let it stop me."

Damn.

Waylon didn't have a response to that, so he kept driving, letting her words linger between them.

The truck climbed higher into the mountains. By the time they reached Idaho Springs, the awkwardness of Waylon's encounter with Derek had mostly melted away. If it weren't for the roses still resting on the dashboard he could've forgotten all about it.

Waylon pulled into the meeting spot, a mostly full public parking lot behind a row of restaurants, between Idaho Street and I-70. Waylon parked and turned to her, one hand resting on the back of the seat. "You good?" He nodded at the roses. "I saw a trash can at the end of the row."

Frankie smiled and nodded. She reached for her pack as Waylon got out and went around the truck to open her door. By the look of surprise on her face, he knew she wasn't used to a guy getting her door. She tucked the port pillow back into her pack, undid her seat-belt, and grabbed the bouquet of wilting flowers. Waylon looked for Stephanie as they walked to the trash can, wondering what they must look like.

Frankie blew out a breath as she dumped the bouquet flowers-first into the trash. Waylon took a ticket from the self-park kiosk and walked back to the truck to set it on the windshield. He noticed a stray petal on the dashboard. He snatched it and dropped it onto the ground beside the truck, then ground it into the gravel with his boot heel.

She loves you not, Derek. You don't deserve her, anyway.

Feeling oddly satisfied, he looked up to see Frankie had found Stephanie and the others by the side of one of the buildings. Even though she had no idea what the adventure was, the little pixie looked excited. He felt his heart thump.

I'd never deserve her, either.

TWELVE

Frankie caught sight of Stephanie and the rest of the Buddies beside one of the buildings. She was annoyed that she and Waylon were almost late thanks to Derek. At least Waylon had deterred him. She was happy to let Derek continue to believe Waylon was her boyfriend, even if the idea was ridiculous.

My friends and I ...we can do something about that.

Nope, ridiculous she told herself as she bit her lower lip. *Besides, you aren't sticking around once you get the all-clear.*

Or was she?

She shook her head. If she was staying, it wasn't for Waylon. He wasn't her only consideration.

Speaking of, Waylon was still back at the truck, looking down at something in the dirt. Frankie felt a moment of doubt. Did he really want to be here? Was he having second thoughts?

When he caught up to her she glanced up at him to judge his mood. He didn't look as annoyed as she'd expected, but something was eating at him. She wouldn't have known that a week ago, but since Pickleball, she'd come to know his resting face wasn't a scowl after all, not around his friends.

Only around her.

Frankie greeted the group with a casual wave. "Hey, everyone! Sorry we're late."

"Everything all right?" Stephanie asked. "I was afraid you'd both backed out."

"No way," Frankie answered. She glanced at Waylon. "At least not me."

"Me neither," he said, his voice defensive. "I'm here, right?"

"You are indeed," Stephanie said, studying him before turning away. "Well, now that we're all here, let's meet our guides." Stephanie started around the building to the street where a shuttle gleamed under the bright Colorado sun, a bold *Wild Side Zip Lines* logo on the side.

"Sweet!" Frankie exclaimed.

"Have you ever been?" Stephanie asked.

Frankie hesitated. "Nope, but it's something on our..." The words caught in her throat, and her smile faltered as the thought of her "list" resurfaced, breaking her heart just a little. She pushed on, trying to sound upbeat. "Something I've always wanted to do."

Stephanie tilted her head slightly, clearly noticing the pause, but didn't press. "Well, today's your lucky day." She pivoted to the group. "All right, Buddies! Get ready for an action-packed day zipping along cliffsides and over canyons."

Two guides stepped out of the shuttle and approached. The taller of the two, a lean man with sun-streaked hair and an easy demeanor, waved. "Hey, everyone! I'm Jacob, and this is Kai. We'll be your guides today."

Kai, a shorter guy with a wiry build and a mischievous smile, added, "Who's ready to fly?"

The Buddies erupted into a mix of cheers and nervous laughter. Frankie felt her heart speed up as she ignored her fear of heights and told herself she'd be fine.

Waylon stood close enough for her to feel the heat radiating from his body. "This your first time ziplining?" he asked, his tone casual, though she caught the trace of a smile tugging at his lips.

"Yup." Frankie glanced up at him, feeling her pulse quicken—not from fear, but something else entirely. "I suppose you have?"

"Not exactly." His grin grew wider. "But I've had to rappel many times as a Ranger. I trained in Georgia at Mt. Yonah. I had to learn how to rappel with an injured teammate on my back, and stretcher-assisted rappels."

"Oh, good," Frankie shot back, her tone teasing. "You'll be able to rappel me down when I break my neck."

Waylon's eyebrows shot up in mock surprise. "You? Nope, I don't buy it."

Jacob clapped his hands, drawing everyone's attention. "All right, folks, if you'll hop on the shuttle, we'll head to the course."

Frankie followed the group into the shuttle, settling into a seat near the back. Waylon slid into the seat beside her. His knee brushed hers, a brief and accidental contact that sent a jolt through her. She looked out the window, focusing on the little town of Idaho Springs as they began the ride to the course.

"Any rules we should know?" Stephanie asked Jacob.

"Just the usual," Jacob replied. "Listen to your guides, keep your helmet on at all times, and have fun. Oh, and scream all you want—it's good for the soul."

Kai chimed in, "And it keeps the squirrels entertained."

Laughter rippled through the shuttle, breaking any lingering tension.

As they arrived at the course, Frankie craned her neck to take in the view. High above, she could make out the first platform built along the side of a cliff, connected to a second by a network of cables, and beyond that, a sprawling canyon opened up, the river below glinting like molten silver.

Jacob led the group to a gear station where the guides handed out harnesses, helmets, and gloves. While Kai and Jacob were busy with Stephanie and one of the other Buddies, Frankie adjusted her harness straps, trying to get the port pillow to stay in place but it kept slipping. She bit her lip against frustrated tears.

I can't believe I'm letting this stupid little thing get to me.

"Can I help?" Waylon asked. He waited instead of just stepping in and doing it for her, which Frankie appreciated.

"Yeah, I think I need it. Thanks, Buddy," she said.

"Anytime." He reached into his pack and took out a plastic circle. "Mind if I tape it in place?" He waved the circle—a roll of some sort of medical tape.

Frankie nodded. "Whatever works."

Waylon dropped to one knee in front of her, which emphasized their size difference. "It'll come off without damaging the pillow or the harness." His voice was low as he adjusted the straps with practiced ease. He slid the pillow into place over her port and Frankie inhaled quickly, her mother's voice in her head.

Gross. Disgusting. Deformed.

Waylon quickly looked up as his gaze flew to hers. "Did I hurt you?" He looked at her like he'd just ripped her arm off.

"No, not at all." She smiled as embarrassment heated her cheeks. He held her gaze with tenderness in his, searching.

No, I'm imagining it. He's only assessing me like a patient.

She broke eye contact and cleared her throat. Waylon tore off a length of tape and wrapped it around the pillow and harness, securing it. His hands lingered a second longer than necessary before he rocked back and stood up.

"That should hold. If it starts to fray, I've got plenty more." He tucked the tape into the pack's front pocket for easy access.

"Thank you."

"How we doing over here?" Kai asked, eyeing the pillow. His brows lifted slightly, then he jumped in and took over, demonstrating how to clip onto the lines and explaining the safety measures. Frankie listened as she tried not to be annoyed as he readjusted her harness without bothering to ask. Waylon looked none too pleased as well.

Kai turned to him. "Whatcha weigh, my friend? A side of beef like you might be over our weight limit."

Waylon snorted. "Calling me fat?"

"Hell no, friend. Military?"

"Former. I'll make the weight limit. Barely."

Kai made a fist for Waylon to bump. Frankie nearly sprained her eyes to keep them from rolling. When Kai walked away, she and Waylon exchanged a look that now had her almost spraining her lips not to laugh.

Her nerves kicked in when they started up the steep path to the platform as she imagined soaring over the canyon.

Waylon nudged her. "You nervous?"

Frankie shook her head, though the butterflies in her stomach told a different story. "Excited."

He raised an eyebrow, clearly not buying it. "You've got this, pixie." His eyes went wide as the name slipped out.

She laughed. "Pixie, really?"

"I'm sorry, I, uh—"

"It's the hair, right?" She ran her gloved hand over her spiky, curly hair.

"Well, that and you're so tiny."

Frankie laughed. "Anything's tiny to you, Side O' Beef." She punched his arm playfully. "Ouch, he wasn't kidding." She shook out her hand, pretending she'd injured it—though considering his guns felt like they were made of actual metal, if she'd punched him for real she'd be dealing with broken knuckles.

Before cancer, she'd never been accused of being tiny. *You should see me in a swimsuit now* she thought, glad that she'd packed a shirt to wear over it.

I...did pack it, right? She remembered pulling it out, but did she actually put it in her pack before Derek interrupted her?

By the time they reached the first platform, Frankie felt her confidence disappear. All she could focus on was trying not to tear open her pack to make sure she brought her shirt.

"You okay for real?" Waylon asked.

"Yup, just fine." *For now.*

Stephanie went first. Jacob hooked her harness to the trolley and gave her a few last-minute pointers. She grabbed the handlebars and jumped, then yelled like Tarzan the entire way across. Everyone cheered as her voice echoed through the mountains.

Waylon cupped his hands and shouted, "I think they heard you in Idaho Springs!"

"I hope they heard me in Idaho!" she shouted back. "That was fun!"

When Frankie's turn came, she stepped up to the edge. The line stretched out before her like a thread of silver spiderweb to the next platform. She'd never had trouble with heights before, but when she looked down at the river below, her knees locked as vertigo hit her.

"How about I go next?" Waylon said.

"I'm just having a little vertigo. I'm not chickening out."

"Never said you were." His mouth twitched into that maddening grin. "You've got this, Pixie. I'm just giving you advice for your first jump. When I started rappelling, I focused on something at eye level. Took the jitters right out of it. I figure a side of beef like me will be pretty easy to spot from a few hundred feet away."

Frankie's laugh came out unexpectedly, steadying her nerves like nothing else had. "All right, Beefcake, I'll give a try."

He squeezed her shoulder, which steadied her even more.

"Thank you," she said quietly.

Waylon nodded. Jacob hooked him to the line, then he took off like he'd done it a hundred times before. She watched him sail across, wind tugging at his flannel, until he landed on the next platform and turned to wave at her.

"Okay," she whispered. "If I can survive cancer, I can do this."

Besides, I'm never going to hang glide naked if I can't, and nothing in this world will make me take it off the list.

Jacob hooked up her harness to the trolley. "Ready?" he asked.

Frankie took a deep breath and nodded. "Ready."

She leaped off the platform into the air. The wind whipped past her, and the canyon below blurred as she hurtled toward Waylon. Her grip tightened as she laughed, exhilaration rushing through her veins. When she landed, her knees buckled slightly, and Waylon grabbed her arm to steady her.

"What'd I tell you?" he asked, grinning ear to ear.

She blinked up at him, still catching her breath. "Oh. My. God. That was awesome!"

"Told you, you've got this," he said, his grin as wide as the canyon. His pride in her sent an unexpected warmth through her chest.

"Yeah, yeah." She shook her head, but her smile matched his.

As the group hiked to the next platform, Frankie found herself laughing more, feeling lighter than she had in months. And every time Waylon caught her eye, that feeling only grew stronger. She went ahead of him at the next line, which was about a third longer and gave her an amazing view of Idaho Springs far below.

By the time they reached the final line, a race across the canyon on parallel lines, Frankie was ready. Adrenaline had transformed her nerves into giddy confidence.

"Loser buys lunch," she declared, narrowing her eyes at Waylon like a gunfighter in an old Western.

"You're on," he shot back, his competitive grin sending her pulse racing. "But let's make it dinner."

Frankie's eyebrows rose. "Dinner, huh? Okay, Buddy, but just so you know, I've got a crazy dinner planned if you win."

"You trying to psych me out?" He winked. "I've got a crazy dinner idea myself."

"Heck no. Let's do this!"

The whistle blew, and Frankie threw herself into the race with everything she had. Wind tore at her hair as she shot across the canyon, the river below a blur of shimmering silver. Waylon pulled ahead, but she wasn't far behind.

"Lean into the line!" he shouted back at her.

Frankie adjusted her position, feeling the difference immediately.

"Thanks! Keep your weight back a little!" she called, spotting the way his posture shifted.

Their combined laughter carried across the canyon.

Frankie knew she had no chance in hell of winning, and honestly, she didn't want to. 'Fancy dinner for two in Denver' was on her list and she couldn't go without a guest.

Frankie just never imagined Waylon would be her plus-one.

Waylon beat her to the platform, and when she landed, he reached out to catch her.

"Dinner's on you, Pixie," he said with a cocky grin.

Frankie pulled off her helmet and shook out her hair. "All right, Beefcake. But if I'm buying, you're not allowed to complain about my crazy menu."

"Deal." His grin softened into something that sent an unexpected flutter through her stomach. This was supposed to be just fun. Why did it feel like so much more?

ONCE THEY WERE BACK on the shuttle to Idaho Springs, Stephanie announced their next stop.

"All right, after all the excitement, I thought we'd spend the rest of the day relaxing at the hot springs. Who's been before?"

Frankie looked around to see almost every hand shoot up, including Waylon's.

That's when she remembered to check for her shirt. She'd completely forgotten during the excitement of the zip lines. Frankie grabbed her pack off the floor and opened the top.

"You forget your swimsuit?" Waylon asked as he watched her.

Now that was an idea...except her suit was right at the top and very obvious. It was also obvious she'd left her shirt on the bed.

"Nope, suit's right here," she said lamely.

"Good. You'll love this place. They have a huge indoor pool and if you want a real adventure, there are individual pools in the caves beneath the resort."

"Wow, sounds great." *Maybe I can hide in a cave.*

Wait.

"Did you say it's a resort?"

"Not a big one. More like a hotel."

"But you can buy things there?"

He looked at her funny. "I guess. What do you need? They supply the towels if that's what you're worried about."

"Nope, I'm good," she said. Especially if they sold t-shirts. She could just buy an extra-large and throw it on over her suit. Easy-peasy.

"WHAT DO you mean you're out of extra-larges?" Frankie implored the woman working the front counter. Behind her, way up on the wall, hung shirts with the hotel's logo emblazoned across the front—in all sizes. Frankie had lingered at the front desk after everyone else grabbed their complimentary towels and headed for the locker rooms.

"No medium, 2xl or larges, either, sorry, honey. We've only got extra-small until the next order comes in, that's it."

The extra-small looked like it *might* fit a three-year-old.

"Could I buy that one right off the wall?" Frankie pointed at the extra-large tee.

"Display only, sorry. They were a pain to get up there, and I'd probably lose my job if I took one down."

Frankie swallowed hard as the woman moved on to the next customer. The white towel in her hand felt like the size of washcloth, and she couldn't exactly go in the water with one wrapped around her anyway. Waylon had driven, so sneaking away wasn't an option. Maybe she could hide in the locker room—

"Hey, what's the holdup?"

Frankie whirled around and faced Waylon.

In his swim trunks, with one of the tiny white towels draped around his shoulders.

Nothing else.

Good Lord. All those abs.

So many abs just abbing away on his abdomen.

"I...was going to buy a shirt," she stammered.

"Then buy a shirt and let's go. Come on, the water's incredible."

"They're out."

Waylon frowned and tilted his head. "Okay...so...?" He held his arms out like *what's the holdup?*

"I can't...I should wear a shirt." She looked down at herself. The scars. He hadn't seen those. Would they show if she moved wrong and her suit shifted? She knew the port wasn't visible under her clothes, and it wasn't like Waylon didn't know she had one.

But still.

"Why?" Waylon scoffed. "You've got a suit, right? You're good."

She blinked as she looked back up at him. She saw genuine confusion in his eyes, then watched it clear.

"You're fine, Frankie." He mock-punched her arm. "Come on, *Adventure* Buddy." He turned, then said over his shoulder, "If you aren't in the pool in five minutes, you're buying me two dinners."

Frankie grinned at his retreating back.

I keep telling other people not to treat me like glass, then I turn around and do it to myself.

"Ten minutes," she called after him.

"Eight. Final offer."

"Ugh. *Fine.*"

Frankie had about one minute left when she stepped out of the women's locker room and into the hallway, towel clutched in front of her chest. Warm, steamy air greeted her. Her flip-flops clopped on her feet as she made her way down the hall leading to the pool area. It looked more like a botanical center than a pool room. Entire trees reached for the glass ceiling arching over the space—broad-leafed fig trees and skinny palms. Everywhere she looked was full of exotic greenery.

"Something else, huh?"

Frankie jumped and spun around. Then she tried to ignore the water beading on Waylon's chest and the way his wet trunks clung to his...

Oh. Lord.

"Jeeze, do you always creep up behind people?" she asked him as she tore her eyes away from the obvious and sent them back up to his face.

Waylon laughed. "Well, that did used to be part of my job."

"I'm not an enemy combatant."

He tilted his head and pursed his lips while he stroked his chin as he studied her.

"Okay, I'm not *that* combative."

Waylon broke into a grin as he shook his head. He jutted his chin out. "Come on. You won't believe how warm the water is."

She turned back around and clutched the towel tighter.

Waylon placed his hand on her shoulder and took a step forward. Frankie found herself walking beside him under the encouraging weight of his hand. They went to one of the poolside tables. Waylon pulled the towel from around his shoulders and dropped it on the table.

The moment of truth.

Frankie gave her shield of a towel one last squeeze and set it down next to his.

"All right," he said, gesturing toward the steaming blue water. "After you. You're gonna love it, Pixie."

He was right. She loved it. Loved the warm, silky water. Loved the jungle all around the pool. Loved the light streaming down through the curved glass ceiling.

But she mostly loved the way Waylon didn't make a big deal about her body while at the same time not making a big deal about not making a big deal about her body. It was simply not a factor. He treated her like, well...a buddy.

Which was fine. Totally fine. Yup, she didn't want anything more than that. Certainly not an *actual* boyfriend.

Just Buddies.

———

ON THE RIDE back from Idaho Springs, Frankie and Waylon talked about the other Buddies, who they got to know during dinner and beers at the local brewery without the distraction of hiking or ziplining. They were all really cool people. One woman was a nurse at the hospital. They also talked about Stephanie.

"Do you think she'll ever bring Dr. Boyfriend along?" Frankie asked.

Waylon yawned before answering. "I doubt it. They've been dating for a couple of years, but I've never seen him. Have you?"

"Nope. All I know about him is that he treats her like a queen and he's younger." Frankie grinned and said, "Cougar," which got a chuckle out of Waylon.

The rest of the ride passed quietly, but it was a comfortable quiet. Frankie felt completely relaxed, her body had that pleasant heavy feeling from spending time in the water. Waylon seemed relaxed, too, humming along with the radio whenever a song he liked came on. So different from the scowly, uptight guy she'd met a week ago.

It was dark when Waylon parked at the curb in front of Frankie's house. Frankie reached for her bag, but something in the air stopped her. A sudden, strange heaviness between them.

"Well, that was fun," she said lightly, trying to break the heaviness.

"Yeah, it was." Waylon's voice was softer than usual. "You did great out there, Pixie."

A smile tugged at her lips. "You're not gonna let that nickname go, are you?"

"Not a chance." He grinned, but it faded quickly as his eyes dropped to her mouth—just for a second. His gaze flicked back to hers, and Frankie's breath caught.

For a brief moment, she thought—no, felt—that he might lean in. Her heartbeat thundered in her ears as the world around her seemed to telescope down to just the truck. More precisely, to the two of them sitting in the dark. She scooted toward him.

But then Waylon shifted in his seat and rubbed the back of his neck. "Well, uh, I should walk you to the door, then head home. Long day."

Frankie blinked, feeling the spell break with a little stab to her heart, and nodded quickly. "Right. Thanks for the ride, Buddy, but I think I can find my way to the front door by myself."

"Nope. I'll walk you." Waylon was already opening his door. He stepped out of the truck and abruptly stopped. He looked toward her house.

"Way—"

He held up a finger. A moment later, he asked, "Do you have a burglar alarm?"

Her eyes widened. "Yes." Then she heard it—a faint, high-pitched whine coming from inside her house. Her heart dropped into her stomach.

"Connected to the police?"

"Should be." But where the heck *were* the police?

"Stay here." Waylon reached for something under his seat, then slammed his door and sprinted around the front of the truck toward the house. She watched him through the truck window, her stomach twisting with every second that passed.

Waylon's movements were swift and precise as he approached Frankie's porch, his body low and his head on a swivel, scanning the surroundings like a predator tracking prey. Every step he took looked deliberate, his focus unshakable. He didn't just look at the house—he analyzed it.

Frankie wondered again where the police were. The station

wasn't far away. The time she'd accidentally set the alarm off, she'd gotten a call from the security company almost immediately and the police had arrived within five minutes. She grabbed her phone and unlocked it. No calls. What the hell?

Did someone *just* break in? Were they still in there?

Was it Derek?

Ignoring his order to stay put, Frankie grabbed her keys, then slipped out of the truck. Crouching, she got halfway across the front yard when Waylon shot her a sharp look over his shoulder and raised his hand to halt her.

"I told you to stay in the truck." His commanding tone was low, calm, and controlled, keeping her panic in check.

"Are you kidding? I'm not letting you do this alone. What if someone's still in there?"

Waylon exhaled hard through his nose. "Dammit, Pixie. Back in the truck *now*." He turned his attention back to the front door and the windows. The curtains were drawn and nothing on the porch indicated a break-in. No broken glass, no signs of forced entry. Maybe they'd gone in through the back door.

"Truck, Frankie. Don't make me say it again."

Frankie bit her lip as she stood her ground, her phone clutched tightly in one hand, thumb ready over the emergency call button.

"No fucking way. I'm not leaving you."

He shot her a look of pure fury. "You're safer in the truck than with me."

"I'm not worried about *my* safety, I'm worried about yours."

Fury turned to confusion. Something bright and painful to see flashed in his eyes, something that hurt her heart on his behalf.

"Please. Go."

She tossed him her keys. He caught them with one hand and that's when she saw the gun in his other.

"Go," he growled again, then headed for the porch steps.

THIRTEEN

Waylon crept up the steps, his boots making no sound despite their size. He crouched as he examined the door handle. It looked untouched. He tried to turn it but it was locked.

Whoever broke in must have entered through the back.

He inserted the key into the lock and turned it slowly, listening for the faint click of the lock. Waylon pushed the door open an inch and waited, listening intently for any sound from inside the house. The alarm's whine grew louder when he opened the door, but beyond that, the house was silent. He eased the door open and stepped inside, his eyes sweeping the front room. Nothing looked disturbed.

Waylon moved through the house methodically, clearing it. He checked every room. No broken windows, no signs of forced entry through the back door. Satisfied there were no intruders lurking in the shadows, he headed back to the front room.

When he reached the control panel for the alarm, he frowned. The display flashed an error code along with the word MALFUNCTION.

Waylon let out a low breath, his tension easing slightly. He canceled the alarm, silencing the whine, and opened the front door.

Frankie waited on the front porch.

Dammit. Waylon's heart pounded in his chest.

"Christ, Frankie, you're supposed to be in the damn truck, not on the lit porch. Anyone could have seen you."

Taken you. Hurt you.

"I told you I wasn't leaving you." And there was that fierceness in her eyes. His heart swelled.

"Get inside." He looked out across the yard and both ways down the street as she scooted in past him. No sign of anyone.

Frankie's gaze darted around the room as if she expected someone to jump out from the shadows. "What happened?" Her eyes went to the gun in his hand. "Was anyone here?"

Waylon shook his head. "No one's here. Your alarm malfunctioned." He set the gun down on a small table beside her front door.

Frankie frowned. "Weird I didn't get a call. But at least it didn't alert the police, either." Another glance at the gun.

How scared is she of me now? An old familiar feeling of shame washed over him.

Then Frankie studied the code on the display. "I'll call in the morning and ask them what the code means. Maybe I can fix it. If not, they'll send someone out." She turned to him and he expected her to tell him to take his gun and get the hell out.

"Sorry that my alarm went off. I'm sure you're pumped full of adrenaline now." She let out a shaky laugh. "I know I am."

"No, Frankie, I'm sorry *I* scared *you*."

She squinted at him. "What are you talking about?"

Not a trace of fear.

"The way you looked at the gun. Some women think a guy carrying a gun is... What? What'd I say?"

Frankie was laughing at him. "You're kidding me right now. Please, *please* tell me you're joking. I was *admiring* your gun. M9

Beretta. I have a Glock 19 myself. It's a little longer than the 17 but it's lighter, which is why I like it."

Waylon just stared at her.

"Dude, pick your jaw up off the floor, please." She rolled her eyes. "My dad gave me my first rifle when I was ten. A .22 I called Ze Pop Gun." She said the name with an exaggerated French accent. "He wanted to make sure I knew how to shoot in case I ran into anything nasty when I was out riding fences."

Right. Cowgirl. I think I'm in love.

Fuck. Shit. No! Just a Buddy...just a Buddy...just a Buddy...

His body wasn't telling him that. His body was telling him she was anything but.

Frankie smirked. "You look a little pale, Buddy. Adrenaline dump getting to you?"

"You're coming home with me tonight."

Now she looked alarmed. "Excuse me?"

He nodded toward the panel. "You aren't staying here tonight with that out of commission."

Her lips parted slightly and she looked at the floor. "Waylon, seriously, I'll be fine."

"Nope. Pack a bag and get back in the truck."

She snorted. "Aren't you the broken record."

"Pixie," he warned.

Alarm turned to anger. "I'm not a pixie. I'm not some frail, weak little creature. You should have seen me before the cancer. Pixie's the last thing you would have called me then. More like..." She shook her head as she quickly looked away, but not before Waylon caught the way her eyes turned glassy.

"More like what?" he gentled his voice.

"Nothing good. Never mind." Frankie waved him off and wiped her eyes. Then she smiled at him like nothing was wrong. "Seriously, I'll be fine. It's a safe neighborhood, *and* I own a Glock. I don't even know why this house has an alarm."

"So come to my place for *me*." Waylon's words surprised them both.

"For...you?" She blinked rapidly. "As in like, um..."

"No, no, not *that*," he said quickly. "We're just...."

"Buddies. Yeah, we are that," she said just as quickly. "I mean, you know, Steve can be insufferable when she knows she's right."

Waylon nodded like a Bobblehead. "We can't give her the satisfaction of thinking that her plan worked."

"Nope. No way." Frankie rolled backward and forward on the balls of her feet as she clapped her hands once.

"You're still packing a bag, getting in the truck, and coming home with me."

"Oh my God, you are impossible!"

"I've been told worse." He crossed his arms. "Or should I pack for you?"

"Like hell you're seeing the state of my bathroom or my underwear drawer." She grimaced at what she'd just blurted out and turned bright pink.

"I already saw your bathroom when I cleared the house. I did not look in your underwear drawer."

"Well, thank God for small favors. The bathroom is bad enough, but at least I don't keep my..." The pink turned to beet red. "Never mind."

Waylon smirked. "But if you don't pack a bag and sit your ass down in my truck in five minutes, I will *thoroughly* search your underwear drawer."

Her gorgeous eyes narrowed. "You. Wouldn't. Dare."

"Try me." He checked his watch. "Four minutes."

She blew a short, hard breath out her nose. "Ten minutes."

Ha! Got her. "Eight minutes. Final offer."

"If I don't have time to pack my toothbrush and deodorant, you're the one who suffers."

Her hair smells like rosemary, like a breath of fresh air, like a sudden sharp laugh or a challenge or a dare.

Those were the thoughts that had been tumbling through Waylon's head all day. He'd had to fight himself not to lean in close and bury his nose into the top of her head every time she ziplined into his arms. Even her sweat smelled good.

"I can live with that," he told her. "Three minutes."

"I *hate* you." Frankie rolled her eyes and turned on her heel.

The smile she shot him over her shoulder before she disappeared into the hallway slayed him.

"WE'RE HERE." Waylon reached across the cab and gently touched Frankie's shoulder. She'd fallen asleep before they'd even gotten out of her neighborhood. She lifted her head and looked around fuzzily at his apartment building's parking lot, eyes at half-mast.

"Oh, right. Forgot I'd been kidnapped."

Even though he knew she was joking, Waylon suppressed a wince.

Frankie wiped her mouth. "Oh, good, I didn't drool too badly."

And as quickly as she'd unknowingly cut him, she put him back at ease, even pulled a chuckle out of him.

"You laugh, but it's your upholstery."

"I need to get you to bed." *Damn.* Why did everything he say have to sound like he wanted to sleep with her?

Probably because I want to sleep with her.

Nope. Nope. Buddies. Nothing serious going on here, and that's not going to change.

"Sorry, I didn't realize I was this tired." She barely got the words out before she yawned.

"Long day that ended stressfully, I don't blame you."

"Fun day though. Best I've had in a long time." She stretched and looked at him. "Even the false alarm."

Waylon raised his eyebrows. "*That* was fun?"

"Yup. Fun like... a roller coaster ride that feels like it might kill you but in the end, didn't. A safe adrenaline rush. I'm making no sense, am I?"

Waylon laughed again. "Bed. Now."

Shit. Really, you had to say it that way?

The corner of Frankie's mouth turned up suggestively. "I'm that irresistible, huh?"

Yes. No. Yes. Shit.

"You're a knockout, actually." The words slipped past his resolve.

She scoffed and tagged him in the shoulder. "And you're cute when you lie."

He wasn't lying, he really did think Frankie was a knockout. Not his usual type by a longshot, but it didn't matter, he still found her attractive. He opened his mouth to refute her as she watched him eagerly. He looked away instead. Anything else he said was going to give her the wrong impression—that he wanted to start something distinctively non-buddy-like.

But holy hell, she *was* irresistible. So irresistible, he'd almost kissed her when he first dropped her off. And she'd wanted him to, judging by the look on her face and the way she leaned toward him.

Good thing he didn't, because he couldn't afford the chance he might not stop.

"Hang on," he told her as he opened his door. "I'll come around and get your door and your bag."

"Oh, okay," she said softly. The hint of disappointment in her voice killed him.

She's just tired.

He circled his truck and opened her door. She handed him her overnight bag and he offered his arm. She didn't argue, just used it to keep her balance as she hopped out of the truck. Wearing only a light jacket, she shivered in the cold night air. Waylon took off his flannel and put it around her.

"Sorry, thanks. It was so warm today, I didn't think to bring my winter coat."

"You can borrow one of mine. It's going to be even colder tomorrow. Winter's giving us a preview." He gestured toward the apartment building and they started walking. She surprised him by taking his arm. Did he really think the first time he saw her, that he didn't want some woman leaning on him, pretending to be weak? Instead, her hand felt so good there that he fought the urge to wrap his arm around her and pull her in closer. Or hell, just pick her up and carry her.

And she would love it, he knew she would, the way she was flirting. Dammit, no way he would've let her stay in an unsecured house, especially the way her ex stormed away that morning. At the moment, there weren't any empty apartments in his building that he could put her up in, and there wouldn't be any furniture in one anyway. But bringing her back to *his* apartment? Worst idea ever.

But what was I gonna do? Call Watchdog and ask to use one of their safehouses just because a woman was in danger of spending the night alone in her own house?

Shane would've been on his ass immediately, bringing up the past. His other brothers, too. Another intervention, no doubt.

They reached the building's entrance and Waylon swiped his keycard at the door. The heavy glass door clicked open, and he held it for Frankie. She stepped inside and he noticed how she trembled slightly. Whether it was from the chill or the adrenaline still lingering from the alarm scare, he wasn't sure.

"I'm on the second floor," he said. "There's an elevator at the back of the lobby."

"We can take the stairs right here," She gestured at the open stairway across from the mailboxes.

"You sure?"

Frankie smirked. "It's one flight of stairs, Beefcake. I can handle it."

He chuckled softly, letting her take his arm again as they climbed the steps. "If you get tired, I could always carry you."

Dude, shut up.

Frankie glanced up at him, her lips curving into a mischievous smile. "Careful, I might take you up on that."

Waylon just looked away.

She let go of his arm. It felt like he'd lost his.

They reached the top of the stairs and walked down the hall in awkward silence. Waylon opened the door to his apartment, motioning Frankie inside. She stepped in, her gaze sweeping over the space. It was spotless but sparse—no pictures, no decorations, just bare walls and the essentials. Her gaze landed on the couch in the living room. It was so short it looked like it came out of a dollhouse. It fit Waylon comfortably when he was home alone in front of the TV— not so much as a guest bed. Not that he was going to let her sleep on it.

"This is...cozy," Frankie said, setting her overnight bag down on the couch.

Waylon rubbed the back of his neck. "Yeah, well, it gets the job done." He avoided her eyes. What was he supposed to say? That he hadn't bothered making it feel like a home because he didn't think he deserved one?

Her expression softened, and she glanced back at him. "Thanks for letting me stay. I'm sorry for all the trouble tonight."

"What are you apologizing for?" he said immediately, his voice firm. "I pushed the issue, if you recall." He walked toward her, stopping a couple feet away. "You're no trouble at all, Pixie."

For a moment, neither of them said anything. Frankie looked up at him, her gaze searching his face. The air between them felt heavy again, charged with something unspoken.

"Dammit. You're really good at this," she said softly.

"Good at what?"

"Helping me."

Waylon's chest tightened at her words. He took a step closer, close enough that he could see the way her lashes cast faint shadows on her cheeks.

"It's nothing. That's what Buddies are for, right?" he said quietly.

"But, see, you do it without making me feel...weak." She gave him a sad smile. "I misjudged you at the beginning. I thought all you would see was the cancer."

He smiled ruefully. "That wasn't exactly on purpose."

She tilted her head.

"Truth? I handle acute trauma, not chronic illness. So, I didn't recognize the signs immediately. But even if you hadn't been having an off day and hadn't told me, I would've just thought you're thin because you're so active. You're always go, go, go. The way you savor everything, the way nothing gets past you. Everything that comes your way, you drink it down, the good and the bad, it doesn't matter, there's still joy in it for you. Frankie, you're one of the most alive people I've ever met. I still don't see the cancer. I see *you*."

Stunned, her eyes widened. "That's...no one's told me that."

Frankie swallowed, her gaze flicking to his mouth for the briefest of moments before darting back up. Her lips parted slightly, and Waylon felt the pull, the magnetic draw that made his body tense and his heart pound.

Don't do it. Don't screw this up.

Before he could decide whether to act or back away, Frankie took a small step closer. Her voice was barely above a whisper when she spoke.

"Waylon..."

Frankie's phone buzzed loudly, shattering the tension like glass. He stepped back as she pulled the phone out of her bag. When she looked at the screen she cringed.

"It's my mom. I've got to take this." She gave him an apologetic smile he hated.

"No problem. Go right ahead." He walked toward the kitchen. The phone call gave him the excuse to shift gears. He'd been this close to kissing her.

"Hey, Mom," Frankie started, but she didn't get any further than that before Waylon could hear the woman shouting through the phone.

"Sorry, I was gone all day."

More shouting.

"No, I was doing something where I couldn't get to my phone."

Pause. "No seriously, I was."

Frankie heaved a sigh. "I was ziplining, and then in a hot spring pool."

Waylon couldn't hear her mother's voice anymore, but whatever she was saying was draining all the color out of Frankie's face.

Oh, shit. Did someone die? Waylon braced for the news as if he were receiving it. The look on Frankie's face killed him. He'd do anything she needed—take her to the airport, hell, drive her across the country if that's what it took to take that devastated look off her face.

"Yes. Of course I wore a swimsuit into the pool."

What the hell?

"No. Nothing over it. They didn't have a big shirt." Her voice had gone soft—a child reasoning with a parent.

Waylon's heart clenched. He'd been right earlier—the shirt she'd wanted to buy at the front counter was meant to cover up her body. As if a beautiful woman like her had anything to be ashamed of.

Jesus.

The yelling started again and Frankie squeezed her eyes shut.

"Of course there were other people there. No. No, I'm not seeing any— No." Her face flushed red. "Not because of that, because *I'm* not ready."

Fuck. Was her mother honestly giving her shit about her body? About *dating*? Like maybe her boyfriend would judge her?

She sighed. "Mom, I need to go. My phone battery's almost dead, it's late, I'm tired, I'll call you tomorrow." Frankie pulled the phone away from her ear and tapped the screen. She looked up and gazed not at, but through, the wall with her thousand-yard stare. Then she seemed to remember Waylon was there and she turned. She looked embarrassed. Lost. Not at all his brave Pixie.

My Pixie?

I'm not ready she'd just told her mom. Message received loud and clear.

The lost look quickly vanished under a smile. "My mom. She's just protective."

She's just a mean, nosy bitch, more like.

Waylon walked toward her. "You okay? You want to talk—"

"I'm really tired," she said quickly, then looked away.

This time, Waylon's phone buzzed.

"Sorry," he muttered, glancing at the screen. "It's just a weather alert. Freezing temps tonight and into tomorrow." He put his phone away and grabbed her bag. "Bedroom's this way. I'll take the couch."

"Excuse me?" She poked the couch's armrest with her finger. "You're really planning to sleep on this tiny thing?"

Waylon shrugged. "It's fine. I've slept on worse."

Frankie snorted. "Waylon, come on. Your legs are gonna hang over the end halfway to the floor." She folded her arms and turned to face him. "Just take the bed. I'll sleep out here."

"No way," Waylon said immediately, his voice firm. "I'm not letting you sleep on the couch after I dragged you over here. You're taking the bed."

Frankie uncrossed her arms and planted her hands on her hips. "I'm not gonna kick you out of your own bed, Buddy. That's ridiculous."

"And I'm not gonna make you sleep on this sad excuse for a couch. End of discussion."

Frankie huffed and threw up her hands. "Fine. We'll both sleep in the bed. Problem solved."

That's what you think. "Frankie—"

"Oh come on, Buddy. It's a bed, not a minefield. We're adults, right? Nothing's going to happen." She arched an eyebrow, daring him to argue. "Obviously," she added softly.

Unless I have another wet dream. Waylon cleared his throat, feeling heat rise from his chest to his neck. "Obviously."

Frankie nodded. "Can't let Stephanie win, right?" She turned and headed toward his bedroom like it was no big deal, but Waylon caught the slight redness in her cheeks.

Stephanie, or your mother?

Waylon stood rooted in place for a moment, his mind racing.

I'm not ready.

Sharing a bed with Frankie was an even worse idea than bringing her to his place. Especially now that he knew where she stood on dating. Not that it made any difference, he told himself. She wasn't for him. Waylon hated the way that felt, like a hole had been blasted through his chest.

I'll move out to the couch after she's asleep. Shouldn't be long.

He headed for the bedroom. Halfway down the hall, he remembered what was sitting out on his dresser.

Oh, great.

He picked up his pace, hoping she'd gone straight into the en suite bathroom without noticing it.

Her loud exclamation told him that yes, she did indeed notice.

FOURTEEN

"Oh my God. You're kidding me, Beefcake. *Really?*"

Frankie turned to see Waylon rush to the doorway, cheeks red, alarmed expression on his face.

"It's not what you think," he stammered.

"Oh bullshit. It's exactly what I think." She grinned. "And I think it's adorable." Frankie reached for the old, stained, and scruffy World War I ace pilot Snoopy sitting on the dresser, back propped against the mirror. She picked him up and studied his scuffed-up leather jacket and the black pom-pom for a nose hanging by a single piece of yarn. "You still have your Snoopy from when you were a kid."

Even more adorable than the Snoopy was the way Waylon defended himself.

"It's not... I don't... I just found him in a box the other day and thought I'd give him away."

"Ooo, then can I have him?" she teased, clutching Snoopy to her chest.

"No." He crossed his arms.

"I'm kidding. I'd never take your beloved childhood Snoopy away."

"He's not my *beloved* childhood Snoopy. I just, you know, found him in a box again, that's all."

"Oh, stop lying. You did not just find him in a box. You don't have boxes. You barely have anything here."

Ooops. Why the hell did I just say that?

It wasn't said out of maliciousness, and it wasn't pity. Frankie had felt a strange kind of sorrow when she'd walked into Waylon's apartment. It hung in the air, totally unexpected. When he let his guard down, Waylon struck her as carefree, someone who loved to have a good time. And this apartment was just...sad.

No art. No throw pillows. From what she'd seen of the kitchen, it looked bare, nothing on the countertops. The front room only had that tiny little beat-up couch with a folded-up TV tray propped against it, and a small breakfast table with two mismatched chairs off to the side. The TV hanging on the wall looked like an expensive one, the only thing he'd splurged on.

His bedroom was just as sparse. A plain wooden dresser, mirror, and a double bed without a headboard. Only a single bedside table with a lamp.

A bedroom designed for one.

No. A whole apartment—a whole *life*—designed for one.

And not much of a life. The only hint of a personality was his sentimental little Snoopy doll on the dresser.

It almost made her cry.

Looking at Waylon's face after her snotty little comment, she did want to cry.

I'm as cold and thoughtless as my mother.

"Waylon, I'm sorry, I didn't mean—"

"Doesn't matter." He held out his hand for the Snoopy and she gave it to him. He opened a drawer and stuffed him inside.

"You don't have to...do...that..." She stopped. His expression might as well have been a closed door.

"It doesn't matter, Frankie." He gestured at the bathroom door.

"Go ahead and get ready for bed. I'll change in the main bathroom."
He set her bag on the dresser.

She picked it up. "No, I'll use that one. Your toothbrush and stuff
are in this one, right?"

"As you wish." He walked past her at the same time she scooted
by him into the hall.

She felt sick to her stomach. One minute, she thought for sure
they were going to kiss in his living room—or in his truck—or in *her*
living room—and the next, she was insulting him.

God, I'm an asshole.

She turned on the light in the spotless bathroom and was not
surprised to see it was empty except for a hand towel and a bottle of
liquid soap next to the sink. Nothing, not so much as a travel-sized
bottle of shampoo, graced the shower.

He doesn't even expect *to have guests here.*

She turned and closed the door, then stood facing it.

What the hell happened to you, Beefcake?

She sighed and opened her overnight bag. She took out her nightshirt and glared at it, tightening her jaw. It was supposed to be funny
when she packed it. Now, it just felt cruel. She undressed, slipped
the nightshirt over her head, then stared at the screen-printed Snoopy
in the mirror.

Frankie washed her face, brushed her teeth, and left her bag in
the bathroom. She went into the kitchen with her mostly-dead phone
and charger and found an outlet. She tried to think of something,
anything, to delay her return to the bedroom. Maybe she could just
curl up on the couch and pretend she was sleeping…

No. He'd come looking for her, pick her up, and carry her into the
bedroom. Then he'd for sure sleep on the couch and that image just
hurt her heart.

Frankie took a deep breath and walked down the hall to the
bedroom. The overhead light was off, the single lamp on the bedside
table casting a small circle of light on Waylon's side of the bed.

Waylon lay there on his back, arms at his sides, eyes closed. Frankie crept to the lamp, hoping to turn it off before he could see her nightshirt.

As she bent and reached for the lamp cord, Waylon's eyelids snapped open. His gaze couldn't help but go straight to her nightshirt since it was right there in his face. He stared for a moment, blinked, and looked up at her.

"Sorry, I thought you were asleep," she said lamely.

"Get settled in bed. I'll turn it off."

Frankie went around the foot of the bed, pulled back the dark-gray comforter, and slipped between light-gray sheets. She laid her head down on her pillow—surprised he even had two pillows—and pulled the comforter up.

"Good?" Waylon asked.

She nodded. "Good."

He turned off the light.

Waylon kept his body stiff and still, lying on his back. Frankie closed her eyes, trying to ignore the ache in her chest. Silence stretched between them, heavy and charged.

"I'm sorry I made you come over here. I was being over the top." His voice was low, almost strained.

The knot in Frankie's stomach eased a little. She rolled over on her side to face Waylon.

"No you weren't. It was sweet."

"It was too much."

"It's *fine*, Waylon. Really." She hesitated. "I'm sorry I said what I said. About the boxes."

"Don't be. It's just the truth." His tone was perfectly flat.

Eventually, Frankie shifted and turned over, pulling the blanket tighter around herself. "Goodnight, Waylon."

"Goodnight, Frankie."

Frankie. Not Pixie.

FRANKIE EVENTUALLY DRIFTED off on a cloud of guilt. Her dreams were scary and awful—she was late for her chemo appointment but it didn't matter because her insurance was canceled anyway. They gave her too much chemo by accident, she had only an hour to live, and she raced from one medical person to another but no one would do anything.

Until someone finally wrapped their arms around her from behind and pulled her to their chest. She struggled, thinking she was about to be hauled out of the clinic for making a fuss, but a man's voice calmed her instead.

"It's okay. You're safe. I won't hurt you."

She stopped struggling and her scary dream melted into softness and warmth. She wanted to stay there in a protective cocoon forever, but eventually, she couldn't stop herself from floating back up to consciousness. Strange thing was, she brought the cocoon with her. Frankie still felt arms around her, felt safe and warm and happy.

And then she remembered where she was.

Her back was pressed up against Waylon's chest. Knees bent, the backs of her thighs were against the front of his. They were spooned together perfectly. She felt Waylon's deep, steady breaths and realized he was sound asleep. Had she cried out from her dream, and Waylon instinctively pulled her close without even waking up?

Er...well, there's one part of him that's awake. Either that, or he'd shoved a steel rod into his sweats. She felt the length of his hardness pressed against her ass.

I should be mortified. Why am I not mortified?

What if he wakes up and he's mortified?

He'd made it crystal clear he wasn't interested in anything romantic. What if he woke up with a hard on? Would he freak out? Would he never want to see her again?

Would he kiss her? Would they do more than spoon?

Did she *want* to do more than spoon?

Waylon shifted, made an incredibly sexy sound in his sleep, and pressed against her even harder.

Hoo yeah, I want to do more than spoon.

Waylon moved his arm up from around her waist toward her chest. With a sharp intake of breath, she grabbed his arm and stopped him.

Scars are a turn-off. Her mother had reminded her of that only a few hours ago, mortified that her scarred-up daughter didn't cover herself in public.

Waylon made a frustrated sound. Which meant she should scoot her ass out of bed and move to the couch right now before he woke up.

But oh, man did she feel good right where she was. The bed was soft and warm, Waylon was holding her just right, and how long had it been since she'd slept beside someone?

Not that long ago.

She flinched at the pain the memory brought.

Waylon mumbled, "'S okay," stroked her arm, and that's when her heart melted into a confusion of feelings. Here she was, cuddling in bed with a man she was deeply attracted to, who was friend-zoning her at best and hated her at worst—at least when he was awake—while thinking about her soulmate.

Frankie bit her knuckles, trying not to sob. She couldn't stay and risk waking Waylon with her sobs. He'd ask her why she was crying, and that was the last thing she wanted to talk about. Slowly, carefully, she inched his arm off of her and scooted to the edge of the bed.

"Camille. Don' go. Stay wi' me." Waylon reached out and brushed her back.

Camille.

He was dreaming of someone else. Of course he was.

Frankie froze until he settled again. She slipped out of bed with her pillow and tiptoed to the living room. The couch fit her *if* she bent her knees, but she felt exposed without a blanket. She got back up and opened the front closet door, hoping Waylon might have a blanket stashed away. No luck, but he did have a winter coat that would work just fine. She slipped it off its hanger.

Oh, man, it smells like him.

Instead of taking it to the couch, Frankie slipped the coat on. Now she was completely surrounded by Waylon's scent—a clean soap smell like cedar or sandalwood, a hint of pine, and the barest trace of eucalyptus, along with a deeper smell that was simply...him.

Before she settled onto the couch, she decided to hit the bathroom. As she started down the hall, Frankie slipped her hands into the coat's pockets and absently jangled the spare change in them. Something that wasn't a coin bumped against the back of her right hand.

Hmm. What's that?

She shut the bathroom door behind her before turning on the light. Frankie closed her fingers around the mystery object and then she recognized the shape. She pulled it out.

As soon as she laid eyes on it, her whole world shrank down to the single earbud.

It can't be.

Frankie set the earbud on the vanity. She shoved her hand back into the right-hand pocket and felt around for an earbud case while her left hand rummaged the other pocket for a second earbud. He'd probably taken them out one day and shoved them in his pockets, then forgot to put them back in their case.

Nothing but spare change.

Frankie stared at the earbud.

She'd forgotten that day on the bus. No, more like actively tried to make herself forget and was mostly successful. She was listening to a hilarious podcast about a woman traveling the world alone and finding herself in a penis museum in Iceland of all places. Frankie wasn't listening to the podcast alone. She'd tossed an earbud to an incredibly hot guy who wanted to know what she was listening to. They never spoke a word to each other, but she could hear his laughter despite all the annoyed people standing between them.

She'd tried to forget that day because it was her last day of normalcy.

Frankie had been tempted the entire bus ride to keep on keeping it a normal day, and here she had the perfect excuse. She could skip her stop, stay on the bus, make her way back to him, and see if he wanted to go for coffee. She could pretend nothing was wrong, nothing at all, and never show up to her surgery.

Frankie started to push past the crowd to get to him. Just as she got to the middle door, the bus stopped. She forced herself to get off right then and there, wherever it left her. She was two stops ahead of the hospital, and standing right in front of a church just as the freezing cold day decided to turn its snow loose. A song went through her head, 'California Dreamin'' but she didn't have time to stop into the church and get down on her knees to pray, let alone talk to a preacher about the cold. She had a double mastectomy to get to.

Frankie watched the bus continue down the road, carrying both the hot guy and her right earbud away. Everything that was normal was on that bus and she was standing in the falling snow watching it grow smaller until it disappeared.

She stopped the podcast and put her lone earbud into its case and put the case into her coat pocket. She tucked her long, dark hair into her coat and lifted the hood over her head. Then she started walking in the direction of the hospital, the surgery, the chemo, the life after cancer. If she lived.

In Waylon's bathroom, Frankie's eyes filled with tears. She'd rubbed her thumb against the earbud case like a worry stone the entire way to the hospital, thinking more about her lost earbud than the guy, if she was being honest. The earbud was still in the normal life—the BC life—and she was not.

It wasn't until her first day of chemo, where she met her ridiculously optimistic soulmate, that the idea of her earbud being lost to her in the normal world became instead her anchor back to it.

And here it was in her hand, fished out of her Adventure Buddy's pocket by pure chance.

If this was the same earbud.

It couldn't be. No way.

She closed her eyes and tried to bring up Hot Bus Guy's face. It had become a blur, an abstract idea of what she could never have again. The chemo brain fog didn't do her any favors either. Frankie pictured the bus, pictured the guy, watched as his face came into focus...

It was Waylon.

Or was her imagination only trying to fill in the blanks, show her what she wanted to see?

But the first time I heard Waylon laugh. It sounded so familiar. Didn't it?

Welcoming.

But if it was Waylon on the bus, wouldn't he have said something by now? Unless he didn't recognize her. Or, he'd forgotten about her entirely.

Frankie opened her eyes and examined the earbud. She turned it this way and that, studying every little nick and scratch.

No. It might be the same brand—a common one, she had to admit —but no way was this her wayward earbud. Hers had been brand new and this one was all scratched up. Besides, why would a guy keep an earbud from a rando he met on the bus who ghosted him?

This is crazy. This is just my stupid little brain reacting to a stressful situation. One more story to make Dan laugh.

Frankie put the earbud back into the pocket and took off Waylon's coat. She used the bathroom and washed her hands on autopilot, contemplating the earbud.

I should get dressed, call a rideshare and go. The sooner I leave, the better. If she stayed much longer she'd probably end up comparing their horoscopes and claiming they were soulmates. Frankie already had one of those; she didn't have to make up another one.

She looked at her bag. It would be easy to take off her ridiculous Snoopy nightshirt and shove it down into the bottom of her bag, then get dressed, brush her teeth, summon a rideshare, and slip out.

And Waylon would think what?

His mumbled words came back to her. *It's okay. You're safe. I won't hurt you.*

He would assume that she was afraid of him and decided to sneak out in the middle of the night and take her chances in a house without an alarm.

I can't do that to a guy whose only possession that shows any personality is a Snoopy doll from his childhood.

Was it pity she felt? Hell no. But she wasn't ready to name the feeling that made her heart swell and beat faster whenever she even thought about Waylon. Ram. Beefcake the Adventure Buddy.

Because that's all he wanted. To be a Buddy to her. He'd made it abundantly clear, and it would be best for her to continue reminding herself of that at every opportunity.

She slipped the coat back on. She turned off the bathroom light and opened the door. The couch was to the right, Waylon's bedroom to the left.

She turned right.

Frankie drifted off, this time, without nightmares.

FRANKIE WOKE to the sound of movement somewhere close by, then a faint whistle that was quickly cut off. She heard water pouring, then the scrape of metal against metal. It sounded like Waylon was putzing around in the kitchen.

She slipped her arms into his coat and sat up. With only a peninsula separating the kitchen from the living room, she could see he had his back to her, doing something on the opposite counter. He was in the same tee and sweatpants he'd worn to bed the night before. Frankie bit her lip at the memory of how his cock had felt pressed up against her backside.

Waylon turned to take something out of the refrigerator and saw her. She registered a look of annoyance on his face before his features smoothed into something neutral.

"Sorry I woke you."

"It's all right. What time is it?"

"Seven-thirty. There's coffee here in a minute if you want some."

Funny, she didn't smell coffee now and she didn't see a coffeemaker the night before.

"You're going out to get some?"

He smirked. "God no. Most of it is burned or so full of sugar it's no longer coffee. I make my own."

Frankie stood up and wrapped Waylon's coat around her like a robe. She zipped it up partway before walking toward the kitchen until she got to the peninsula. Ah, that's why she couldn't smell coffee—a metal French press sat on the opposite counter, capped and waiting for Waylon to press the plunger down.

She nodded toward it. "Good man." She tried out a smile on him to see how he would react. Waylon turned away and opened the fridge. She didn't think the sudden cold that hit her was from the appliance.

"It's got a couple minutes to go." He set a carton of eggs on the counter along with a gallon of milk.

"French press is always worth the wait. And yes, I will have some. I might even fight you for it," she added, hoping for a smile.

He rewarded her with the barest grin, so quick she wasn't sure she'd actually seen it between scowls, and turned the burner on.

"Sorry I grabbed your coat. I'll go get dressed."

He shook his head. "I told you last night coming in you could use it. Sorry it wasn't warm enough in here for you."

"Oh, no it was fine. I was just—"

"You like fried eggs?"

"You don't need to make me breakfast."

"That didn't answer my question."

Frankie sighed. "Yes, I like fried eggs."

"One or two?"

"Just one, thanks."

He grunted. Frankie didn't know if she should go get dressed or stay right where she was. There was probably no right answer, except to leave as soon as possible.

Waylon poured milk into a skillet and plunged the French press. He opened a top cabinet and took down a mug—Frankie was afraid it might be his only one—and poured the coffee.

"Milk and sugar?" His voice was brusque.

"Both, please." God, the tension in the air was about to kill her.

He set the coffee in front of her with the milk. He opened a drawer and took out some raw sugar packets. He gave her two and kept two. He opened another cabinet and took down a second mug—much to Frankie's relief. She fixed her coffee while Waylon cracked three eggs into the skillet.

She took a sip of coffee and tried not to moan. "This is the best cup of coffee I think I've ever had."

Another small smile, quickly hidden again.

"And I've never seen anyone cook eggs in milk before."

"I picked it up from working out of a fire station. Best method I've found."

"I've always heard firefighters are the best cooks."

Waylon set two plates on the counter beside the stove and slid the eggs onto them. He grabbed some silverware from a drawer, turned and set everything down on the peninsula.

"You tell me," he said, watching her take the first bite. Frankie noticed the barest sparkle in his eye. She took a bite.

"Oh my God. These are incredible."

Finally, a true smile. "Thanks."

"You're spoiling me with this. I should have asked for two."

"I can make another."

She held up her hand. "No, it's all right. If you make me a second one, I'll end up asking for a whole dozen."

"You could use a whole dozen." Waylon's eyes widened.

Too late, his words already stung. Ironic, how BC, she was

constantly trying one diet or another to slim down. Now, she'd give anything to have those pre-cancer curves back. To be perfectly healthy.

To be back in her normal world with a body that wouldn't betray her this time. One that Waylon would never criticize.

Red rose up his neck. "I mean, you're fine, Frankie, but it's just that you need protein, you know?"

"Yeah, I get it." She took the last bite of egg, then downed the rest of her coffee. "Great breakfast. I should call about the alarm and get out of your hair."

Waylon rubbed the back of his neck. "Frankie, I'm sorry."

"About what?" She shrugged. "It's just the truth."

Which was exactly what he'd said the night before after her snide comment.

Shit. He's going to think I'm mocking him.

Mortified, she turned and headed for the bathroom where she'd left her things. She absently put her hand into the coat pockets and rediscovered the earbud.

What would it hurt to casually tell him you found a stray earbud in his pocket? Just to see his reaction?

Frankie shook the thought out of her head. It wouldn't matter at all. She got dressed, brushed her teeth, packed her things, and carried her bag to the living room. Waylon had changed into a pair of cargo pants, a fresh thermal, and a flannel shirt—the typical Colorado male's winter uniform. As soon as he saw her, his expression went from sad to perfectly neutral to scowling in the space of a moment.

Waylon lifted his chin toward the kitchen. "Call the alarm company and I'll get you back home ASAP."

It's not the same earbud. It's not.

Frankie nodded and headed for the kitchen, which was once again bare except for her phone on its charger. She found the alarm company's number in her contacts and called. The man who answered looked up her account and listened to her story. He said someone would be over in the next hour.

Waylon in the meantime had turned on the TV and sat down on the loveseat to watch some sports show talking about the Broncos' odds of making it to the Super Bowl. When she finished her call, he clicked off the TV and stood. Frankie started toward the closet to hang Waylon's coat up.

"You'll want to wear that. It's snowing outside," he said without looking at her.

She blinked hard against the memory of walking to the hospital in the snow. Then she put the coat on, aching to shove her hand into the pocket and find the earbud.

It doesn't matter if it's mine or not. And last night doesn't matter, either. He's back to wanting as little to do with me as possible.

And who can blame him? her mother's voice added, oh so helpfully.

They spent the ride to Frankie's house in silence. Not once did she put her hand back into the pocket. When they pulled up in front of her house, Waylon killed the engine.

"I'm coming in with you to wait for the alarm tech."

That took her by surprise. "I'm sure you have better things to do today. It'll be fine, I'm sure."

He shook his head. "I want to make sure he actually fixes it."

Frankie tried to ignore the excited little tingle at the back of her neck. She shrugged. "It's your morning."

Waylon nodded. He got out, went around the truck and opened her door. He carried her bag as he walked her to the front porch and she let them in. He looked around the front room as if he were expecting someone to jump out at them.

"I'm sure no one broke in while I was gone."

Waylon nodded absently. "It just...bothers me. The timing with Derek."

Frankie scoffed. "Really, it's just a coincidence." She took his coat off and set it on the couch. "You can look around again if you want. You've already seen the place."

So he did just that. Waylon went from room to room, Frankie

trailing behind. She wasn't sure how she was *supposed* to feel about all this attention to her safety, but she liked it. When they got to her office, she remembered she'd left her map and list of adventures spread out on her desk.

"I only got a quick look at this last night," Waylon said.

"It's nothing. Well, not nothing. It's all the things I want to do. Eventually."

He nodded without saying a word as he studied it.

The doorbell rang. Frankie turned but Waylon moved past her and got to the door first. He looked out through the window before answering it.

"Frankie Whitmore?" the guy asked Waylon. He looked confused.

"That's me, actually," Frankie said as she peered out from behind Waylon. "Come on in, the alarm's right next to the door."

Waylon stepped back to let the guy in, who smiled and nodded at him, then turned his attention to Frankie. She explained what happened the night before and he got to work. He tinkered with the alarm for a few minutes, then tested it. Waylon watched him like a hawk the entire time.

"You should be good to go," the guy told her. "The repair's free, it's under warranty."

Waylon crossed his arms. "What happened to it?"

"It's an old glitch that sometimes goes off when the software is patched. It should be all right now."

"Thank you," Frankie said as she opened the door for the tech.

"Let us know if you have any other issues. Have a great day." He gave Frankie a smile, nodded at Waylon, and left.

"Thanks for sticking around," Frankie told Waylon. "Would you like—"

"Now that it's fixed, I should go."

Frankie's heart stuttered. "Yeah." She picked up his coat and handed it to him. He took it without a word and she let him out.

Frankie watched him walk back to his truck. He tossed the coat into the passenger side before getting in. He sat for a moment, then pulled away.

She took out her phone and called the rec center, hoping Stephanie was there.

FIFTEEN

Waylon lay on his back in bed staring at the ceiling, his thoughts a chaotic mess. It was early Saturday morning, still dark outside. His alarm would ring soon, telling him it was time for another fun-filled day with the Adventure Buddy Club.

He scrubbed his hand down his face. He was so damn tired, but sleep had been a joke all week. It didn't matter how many hours he *technically* spent in bed—his brain wouldn't shut the hell up.

Most of it was replaying that damn night.

Frankie, curled up against him, soft and warm and so damn perfect.

Frankie, slipping out of bed in the middle of the night, leaving him cold.

Frankie, standing in his kitchen the next morning, drowning in his coat, looking like she belonged in his life.

He groaned at the idea and grabbed the other pillow to put over his face.

Which was a really stupid idea because it smelled like her. Rosemary and sleep-warmed skin.

He slammed it back down on the other side of the bed but it was too late. Her scent was in the air and his cock was standing at attention. His entire body lit up, every nerve ending crackling, hoping Frankie was there again so that this time, he could take her in his arms, breathe in her scent, and make love with her.

He hated how much he'd liked having Frankie close last Saturday night. How good it felt, after all these years, to fall asleep next to someone. He'd fully planned on waiting for her to fall asleep first and then move to the couch. He even played possum when she came out of the bathroom, thinking she'd just lie down instead of trying to talk.

When he felt her standing right beside him, he was positive that she was leaning in to kiss him. His eyes popped open only to see her inches away. He wanted to reach out and grab her in her adorable Snoopy nightshirt—he was sure she'd packed it just for him as a joke —then he realized she was only turning out the light.

Of course she was. Why would she want to kiss him after he screwed everything up? More importantly, why did he think he deserved her?

To make matters worse, he'd dreamed of Camille, and that she was upset. He'd taken her into his arms, reassuring her that things would be different this time. He dreamed of holding—then losing— Camille all over again. Suddenly, Camille was Frankie, and Waylon had felt such relief, such peace. He'd held his dream Frankie, promising he'd never hurt her. About the time he realized he was holding her for real, she was slipping out of his arms. Heart pounding, he waited for her to come back.

He couldn't blame her for choosing the couch instead. He'd betrayed her trust in his sleep. He fought every instinct to go after her, remembering how that had turned out with Camille. Waylon could barely look at Frankie the next day. He was relieved that she'd let him back into her house to wait for the alarm to be fixed. No way was he going to leave her defenseless.

It's not over the top, he'd told himself. *It's just one friend looking out for another.*

Right?

MONDAY, Waylon had dragged himself into work. Elias had taken one look at him when he walked into the ambulance bay and just grinned.

"Oh, this is gonna be good."

"Shut up."

"I didn't even say anything."

"You were about to."

Elias smirked as he leaned against the rig.

"You sleep at all last weekend?"

"I got a solid four hours."

"Total, or per night?"

"What do you think?"

"I think I haven't seen you this wrecked since RAP Week. And even then, you at least *pretended* to function."

"I'm fine." Waylon rubbed his eyes.

"This is incredible. I haven't seen a denial spiral like this since, well... *me*."

Waylon's jaw clenched. He already knew where this was going.

"Don't."

"Oh, I'm doing it, brother. Because if I remember correctly, we were at the rec center when *you*—"

"Elias—"

"—told me I was smitten before I even realized it. That I was *breaking our protocol*," he air-quoted, "because I spent more than one night with Wren. And now—look at you." Elias gestured at Waylon's entire pathetic state. "I'm not saying karma is real, but damn, brother, it is punching you in the face right now."

"You done?"

Elias pushed off from the ambo, smug as hell. "Not even close."

Waylon exhaled sharply and pinched the bridge of his nose. He walked around to the back of the ambo, Elias on his heels. "Don't we have a job to do right now?"

"I also think you're having a full-blown existential crisis."

Waylon grunted and tossed his gear in the back of the ambo.

Elias nodded. "That's a yes."

Waylon climbed into the rig, then dropped into the seat like his bones had been replaced with lead. "It's not a crisis."

Elias climbed in beside him, all smug amusement. "That's what *I* thought once. Maybe you remember?"

Waylon shot him a glare.

Elias cackled. "You're in the denial phase, brother. Trust me, I've been there. Next comes the part where you pretend you're *fine*, but deep down, you're already gone."

Waylon leaned back, crossing his arms, jaw tight. "Told you, I *am* fine."

Elias ignored him. "And after *that*, comes the part where you know for certain you can't live without her—"

"Yeah, well, I'm not you."

Elias nodded slowly. "You're right. Because I did something about it."

Waylon didn't have an answer for that.

Elias' expression turned serious. "Frankie's incredible, brother."

She is.

Elias held up his hands. "Look, brother, I get it. I was right there along with you. For years, you've kept it fun, kept it easy, picking up a new hottie every Friday night. But now you've got *feelings* and you don't want them. It's a bitch, realizing you actually *care* about someone."

Waylon opened his mouth to shut that down—except nothing came out.

Elias watched him carefully as amusement gave way to something a little more serious. "You think keeping your distance is safer."

"Because it is."

"It was a long time ago, Ram."

"Doesn't matter."

Now lying in bed a week later, Waylon hated that Elias might have had a point.

Because yeah, he did want more with Frankie.

But he wasn't supposed to want her. Not when he knew exactly how that story ended.

Waylon sighed heavily, shoving the covers off. He wasn't gonna lie here and wallow. He had a plan. Keep it simple. Just fix things with Frankie—keep it friendly, lighthearted.

He got showered, dressed, grabbed his keys, and headed for the rec center.

WAYLON WAS ALMOST to the meeting room when Stephanie called to him.

"Hey, Ram, wait up." Stephanie jogged down the hall after him.

Waylon stopped. "Hi, Steph. What's up?"

"Good news." She beamed at him.

Waylon frowned. Stephanie's good news usually meant bad news for him.

"You're off the hook."

Waylon blinked. "Off the hook?"

"Yeah! No more Adventure Buddies for you. I found your replacement."

A pit opened in Waylon's stomach.

"My replacement? For Frankie?"

"Mmm-hmm. He's new to town and looking to make friends right away. He's a real hottie too, whew!" She fanned herself.

"He? New? Friends?"

Hottie?

The pit became bottomless.

"Is there an echo in here?" Stephanie laughed. "I did like I promised and found your replacement as quick as I could, just as you wanted." She tagged his arm. "I wanted to catch you before you went in so you can get on with your weekend." Steph made shooing motions at him back down the hall toward the door. "Go on, scram, kid. Go do something fun *you* want to do. Your job here is done."

He was free. No more Adventure Buddy Club. Just what he'd wanted.

Except...

"Why aren't you scampering out the door?" Stephanie asked. "I'm honoring our agreement, remember? You said, and I quote: the second you find someone else, I'm out, no exceptions."

Shit.

"Did I say that?"

"Mmm-hmm, Mr. Gaslighter, you did. So you're out. Make like a prom dress and off with you. Isn't that what you wanted?" She turned and started walking down the hall.

IT WAS EXACTLY *what I wanted. I'm free now. No messy emotions. Frankie's got someone new.*

Then why the hell did he feel so desperate?

"Steph, wait. I don't even know what I want to do with my day."

She stopped and turned. "Not my problem. Go do what you used to do."

Cocks and Strippers. Casual hookups. Someone who wouldn't mind if I left after. Who isn't a stubborn little pixie who makes me question what I want.

"But I'm a planner kind of guy, and I already planned for today to be an Adventure Buddy day."

"Are you? Did you?" She quirked up an eyebrow.

"Yeah." He gave her a firm nod. "I am and I did. So, there's no point in me doing anything else today."

"Really?"

"Yeah."

Stephanie tilted her head. "Why is that, I wonder?"

"It's...my medical training." He nodded, hoping to convince her.

"And my military background. I make a plan, I enact that plan. And this," he jabbed his index finger toward the floor, "is my Saturday plan now."

"Ram. I can't let you be an adventure buddy on your own. Rules."

Shit. He hated the way his belly dropped through the floor.

This guy is a total stranger. He doesn't know Frankie. What she needs.

"Then...I'll be *your* adventure buddy, since Frankie has a new one."

And that way I can keep an eye on the new guy. For her sake.

"I don't need one, remember?" Stephanie tilted her head in the other direction. "But let me ask you something. As part of your training, don't you also evaluate a plan to see if it's working?"

"Well, yeah, of course."

I'll just be evaluating the new guy. Make sure he's treating Frankie right, that's all. Makes sense.

"So. You're telling me that you've evaluated your Saturday Adventure Buddy Club plan and it's working for you the way it is. Partnered up with Frank."

Waylon opened his mouth to protest...

...And he couldn't. Not a single word came out of his mouth. He clenched his jaw shut.

Dammit, how does she do that?

"Well, good news for you," Stephanie said. "New guy isn't here yet. But Frankie is."

Waylon snapped to attention.

"She's already here?"

Stephanie nodded toward the meeting room. "Sure is. And I'll warn you—when I told her about her new partner? She seemed pretty damn excited."

Waylon's heart twisted.

Excited.

To be rid of me.

Waylon just stared at Steph.

"I'll be up front waiting for the others. You two work it out." She walked off, leaving him standing there pissed off, confused, and absolutely not leaving.

No way in hell.

You bet I'm gonna work it out.

Waylon strode down the hall, trying not to sprint as if the *hottie* would suddenly appear out of nowhere and run past him to get to Frankie first.

When he got to the doorway, Frankie was standing at the window at the back of the room. She spun on her heel.

"Nice to meet you, but I was wondering if you'd be willing to—"

She stopped abruptly when she saw Waylon. Her eyes went round, like a fox caught in headlights. "Oh. It's you."

"Willing to...what?"

Frankie shook her head and crossed her arms. "What are you doing here? I thought you dumped me."

"*Dumped* you?"

"Yeah. I talked to Stephanie on Sunday. She said she'd found your replacement. At your request."

Dammit! She wasn't wrong, but that had been before he'd met her.

Frankie shrugged. "I figured I'd never see you again."

Waylon couldn't believe what he was hearing. "You think I'd just turn around and go out the door without saying goodbye?"

A deep look of pain flashed across her face. "Par for the course," she murmured.

Waylon's temper flared. How dare she think he was such a selfish jerk that he'd just walk away?

"It's okay, I'm used to people ghosting," she added.

He came this close to saying *Well, so am I* when insight hit him. His anger cooled immediately. She wasn't talking about him but about what other people had done to her. And what did Waylon expect? He was the one who'd been such an asshole. Of course she thought she'd never see him again.

But she looked...upset about that.

Waylon's mouth went dry and he swallowed around what felt like a boulder in his throat.

"When you thought I was the other guy just now...what were you going to ask him?"

Arms still crossed, Frankie looked to the side. "Does it matter?"

"Yeah, it matters." Waylon took a step into the room and closed the door behind him.

She met his eyes, her gaze piercing. "What are you doing? Why aren't you leaving?" She dropped her arms to her sides.

"Because I want to know what you were going to tell him." He ran a hand through his hair and watched Frankie's gaze follow his hand. "It matters. A lot."

She blinked slowly. Her gaze moved over his face and he felt it as if it were her fingertips gliding gently over his skin. Goose bumps actually rose on his arms.

"I was going to ask him if he wanted to pair up with Stephanie instead," she said quietly.

Now Waylon blinked. "Why? That would have left you without an Adventure Buddy."

She shook her head. "Not if I went home."

Waylon frowned. The boulder in his throat doubled in size. "Why would you go home? Aren't you feeling well?"

Her eyes flashed. "No, I'm feeling just fine. Amazing. Why would you ask?" She touched her face. "Am I looking pale?"

"Now that you've mentioned it, yeah, you do look pale."

"Well, I'm not. I'm fine. See, that's why I didn't want to be paired up with a medic. They're always telling you that you don't look good, or you should rest, or take it easy. And I don't want to take it easy. I want to get out there and *live*."

She looked Waylon up and down and by the time she was done, it wasn't just the goose bumps threatening to rise.

"Then we'll get out there and live."

She cocked her head. "What do you mean, *we*?"

"I'm your Adventure Buddy, aren't I?"

"Are you?"

"I am. New guy can team up with Stephanie. Just like you wanted."

Dammit! Why did I say that?

"Like *I* wanted? So, you're sticking around for *me*?"

"Yeah." Waylon crossed the room until he was standing right in front of her. "The new guy doesn't know you. He doesn't know how you hesitate just a moment and take a deep breath right before you have to do something involving heights, but that you go ahead and do it anyway. He might tell you to stop. He might underestimate you. I don't. I know you're gonna overcome any last bit of doubt and make that leap."

He took another step until he was in her space and she was looking up at him. "He's only gonna slow you down. I won't. I'll be cheering you on. And I'll be the one catching you on the other side every time."

Frankie stared into his eyes. She took a step toward him, almost closing the gap.

The door opened behind them. Waylon whirled around, ready to chew out the new guy if he dared step in.

"Oh, hey," Stephanie said. "Got the new guy on the horn. He's not sure if he can make it now, but he can try and rearrange—"

"No," they said in unison.

Waylon turned and looked at Frankie who was already staring at him again, so he didn't see Stephanie close the door as she muttered, "Okay, okay, don't mind me, just trying to be helpful..."

SIXTEEN

Standing toe to toe with Waylon, Frankie fought the impulse to throw her arms around him. Waylon was here. With her. He wasn't walking out. A fact that settled into her chest, warm and unnerving all at once.

When she'd called Stephanie on Sunday, it was to thank her for signing her up for the club, but that she wouldn't be continuing. Stephanie would just have to find someone new for Waylon.

Stephanie had shocked Frankie when she said that she'd already found her a new partner. At Waylon's request.

Shocked and hurt.

He must have called Stephanie when I was in the bathroom at his apartment.

At least he'd stuck around long enough to make sure the alarm worked and she was safe.

"New guy's a hottie," Stephanie told her. "He's looking forward to meeting new people. I figured you knew how that felt, so I told him I had the perfect partner in mind. I'd hate to let him down, Frank."

Grrr!

"Fine. I'll see you both on Saturday."

The week sucked. Dread took up residence in her stomach. She debated going back on her word, calling Steph and telling her sorry, but the damage was done.

But then on Wednesday, Derek texted her a long apology for bothering her when she obviously had someone in her life already. So, could he take her out—only as friends—the following Saturday morning to make up for it?

Frankie almost threw her phone across the room. Instead, she texted back that all was forgiven, no worries, but that she was busy Saturday mornings for the foreseeable future. He never texted back with a different suggestion, thank goodness.

She'd dragged herself into the rec center Saturday morning, and was in the middle of debating whether or not to give the 'hottie' a chance, when the door opened behind her. In that instant, she knew —it was Waylon or no one.

And there he was.

He was standing *this* close to her. All it would take was lifting her arms, finding the nape of his neck, then standing on her tiptoes to reach his lips.

I'll be the one catching you on the other side every time.

God, she wanted to believe that.

But, she knew better.

Just like she *knew* that earbud she found in his coat pocket couldn't be hers.

It wasn't possible. It was just the same brand, the same color. A coincidence.

But what if it isn't?

No. Even if it *was*, what would that change? It wasn't like Waylon had said anything. And she wasn't about to bring it up and sound like some hopeless romantic who thought fate had been scheming behind the scenes. He'd laugh. Or worse—look at her like she'd lost her mind.

Too good to be true. That's all it was.

She shook off the ridiculous thought and turned away, rummaging through her pack for something, anything.

"Frankie?"

She looked up and beamed a smile at him. "Glad to have you back, *Buddy*." She went back to searching for God-knew-what.

"Good to be back, *Buddy*."

———

STEPHANIE PARKED the bus along the road at the start of the Eldorado Mountain Trail. "All right, Buddies. Today we'll be going along some challenging trails, but the view at the top of the Rattlesnake Trail is totally worth it. Since they got some snow up there a couple nights ago, I'll be handing out poles. Trail's bound to be a little icy in the sun, and I don't want anyone slipping down the side of the mountain. On the way back, we'll reward ourselves with a stop at a brew pub. Any questions?"

"Yeah, how about hitting the brew pub first and staying there?" Mateo said, and everyone laughed. Out of all the other Buddies, Frankie thought he was the funniest, having gotten to know him better at dinner the week before. He was a California transplant and not a fan of the cold.

"Fun fact—beers and burgers taste better after hiking through snow," Stephanie said. "And I promise—the views we're about to see are worth it."

The air was crisp and cool, a bite of winter air mingling with the sharp scent of pine as they ascended the trail. Frankie was thankful for the poles once they hit the snow. The trail had narrowed along a rocky ridge, demanding all her focus. Stephanie, at the head of the group, kept her pace steady and deliberate.

"Everyone doing okay?" she called back.

"Living the dream," Mateo deadpanned from the middle of the line, mimicking her tone with a smirk.

Frankie, laughed along with the others. Stephanie's enthusiasm was infectious, even when the hike grew grueling. The woman didn't just walk trails; she owned them.

Frankie had to admit, the views of the sharply peaked rocks were already breathtaking between the trees and they weren't even at the top yet. She kept glancing down at the snowy footing, her steps careful but slower now. Frankie caught Waylon's eye, and they shared a brief, wordless exchange.

I'll be the one catching you on the other side every time.

The trail widened into a flat, grassy space, reddish rocks on one side, a steep drop-off into the pine forest on the other.

Stephanie stopped. "Five-minute break," she called out, sounding winded. "Enjoy the view, hydrate, pretend you're not regretting your life choices."

Frankie bit back a grin as she reached for her water bottle. Waylon gave Stephanie a pointed look, but she waved him off. "I'm fine, don't even think about babying me, Ram. Save it for someone who needs it."

The group spread out, some taking photos of the mountains, others rummaging for water or snacks.

"The trail gets steeper from here," Stephanie said, gesturing with her trekking pole. "Should be—"

She stopped talking and tilted her head, listening.

"Steve?"

Stephanie put her finger to her lips. Then Frankie heard it—a faint whimpering sound carried on the breeze.

"Do you hear that?" Stephanie asked.

"Sounds like an animal," Frankie said, stepping up beside her. "Coyote?"

"Dog," Stephanie said. She scanned the steep incline below. "There, under that pine. Do you see it?" She pointed.

Frankie squinted, following her finger. Sure enough, a small, scruffy dog huddled against the trunk of a tree about fifty feet down.

"Oh no," Frankie whispered. "It looks terrified."

"Poor thing," Stephanie said, inching closer to the edge for a better look. "We can't leave it."

It happened in an instant.

Her words cut off abruptly as her boot slipped on loose, icy gravel near the edge. The pole skidded uselessly across the rocky surface. Then, with a startled yelp, Stephanie slid over the edge.

"Steph!" Frankie cried as she tried to grab her but missed.

Waylon was suddenly at her side, peering over. Stephanie had slid down the incline, slippery with pine needles. She came to a stop just above the dog, where a scraggly pine jutted out from the steep slope. She grabbed the trunk to pull herself up, then groaned, her face pale and strained. One arm hung at an awkward angle.

"Steve!" Frankie's heart pounded as she looked down at her friend, then at the trembling dog just a few feet below Stephanie.

"I'm fine," Stephanie called up, her voice strained but defiant. "I just bumped my arm on the way down. Just help me with the dog. There's rope in my pack and a first aid kit. Actually, dump everything out of my pack. We can use it to bring the dog up."

Frankie rushed to Stephanie's pack and tipped it upside down. She picked up the rope and ran it and the empty backpack to Waylon, who crouched near the edge, eyes scanning the slope below.

"Trish, call 911," Waylon said, his voice calm but commanding. "Anna, get the first aid kit and be ready to stabilize her arm when she's up."

"Lower me down. I can get her," Frankie told Waylon.

"No, I'll go down," he said, his tone brooking no argument.

Frankie grabbed his arm. "Let me. I'm smaller, lighter—"

"And not trained for this," he interrupted. "Pixie, I know you're brave, but I've done this before. I'll get them both. When I signal, I'll need you to tell the others to hold the rope steady while I get Steph ready for the ascent. Got it?"

She nodded, already uncoiling the rope as Waylon studied the terrain. He wrapped the rope around a tree, tying it into a secure anchor point. "This'll hold a tank," he muttered, double-checking the knots. Then he looped the rope into a makeshift harness for himself. His movements were fast, efficient. "Trish?"

"Ambulance is on its way, but we'll have to start back down the mountain toward the trailhead. They'll start up the trail until we meet."

Waylon nodded. He took off his flannel and draped it over his neck and shoulders.

"Pixie," he said, his voice softer as he glanced at her. "Keep your focus on the rope and the terrain. If anything feels wrong, yell. Got it?"

"Got it," she said, gripping the rope tightly.

"Mateo, Sebastian, Chris, you guys get ready to pull us back up. Anna, you good with the first aid kit?"

"Yup, got it," she answered.

Waylon gave Frankie a smile. "All right, Buddy. You've got this." He slid over the edge.

Frankie watched as Waylon descended the steep incline with practiced ease. The knots held firm. Frankie's nails dug into her palms as she watched his steady progress. When he reached Stephanie, he crouched low, assessing her arm with quick, practiced hands.

"I'm gonna stabilize Stephanie's arm before we move," he called up to Frankie.

Frankie glanced back at Anna, who had the first aid kit ready. "He's stabilizing her arm." Then she watched Waylon wrap his flannel around Stephanie's arm, tying it snugly against her chest. His movements were calm, precise, like he'd done this a hundred times.

He slipped out of the harness then secured the rope around Stephanie's torso, reinforcing the harness with loops under her arms and around her waist.

"You're stable. Now for the pup."

Stephanie tilted her head toward the trembling bundle of fur below her. "Poor thing's been crying for hours, I bet."

Frankie watched as Waylon eased himself down another few

feet, his boots sending loose dirt cascading below him. The puppy let out a frightened yelp and tried to back farther into the tree's roots.

Waylon crouched, extending his hand palm-up. "It's okay. I'm here to help."

The dog whimpered but didn't move as Waylon carefully slid down until he was level with the dog. He slid his hand under the dog's belly.

"Gotcha," he said, lifting the trembling pup into his arms. He tucked the small dog into the empty backpack and slipped his arms through the straps. He climbed back up to Stephanie and examined the rope around her torso one more time.

"All right, Steph, you're going up first. I'll be right behind you."

Then he signaled to Frankie.

He's going up without a rope around him. God, please, please don't let him slip.

Frankie nodded to Waylon, then turned her head. "All right, guys, start pulling, slow and steady. Don't rush."

As the men worked together to bring Stephanie up, Waylon climbed behind her, one hand on the rope and the other around Stephanie, making sure she wasn't getting banged up on any rock hidden under the pine needles. Frankie's heart was in her throat as she watched them come closer and closer.

When Stephanie neared the top, Frankie pulled her onto the trail. Stephanie's face was pale with pain and fear.

Waylon clambered up seconds later, as he pulled himself over the edge. Frankie reached out instinctively, grabbing his arm to steady him.

Safe!

Frankie held the backpack steady as Waylon shrugged it off. She looked inside it at the frightened dog who gazed back up at her with the saddest brown eyes.

"Well," Stephanie said, sitting on the ground, her injured arm cradled in Waylon's shirt. "That was a hell of a lot more excitement than I planned for today."

Anna and Waylon knelt beside Stephanie, checking her over and offering her water.

"I can't believe I'm so clumsy," Stephanie muttered, wincing as Anna examined her arm. "It's just a sprain. Probably. Right?"

Anna arched a brow and exchanged a look with Waylon. "Steph, it's not just a sprain."

Stephanie ignored Anna. "How's the pup?" she asked Frankie.

"Fine. But we need to get you off the mountain. There's an ambulance on the way." She looked at Waylon. "We've got a tarp. Would that work as a litter to get her down?"

Waylon grinned. "Hell yeah, Pixie."

"Guys, I broke my arm, not my leg. I can walk just fine." Stephanie started to stand.

"Uh-uh, no," Anna said. "You took a big tumble, *and* you're at risk for shock. We're bundling you up and carrying you out." She grinned. "If I had a roll of bubble wrap, I'd wrap you in it right now."

Waylon chuckled. "Yeah, me too."

Trish had gone to grab the tarp and came back with it. Stephanie continue to protest—though not as hard—when everyone took off their flannels and jackets to make a 'nest' for Stephanie in the tarp. She finally conceded to being carried back down the trail, swaddled in everyone's jackets. Waylon and Mateo carried each end, creating a hammock. Anna monitored Stephanie while Frankie cradled the dog, still wrapped in the backpack.

The trail back down went much faster than the way up, and pretty soon, they met up with four paramedics carrying a litter. Waylon and Anna gave reports to the paramedics while they transferred Steph after more grumbling—though Frankie thought it sounded like a token protest. They carried her to the ambulance waiting in El Dorado Springs.

"Take the van keys." Stephanie handed them to Waylon before they loaded her into the ambulance. She appeared absolutely devastated as she looked at each Buddy one by one. "I'm so sorry. I think this is the end of the club. The rec center probably won't let me continue after this. So, you all had better hit the brewpub on the way back to the rec center."

Everyone told her not to worry about it, that she was way more important. The ambulance doors shut with a final *clunk*, and the sirens wailed as it pulled away, carrying Stephanie toward Foothills Hospital. The rest of the Adventure Buddies stood in a loose cluster near the rec center's van, watching the taillights disappear down the road.

"She's going to be fine," Anna reassured everyone. "She's not in shock, and doesn't appear to have a head injury. I'm betting her arm was a clean break."

Mateo blew out a relieved breath. "Damn, Steph scared the hell out of me. And of course, her biggest concern was whether we'd still hit the brewpub afterward."

A few chuckles rippled through the group.

"Do we want to follow the ambulance to the hospital?" Waylon asked.

All hands went up.

As they rode to the hospital, Frankie sat in the back with the dog —a puppy, she realized—who seemed to be fine, and was becoming curious now that he was safe and warm. He poked his grayish-white snout out of the bag, followed by his whole head. He was an adorable little black-and-gray mutt, filthy as he was. They took turns petting him on the drive to the hospital, which turned out to be only about fifteen minutes away. Waylon parked in the visitors' lot and everyone got out.

"Go ahead in without me," she told Waylon. "I'll stay here with Sn...I mean, this little guy."

Waylon grinned. "You were about to name him something. What is it?"

Frankie rolled her eyes. "I think you know."

He handed her the van keys. "I'll keep you informed. Text me if you need anything." His grin turned to a full-on smile. "Then after we drop everyone off at the rec center, we'll go get Snoopy checked out."

SEVENTEEN

"I thought we were going to get Snoopy checked out," Frankie said. "Are you sure there's a vet up this way?" She absently petted Snoopy's head as they turned onto a road winding up a foothill a few miles outside of Lyons.

They'd waited at the hospital for a couple of hours. Stephanie was lucky—the break was a clean one as Anna had suspected, and she didn't have any other injuries besides a few scrapes and bruises. Once she got the all-clear and was released, Waylon drove them all in the van back to the rec center. Gabe had been beside himself over Stephanie. The Buddies left the two of them arguing over the fate of the Adventure Buddy Club, but it wasn't looking good.

"We are getting him checked out, just not at a vet hospital," Waylon answered. "We're taking him to some friends of mine who know dogs. Snoopy deserves the best." He reached over and scratched the scruffy dog's head. His fingers brushed Frankie's, and he fought the impulse to take her hand in his. The same impulse he'd been fighting all day, ever since their confrontation in the meeting room.

I'll be cheering you on. And I'll be the one catching you on the other side every time.

His words had surprised him even as he'd said them. No, not his words—his feelings. For her. His Pixie.

No, your Buddy and that's all.

She'd been great during Stephanie's rescue. Calm, cool-headed, resourceful. Brave enough to offer to rescue her, and she didn't push the issue when he'd explained why she couldn't. Waylon wondered what she'd been like before the cancer—probably unstoppable. As it was, he usually forgot she'd even been sick.

He absently pictured her with long hair and a few more curves, something he'd been doing all day—oh, hell, be honest—since after the moose. He stopped and focused on the road. But there was something about his mental image of pre-cancer Frankie that tickled his memory. Was it possible that he'd seen her at the hospital in passing? That felt almost right. But he wasn't even sure where she'd been treated. Waylon didn't know how to bring it up without making her think that he only saw her as a cancer patient. And besides, what was he going to say—maybe you had bigger things on your mind, but do you remember ever seeing me in passing at the hospital, before you lost all your hair and a ton of weight? God, how messed up did *that* sound?

"How do you think Snoopy got up there?" Frankie asked. "He's just a puppy, and El Dorado Springs is too far away for him to have run away, don't you think?"

"He doesn't have a collar, either." Waylon sighed. "Most likely, he was dumped in the woods."

Frankie flinched. "I hate that thought. I was hoping you'd tell me something different." She leaned forward and kissed the top of Snoopy's head. "Someone dumped a litter of puppies at the ranch gate when I was little. Thank God my dad saw movement in the tall grass and stopped to see what it was. He was driving his truck, and I hate to think he could have run one over. Anyway, there were four of them. We kept one and gave the others to a couple neighbors. When they got older, they all used to find each other and run together like a pack." She smiled at the memory. "I hate to think Snoopy has brothers and sisters out there."

"Belle and Spike," Waylon said.

Frankie looked at him. "Exactly. If we found them, that's what we'd name them."

We.

Let it go.

"So, who are these friends of yours who are better than a vet?"

Waylon was relieved at the change of subject. "Actually, one of them is a vet, or would have been if she'd stayed in vet school. I grew up with her. She's the little sister of one of my oldest friends. Arden Volker McGuire. Her husband runs a security company. Watchdog. They have a kennel and train guard and service dogs."

"Oh, cool. Do they know we're coming?"

"Yeah. I called my friend, Shane. He's one of Watchdog's bodyguards, but he also works with the kennel. He, Kyle, and Arden will meet us there."

They pulled up to a gate with a gatehouse. Waylon rolled down his window, told the gatekeeper who he was, and drove on after the gate opened. Frankie's attention turned from Snoopy to their surroundings.

"Does this all belong to Watchdog?"

"Sure does. They bought damn near the whole mountain a few years back."

"Seems like more than just a security company." She side-eyed Waylon.

The corner of his mouth turned up. "Might be."

They passed the front offices and followed a sign to the kennels. They parked in the lot in front. Frankie waited for Waylon to come around and open her door. He liked that she did that. She handed him Snoopy, then he held out his hand for her to step out—which was the reason he liked that she waited; it was an excuse to touch her. She gave him a faint smile once she was out of the truck that made his heart thump against his chest.

Waylon held the door open for her and they went inside. Shane was waiting for them beside the receptionist's desk. He grinned when he saw the pup. Waylon was pretty sure Shane liked dogs better than he liked people, with the possible exception of April, a barista in Lyons.

"Hey, Ram. Who do we have here?" Shane only had eyes for the puppy as he reached out for him.

"This is Snoopy."

"Hey, Snoop. You've had quite an adventure, huh?" Shane took the puppy and cradled him. He finally looked up from the dog and acknowledged the two humans in front of him.

"This is Frankie," Waylon said. "My—"

"Adventure Buddy, yeah. Nice to meet you. Elias mentioned you."

Great.

"Oh, are you friends, too?" Frankie asked.

"More like brothers. Him and this guy here." Shane pointed his chin at Waylon. "She met Bear and Ben yet?"

Yet? Waylon watched Frankie's eyebrows rise ever so slightly as she glanced at him.

"Nope, just Elias and Gabe, and now you. Arden here? Should we check out Snoopy now?"

Waylon didn't miss Shane's smirk. "Yeah, she and Kyle are in the exam room." He turned and they followed him down the hall.

"So," Frankie said. "Which animal are you, Shane?"

Shane almost dropped Snoopy. He laughed. "You know about that, huh?" He gave Waylon a look that said *just buddies, huh?* "I'm Elk. Ben is Moose, Bear is obviously Bear, and Badger and his wife should be back in town here soon."

"Got it." Then with a wink, Frankie bumped her hip into Waylon's thigh, which did all sorts of things to his chest and sent a message to his cock to stand by.

Shane opened a door with a sign reading EXAM ROOM. "Whoa, sorry." He chuckled as Kyle and Arden sprang away from each other, Arden's face flushed.

"Well, the door does say exam room, so we were doing some examining," Arden joked. Her gaze went straight to Frankie and she held out her hand. "Hi! You must be Frankie, and God knows what your first impression of us and Watchdog is."

Frankie burst out laughing. "Pretty awesome. Nice to meet you." She shook Arden's hand, while Waylon bathed in the sound of her laughter. He loved how she never held back when she laughed.

He almost...remembered? What? It was maddening, the déjà vu that hit him sometimes when she laughed.

Kyle clapped a hand on his shoulder, interrupting his thoughts. "Good to see you, brother."

Frankie looked at Kyle. "Brother? Oh, are you an animal, too?"

They all laughed and Shane answered for him. "Actually, yeah, he's The Pup."

"So you grew up with these guys, too?"

"Negative." Kyle put his arm around Arden's waist. "I married into the group."

"After I nearly shot him," Arden added.

"Ha! Now there's a meet-cute."

"Yay! A romance fan." Arden high-fived Frankie. "You need to join my book club."

"Fun! Count me in."

Waylon thought it was amazing, the way Frankie fit right in with every one of his friends, like she already belonged. Amazing, and a bit unsettling. It made him want things he wasn't supposed to want.

In the meantime, Shane had put Snoopy on a blanket draped across an examination table. Kyle and Arden turned their attention to the little dog.

"So, this is Snoopy," Kyle said, putting his hand out, palm up, under the dog's muzzle. "Hey, little buddy."

Snoopy wagged his tail and licked Kyle's hand.

"Has he eaten?" Arden asked.

"Yeah," Frankie answered. "Food and water. I went and picked up some kibble while we were all waiting for Stephanie. I didn't give him too much just in case, but he's kept it down. And he's gone number one and number two. I scooped up the poo and put it in a plastic bag if you need to check it."

Arden nodded. "Excellent, that answers my next question, thank you. He's definitely malnourished," she said as she felt along the puppy's sides, then cupped his tummy. "But if he's keeping food and water down and having bowel movements, that's a good sign. No obvious injuries, either. And no fleas or ticks." She examined the puppy's mouth, then looked at Shane and Kyle. "What do you think? Shots, dewormer, heartworm medicine, and a bath?"

"Sounds good to me," Kyle said as Shane nodded. "Do you want us to keep him overnight or long-term, or is one of you taking him?" He looked back and forth between Frankie and Waylon.

"Um." Frankie looked at Waylon, uncertainty in her eyes. "We hadn't really discussed that yet. My landlord is strict on no dogs or cats. Does your apartment allow pets?"

To Waylon's alarm, everyone gave Frankie a funny look, then side-eyed him.

"Well, yeah, it does. Because I say it does."

Frankie looked confused. "What do you mean?"

"I own the building."

Her confusion only grew. "You...do?" She looked at the others, who nodded.

"He didn't tell you?" Shane asked.

"Nope." Now she looked amused. "Ram's apparently full of secrets."

"It never came up," Waylon said in his defense. "So, yeah, I can take Snoopy home. If you don't think he needs to spend the night, Arden."

Frankie looked crestfallen but quickly hid it. Something twisted in Waylon's chest. He hated that look, knowing she was disappointed that she couldn't be the one to keep the puppy.

"I don't think he does," Arden said. "He seems healthy, other than malnourished, poor little guy." She ran her fingers over his coat. "We can immunize him, check his stool for parasites and treat him for that if necessary, give him a bath, then he's all yours. You'll bring him back in if he starts coughing or shows any signs of digestive issues." The last was a statement, not a question.

"Of course."

"What kind of breed do you think he is?" Frankie asked.

Arden smiled. "He looks to me like he's a purebred mutt." She ruffled the top of Snoopy's head. "The best kind." Then she grinned at Kyle. "Except of course for any well-trained Malinois and a certain black-and-gold Lab named Camo."

"That's my dog," Kyle said, grinning back at Arden.

"He's *my* dog," she said, smiling sweetly back. "And I have the shotgun to back that up."

"*What?*" Frankie asked, clearly amused and overjoyed. "Please tell me everything about your meet-cute."

"Girl, we'll talk. Now you definitely need to join the book club." Arden laughed. "Just be careful when you're fighting over a dog." She gave Frankie a pointed look. "You never know where it might lead."

"I'M SPENDING the night at your apartment, fight me." Frankie nuzzled Snoopy on her lap—who turned out to be a black-and-*white* dog once he'd had a bath. Snoopy also had a clean bill of health—no parasites. They were in Waylon's truck headed back to the rec center where Frankie had left her car.

At Frankie's declaration, Waylon's heart felt like it flipped over. *Yes, yes, please spend the night* that flip said.

"Not gonna fight you," he said. "I know I'd lose."

"Yup, you sure would." She beamed at him.

"I'm sleeping on the couch this time though." He grinned at her. "Fight me."

Her smile faded ever so slightly. "I'll win that fight, too."

And either way, I lose. God, he wanted Frankie with him in his bed again. Wanted to hold her close, breathe in her rosemary scent. He'd noticed his truck smelled like her now, which was going to drive him insane the next time he got in without her. Just like the pillowcase he hadn't washed yet.

"So. You own the *entire* building?" she asked.

"All four buildings, actually. The whole complex."

"Four? I only saw three buildings."

"The fourth is across the street. Thirty-six units all together."

"Oh." She got quiet.

"What? Why'd you go quiet?" He grinned ruefully. "When you saw my apartment did you think I was dirt-poor?"

"*No.* That's not what I was thinking."

"Because I'm not dirt-poor."

"Pfft. Obviously. And for the record, I never thought so. You've got a good job and the military probably gives you something, too." She looked frustrated as she shook her head. "I mean, it doesn't matter either way."

"It doesn't?"

"No. Believe it or not, I'm not contemplating your net worth right now, Beefcake."

"What *are* you thinking about then?"

He got nervous when she didn't say anything for a moment. Then, "Why don't you have any furniture, Waylon?"

Shit. "What do you mean? I have furniture." He sped up. The rec center was only minutes away—maybe he could get there before this stupid conversation went any further.

"Only the barest of necessities."

"That's all I need." He shifted in his seat. "Makes cleaning a breeze."

Frankie sighed. She petted Snoopy, who had gone to sleep curled in a tight ball in his baby blanket on her lap. Kyle had given Waylon puppy supplies, including a crate and a small, soft-sided carrier, which lay at Frankie's feet—she'd insisted on holding Snoopy.

"Have you ever lived with anyone?" Her voice had gone quiet. "I mean, besides in the barracks?"

He turned into the rec center and parked beside her car. "Here we are. You remember where I live, or do you need the address? I'm sure you want to go home and get some clothes and stuff first."

She just looked at him. Disappointment filled her eyes. "I remember."

Waylon nodded and got out of the truck. By the time he went around and opened Frankie's door, she'd tucked Snoopy into the carrier with his baby blanket. She left the carrier on the passenger seat as she slipped out of the truck. She didn't take Waylon's offered hand, which felt like a gut punch. She walked the three steps to her car, unlocked it with her key fob, then she reached for the door handle. Maybe now she'd just go home and stay there, which was absolutely for the best. And no more Adventure Buddy Club, either. Exactly what he wanted. Perfect.

"You still coming over?" he heard himself ask quietly in the space between heartbeats.

Still gripping the door handle, Frankie turned, face expressionless.

The corner of her mouth quirked up. "Fight me, Beefcake?"

Waylon felt his heart beat again. "I'd lose."

Her smile bloomed. "Yeah you would."

EIGHTEEN

Frankie had obviously touched a big honking nerve when she asked about the furniture. She'd outright stomped on one with her question about ever living with someone.

Camille. It had to be connected to her.

Frankie didn't ask out of jealousy—who cared if Waylon had been in previous relationships? So had she. She just wanted to know what the hell had hurt him so much that he lived like a monk. It obviously wasn't a happy lifestyle choice or he wouldn't have pushed her away when she asked. She was disappointed that he didn't trust her, and it hurt. She'd been ready to walk away.

Except she knew what it was like to be poked and prodded and hurt by someone who was only trying to help.

Not just during my cancer treatments. I pushed Waylon away at the beginning out of my own pain and fear of being reminded or held back.

Even when I pushed, he caught me anyway.

Now she found herself on the other side. She was the one doing the prodding.

Frankie smiled to herself as she drove home. Waylon could push all he wanted but he wasn't fooling her. The look on his face this morning when he thought she had a different partner said everything. Then he'd had the chance to tell her goodbye forever tonight.

You still coming over?

And didn't take it.

Frankie pulled into the alley behind her house then parked in her detached garage. She hadn't picked up her mail, so she cut through the side yard to the front. As she approached her front porch, she noticed she had a package. She ordered things all the time, God knew what it was. It weighed next to nothing when she picked it up and unlocked her door. The burglar alarm chirped, but when she went to punch in the code, she saw the same damn error message on the screen.

"No time for it now," she mumbled to herself, thankful that at least it didn't go off this time. Besides, she wasn't spending the night in the house, and as she'd told Waylon, the neighborhood was a safe one. She set the mail and the package down on a table and went to pack an overnight bag. Her phone buzzed with a text from Waylon.

Let me know when you get here, Pixie.

Three dots bounced as he typed another message before she could respond.

Snoopy misses you already.

Then:

I'm sorry about earlier. Really sorry.

HER CHEST WARMED.

Fifteen minutes later, she was back in her car and driving to Waylon's.

FRANKIE PARKED beside Waylon's Dodge Ram. She took out her phone to text him, then saw a man walking toward her car from the apartment. She recognized Waylon's silhouette and realized he'd been waiting outside for her. She stepped out of the car.

"Hey, Beefcake. Thought you were going to wait for my text."

He shrugged. "Figured you'd be along." He looked up at the sky. "It's a nice night, probably one of the last warmish ones we'll have this year. I didn't mind waiting."

"Ah, of course. Just out enjoying the weather." She grinned as she bounced on the balls of her feet. "You're forgiven, by the way. I'm sorry I pushed."

He shook his head. "No. It's all right. Is your bag in the back?"

"Yeah. Thank you." She opened the back passenger door on her side. He reached in and picked it up. She closed the door, and when she started walking, he placed his hand on the small of her back. It felt like the most natural thing in the world.

"Snoopy settling in okay?" she asked.

"Just fine. He ate some more, I took him for a quick walk outside, and he settled right into his crate." He swiped his keycard and opened the door for her. They walked to the stairs.

"Aw, well, he doesn't even need me here then," she teased as they climbed the steps.

Waylon laughed softly. "I told you, he missed you." Then when they reached the landing, he dropped a kiss on top of her head like it was nothing. He didn't even slow his step. Meanwhile, Frankie had to concentrate on keeping her knees from buckling.

"*He* did, huh?" Her voice barely quivered—a minor miracle.

"Sure did, Buddy."

Buddy.

Okay, fine. Sure. We can keep up the 'Buddy' thing. Sure.

Waylon opened his apartment door. The first thing Frankie saw was the little table with the mismatched chairs. Only now, it was covered with a red-and-white checkered tablecloth. An unlit tapered candle waited in its candlestick holder between two sets of dishes and silverware.

"Oh my." She sniffed the air. "Something smells delicious."

"You still owe me a dinner," Waylon said. "But I thought I'd treat you first."

"Wow, fine by me." She spotted Snoopy's crate and walked over to it. The puppy was curled in a little ball in the corner on a nest of blankets, his back to her. As soon as she opened the crate door, he lifted his head, then stood up, tail wagging. She reached in to pet him, listening to Waylon flick a lighter behind her. Snoopy yawned and curled back up. She gave his adorable head one last scratch and closed the crate door. The candle was lit.

"So, what's for dinner?"

"A real treat." Waylon grinned at her from the kitchen. "Sit down and I'll bring it out."

Frankie took a seat. Waylon came up behind her and set a rectangular brown bag on her plate. He sat down across from her with his own bag and a bottle of water.

"Um. Is this an MRE?" She picked up the bag by its corner.

"One of the best," Waylon said, tearing his open.

"Menu twenty-one." She read the meal description. "Oh, God. Lemon pepper tuna?"

Waylon nodded.

"I'm not really a fan of tuna."

"Where's your sense of adventure?" Waylon tore open a little packet of what looked like salt and cracked open the bottle of water. He poured both into another bag, then plopped a smaller bag inside and closed it up.

"What are you doing?"

"Cooking my chili mac."

Her eyebrows rose. "Seriously? You have a microwave right over there."

"It doesn't have the same Jenny Sayqwah." He butchered the French words and she snort-laughed. He nodded his chin at her MRE.

Frankie tore her bag open, dreading the idea of cooking tuna from an MRE. How old was it, anyway? She took out each package.

"Okay, the tuna is in a camouflaged bag. Cute. Is that in case you need to hide it so that you don't have to eat it?"

Waylon laughed. "You'll love it."

"Uh-huh." The other packages contained mayonnaise, crackers, tortillas, cheese spread that felt like it might be the bright-orange fake stuff.

"Lemon-lime powdered drink."

"It pairs well with the lemon pepper tuna."

"I bet. Oh, hey, candy." She shook a bag of yellow and orange peanut butter candies.

"That's for dessert, along with the pound cake."

"I'm looking forward to it." She opened a clear plastic package and took out a spoon, a packet of salt, some breath mints, and another little brown package. "What's this? Oh. Toilet paper. Is this a horrible warning?" She shook the package of TP at him while he chuckled.

"Let me pour you a drink." He reached across the table and grabbed the lemon-lime packet, dumped the powder into her wine glass, then filled it with the rest of the water from his bottle. Then he picked up the bag heating his chili mac and opened it. "Mmm. Dinner's ready."

Frankie eyed the camo bag o' tuna. "Is there any chance I could trade with you?"

Waylon tilted his head, considering. "I'll only give you a bite of mine, because this is the best one."

"You are a sadist. I don't think I can let our...I mean, your dog stay here."

Waylon meanwhile dunked his spoon into the bag and scooped

out some chili mac. He stretched his arm across the table. The spoon inched dangerously close to her mouth.

"You know, the adventures I want are fun, not, um...this."

He smirked. "Try it."

"Fine." She opened her mouth and took the food off the spoon. She chewed.

"Actually, it's not half bad."

"See?"

"It's not half good, either."

"Food snob."

"Maybe." She poked at the unopened package of tuna on her plate. "Do I *really*?"

Waylon burst out laughing. "No, of course not." He put all the bags on his plate and stood up. He grabbed Frankie's plate with everything on it, dumped it onto the other one, and tucked her plate under his. He carried it all into the kitchen.

"Actually, *this* is our dinner." He held up a big paper tote bag with a receipt stapled to it. "There's a French restaurant down the street that does carry out."

"*That's* what I smelled! Oh thank God. You are *evil*." Frankie laughed as Waylon plated up their food. "French food in honor of a certain World War One ace pilot?"

"But of course," Waylon answered in a cheesy French accent. He set the plates on the table. "I borrowed the tablecloth and candle from the restaurant, too."

Frankie rested her elbow on the table and put her chin in her hand. "I had a feeling."

Waylon went back to the kitchen for a bottle of wine and a new glass for Frankie.

"They couldn't sell me a bottle of wine, but suggested this one so I picked it up from the liquor store across the street from them." He popped the cork and filled her glass, then his.

Frankie lifted her glass and waited for Waylon to lift his.

"To Snoopy," she said.

"To adventurous women," Waylon added, making her laugh again as they clinked glasses.

FRANKIE STOOD in the main bathroom staring at her reflection just as she had the week before. Dinner had been incredible, and not just the food. She and Waylon talked throughout as if they'd known each other forever. No strain, no stress, no awkward pauses.

No landmines either. The conversation was kept to the present, except when he asked her about growing up on the ranch. It was cute the way he avoided eye contact, as if he were simply curious. Feeling slightly evil herself, she kept the details to a minimum and blatantly steered the conversation to other topics. She helped with the dishes even though he insisted that he would do them himself. Frankie tried to tell herself it was just her imagination when sparks flew every time their hands brushed accidentally.

Now she was in her nightshirt—the Snoopy one, what else?— rustling up the courage to share a bed with him again. She took a deep breath, opened the bathroom door, and flicked off the light. His bedroom was only a few steps away.

We're just Buddies. Keep reminding yourself of that.

Smiling ruefully to herself, she started back down the hall to the bedroom.

Waylon was facing away from her side of the bed, eyes closed. Frankie slipped under the covers and he turned out the bedside light.

They both lay there perfectly still. Frankie was wide awake and judging by Waylon's breathing, he was, too.

Finally, he said, "You took a while in the bathroom. I thought you'd headed for the couch." A question lingered in his voice.

I'll remind myself we're Buddies.

Starting tomorrow.

In no universe could Waylon be called the little spoon, especially when compared to Frankie. She damn near giggled at the idea as she slipped her arm over his waist and snuggled into him.

"Nope." She snuggled closer. "You insisted. Just two good Adventure Buddies sharing a bed."

"You have your arm around me."

"Really? I hadn't noticed."

"Frankie." His voice was low, guttural.

"Can't a Buddy side-hug another Buddy?"

Waylon's body shook and she hoped it was because he was suppressing a laugh.

"This isn't a side-hug, Pixie."

Yay, we're back to Pixie!

"Sure it is. I only have one arm around you. Side-hug."

He shook again. "We're lying down in bed. What you're doing is called spooning."

"Hush now, Little Spoon."

Now his shaking was accompanied by a snort. "I've never been anyone's little spoon."

"You know, I was just thinking that myself, that you're much too big for a little spoon." She paused. "So, should we change spoons?"

Please?

"Frankie."

"Come on. Think of it as a mini-adventure with your Adventure Buddy."

He snorted again.

"Well, maybe not *mini*," she teased.

Waylon went perfectly still. "What do you mean by that?"

"I mean, well, you started it after all."

"I...did?"

"Mmm-hmm. You did. Last week."

"I thought I was only dreaming," he said, dragging out the words.

"Well, technically you were dreaming, but you were also doing."

Waylon's body stiffened. "Doing...what?"

"Nothing bad. You were talking in your sleep."

He jerked. "What did I say?"

Frankie wondered if he remembered dreaming about Camille. "Nothing important."

Waylon slumped as much as a person lying down could. "You said I did something. Did I...scare you?"

"No. Not at all." She gave him a squeeze. "You were reacting to a nightmare I'd just had. You told me I was safe. Then you spooned me." She fought the impulse to plant a kiss between his shoulder blades. Buddies hugged but they didn't kiss, did they? Wait, yes they did, as of tonight on the stairs. "The spooning was nice, Waylon. I enjoyed it."

"It was? You did?"

"Absolutely. Not scary at all," she added. "So how about it? Wanna be the big spoon?"

She waited.

"It...might be best if you stay the big spoon."

"Why?" *Oh.* "You afraid I'll feel your spoon handle?"

That did it. Waylon couldn't hold back his laughter—music to her ears. Just like on the bus.

No, that's just your imagination playing tricks on you.

"Yeah, Pix, you might feel my handle."

Frankie shivered at the thought, half-desire, half-worry now that she had poked the bear—or rather, the Ram. She ignored the voice in her head telling her she needed to stop now; that if she didn't, he'd see her naked and think she was ugly.

Desire won out.

"You want the truth?" she asked.

Waylon groaned. "Oh, no. Let me guess."

"Yeah, I, um. Might-have-already-felt-it." She ran the words together as fast as she could then pressed her face against his back.

"Oh, shit."

She eased her head back. "No, not shit at all. Actually, pretty impressive. Thus the 'not mini' comment."

"Please tell me you're joking right now."

"Not joking. You have an impressive spoon handle. I'm gonna stop calling you Waylon and start calling you Way-*long*."

Waylon shook with laughter. "You're something else, Pix."

She lifted her head until her mouth was close to his ear. "So, you gonna be my big spoon? Or am I—"

Waylon turned so quickly, he took Frankie entirely by surprise. One second she was behind him, whispering in his ear, and the next, she was flat on her back under him. Their faces were inches apart, close enough that all she had to do was lift her head the tiniest amount to touch his lips with hers. Her heart pounded as her entire body shuddered with need. How long had it been since she'd been pinned under a lover?

Since way back in the BC days. Back when her body was worth making love to.

"Damn, Pixie," Waylon breathed. "You are impossible, you know that?"

"I do my best."

He closed the gap between them when his lips met hers.

NINETEEN

Waylon parted Frankie's lips with the tip of his tongue and found no resistance. In fact, her tongue darted into his mouth the second he offered the invitation. He groaned, excited by her eagerness.

There is nothing better in the world than a woman who wants you.

And Frankie was giving every indication that she did want him. Her hands ran over his back and through his hair, causing his skin to prickle with goose bumps.

God, what am I doing? This was Frankie, his Adventure Buddy, his gal pal, his not-a-girlfriend, who—Jesus!—he'd almost fed a damn MRE to as a joke.

No romance. That's what we agreed on from day one. No dating, no romance, just two adventure buddies doing fun stuff together.

The sudden image of her bare ass waggling in the air at him from his bed filled his brain like an incoming nuke.

Not fun bed stuff. Outdoors stuff. Like hiking with Snoopy. Not doing it doggie-style.

But her soft touch when she'd wrapped her arm around him had brought his cock roaring to life. And now she was kissing the life out of him.

God, she tasted so sweet, so good, as he realized just how much he'd wanted her from the moment she'd looked at him in the rec center. She'd gone from an intriguing—sometimes infuriating—woman, to an Adventure Buddy he could talk to about anything, and now to this.

Was it right?

Did he care if it was right or wrong?

Yes and no, in that order.

Then she whimpered under him and his heart stuttered.

No! He broke their kiss.

"Pixie, I'm sorry. Oh, God, I don't mean to be forcing you to do anything. I misread the situation."

"No, you didn't misread anything." She kissed him quickly, confusing him even more. "I want this. More than anything." When she went in for another kiss, he stopped her, pulled her close, and rolled sideways until they were both on the bed lying face to face. She tucked her head under his chin and pressed her cheek against his chest.

"Pixie, talk to me."

Her body heaved. His t-shirt was suddenly wet.

"You're crying." Unexpected tears made his eyes prickle. He felt his Pixie hurting, and if it wasn't anything he did, then he had no idea what was causing her pain. "What is it? You can tell me anything."

"It's not you," she reiterated, her voice muffled against his chest.

"Okay."

"It isn't."

"All right."

She shifted until she buried her face in his neck and he let her cry while he held her, hoping that his arms were enough. His mind raced through all sorts of scenarios. Had a man hurt her in the past?

"You can talk to me, Pix," he whispered as he stroked her hair. "You can tell me anything. You're safe with me." The words came out before he could think about them. *Safe. With him.*

Finally, she said, "I'm ugly."

Waylon flinched. "What? What do you mean? You're beautiful. *Jesus*, you're beautiful."

"No. Under my nightshirt. I'm ugly." She hiccupped. "*It's* ugly."

"There is not a damn thing ugly about you, Pix, inside or out."

She shook her head. "There is." And then she added so quietly he barely caught it, "My scars."

Oh. Wow. He never would have thought her surgical scars would bother her—not his Pixie, so full of life she practically roared every morning to greet the day.

"You're afraid to let me see your scars?"

She nodded into his chest. "Women aren't supposed to have scars."

"Who told you that?" Though he was pretty sure he already knew the answer.

"My mother. She says men hate scars on women, that they...get turned off."

Oh, fuck me. That insufferable woman.

Waylon tilted Frankie's head up so that she could look right into his eyes.

"No, no, she's completely wrong. I love a good scar, Pixie. That scar means you have a story. That scar means I get to hold you in my arms. It means the woman I—"

Love.

"—care deeply about is alive and with me."

She hesitated. "You'll still want me if you see it?"

He squeezed her gently. "More than ever."

Then she blinked as if his words had just caught up to her. "You...care about me?"

I love you.

Waylon shut that thought down quickly. He barely knew her. And love wasn't real anyway.

But he couldn't deny the warmth flooding his chest, the tender way he felt about Frankie. It didn't have to be full-blown love to care about a woman. Right?

Waylon stroked her cheek as gently as he could. "Yeah, I care about you greatly, Pixie." He kissed her forehead. "No scar's gonna change that. It's gonna do the opposite. It's going to show me how precious you are and how lucky I am to have you in my life. And if you aren't ready for more, I can hold you all night."

She was already shaking her head wildly. "I want more. I really, really want more."

"Then trust your body and don't be afraid," he whispered. "Jump, Pix. Jump and I'll catch you."

She inhaled sharply at his words. Then she shifted out of his arms and sat up. He sat up with her. She grabbed the hem of her nightshirt and pulled it over her head. In the faint light coming from his windows, he could see the marks cancer had left her.

"Even this?" she asked, and touched the scar under her right breast, slightly larger than the one on the left.

Waylon only chuckled and shook his head. "A little scar like that? Doesn't bother me." He leaned forward and planted a kiss in the middle of her chest, then moved down and feathered his lips over first one scar, then the other. He left Frankie gasping.

He looked up into her eyes, a moment's sadness there. "Someone tell you they're ugly?"

She nodded. "My mom. Last time I saw her. She wouldn't leave me alone until I showed her. Just the one on the right. She looked at it like it was a disgusting worm and asked why I hadn't gotten plastic surgery yet. That no one could love a woman who was so disfigured."

Waylon closed his eyes as his fists clenched. He took a calming breath and opened them. "You believe her."

"Yeah."

"It's not true."

She looked away. Waylon reached out. His fingers brushed her chin and she looked back at him.

"Let me show you how little it matters."

Waylon gently pulled her into his arms. He kissed her tenderly, caressing her back and shoulders. His hands traced delicate patterns over her skin until he felt her shiver under his fingers.

Slowly he lowered her down, his body covering hers like a warm blanket. He trailed kisses along her jaw, down her neck, grazing her collarbone. He wanted her to forget her self-consciousness, to feel beautiful, the most desired woman in the world. Because that's what she was to him.

Waylon slowly dipped his head and pressed a tender kiss to the scar on her right side. Frankie gasped and shivered, her body tensing up at the sensation. He soothed her with soft words of reassurance as he continued to rain gentle kisses along the length of the scar, his lips like feathers against her skin.

"I've never wanted a woman so much."

"You...you really mean that?"

"I wouldn't say it if I didn't," he replied.

Frankie ran her fingers through his hair, clutching him close.

He moved lower, his tongue leaving a wet trail down her stomach. He gripped her hips, holding her still as he reached the waistband of her panties. They were soaked through, the thin fabric clinging to her, teasing him with its outline. Waylon hooked his fingers into the sides of her panties and pulled them down, revealing her glistening pink folds.

He stroked her thighs as his cock hardened to an impossible degree, until he couldn't take it anymore. He buried his face between her legs. Waylon dragged his tongue through her folds in one long, slow stroke, from the base of her pussy to her clit. Frankie gripped the sheets, twisting them as he repeated the motion, over and over, adding a spiraling swirl around her clit until she was moaning and shaking with need. When he finally closed his lips around her clit and sucked, she nearly came off the bed.

"Waylon!" she moaned.

Waylon moved back up her body, kissing her all the way, until he was face to face with her. There was no hesitation now, no shaking, no tears. only warmth and desire in her eyes.

Frankie leaned upwards and captured his lips in a searing kiss. Waylon moaned into her mouth, deepening the kiss as his arms wrapped around her. He pulled back only to open the nightstand drawer and take out his wallet. He opened it and found a condom. Waylon looked into Frankie's eyes again and she nodded.

"Yes," she breathed. "Please. I need to feel you inside me." She slid out from under him and sat up. Frankie plucked the condom out of his hand. "But first, you're wearing way too much clothing. Let me hang onto this," she held the condom up between her first finger and thumb and shook it, "while you fix that problem."

Waylon looked down at himself. "I should, shouldn't I?" He grabbed the back of his tee and pulled it off in one swift move, then tossed it into the hamper beside his dresser. He pulled his boxer briefs down and savored the look of pure lust on Frankie's face when his cock sprang free.

"Yup. You will now forever be known as Waylong."

He laughed as the briefs joined his tee in the hamper.

Frankie reached out and her fingers circled his shaft. Waylon groaned at her touch. It was true—he'd never ached for a woman so much. He'd been a fool to fight his feelings for Frankie.

"You're so beautiful, Pixie," he murmured. "Every inch of you." Then he closed his eyes in ecstasy as her hand moved up and down his cock until it wept. Waylon groaned, his hips bucking into her hand as she tightened her grip and started pumping him. She set the condom on the bed then cupped his balls, rolling them gently in her palm as she worked his cock.

"Fuck, Frankie," Waylon growled, his voice rough with need. "You're going to make me come if you keep that up."

She smirked, leaning up to give him an open-mouthed kiss. "Good," she whispered against his lips. "But I want you inside me first."

Waylon didn't need to be told twice. He grabbed the condom off the bed and tore the package open, then wrapped his hand around Frankie's, stilling it.

"Let me," Frankie said.

"No way. If I let you put this on me, I'll end up coming in your hand."

She let go of him and he rolled the condom on in one swift motion. Frankie lay back against the pillows and Waylon spread her legs. He rubbed the tip of his cock up and down her soaking wet pussy. She closed her eyes and arched her back.

"You want this, Pixie?" Waylon stopped and pressed against her entrance.

"God, yes, please, Waylon. I can't stand it." She reached down to grab his cock but he caught her hand and kissed her palm, then placed it on her belly. He lined himself up, then pushed inside her slowly. God, she was tight. Every inch he gave her felt like heaven.

"More," she moaned. "Please."

Waylon sank himself into her hot, wet pussy up to the hilt. He paused, savoring the feeling of being inside her. He reached between them, his fingers finding her clit and rubbing frantic circles around it as he pumped in and out, gently at first, then faster and harder as he felt Frankie clenching around his cock. It didn't take long before Frankie came again, her pussy clamping down around his cock like a vice as she screamed his name.

Waylon wasn't far behind. With a growl, he buried himself deep inside her and let go, his cock pulsing as he came. He collapsed on top of her, both of them gasping for air as they came down from their high.

"Damn, Frankie," he panted. He pressed a kiss to her sweat-soaked forehead. "You're going to be the death of me."

Frankie laughed, the sound like sweet music to Waylon's ears. He rolled off of her and pulled her into his arms. They lay there, tangled together, as their breathing slowly returned to normal and they drifted off to sleep.

"SO, I can't stand it anymore and we're going to do something about this," Frankie said over breakfast the next morning.

"What?" He took a sip of coffee.

"This. It's no good."

Waylon nearly choked on his coffee as his heart stopped. Frankie leaned across the table and awkwardly tried to pat him on the back. "You okay?"

"What? No! Not that. That was," her eyes practically rolled back in her head, "*amazing*, and we should do more of it. I'm talking about your *apartment*, Waylooong." She winked.

Waylon tried to ignore the stirring that caused, since they'd made love twice before getting up and eating, and one more time with her would probably send him to the ER.

"What about my apartment?"

"Buddy." She looked him dead in the eye. "It's not you."

Buddy?

"What do you mean it's not me?"

"It's bleak. The only life in here is real Snoopy," Frankie pointed at the puppy sniffing around their feet hoping for crumbs, "and stuffed Snoopy," she pointed back toward his bedroom. "So, like I said, we're doing something about it. Today." She crossed her arms, signaling the end of the discussion. Then she told him their plan for the day.

"We're going *where*?" Waylon asked.

Frankie grinned. "Come on. Or are you chickening out?"

"Chickening out? Nope."

"Okay then, finish your coffee and let's go." She stood up and grabbed her empty plate and silverware, then headed for the kitchen. She turned suddenly, and with a mischievous gleam in her eye said, "You have five minutes."

Waylon laughed. "Gimme ten."

"Eight. Clock's ticking." Then she strutted into the kitchen, taking Waylon's heart with her.

AFTER DROPPING Snoopy off at Watchdog, they drove south on I-25 through Denver, past the amusement park—also on Frankie's list —and the stadium—which was not—until the massive blue box rose from the ground like a square piece of the sky. Four giant letters dominated one side.

"Here we are, good old IKEA." She glanced at Waylon. "You're serious, you've never been here?"

"Dead serious." Waylon eyed the giant blue warehouse like he was looking for snipers. They drove into the covered parking lot. Waylon got the impression that they'd driven into some sort of space-ship. The place was totally alien to *him* at least. He parked and opened Frankie's door for her. She hopped out and walked toward the store-end of the parking garage, determination in every step.

"Couldn't we have done this online?" Waylon asked when he caught up to her.

Frankie abruptly stopped, turned, and put her hands on her hips. "Chicken," she said. "Of course not, I told you this would be an adventure."

God, it was fun to get a rise out of her. She looked like an angry baby chick, the way her hair was standing up in all directions. "I have a feeling it's payback for the MREs."

She pursed her lips and tilted her head. "Maybe a little. But it's also going to be fun. You'll see." She laughed and grabbed his hand, drag-ging him with her, and it felt like the most natural thing in the world.

They took a baffling number of escalators before they even got into the store itself. The first thing Waylon noticed was the sweet smell of cinnamon rolls.

"I promise I'll buy you an entire box when we're done," Frankie said. There she went, reading his mind again.

"So how does this even work?" Waylon said, already confused as he looked around.

"It's the easiest thing in the world. There's a dotted line that we follow. That will take us through the entire store. Everything's set up like rooms, so you don't even have to guess what things will look like together or how much space they'll take up. You'll see. It's kind of like being on a movie set, actually." Mischief returned to her eyes.

"What are you thinking?" Waylon asked.

She didn't answer him. Instead, she grabbed his hand again and led him along the dotted line until they reached a display that looked like a living room.

"Isn't this nice?" she asked, running her hand along the back of the couch. "And this rug is perfect." She cupped her hands around her mouth. "Lucy, I'm home!"

To Waylon's dismay, half the store stopped and looked at them. Frankie just grinned, completely unbothered by the attention, while Waylon felt his face heat.

"Frankie," he hissed under his breath, stepping closer. "What the hell are you doing?"

"Having an adventure." She batted her lashes at him, then turned back to the imaginary living room. "Lucy! You've got some 'splainin' to do!"

Waylon glanced around, expecting people to be annoyed, but instead, amused chuckles rippled through the crowd. An older couple actually clapped.

"Oh, God," he muttered, running a hand over his face.

Frankie elbowed him. "Come on, Beefcake. Live a little. Haven't you ever wanted to be in a sitcom?"

"No."

Her eyes gleamed. "Well, how about a soap opera then?" She grabbed his arm and pulled him toward a kitchen display. "Ooooh, perfect! Here we go."

"What—"

Before he could protest, Frankie turned to him, her expression morphing into pure soap opera-level angst. She clutched his arm, eyes wide with mock devastation.

"Waylon, the cinnamon rolls you made for me... I think I'm allergic to them!" Frankie dramatically pressed the back of her hand to her forehead, spun around three times, and stumbled toward a barstool beside the countertop.

More laughs came from a few nearby shoppers, as Waylon realized to his horror that they now had a small crowd following them.

"Your turn. Go on!" she whispered. Then she grabbed her throat and pretended to gasp for air as she made the funniest faces.

More laughter.

Waylon's jaw worked as he stared at her. He was torn between mortification and something dangerously close to having fun.

She peeked at him through one half-opened eye, her mouth twitching.

And then, telling himself he was a damn fool, he gave in.

Squaring his shoulders, he stepped forward and grabbed her shoulders. "No, Frankie! Don't give up now! You've still got so much to live for!"

Frankie sucked in a breath. "But what's the point, my darling, if I can't have your cinnamon rolls?"

Waylon exhaled dramatically, then lifted his gaze to the heavens. "I'll find another way to show you my eternal love and devotion, Pixie. I swear it. Wait." He snapped his fingers. "Waffles."

The audience—their actual audience—laughed and applauded.

Frankie turned and did a little bow, beaming. "Thank you, thank you. We'll be here all day. Tip your waitress. Try the meatballs."

As the crowd dispersed, Waylon chuckled, shaking his head. Frankie looped her arm through his.

"You're ridiculous, you know that?" he told her.

"And you love it," she said, nudging him.

He didn't deny it.

They followed the dotted line deeper into the store, pausing every now and then to test out chairs or inspect lamps and knick-knacks. Frankie couldn't seem to stop grinning, and Waylon found himself watching her more than paying attention to the furniture. God, she made everything fun.

"Okay," she said eventually, plopping onto a sleek black couch. "We've been through the entire showroom. See anything you like? What's your vision for your space, Beefcake? You want a man-cave? Or maybe you want everything in pink?"

Waylon grinned and sat beside her, stretching his arm along the back of the couch. "I don't know." He looked around. "Something simple. Functional."

Frankie rolled her eyes. "Okay, like what you already have. That's not why we're here." She grabbed his other hand in hers and ran her thumb over the top. "What makes you *happy*? What's *you*?"

Waylon hesitated. What made him happy?

Frankie.

He looked at her hand in his. "Comfort," he said finally. "And warmth. And maybe...a little color. *Not* pink though."

Frankie beamed. "Now we're talking."

"And I..." He hesitated. "I want to keep the checkered tablecloth."

Frankie's eyes went slightly unfocused. "Why's that?" she whispered.

Because it will always remind me of our first date.

No way was he going to say *that*. So he shrugged. "First real table-cloth I've had in a while."

Frankie tilted her head and grinned. "First real *tablecloth* in a while, huh?"

She stood abruptly and rubbed her hands together. "Come on, Beefcake. Let's put together a home." She caught what she'd just said at the same time he did. "For you," she added quickly. "A home for you and Snoopy."

A home.

Waylon didn't know why that single word almost knocked the air out of his lungs. It had been a long time since he'd thought about a place that way.

Camille never did.

He glanced at Frankie, who was already marching ahead, acting completely unbothered by what she'd said. Or maybe just pretending she hadn't said it at all.

Probably for the best.

Still, the word stuck in his head like an earworm he couldn't shake. And just like that, with his heart in his throat and a woman who *should* have terrified him but somehow made everything feel *right*, Waylon let himself imagine—for the first time in a long time— what home could really be.

And then, just as quickly, he slammed the door on the thought. *No. Not for me. Not with her. Not with anyone.* He wasn't built for that anymore. He was having a fun day with his *Buddy.* A good time. An adventure.

No strings.

He focused on the present. On Frankie marching ahead, already running her fingers over throw pillows like she was picking out a horse for the ranch she grew up on. His blood heated.

Stop thinking about that.

He followed her back through the winding IKEA maze, letting her chatter on about area rugs and coffee tables. He threw a blanket over the part of himself that had started hoping for more.

An hour later, they were in the loading area, fitting a pile of flat-pack boxes into his truck bed like they were playing Tetris. The sofa and a few other things that couldn't be flat-packed would arrive at his apartment via delivery truck later.

"I still don't know where I'm going to put all this," Waylon muttered, shifting the last box, labeled LÖVBACKEN, into place. He jumped down to the pavement.

"This is just a start," Frankie said, wiping her hands on her jeans. "We didn't even look in housewares for kitchen stuff."

"You really think I need this much furniture?"

Frankie smiled, brushing against him as she leaned into a shopping cart and pulled out the last, crucial item. "Nope. I know you need it. Along with this well-earned box of cinnamon rolls." She held the box in one hand and tapped his chest lightly with her other fist, playful. Casual. Like nothing had changed.

Like he hadn't just spent the last hour trying—and failing—not to imagine what life would be like if she were always in it.

But this wasn't the time for thoughts like that. This was fun. That's what they agreed on.

She stretched, then pushed off the truck with a grin. "Come on, Beefcake. We've got a full day of putting this stuff together ahead of us. If you play your cards right, I might even let you use an actual screwdriver instead of that weird little doohicky they always include."

Waylon caught her by the waist before she could escape and pulled her close to his chest. He'd meant to give her a quick kiss and let her go, but those eyes held him captive the same way they had on day one. He brushed a stray curl off her forehead as he gazed into her eyes. Her cheeks pinkened. Then he kissed her, slow and sweet, leaving them both breathless.

Frankie pulled back just enough to smirk up at him. "Let's just keep this fun, okay?" she said, her tone light. "Nothing romantic, nothing...you know." She shrugged a shoulder, "Just buddies who adventure. Together. Sometimes in bed. Easy-breezy, just like we both wanted. Want. Still want. Right?"

Waylon chuckled, low and rough. "Easy-breezy," he echoed, brushing his thumb over her cheek before stepping back.

The second she turned to get into the truck, he let out a slow breath and rolled his shoulders like he could shake her words off.

No strings. No big feelings. Just fun.

And that was exactly what this was.

Exactly what he was used to. Exactly what he needed.

TWENTY

Frankie flipped a fourth pancake onto Waylon's plate. He glanced at the stack in front of him, then at the single pancake on her plate, and arched a brow.

"You trying to fatten me up?"

She smirked, pouring a generous amount of syrup over her own pancake. "Nah, just keeping you fueled up. You've got a long day of saving lives ahead of you, Beefcake."

Waylon made a sound suspiciously close to a chuckle and she caught the way his mouth twitched like he was holding back a smile. Her heart warmed in her chest. He cut through the stack and took a huge bite. His eyes closed as he chewed.

"You like?" she asked.

"I love." He opened his eyes and looked at her, making her heart flip.

"Thank you." She grinned and looked down at her plate before she could lose her cool. The entire weekend had been nothing short of perfection. But now it was Monday morning, time for them to part ways until their next adventure.

Except, there was no more Adventure Buddy Club. They'd

gotten a group email late last evening saying it was officially cancelled since Stephanie had broken her arm. Neither one had said anything, but they'd looked at each other after reading it on their phones, then gone back to work on the last of Waylon's furniture. She'd hated the thought of leaving the next morning, of getting a promise that Waylon would call and they'd go do something, and then never hearing from him again.

"So. I guess the Adventure Buddy Club is over, huh?" Frankie finally broke the silence.

Waylon had been looking down, tightening a screw. His head shot up so fast she swore she heard the sound barrier break.

"Hell no."

Frankie felt her tight chest loosen. "No?"

He shook his head. "You still owe me dinner, so don't even try to weasel out of it."

Frankie laughed, surprised. "Well okay then." She turned serious. "What about after dinner?"

"I see no reason why we can't keep up our own adventures." Then with a wicked gleam in his eye, he set the screwdriver aside, picked her up, and carried her to the bedroom.

Waylon ordered her onto the bed. "On your hands and knees," he'd said, and Frankie couldn't obey him fast enough. He came up behind her and laid his hands on her hips. She shivered in anticipation of what he'd do next. He kept her in suspense until she felt his warm tongue caress her folds, he ate her out until her legs shook and her whole body tensed, then he held onto her while she came long and hard for him.

"I love your gasps, Pixie," he said, his voice low and heavy with need. She tried to answer him with something clever, but her brain was short-circuiting.

Feeling the tip of his cock press against her opening did not help clear her head.

"I need to be inside you," he breathed against her ear, which made her already-soaking wet pussy gush. "Do you want this, Pix?"

He let go of one hip and grabbed his cock. He rubbed the tip achingly slowly up and down her lips.

"Oh God, yes," she gasped. "God, yes, please, right *now*." She tried to back up, to take him in, but he grabbed both hips again and held them firmly, the sadistic bastard.

Waylon chuckled. "So damn sexy when she's hungry."

"So damn annoying when he's in charge," she countered. Which made him laugh.

"All right, Pix." She lost the touch of his hand as he fisted his cock again, then slid achingly slowly into her.

Blessed relief.

He moved gently inside her as his hand slid over her hip to find her clit. Relief turned to torture.

"You won't break me, Waylon," Frankie told him. "I know you can go harder."

"Pix."

"I mean it. *Please*."

He pounded into her, his grunts of pleasure driving her wild—just like everything else he did. His fingers stroked her, his cock slammed deep inside—softness versus a good, hard fucking. Soon she was climbing to the peak of orgasm again. She cried out his name as waves of pleasure rocked her body. As Waylon tensed, he groaned out her name.

"Frankie. *Fuck*. So good." She felt his cock pulse as he emptied into her. He kissed the nape of her neck and nuzzled there.

"I love the way your hair smells."

"Rosemary oil. It's supposed to help my hair grow faster."

"Did you used to wear it long?"

"Oh yeah. Almost to my butt."

He shivered at that.

"I take it you like long hair?"

"Love it. I like to be able to do this." He lifted his body, tangled his fingers in her hair, and made a fist. He pulled her head back. "It's easier with longer hair, but it still works with yours."

That was the start of round two—round two of three that night.

She was still pleasantly sore.

Frankie couldn't recall the last time she'd been this happy. She had a hard time remembering that they were only Buddies.

Buddies with the best benefits ever.

They'd agreed to keep things simple and fun—which included sex because dammit, why not?

She ignored the voice in her head telling her she needed more.

They ate in comfortable silence for a minute, the occasional clink of forks filling the quiet along with Snoopy's hopeful yips for a piece of bacon. They both found it hard not to spoil him rotten and slipped him tiny crumbs when they thought the other wasn't looking. Waylon reached for his coffee, then hesitated before he took a sip.

"So. I guess you're going back to your place today."

Was that reluctance in his voice? Did he actually want her to stick around? Butterflies rose in her stomach.

"Yeah, I..." And then she remembered.

"What?"

Frankie cleared her throat. "So... funny thing."

Waylon set his mug down. "Yeah?"

Frankie focused very hard on cutting her pancake. "You remember my alarm?"

His entire body went still. "What about it?"

She winced. "I forgot. When I went home to pack a bag Saturday night, that same malfunctioning message came up."

"*Frankie.*"

"I know, I know." She held up a hand before he could launch into whatever protective, exasperated speech was coming. "I'll call and have the repair guy come back out today. It's probably just a glitch."

Waylon didn't look convinced. His jaw ticked, and he dragged his hand down his face. "I don't like that it keeps glitching and that it didn't get fixed the first time. I should have my friend Bear come take a look. Hell, I should have him put in an entirely new system for you."

"Waylon, that's not necessary. Besides, I don't want to spend money on an expensive system. I'm saving up my money for my next trip."

"It wouldn't cost you a thing," Waylon said softly.

"Oh, don't even think about paying for it." Frankie braced, ready for a fight.

"Fine. But I don't like you being there alone overnight when it keeps breaking. Why don't you—"

"Don't say stay at my place until it's fixed," she cut in, pointing her fork at him. "I can handle a repair guy in broad daylight."

His expression darkened and she could see the wheels turning in his head.

"Waylon, I've been handling everything by myself for a long time without someone monitoring my every move."

He sat back and let out a long breath as if she'd gut-punched him.

"I meant that as a joke, Beefcake. I'm sorry, I didn't mean to—"

Waylon waved his hand. "No. You're right. I'm overstepping."

Frankie sighed. "You aren't. You're just being sweet."

"You don't have to say that. I'm not going to..." He trailed off as he looked away.

"Not going to what? Waylon, look at me."

He did and she could read his thoughts in his pain-filled gaze.

"Why do you think you scare me?"

Waylon flinched as a look of surprise overtook his face.

Frankie nodded slowly. "You think you scare me, or that I think you're going to hurt me if I don't agree with you."

Waylon closed his eyes.

"Why? Why would you think that?" She reached across the table and grabbed his hand. "All you've ever done is shown me kindness. Even last night, I had to convince you in bed that I'm not made of spun glass."

His expression went neutral as he opened his eyes. He'd locked it down tight, whatever was going on inside his head. She wanted to pry, to poke, to make him tell her what was rattling around in that stubborn skull of his.

"Talk to me." She gave him a soft smile and squeezed his hand. "Buddy."

He returned her smile with a sad one of his own. "I know what men can do to women, Pixie."

My friends and I... We can do something about that.

She wondered just how much domestic violence Waylon had seen.

Enough to convince him that because he's big and tough, women are automatically afraid of him she guessed.

"I know you know, Waylon. But think about this. I won't let Derek back into my life under any circumstances. I have very good boundaries, I assure you. So do you really think I'd be here if I thought you were going to hurt me?"

He searched her face as if he were looking for the tiniest sign that she was lying to him.

"You aren't, are you?"

"No. Not in the least." She grinned. "You're my Buddy. You've always got my back."

Without breaking eye contact, Waylon stood up and walked around the new table. He took Frankie's hand and as soon as she stood, he pulled her close and wrapped his arms around her. They stood like that until Waylon asked, "You'll text me as soon as the repair guy gets there?"

She shook her head and looked up at him. "I don't want to bother you at work."

"Pix, it's not a bother at all. Believe me." She saw that brief flash of pain in his eyes and wondered again what had happened to him.

"Promise?" She gave him a small smile. The pain in his eyes disappeared.

"Yes."

"Okay then."

"And text me again when he's done."

Frankie chuckled. "Yes, sir. I will."

Waylon gave her a small nod. "All right." He kissed the tip of her nose.

"Actually, is it okay if I stick around here for a while after you leave?"

His whole face lit up. "Stay as long as you like."

"I thought I'd make a couple phone calls and shoot off some emails for work. I can do that from anywhere. I figure Snoopy's gotten used to having people around."

"Snoopy. Yeah." Waylon's expression flattened as he glanced at the clock and dropped his arms. "I gotta get going. Thanks for making breakfast."

Frankie watched as he grabbed his jacket. Waylon picked up his keys from the kitchen counter, hesitated, then opened a drawer. He walked back to her and held up a key.

"This is to the apartment." He held up a card in his other hand. "And this will get you into the lobby."

Frankie bit her lower lip as she took them. "Thank you."

Calm down. Of course he's going to give you the key to his apartment if you're staying here. He'll probably ask for it back tonight.

"Call if anything feels *off* at your house today," he said, voice firm. "I don't care if it's nothing."

Before she could react, he hooked an arm around her waist and pulled her against him. His lips brushed her temple and then found her mouth.

He left her breathless. Before she could get a grip on herself, he was out the door.

And she was left staring after him, trying to shake the feeling that something huge had just shifted between them.

FRANKIE HAD BARELY HIT *SEND* ON an email when her phone buzzed with a text from Wren.

Coffee? Riversong? Bring Snoopy. I'm
dying to meet the little guy!

Frankie grinned at the message. She set her phone down and stretched her arms over her head. She'd had a productive morning. She'd sent three emails off to potential donors and convinced a current donor to increase her company's yearly donation. She'd also called the alarm company, which apologized and promised to send the repair guy out that evening even though he was booked for the day. She'd sent off a text to Waylon telling him the appointment time and he'd responded with a thumbs up. And a heart.

Definitely productive enough to warrant a coffee break.

Twist my arm, why don't you?

I live to enable. See you in half an hour.

Frankie glanced down at Snoopy, curled up on the couch beside her with his face buried in a blanket. She ran a hand over his scruffy fur. "Up for a field trip, buddy?"

His tail thumped immediately.

Five minutes later, Snoopy's carrier was in the passenger seat, the puppy turning in circles and trying his best to look out the window. Frankie smiled as she drove, glancing now and then at him, eager to show him off. In the back of her mind, the conversation at breakfast played and rewound and played again.

She shook it off as she pulled into Riversong's parking lot. She grabbed a tote bag and took Snoopy out of his carrier and hooked a leash to his collar, though she decided to carry him in. She could see Wren and Rochelle sitting at a table by the front window, deep in conversation.

The second Frankie stepped into Riversong, Snoopy tucked under one arm, Wren and Rochelle's heads snapped up.

"Awww!" they said in unison. Then both women got up and hurried over, completely ignoring Frankie in favor of her puppy.

"Who's the cutest little adventurer?" Wren cooed, scratching behind his ears. Snoopy wriggled with joy, his entire body vibrating in excitement.

"I cannot handle how adorable he is," Rochelle declared, running a gentle hand down his back. "This is criminal levels of cute."

Frankie smirked. "Glad to know where I rank in this friendship."

Wren waved her off. "You're great. But he's *tiny* and *fluffy*. You can't compete."

Frankie rolled her eyes. "Come on, I've been working all morning and I need coffee now." She turned to the counter where two people were working. One was a broad-shouldered man with his back to her as he tinkered with the huge espresso machine. The other was a woman with dark, curly hair and an air of effortless confidence leaning on her elbows, watching the interaction with a big smile. Frankie had never seen her before, but she didn't need an introduction to know exactly who she was. April Taylor, one of the owners of Riversong. Wren had mentioned her in passing.

"Is it okay that I brought him in?" Frankie asked April. "If not, his carrier is in my car."

"Oh, don't you dare keep him outside," April answered. "Bring that little guy up right up here." She waved them toward the counter. "Wren told me you were bringing in a little rescue puppy. Snoopy, right?"

"Yup. Waylon rescued him along with Stephanie."

"I heard about that, too. Shane told me." Frankie noticed the slightest tinge of pink in April's cheeks when she mentioned Shane. "He said he looked Snoopy over at Watchdog." April held her hands out and Frankie handed her the puppy. She immediately cradled him like a baby against her shoulder. "He's a little love, isn't he?"

Before Frankie could say anything, a loud metallic clunk came from the machine, followed by a gruff, irritated voice.

"April, you're overloading the damn grinder again," the man muttered. He turned and Frankie noticed he had the same eyes as

April—but where she radiated effortless control, he radiated exasperated dad energy.

April didn't even look at him as she rolled her eyes and said, "No, I'm not, Sonny."

"You're about to burn out the motor—"

"It's *fine.*"

"You said that last time."

"And I was right."

Sonny muttered something under his breath about "stubborn kids" before shaking his head and going back to work.

Frankie grinned. *Oh, I like these two.*

April handed Snoopy back to Frankie. "What are you drinking?"

Frankie looked at the menu board on the back wall. The coffee shop smelled divine, and the pastries in the display counter made her mouth water. "Everything looks so good, I can't decide. Surprise me."

April nodded once. "You got it." She turned and grabbed a bottle of chocolate syrup.

"You're off to a good start," Frankie said.

April tossed her a smile over her shoulder.

"April has a sixth sense for what people want," Rochelle said.

"Who doesn't love chocolate?" April shrugged. She finished Frankie's drink and set it on the counter in front of Frankie.

"What do I owe you?" she asked as she passed Snoopy to Wren.

"On the house." April snatched a black-and-white cookie from the display. "Here, this matches Snoopy."

"Aw, thank you."

April poured another mug of coffee. "I'm going on break, Dad."

"Figured." Sonny didn't look up from the machine.

April walked to the end of the counter and opened a half-door, letting herself out. The four women headed back to the table by the window seat.

"I love this place," Frankie told April, who smiled proudly.

"I practically live here," Rochelle said as she sat on the cushioned bench under the window. "It's a safe space for introverted caffeine addicts."

Wren set Snoopy on the bench beside Rochelle and picked up her coffee mug. "And for extroverted caffeine addicts." She clinked her mug against Rochelle's.

Frankie took a sip of her drink and nearly moaned. "Oh my God."

April smirked. "Good?"

"Life-changing."

April leaned back in her chair, satisfied. "Then my work here is done."

Across the shop, Sonny snorted. "Your work would be done if you'd listen to me about the damn grinder."

April rolled her eyes. "Ignore him. His doctor told him he needs to lay off the caffeine."

"Where does he think I work?" Sonny grumbled.

Frankie laughed. Yeah, she was really going to like it here.

Wren set her drink down. "So, we were just talking about Steph."

Frankie perked up. "How's she doing?"

"She's bored out of her mind," Rochelle said. "Which is why we're planning a chocolate, flowers, and smut delivery."

Frankie grinned. "Solid plan."

"We're thinking of getting her the next book in the *Fate of a Pineapple* series," Wren added.

Frankie frowned. "I'm sorry, the *what*?"

April groaned. "Oh *no*. Don't bring her into this."

Wren grinned. "Oh *yes*, bring her into this."

Rochelle clapped her hands together. "Okay, so picture this. Regency romance, but reverse harem."

Frankie blinked. "Wait. Like—"

"Three men. One heroine," Wren confirmed.

"And *pineapples*?" Frankie burst out laughing.

"Pineapples were a status symbol. They are historically accurate in the book," Rochelle said, straight-faced.

"Reverse harems, maybe not so much," Wren added.

"And it all goes downhill from there," April muttered into her coffee.

"You *love* it," Wren shot back.

April sighed dramatically. "I do."

Rochelle turned to Frankie, eyes gleaming. "Stephanie started a book club just for the series. You in?"

"Arden mentioned a book club. Same one?"

"It is."

Frankie smirked. "Hell yes."

Sonny groaned from behind the counter. "God help us all."

They laughed and high-fived. After that, the conversation drifted from one topic to another. Frankie took Snoopy out for a potty break. At one point, April got up to handle the lunch surge, then brought back sandwiches for everyone and took another break. While they ate, Rochelle filled them in on her latest translation and Wren showed them some photos she took with her drone on her honeymoon in Hawaii. April had the latest Lyons gossip.

"You can't believe what people will tell their barista after three shots of espresso," she said. "Even when said barista and her family has a 'past.'" She rolled her eyes as she air-quoted.

"Speaking of gossip..." Wren looked Frankie dead in the eye.

"Oh, no." Laughing, Frankie covered her face.

"So," Wren drawled. "Elias texted me IKEA. With Waylon."

April's eyebrows rose. "Wait, what?" She slammed her hands on the table. "And here I was bragging about how I have all the gossip. You went to IKEA with *Waylon*? Spill it, girl!"

"I did," Frankie admitted. She hesitated; was she betraying his trust? "His apartment was just...sad."

Wren nodded, more serious now. "That's what Elias has said. I've never been, and he's only been there a couple of times."

"I walked in and it was worse than a monk's cell. I couldn't stand it."

"Wait, so you've been there?" April set her coffee down.

Frankie rolled her lips in, then said, "I may or may not have spent two weekends there."

"As *Buddies*, right?" Rochelle grinned.

"Of course."

"Mmm-hmm." Wren sipped her coffee.

April, arms crossed, watched her closely. "So what *is* the deal with you two?"

Frankie sighed. Even if she hadn't heard about the IKEA part yet, of course April knew what was going on. "We're just friends. Buddies. With, you know."

"Benefits?" Rochelle teased.

Frankie pointed at her. "Exactly. Buddies with benefits. No complications."

The three women shared a look.

"What?"

April uncrossed her arms and tapped her fingers against her coffee mug, studying Frankie. "I don't mean to make Waylon sound like a man-whore, but... I don't think he's *ever* taken a woman back to his place since he's come back home."

"Yeah, I got that feeling." Frankie sighed. "So, you grew up with all of them, right?"

April looked uncomfortable.

Shit. "You don't have to—"

"No, it's fine." April waved her off. "We all went to the same high school. Bear, Gabe, Elias, Waylon, Ben, Brock, Sean, and Shane," she counted them off on her fingers as she said their names, "they were all inseparable. They'd met when they were little kids, riding the school bus."

"Elias told me they all lived up in the mountains, so they were always the first to be picked up and the last to be dropped off," Wren said. "So they bonded."

April nodded. "Mountain kids versus townies. Unless we had a game against Denver or Boulder or some other city. Then we were all hicks as far as the city kids were concerned." She laughed lightly.

"I get it. I grew up on a ranch in the sticks," Frankie assured her.

April saluted her with her coffee mug. "Waylon and Elias were hellraisers in high school," April continued. "Non-stop partiers, until Ben talked some sense into them."

"That's Moose, right?"

"Yeah, that's him. You've met him?"

"No." Frankie shook her head.

"I'm not surprised. He's more of a recluse than even Bear and Ellie." April smiled fondly. "Big sweetheart though. Had some issues in school when he was younger I guess, but by high school, pretty much everyone respected him." Her smile softened. "He was always kind to us—my sister and me, I mean—and our cousin, Brianna. Anyway, they all ended up in the military eventually. Waylon..." She stopped. Obviously, Frankie wasn't the only one worried about invading his privacy. "He was the only one who got married."

Frankie tried not to let her surprise show.

Camille was his wife?

"I don't know the details." April glanced at Wren, who shrugged. "But it didn't end well and he won't talk about it. Like, at all."

"He won't even let Elias bring it up," Wren added. "And they're bro-mates."

"Bro-mates?"

"Yeah, like soulmates, but two dudes." She grinned.

"He's been back for years and never dated seriously. So, you going to Waylon's apartment, that's kind of a big deal," April finished.

Frankie's stomach knotted.

Wren grabbed her hand. "I take it by the way your face just turned green he never told you he was married."

Frankie gave her an awkward smile. "It's really none of my business. Like I said, we're just friends."

Wren's squeezed her hand. "Just... Don't assume he doesn't want more."

Before Frankie could respond, her phone chimed—the alarm to

remind her it was time to run some errands before going home and waiting for the repair guy.

She exhaled, grabbed her bag, and stood. "I gotta go. I have a repair guy coming to the house, but I need to drop Snoopy off and hit the grocery store first."

"What broke?" April asked Frankie.

"My burglar alarm."

April frowned. "Your alarm's broken?"

Frankie waved a hand. "It's fine. Just a glitch."

April looked concerned. "Yikes."

"More annoying than anything."

"I've gotta run, too," Wren said, standing up. "And I'll let you get back to work."

Rochelle pulled a laptop out of her bag and set it on the table. "April, you really need to start charging me rent."

The women hugged and made plans for the next book club. Wren walked Frankie to her car.

"So. Not only did you spend the weekend, but Waylon gave you a *key*?"

"It's not like that," Frankie insisted. "It's just so I could bring this little guy back," Frankie said as she kissed Snoopy's head. She opened the passenger side car door.

Wren folded her arms. "Oh, I see. So I guess he told you to leave it in the apartment when you left."

Frankie's eyes went wide.

"He didn't, did he? *Girl*." Wren gave her a warm smile. "I mean this in the nicest way, but I think you're delusional."

Frankie laughed as she zipped Snoopy into his carrier. "Seriously, just Buddies," she reiterated.

"Whatever."

Wren gave her one last hug before Frankie got in the car. "Think about what I said. There's a good chance Waylon's even more delusional than you are about being *just* Buddies."

Wren's words echoed in her head later as she unlocked his apartment door. She looked around at the new furniture. It still looked like a showroom, but after it was worn in a little, his place would look like a home. One she'd helped him build.

She fed Snoopy, then went to the closet. She pulled out his winter coat and felt around in the pocket for the earbud. Still there, of course. She let it go, hung the coat back up, and closed the closet.

"I *am* delusional, just not the way Wren thinks."

DUSK WAS FALLING by the time Frankie got home. She parked her car in the garage and unloaded the trunk—a couple bags of groceries and her overnight bag. She decided to go in the back door instead of walking all the way around the house. It was less of a pain getting in with the alarm off.

Frankie stepped into her house, juggling her bags as she nudged the door shut behind her. The house was silent, save for the click of the lock sliding into place. It felt weird being here alone after two nights with Waylon. She put her groceries away then picked up her overnight bag to unpack it in the bedroom. As she walked past the front room, she spotted the small box still sitting on the table beside the door where she'd left it. Frankie diverted to the table and picked the package up. She'd totally forgotten about it since bringing it in the other night.

Chemo brain? Or just a great weekend? She grinned. *Can't wait to tell Dan.*

It weighed almost nothing. She shook it but couldn't hear any rattling inside. Probably something she'd ordered and forgotten about.

Yup, chemo brain.

She ripped through the packing tape and peeled back the cardboard flaps.

Black lace and red silk. Delicate. Expensive.

"What the hell?"

She picked up the bundle of fabric and let it unfold, revealing an intricate set of lingerie—way too sheer, way too intimate, definitely nothing she'd would've bought for herself. For a moment, she thought it might be from Waylon. But no, that was dumb—the box had been sitting on her porch before they slept together.

A 'suggestion' sent by Stephanie? No. She could be pushy, but she wouldn't go this far.

A small white card rested at the bottom of the box. She picked it up with trepidation and opened it. Her stomach dropped as she read the words.

I CAN'T WAIT *to see you in this. You'll be stunning.*
    —*Derek*

FRANKIE'S PULSE slammed into overdrive. "How *dare* he?" Furious, she dropped the card like it burned her. Of all the offensive things Derek had done, this was a new level.

The doorbell rang.

Frankie jumped. For a split second, panic seized her—*Derek*—but then she remembered the repair appointment.

She dropped the lingerie back into the box and slammed the flaps shut like she was trapping a spider inside. Shaking, she looked out the window. No Derek—just the same repair guy from last time.

Relieved, she opened the door.

"Miss Whitmore," he greeted with a friendly nod, "Sorry to be back again so soon."

"Yeah, no worries," she glanced at his name tag, "Leon. Come on in." Frankie exhaled, trying to shake the lingering adrenaline. *Jesus, calm down. It's just the alarm guy.*

He brushed off his boots on the welcome mat and stepped inside. "Turns out it wasn't a software issue after all—hardware's the culprit.

I've got the parts to swap it out today." Leon studied her for a second, brow furrowing. "You okay?"

Frankie blinked. "What?"

"You look a little rattled."

"Oh." She forced a tight smile. "Just a weird day."

He nodded like he understood completely. "I can come back later if now's not a good time."

"No, no, that's okay. You're already here."

"Fair enough." He set his bag down in front of the panel. "Shouldn't take too long, then I'll be out of your hair."

Frankie didn't linger. She tucked the box under her arm, grabbed her overnight bag, and made a beeline for the bedroom. She sat on the bed, setting the box down beside her, and grabbed her phone. Her fingers hovered over the screen for half a second before she typed:

> Derek, the lingerie you sent me was wildly inappropriate. Do not contact me again.

She hit send and exhaled.

There.

Done.

Then she tapped over to her texts with Waylon.

> Repair guy is here. Same one as last time.

Frankie hesitated before adding:

> Everything is fine!

She listened to the repair guy fixing her alarm in the other room as she tried to get her racing heart under control. His phone dinged, and a minute later he called out, "Miss Whitmore? Another appointment just came in, but I want to show you before I leave, I've got yours working again."

Thank God.

Except now she couldn't shake the dread of facing a night alone in her house.

TWENTY-ONE

Waylon tilted his head side to side to crack his neck as he walked up the stairs to his apartment. The temperature had dropped considerably after the sun went down, and for the last hour of his shift, he'd wished he'd brought his winter coat. The shift had been a good one otherwise—no big surprises and no fatalities, thank God.

Frankie had ridden along in his mind the whole day. He caught himself grinning at times, remembering something funny she said or did over the weekend. He fought the urge to text her just to see what she was up to. Several times he caught Elias giving him a knowing look, the bastard.

When Frankie texted that the repair guy had come by, fixed the alarm, and that everything was fine, Waylon had felt a knot loosen in his chest. The worry was gone, replaced by anticipation. He'd be coming home for the first time to an apartment that actually looked like a home. And now here he was.

He quickly unlocked the door, stepped into his apartment, shut the door behind him, and let out a slow breath as he looked around. His apartment felt so different. Obviously, it looked different too, with the new couch and tables and rugs—but that wasn't it.

Except for the black-and-white ball of fur curled up in the middle of the couch and snoring softly, the space looked too neat, too sterile. Like a showroom. It still looked like no one *lived* there, which was the same way the apartment had looked and felt the entire time he'd been there. So why did it *feel* different now?

No. He had it backwards. The *weekend* had felt different.

Waylon took in the whole space. It looked great. But all the furniture in the world wouldn't make his apartment feel like a home.

His gaze fell on the red-and-white checkered tablecloth.

Only Frankie makes it feel that way.

And now he missed that feeling. Missed *her*.

His phone buzzed in his pocket. He pulled it out and saw her name on the screen. His heart thumped as he swiped to answer.

"Hey, Pix." His shoulders eased and his expression relaxed into a smile.

"Hey," she said. "How's Snoopy? Was he okay by himself for a while?"

"He's fine, but he must have had a big day," he said as he crossed the room. "He's zonked out on the couch. Didn't even twitch when I came in just now." He sat down next to the puppy, who finally woke, lifted his head, and looked at Waylon sleepily. He wagged his tail and yawned. "I was just about to take him out for a walk and then feed us both." Waylon dropped his hand on Snoopy's head and scratched behind his ears.

There was a pause. Not long, but just enough for Waylon to feel it. "I should let you go do that then." Her voice sounded a little raw, like she was getting a sore throat.

It occurred to Waylon that Frankie could've texted. She'd called instead.

"Everything all right, Pix?"

"Yeah," Frankie answered quickly. Her voice now sounded artificially chipper. Before he could press, she added, "Speaking of eating, I still owe you dinner."

"Oh yeah? You thinking tonight?" Waylon's grin turned into a smile that stretched from ear to ear.

"Um. No, actually," she said. Disappointment flooded his chest. "I mean, not for the dinner I was thinking of. That's on Halloween night. I actually made the reservation for Liminal a while ago and it took a lot of work to get in, and I already paid for it, and it's for two people, and...," she smiled and shrugged, "I don't want to go by myself."

Waylon tightened his grip on the phone. He didn't ask who the reservation was originally for. He didn't need to. *Derek.*

"You said it was expensive? We'll split the cost."

"No way. Like I said, I already paid. Besides, you won, I pay. That was the wager."

Waylon exhaled slowly. "You don't have to do that, Pix."

"I want to. Besides," warmth crept into her voice, "I still owe you for that oh-so-delicious MRE."

Waylon chuckled. "Hey, I did feed you a great meal after that."

"Yes, yes you did." She laughed lightly.

There was another pause, and Waylon could *feel* the shift.

"Frankie?" His voice was softer now. "Anything else going on? You sure your alarm's fixed?"

She hesitated again. "Yeah, absolutely. We tried it out and it's definitely fixed."

Waylon's jaw ticked. "But?"

A breath. "Derek...sent me lingerie."

Waylon could barely control his rage. "He what?"

"The box was on my porch Saturday night. I just thought it was something I ordered. I didn't open it until today. I texted him and told him to leave me alone."

"Frankie," Waylon said, "Get in your car and come over. Right now."

She let out a short, scratchy laugh. "Thank you. I told myself it was nothing, and I didn't want to impose—"

Nothing? Impose? Dammit, Frankie.

Now that she'd told him what was going on, she sounded scared. He kept his voice calm and steady. "Put me on speaker and I'll stay on the phone with you while you pack."

"Thank you." He could hear her moving around, opening and closing drawers. She rattled off her things as she tossed them into a bag. "Jesus, at this point I should just leave a suitcase at your place."

"Wouldn't bother me, babe."

Frankie went quiet.

Shit. Did I really just call her babe?

"Keep packing, Pix."

"Yeah, okay."

He heard beeps that didn't sound like the alarm followed by a soft clunk.

"What's that?"

"Just getting my Glock out of the safe."

Right. He'd forgotten she owned a gun.

"Pix, I hate to say it, but bring the lingerie, too. It's evidence."

"Evidence?"

"For when you file a restraining order."

Everything went quiet on her end. "Shit. Right."

A minute later he heard a zipper. "I'm heading out to the car now."

"Wait. Your backyard lit up?"

"Yeah, I have the back porch lights on. They flood most of the yard."

"Good. Grab a flashlight anyway and make it obvious that you're on the phone while you walk to the garage."

Waylon heard her keys jingle followed by beeping as she set the damn alarm.

"Talk to me, Pixie."

"I'm heading out the door now." Waylon heard the door close.

"Everything good?"

"Yeah, the yard's clear." She sounded breathy and he pictured her sprinting through the backyard. He heard the garage door open.

"Look—"

"I'm looking in the back seat of the car," she interrupted, doing exactly what he was going to tell her to do. "Nothing." Then thankfully, her car door open and shut.

He listened to her blow out a breath and start the car.

"I can disconnect now," she said.

"You sure?"

"Yeah. I don't need any extra distractions while I drive. I'll see you soon."

"Drive safe, Pix."

Babe.

"Will do."

The second the call ended, Waylon's thumb was already moving, dialing Shane.

His friend answered on the first ring. "Ram."

"We've got a problem, brother."

Shane didn't miss a beat. "What's going on?"

Waylon took a steadying breath, forcing his grip on the phone to loosen. "Frankie just called. Her ex sent her lingerie. Unwanted. To top it off, her security system's jacked up."

Shane let out a low whistle. "Fucking hell."

"She texted him to back off," Waylon continued, pacing now. "Then she called me after my shift was over. I told her to pack a bag and get the hell over to my place, now."

"Good call." Waylon could already hear Shane switching gears into Watchdog mode. "You want me to run a check." A statement, not a question.

"I do. I need to know what kind of history this guy has. If there's a pattern." Waylon gave Shane a quick rundown about the morning Derek showed up on Frankie's porch. He gave Shane the make, model and license plate number of Derek's car along with a physical description.

"That's about all I know about the guy right now." Waylon pinched the bridge of his nose. "I told her we could do something about him but she brushed me off. Said he was just awkward, not dangerous. I wasn't gonna push. But this?" He clenched his jaw. "This is different."

"Yeah, no shit. Lingerie isn't just a 'Hey, let's still be friends' gift."

"Exactly."

"I'll pull what I can tonight and send it to you. You told anyone else yet?"

Our brothers in Mountain Division.

"No."

"You want *me* to?"

Waylon hesitated. "Am I overreacting?"

There was no hesitation from Shane. "Oh hell no. I know what's in your head. Don't even start down that old road, brother. This is different. If this were happening to Apri—" He cut himself off, clearing his throat. "To *my* woman, I'd do the same thing. Any one of us would, Ram."

Waylon ran a hand down his face. "Do it, then. See what pops up."

"You got it. I'll loop Kyle in. And the rest of our brothers."

"Appreciate it, brother."

"Keep her close, brother."

"Yeah. I will."

Waylon hung up and exhaled, trying to tamp down his anger before Frankie arrived. She didn't need to see his rage.

When he had himself under control, he ordered takeout. He opened his closet and put on his winter coat. Then he headed downstairs to wait for Frankie.

TWENTY-TWO

Frankie held tightly to the steering wheel as she drove through the night to Waylon's apartment. The only time she let go of it was to brush away a tear. They weren't so much tears of sadness or fear—though she felt both—but frustration.

Frankie hated feeling helpless. Hated it more than anything else in the world. Cancer had done that to her, but only at first. After the initial shock, she fought back as hard as she could, knowing that even the toughest fighters didn't always win that battle.

The next tear that fell was pure sadness.

"No." She wiped her nose and gritted her teeth. "He's not going to get the best of me. I'm fighting back right now, even if it feels like I'm running. I'm doing something to protect myself."

After the repair guy had left, she'd set her alarm and sat down on the couch while a voice in her head told her she was overreacting. Then it switched gears and berated her for not blocking Derek's number the first time he contacted her. Maybe if she'd ignored him, this wouldn't have happened. Maybe if she'd been firmer, this wouldn't have happened. Or, maybe if she'd been nicer at the beginning and gone on a date—

"Stop it!" she'd screamed in her empty house. "Just stop it!" She swallowed and her throat felt raw. "This isn't my fault."

She had a choice—call the police or call Waylon.

She chose Waylon.

She'd call the police tomorrow.

We can do something about that.

Or maybe not.

Relief flooded her as she pulled into the lot and parked, followed by a wave of worry as soon as she saw Waylon marching toward her car. Would he rage at Derek? Or tell her she should have let him take care of the problem from the beginning, scold her for being stupid?

Only one way to find out.

She opened her car door as soon as he got there and braced for a lecture.

Waylon pulled her into his arms without a word.

He held her tightly, his body so much bigger and stronger than hers that he practically enveloped her. So warm. Solid. The rock she realized she needed.

"You're not gonna have to face him alone, Pix," he said, reading her mind. "You've got me. You've got your friends. Hell, you've got Snoopy."

"He's only a puppy." She sniffed, fighting back tears.

"Yeah, but we know he's gonna grow up to be an ace fighter. We should probably buy him a Sopwith Camel now."

When did her body start shaking so hard? "Did you know the Sopwith Camel replaced the Sopwith Pup?"

"Babe," he whispered.

Then he tilted her chin up and kissed her.

It was exactly what she needed and it was the best kiss she'd ever had. It filled her with warmth and stopped her from shaking and kept her knees from giving out on her.

But it didn't stop there.

His kiss told her she wasn't alone anymore.

His kiss was a solid promise that she wouldn't be abandoned.

His kiss returned her trust in other people.

"Let's get you inside, babe. It's cold out here and you don't have a coat."

Frankie nodded. It was freezing. She hadn't even noticed as she ran across her backyard to the garage, and Waylon's body kept her warm as he held her.

Wait a minute.

He was wearing a winter coat.

The winter coat.

Which he promptly took off and wrapped around her before he opened the car door to grab her duffel and that horrible 'gift' from Derek.

Her right hand went directly into the pocket and she felt around for the earbud.

Still there.

Her anchor to her BC life.

If it was the same earbud.

I want it to be.

She could pull it out of the pocket *right now* and ask him.

But if it wasn't? If he looked at her like she was crazy?

Devastating.

Suddenly, she was off her feet as Waylon swept her up into his arms and started carrying her to the apartment building.

"I ordered us pizza and some wings. Oh, and breadsticks, and a big salad if you want that instead."

"Salad? I want cookies."

Waylon grinned. "Good thing I also got the big-cookie pizza for dessert."

WHEN THE FOOD ARRIVED, the salad went straight into the refrigerator. Frankie needed cheese and pepperoni and thick, carb-ladened crust *now*. She barely said a word through dinner, shocked at how ravenous she was. Waylon matched her bite for bite. He'd set the oven to its lowest temp and turned it off after a few minutes, then slid a cookie the size of a personal pizza onto a baking tray and into the oven it went. When it was time for dessert, the cookie was soft and warm, the chocolate gooey.

Frankie stabbed her fork into the last bite of cookie, scooped up the drizzle of chocolate and raspberry, then hesitated.

Waylon grinned. "Go on, Pix. You know you want it."

She sighed dramatically. "I *do.* I really do."

"And yet, you hesitate."

She narrowed her eyes at him, then leaned forward and held out her fork. "You take half."

Waylon shook his head. "Half? It's all or nothing. I'll fight you for the whole thing."

Frankie let out an incredulous laugh. "How? You want to arm wrestle?"

"Rock, paper, scissors."

Frankie snorted. "Beefcake, just eat half the cookie."

"No."

"Waylon."

"Frankie."

She met his gaze, deadlocked for all of two seconds, before shoving the fork in her mouth.

Waylon exhaled sharply, laughing as he leaned back in his chair. "Unbelievable. The woman fights *dirty.*"

Frankie chewed, swallowed, and grinned. "*And* I win."

She groaned then, slumping back. "Ugh. Why did I do that? No regrets, but I am *so* full."

"Worth it, though, huh?"

"Oh, absolutely."

Waylon stood up and reached for Frankie's hand. He pulled her up and started leading her to the couch. Snoopy followed on their heels.

"What about the dishes?"

"They can wait." He sat down and pulled Frankie into his lap, folding her against his chest. Snoopy jumped up beside them and curled into a ball. Silence stretched between them, warm and easy. But then Waylon tilted her chin up and said, "So. You gonna file a restraining order tomorrow?"

The question sucked the warmth from the air. Frankie exhaled hard.

"You really think it'll do any good?"

"Not on its own," Waylon admitted. "But it makes it easier to step in..." He caught himself. "For the cops to step in if he doesn't leave you alone."

We can do something about it.

"Then yeah. Yeah, I will."

Waylon nodded. "Good." He rubbed her back. "You don't have to do that alone, Pix. I'm coming with you."

Frankie shook her head. "You have to work tomorrow. I don't want you to miss your shift."

Waylon scoffed. "You think I don't have vacation time? I don't think I've taken a day off since I started."

Frankie turned her head, studying him. "Seriously? You haven't missed a single shift?"

"Nope. If something comes up, I just trade with someone." He smirked. "My boss has been on me for months to take some time off before I lose it."

Frankie huffed a laugh. "I bet you're the only one at the hospital with that problem."

"Pretty much."

"Well," she sighed, "if you're sure."

"It's not up for debate, Frankie. I'm going with you."

She sighed as she thought about the damn box, which Waylon had unceremoniously tossed onto the kitchen counter earlier. "I hate that it's come to this. I don't even know how it got this far."

Waylon's jaw flexed. "I do."

Frankie frowned. "What do you mean?"

"You dated him. He got obsessed. Now he thinks he's got some claim on you."

Frankie's head snapped up so fast she nearly gave herself whiplash. "Wait. You think I dated that guy?"

Waylon blinked. "Didn't you?"

"No!" she blurted. "God, no. I never—Waylon, he was a creep. I never even liked him. No woman at the clinic did once they saw through his little-boy act."

"Little boy act?" He said the words like he was spitting out something nasty and sour. "At the clinic?"

"Yeah. Okay, so—he was one of the doctors at the cancer center. Dr. Sloane, but he insisted on everyone calling him Dr. Derek. He didn't act arrogant like some doctors do, but he wasn't warm and caring like the good ones, either. Not really, though he tried to act that way. He was just...awkward, harmless, I thought. At first. He has this 'aw shucks' thing going on; that's the best way I can explain it. Like, fake-shy."

Waylon nodded. "A shy little boy in a grown man's body."

"Yeah. Creepy, right? But I was friendly at first because I didn't want to be rude and I thought maybe he was socially awkward and I was misjudging him. Really smart people are like that sometimes."

"But your gut told you otherwise."

"Yeah." She blew out a breath. "And then so did a couple patients, *and* the nurses, once he started paying extra attention to me." She looked down. "I was stupid and I gave him an in, made him think I liked him."

"Stop right there. You did nothing wrong, Pixie. He thinks you belong to him just because you were polite? That's not on you, that's on him."

She sighed.

"Does the voice in your head telling you otherwise, by any chance, belong to your mom?"

Again, Frankie thought she'd given herself whiplash with the speed her head shot up.

"I'll take that as a yes." Anger flashed in his eyes and was gone. "It's none of my business but I'm gonna say it anyway. Tell your mom to shut the fuck up."

Frankie's jaw dropped like a marionette's. Laughter bubbled up, shocking her. Even Snoopy looked at her, startled. She slapped her hand over her mouth, which only made her want to laugh harder. "You must think I'm insane," she said between laughs. "Laughing this hard right now."

"Not one bit. You've been through a lot." He reached out and stroked her hair. "Wren does the same thing when she's stressed. Not surprised you're friends."

"I saw Wren at Riversong today, by the way. She wants to come over and see the new furniture."

Waylon's smile froze.

Shit. I shouldn't have said anything.

And then he relaxed. "Yeah, sure."

Frankie blinked hard. "You're okay with that?"

"Yeah. We'll set up a time."

"*We?*" She pointed back and forth and him and herself.

"Yeah, babe. We." He kissed her, brushing his lips softly against hers, making her tremble. "Keep my key."

With that, he picked her up and carried her to the bedroom.

Standing at the foot of the bed, Waylon kissed her softly, reverently, as he reached for the hem of her sweater. His hands were steady as he peeled it over her head. He took his time, trailing his fingers down her bare arms, mapping every inch of her skin like he was memorizing her all over again.

Frankie shivered under his touch.

His eyes darkened as he looked at her, drinking her in like she was the only thing that existed. No hesitation. No flicker of doubt. Just pure, aching want.

"You're so damn beautiful," he murmured, his voice low and thick with heat.

She wasn't self-conscious. Not with him. Not after all the ways he'd already shown her how much he wanted her. How much he adored her.

His lips brushed her collarbone, slow and soft. He worked his way lower as his hands made quick work of her jeans, tugging them down her legs.

"Your panties are already soaked through." He traced his finger over the wetness and Frankie thought she'd lose her mind. When he pressed a kiss to the thin cotton, she sucked in a breath, already aching, already desperate for his mouth.

Waylon smiled against her skin. "Patience, Pixie."

Frankie let out a frustrated whimper, but she didn't get a chance to protest further. He hooked his fingers under the waistband and slid them down, exposing her to the cool air—quickly followed by the warmth of his breath. He tossed the new comforter to the side and laid her down on the bed.

Then, standing beside the bed, he reached for the hem of his own shirt and pulled it over his head. Frankie's gaze locked onto him, watching as he kicked off his boots, unfastened his belt, and shoved his jeans down, leaving only his boxer briefs.

"Take them off," she whispered, her voice husky.

His lips curled in a slow, knowing smile. He pushed them down and stepped out of them, finally bare, his cock thick and hard and curving in an arc toward his belly.

Frankie's breath hitched.

Waylon climbed onto the bed, settling between her legs, his mouth curving against her inner thigh as he kissed his way up.

Her hips jerked when he licked her, slow and teasing, as he dragged his tongue through her folds before circling her clit. He groaned, like he was the one getting the pleasure.

"God, I love the way you taste," he murmured, his tongue flicking just right, just enough to drive her crazy but not enough to send her over the edge.

She buried her fingers in his hair, trying to guide him, but he just chuckled and gripped her hips, holding her still.

"Waylon—"

"I've got you, babe." His voice sounded gravelly, full of heat and tenderness all at once.

Then he stopped teasing.

He licked and sucked, slow and deep, every movement deliberate, raising her higher and higher until she was gasping, trembling, thighs clenching around his head. And when he finally slid two fingers inside her, curling them just right, her orgasm crashed over her like a tidal wave.

She cried out his name, as he kept licking, kept stroking, drawing out every last pulse of pleasure until she was shaking.

Waylon kissed his way up her body, lingering over her skin, until he reached her ear, where he whispered sweet things. Telling her how good she tasted. How soft she felt. How fucking beautiful she was.

Frankie, still breathless, reached between them and wrapped her fingers around his cock. He was hard and hot in her hand, slick at the tip when she ran her thumb over it.

Waylon groaned, his hips jerking into her touch. "*Fuck*, Frankie."

She stroked him slowly, watching his face as he clenched his jaw. She let go so that she could slide down. She open-mouth kissed the head of his cock, pressing her tongue against it, tasting the saltiness there.

"Frankie." His voice was ragged as his hands fisted in the sheets.

When she took him into her mouth, he lost all control.

"Jesus, babe—" His voice broke as she sucked, hollowing her cheeks, taking him deep. She loved the way he reacted, the way his muscles tensed, the way he threw his head back as he restrained himself.

She could tell he was close. So close. But just when she thought he was going to let go, he reached down, twined her hair in his fingers, and gently pulled her away.

Frankie frowned. "I wasn't done with you."

Waylon let out an almost breathless laugh. "You were about to be." He cupped her face, brushing his thumb over her lips. "But I need to be inside you, Pixie."

Her breath hitched. "Yes. God, yes, *please.*"

"Scoot back up." She rested her head on the pillow as he reached for the drawer of the new bedside table and grabbed a condom. She watched, mesmerized, as he rolled it on, his jaw tight, his movements precise.

Then he was on top of her, his body pressing her into the mattress, his weight solid and warm and grounding.

Frankie wrapped her legs around his waist. "Please, Waylon."

His gaze locked onto hers as he slid inside her, slow and deep.

Frankie gasped. He filled her completely. But even better, the way he looked at her—like she was the only thing that mattered— made her heart squeeze in her chest.

Waylon groaned, pressing his forehead to hers. "You feel so good, baby. So perfect."

He rocked into her slowly, driving her crazy. She begged him to go faster.

"I want to savor you, Pixie," he breathed into her ear.

When his fingers found her clit, circling, pressing just right, she shattered all over again, clenching around him.

"So damn beautiful, watching you—"

His body tensed, and then he was gone, groaning her name as he pumped hard into her.

When he caught his breath, he eased down next to her, turning her carefully so that he stayed inside her. Tangled together, breathing hard, neither one was ready to let go.

Waylon brushed his lips over her temple, soft and reverent. "You're mine, Frankie."

She should've corrected him. Should've reminded him they were just Buddies.

But she didn't.

Instead, she melted into his warmth and whispered, "You're mine, too."

———

THEY SLEPT, then woke and made love again. Frankie lay beside Waylon, breathless, still warm from his touch, one hand lying on his chest. His steady heartbeat beneath her palm felt like home.

Waylon shifted and brushed his lips over her hair. "Tell me what you're thinking, Pixie."

She smirked. "I hear you have a thing for cowgirls."

"Oh, man." Waylon closed his eyes as his hand covered his face, fingertips touching his forehead before sliding down his nose and over his mouth. "Busted."

"Yeah you are."

"Who ratted me out? No, don't answer that. Elias."

"Wren, actually." She laughed quietly. "So now I get how you looked at me in the truck when I told you I was raised on a ranch."

"How I looked at you?"

"Yeah."

"What? How did I look at you?" He gave her one of those frown-smiles with narrowed, sparkling eyes that made her tummy flutter.

"Like I was skirt steak."

That cracked him up. "I do love a good skirt steak."

"I know." She closed her eyes, tipped her head back, then opened them and looked heavenward as she dragged her teeth over her lower lip. "Boy, do I know."

"So tell me about the ranch," he said as he traced his finger across her forehead and down her cheek. "Tell me about growing up there."

Frankie shivered under his touch. She moved her hand up to his. She threaded her fingers between his until they were holding hands.

"I was practically born in the saddle. You couldn't separate me from my horse in the summer when I didn't have school. He was a beautiful red roan, sired by Zippo's Mad Match, and his dam was Sunny's Hope. I named him Flicker of Hope." She grinned. "Get it?"

Waylon grinned back. "Of course I do. That's a badass name."

"I was very proud of myself at age eight for that one."

"So do you ever go back and ride him?"

She shook her head. "He's not mine anymore. My mother sold him while I was at college without telling me."

"What?" He propped himself up on one elbow.

"She didn't just sell Flicker." Frankie pressed her lips together. "My dad." She sighed. "He died suddenly my sophomore year."

"Pix, I'm so sorry."

"I came home for the funeral, of course. Pretty much the minute I went back to school, she sold everything. The whole ranch is gone." Her heart clenched. Even after all this time, the betrayal killed her.

"The fuck?"

"Now it's all tract housing." She made a small, disgusted sound. "You can bet she's not living in a tract house herself. Custom build, fancy marble, gold fixtures."

"While you don't have a home."

"That's by choice, not because I don't—didn't—have money. The will stated that I got half if she sold, but Dad never thought she'd sell. He grew up on that land. I did, too. She hated ranch life, but he downplayed how much in his head. She was his blind spot."

"I'm sorry you lost your dad."

"Yeah, me too." She smiled sadly. "That's an old wound now. A scar that doesn't show."

Waylon shook his head. "You're wrong. It shows in your eyes when you talk about him."

She looked away. He reached out and turned her head back toward him. Then he leaned in and kissed her.

When she'd gotten her breath back, he asked her why she chose not to find a permanent place somewhere.

"I don't know. I guess I'm just a tumbleweed. Detached from my roots, rolling where the wind blows me." She grinned. "They pick up and spread seeds from other plants as they tumble."

Waylon smiled. "The original Wwoofers."

Frankie laughed. "Yeah, I guess you could say that."

Waylon squeezed her hand. He brushed his thumb lazily over her knuckles. "So where's the wind blowing you next, tumbleweed?"

Frankie smiled, stretching her arms above her head before returning her palm to his chest.

"Remember our conversation on the way up to Idaho Springs? I'm letting fate decide. I'm getting a whole bag of state quarters to pick—"

She stopped.

Waylon's voice had been light when he asked, but his eyes told a different story. She saw it now—the faint flicker of something deeper, something raw.

He didn't want her to go.

And suddenly, she wasn't so sure she wanted to, either.

For so long, her life had been about movement, about running toward the next thing. But here, wrapped up in Waylon, she wasn't running. She hadn't even given serious thought to the next place since meeting him.

And that scared the hell out of her. But so did losing Waylon.

She swallowed hard, then let her fingers drift lower, tracing idle patterns against his skin. "You know..." She glanced up at him, keeping her tone casual. "You said you've got a ton of vacation time banked."

Waylon nodded, watching her closely.

"So why not use some of it for fun?" She gave him a small smile. "Come with me on an adventure."

Waylon stilled beside her. His breath hitched, and for a second, he just looked at her, like he was making sure he'd heard her right. Then, slowly, a grin spread across his face.

"You serious, Pix?"

"Serious as a shark bite."

Waylon let out a short laugh before rolling her onto her back, pinning her beneath him. His eyes had lost that shadow of doubt. Now, they were full of something else entirely.

"Careful what you promise, Frankie," he murmured against her lips. "I just might take you up on that."

She kissed him in response.

And later, when Frankie drifted off in his arms, her last thoughts were of her and Waylon swimming in warm, tropical waters. Together.

TWENTY-THREE

Waylon woke before dawn, the room still blanketed in darkness. He lay still for a moment, listening to Frankie's soft, even breathing beside him. She hadn't moved much in the night—too exhausted, he figured, from everything that had happened. He hated that she had to deal with any of it, but at least now, she wasn't dealing with it alone.

Careful not to wake her, he slid out of bed, grabbed a fresh pair of boxer briefs, sweatpants, and a tee out of his dresser, and got dressed. He padded barefoot into the living room. Snoopy lifted his head from his dog bed, ears twitching, but didn't get up. Waylon scratched the pup behind his ears, then headed for the kitchen.

His and Frankie's phones were still where they'd left them charging on the counter. He picked his up and called in to work, saying he needed a personal day and hoping his boss didn't die of shock. Then he sank onto the couch. He rubbed a hand over his face. He opened his texts to type a message to Shane to let him know what he'd learned about Derek, but it was unnecessary. A new message from Shane was waiting for him. He saw the time-stamp—2:12 AM and sent a silent thanks to his brother for losing shuteye.

Check your email. Call me when you're up.
Got a full dossier on Dr. Derek Sloane.

Waylon's stomach tightened as he swiped over to his email app. He scrolled through junk mail until he found Shane's message, tapped the attachment, and started reading.

The first part was the usual background check—current address and phone, all previous addresses, where Derek had grown up, where he'd gone to school, his residency in Chicago. He'd graduated third in his class in medical school.

Waylon skimmed over most of it, slowing only when he got to the section about Derek's hospital history. His record as an oncologist was spotless. He'd even won a national award for his contribution to oncology care.

Waylon scrubbed his face with one hand. A guy like him, making women uncomfortable, crossing boundaries—there should've been something.

Then Waylon found it.

Four years ago, Derek had been disciplined at a hospital in Chicago, his privileges revoked for "unprofessional conduct."

Waylon's pulse kicked up.

Derek had challenged the ruling and it went to a hearing. But the person who filed the complaint never showed. Because of that, the ruling was reversed and his privileges reinstated.

Shane had added a note:

That means the hospital was required to file an Action Report with the National Practitioner Data Bank when they revoked his privileges. Then when the witness didn't show up and he got his privileges reinstated, they filed a Revision-to-Action Report which updated Derek's record to reflect the reversal. In other words, if another hospital or medical board looks him up, they'll see both the original complaint and that it's been undone. A neat little loophole that means technically, Derek's slate is clean.

And Derek was free to continue stalking women.

Waylon's jaw clenched as he read Shane's words.

Interesting enough, Derek hadn't gone back to the hospital after the hearing. Instead, he'd packed up, left Chicago, and started fresh in Colorado. Waylon smiled ruefully when he read the name of the first hospital to hire him—Milestone Hospital.

"Figures," he scoffed. A friend of Stephanie's—a man who Waylon and Elias had saved when he had a heart attack at the rec center—had nicknamed it Millstone Hospital. Their predatory billing practices had left him feeling like they'd tied a millstone around his neck and threw him in the river.

A revocation like Derek's should've raised red flags. Even with the reinstatement, it *should* have followed him. Should have made hospitals think twice before hiring him, dammit. But it was Milestone; no surprise they didn't care so long as they were getting an award-winning doctor.

A year and a half ago, Derek had been granted privileges at the hospital and cancer center where Frankie had been treated. Derek hadn't been her doctor, so he wasn't supposed to have access to her records. But somehow, he knew her number. Knew where she lived.

Waylon's grip tightened around his phone.

This motherfucker.

He kept reading, and the reason why Derek left Chicago became clear. Shane had found a restraining order against him filed by a woman named Kathy Rhodes. She didn't work at the hospital but she'd filed it about a month before the hospital disciplined Derek. Shane had added another note:

I'm going to try and locate her. My thought is that he became frustrated when Kathy Rhodes filed the order, then went after some other lucky lady at the work. He must have intimidated her or paid her off to keep her from showing up at the hearing.

"Son of a bitch," Waylon said quietly to himself. He sat on the couch, phone heavy in his hand, the words on the screen burning into his brain. Derek wasn't just some awkward, harmless creep. And

Frankie wasn't his first victim. He was a predator. A careful one. A smart one who made sure nothing stuck to him.

Waylon exhaled hard as he dragged a hand down his face. He needed to tell her. But not now. Not at four in the goddamn morning when she'd barely had a chance to breathe since all this started. He'd let her sleep a little longer, let her have a few more hours of peace before he shattered it all over again with what he'd learned.

He stood and stretched, trying to ease the tension out of his shoulders. Snoopy, still curled up in his bed, cracked an eye open and decided it must be breakfast time. He stretched and trotted over to Waylon, tail wagging, hopeful look in his eye. Waylon couldn't help but smile at the pup, especially when he went up on his hind legs and planted his front paws on Waylon's leg.

"All right, little guy. Let's take you on a quick trip downstairs, then get you fed."

After he got Snoopy sorted, Waylon padded back to the bedroom. He wasn't going back to sleep, but he could at least be near Frankie. He stripped down and slipped under the covers, careful not to jostle her. She was curled on her side, facing away from him, her breathing deep and even. He pressed his chest against her back and wrapped an arm around her waist, pulling her in close.

Frankie sighed softly in her sleep and nestled into him, her body warm and relaxed against his. Waylon closed his eyes, breathing her in, grounding himself in the rise and fall of her chest and the steady beating of her heart. He pressed a soft kiss to the top of her head.

It wasn't going to be enough to tell her to file a restraining order. Wasn't going to be enough to tell her that Derek was dangerous.

We have to stop him.

He wasn't sure how much time passed, only that he lay there, listening to the slow rhythm of her breath, until morning light started creeping in through the curtains.

Frankie stirred. She stretched against him, pressing back into his warmth, letting out a soft, contented sigh before turning her head toward Waylon and blinking sleepily at him.

"Mmm. What time is it?" she murmured, her voice husky with sleep.

"A little after six-thirty is my guess."

She yawned and rolled over to face him. "You're awake early." She studied his face. "I have a feeling you didn't get much sleep."

Waylon hesitated, brushing a dark curl from her forehead.

Frankie's brow furrowed. "Waylon?"

Sometimes it was best to rip the band-aid off quickly. "Shane sent me Derek's full report last night."

She pushed up on one elbow, suddenly wide awake. "And?"

Waylon sat up against the headboard. He told Frankie what he'd learned about Derek. "He probably left Chicago because he had a restraining order filed against him. A woman named Kathy Rhodes."

Frankie's eyes went wide. "Wait. What?"

"She didn't work at the hospital," he explained. "But a month after she filed, the hospital revoked his privileges for 'unprofessional conduct.' Then at his hearing, the woman who filed the complaint never showed. So they reversed it, but he never went back."

"Damn."

Waylon nodded grimly. "And then he shows up in Colorado and gets privileges here, no problem."

Frankie sat all the way up now, pulling the covers around her. "Jesus."

"He's done this before, Pix, God knows how many times," Waylon said, his voice low, controlled. "So I don't ever want to hear you blame yourself again."

"I won't." She sighed. "It's just automatic, you know?"

"A lot of women do it. I think you're taught to." He looked away. "But it's not on them, it's only on the men who decide to become monsters. Some woman hurt them, yeah, but so what? A man can choose to move on, like a fucking adult. When he doesn't, it's his choice, not hers."

Waylon pulled Frankie close, pressing a lingering kiss to her temple. "Come on, babe. Let's get out of bed and get some breakfast in you."

Frankie sighed against him, her breath warm on his skin. "Only if there's French press coffee."

He chuckled. "Do I ever make any other kind?"

"No, thank goodness."

Reluctantly, she rolled out of bed. He watched as she stretched her arms over her head, her naked body still flushed from sleep. She caught him staring. Smirking as she reached for her overnight bag, she asked, "Like what you see, Beefcake?"

"Always," he said, completely serious.

Frankie shook her head, biting her lip as she pulled out a sweater. "You better get dressed, or *I'll* get distracted."

Waylon grinned but grabbed a clean pair of boxer-briefs out of a drawer, then pants and a fresh thermal, and went into the bathroom, As he pulled on the shirt, Frankie joined him. He brushed his teeth, then took a swig of mouthwash directly out of the bottle.

Frankie just stared at him, a slightly disgusted look on her face.

He tipped his head back and gargled.

She winced. "That sounds horrendous."

Waylon spit out the mouthwash, then grinned at her in the mirror. "I could sing opera instead."

Frankie snorted. "Oh, God, no."

But it was too late. Waylon launched into an exaggerated, off-key rendition of *O Sole Mio,* complete with vibrato.

Frankie slapped a hand over her mouth, muffling a squeal of laughter. "Please, stop! Swigging mouthwash right out of the bottle is disgusting, your gargling is bad, but the singing is *painful!*"

Waylon wiped his mouth with a hand towel, grinning. "I don't know, babe. I think I missed my calling."

"If you mean torturing people with your voice, then yeah." She grinned back. "Stick to saving lives."

"Everyone's a music critic," he teased, winking at her as he walked out.

Her laughter followed him down the hall. It felt good to hear her happy instead of scared.

The light moment lingered while they made breakfast, but as they settled at the table, Waylon noticed her gaze darting toward her phone, which she hadn't picked up. Just quick glances, like she was checking on a spider waiting to jump on her.

He poured them both coffee, letting the silence sit for a moment before saying, "So, about today."

Frankie sighed. "Yeah. The restraining order."

"You ever filed one before?"

She shook her head. "Nope. But I'm guessing you know something about it."

Yeah. Too much.

He took a sip of coffee. "I'll download the forms you need to fill out before we go. I've gone with women to the interviews. Sometimes a piece of paper keeps a guy away. Sometimes it doesn't."

Frankie watched him carefully. "And when it doesn't?"

"That's where Mountain Division comes in."

She blinked. "Mountain Division?"

Waylon nodded. "Me, Elias, Shane, Gabe, Bear, and Ben. We look out for women and kids who've slipped through the cracks of the system. Restraining orders help, but some guys don't give a damn about them. So we step in."

Frankie sat back. "You told me the day Derek showed up, we can take care of that. Is Mountain Division like... a vigilante group?"

Waylon huffed a small laugh. "If you want to call it that. But we make damn sure men like Derek understand there are consequences for their actions." He set his mug down. His voice softened. "We helped a woman around a year ago. Felice. She was married to a guy named Preston. Real piece of shit. He controlled her, beat her, made her think she had nowhere to go. The second she decided to leave, we made sure she got out safely."

Frankie's fingers tightened around her mug. "What happened?"

"She told him she was filing for divorce and he beat her up real bad. We stepped in, helped her get a restraining order and served it along with divorce papers, set her up in a safe house at Watchdog while we moved his shit out of their house. He tried to stop us." Waylon grinned at the memory. "Didn't go well for him. He was arrested for assaulting an officer. Now he's serving time for embezzling."

Frankie looked confused. "But not for beating the shit out of his wife?"

Waylon shook his head slowly. "Nope. Felice was lucky she had proof of the embezzling."

"Or she'd still be living in the safe house," Frankie surmised.

Waylon leveled his stare at her. "No, she wouldn't be. We would've made sure of that, one way or another."

Frankie let out a slow breath. "I understand."

Waylon's gut tied itself into a knot. "Do you...have a problem with that?"

She didn't hesitate. "Absolutely not."

Waylon closed his eyes and exhaled. *Thank God.*

"How is Felice now?" Frankie asked when he opened them again.

"She's safe. Free. She's taken shooting lessons and self-defense classes. Her life isn't perfect, no one's is. But it's hers now, and she's a lot happier."

Frankie nodded, then stared down into her coffee. When she spoke again, her voice was quieter. "I hate that this is even necessary."

"Me too, Pixie," Waylon said. "But it is."

She pressed her lips together, then let out a deep sigh. "It is."

Waylon reached across the table and squeezed her hand. "I'll be with you the whole way."

Frankie nodded. "Thanks, Beefcake."

They finished breakfast. More than a few scraps had found their way to the floor where Snoopy hoovered them up. Waylon cleared the table and added the dishes to the ones from the night before in the sink. Frankie wanted to help, but he insisted on cleaning them himself while she filled out her paperwork.

As he washed and rinsed, his thoughts drifted back to the day they'd helped Felice. He grinned, remembering how he'd lost a bet to Elias.

That damn bus.

The memory surfaced so abruptly that Waylon almost dropped a plate. It had been over a year ago, but suddenly, it was *there*—the crowded bus, the gorgeous woman laughing so hard it lit up the whole damn place, the podcast about some woman stumbling into a fucking penis museum.

He chuckled under his breath, even as he felt a little guilty thinking about another woman he'd been seriously attracted to. But no wonder he was falling for Frankie so quickly. Even if she didn't have those luscious curves, she had the same kind of laugh. The same mischievous spark in her eyes. The same...dark...hair...

He stopped scrubbing as he tightened his grip on the dish.

It's not possible.

If it *was* Frankie, wouldn't she have recognized him when they met at the first Adventure Buddy meetup? Said something about the bus, like maybe 'Hey, can I have my earbud back?'

The earbud. *Holy shit.* He'd held onto that damn thing for weeks, played with it like a worry stone until he'd forgotten all about it. Where had it ended up?

Do I still have it?

Don't be an idiot. It wasn't her. Forget about it.

He went back to scrubbing the plate, then rinsed it. His mind wouldn't let go of the memories, instead deciding to oh-so-helpfully fill in some details. He'd been on his way to work. It was dreary and freezing outside because of an early cold front. The podcast was about a woman traveling the world on her own—

Like Frankie wants to do.

—who ended up in Iceland. She went to a penis museum—*no thanks*—then a punk rock museum, which sounded pretty cool.

But he couldn't take his eyes off the woman on the bus. She lit the entire fucking day up. She made him want to forget about going to

Cocks and Strippers for another one-night stand, and ask her out instead. Go on an actual date. Hell, go and check out Iceland together. Maybe have something real again.

Something real *again? Are you serious? Stop lying to yourself. Love isn't real. Besides, you're thinking about a woman who didn't care enough to stick around, so she took off.*

No. He was thinking about *two* women who took off. Who didn't care.

Only, where he'd made the wrong decision with Camille, he'd made the right decision with the woman on the bus. Mostly. Except for the earbud.

If you do find the earbud, fucking toss it in the garbage like you should've that day.

He finished cleaning the plate, grabbed the last one, and scrubbed.

Love isn't real. It isn't. It isn't.

He rinsed the last plate.

Yeah, stop lying to yourself.

Because you love Frankie.

He had shut that thought down before, on the night they made love the first time. But there was no shutting down the way he felt, then or now. He was in love. Madly, stupidly, deeply in love with the Adventure Buddy he never wanted. He had been since the moment he laid eyes on her. Hearing her laugh sealed it in his heart.

But where *did* he first see her and hear her laughter? At the rec center...or on the bus?

Ask her.

He scoffed. How was he supposed to do that? Hey, were you that sexy woman I met on the bus last year? *That* would go over well.

Maybe he could ask her if she ever rode the bus. To the hospital. Where she had her surgery a year ago. *Shit. It lines up.*

· · ·

WAYLON PUT the last plate in the dishwasher and hit the power button. Before he could stop himself, the question was halfway out of his mouth.

"Hey, kind of a weird question, but—"

He turned, dish towel in hand, his gut twisting with anticipation.

Frankie stood frozen, staring hard at the box containing the lingerie. Waylon hadn't opened it, not wanting to upset Frankie any more than she already was the night before.

His stomach dropped. "Frankie?"

She slowly turned to him, her expression tight.

"It's the damn note," she muttered. "I keep thinking about it, even more than the stupid lingerie. I told myself it was just a gross overstep."

She opened the flaps, and Waylon watched her whole body stiffen. She'd looked fine five seconds ago, but now she was pale. Furious.

She took out the note and showed him.

I can't wait to see you in this. You'll be stunning.

—Derek

"Motherfucker," Waylon said, jaw tightening.

Frankie set the note down slowly, deliberately beside the box. her breath measured like she was containing a nuclear detonation. "I am *done*. I am sick of random men thinking they can send me lingerie or dick pics or tell me how I'm *really* feeling."

Waylon's anger softened just enough to let admiration slip through.

"I am taking him *down*," she said. "To-fucking-*day*, Waylon."

"Damn right you are." He took her in his arms. "Except you've got one thing wrong."

"Yeah? What's that?" She looked fierce, like she would chew right through him if he tried to stop her. *Fucking turn-on.*

"It's *we*. We're taking him down. You, me, Shane, Elias, hell, all of Watchdog. We've all got your back, Pixie."

For a moment her eyes shone as the realization set in. She wasn't alone. Not anymore.

Her eyes hardened again. "When does the police station open?"

"Police don't handle it. Lawyers do. We need to go to the Protective Order Clinic at the Justice Center."

"So when do *they* open?"

"Soon. We're lucky it's Tuesday morning. They only hold interviews Tuesday mornings and Wednesday afternoons. If we're lucky, you'll get a hearing today and it can go into effect right away."

"And if not?"

"You're not in immediate danger, like if you were living with him, so we'd go before the judge tomorrow or Thursday. Maybe Friday."

"Wow. They make you wait." She shook her head and looked disgusted.

"System sucks, babe."

"Then let's make sure we get an interview today."

"Let me call Kyle and see if Snoopy can hang out there. We'll pick him up when we're done."

Frankie beamed at him. "Perfect."

She started pulling on her cowgirl boots while Waylon headed to his bedroom to make the call in private. He wanted to ask Kyle for a favor, one he didn't want Frankie to hear. He disconnected with a smile—Kyle was more than happy to help out.

Frankie had leashed Snoopy and she had the car carrier under one arm. Waylon barely had time to grab his shoes as Frankie marched over to the closet. She pulled out Waylon's winter coat and threw it on. Her hands immediately went into the pockets.

TWENTY-FOUR

Frankie was grinning ear to ear as Waylon parked in front of Watchdog's kennels to retrieve Snoopy several hours after dropping him off.

"Do you think he missed us?" she asked.

Waylon gave her a grin. "Of course he did." He ran his hand through her hair, then leaned over and kissed her. "Love seeing you happy, Pix."

"I love seeing justice actually work." After listening to Waylon talk about Felice, she was expecting to be told she'd have to wait for her restraining order. But the stars must have been aligned. Not only had she gotten an interview, she'd been in front of a judge a couple hours later, presenting the evidence on her phone along with the paperwork. She'd granted Frankie her restraining order without hesitation. Derek would receive it that day. Frankie had to restrain herself from hugging the judge.

Frankie knew that in spite of his smile, Waylon was not expecting the order to stop Derek. She couldn't blame him, but at the same time, she couldn't help but feel hopeful. It was her optimism that had helped her mentally get through her chemo. It would get her through this, too.

When they walked in, the kennel's receptionist, Jodie, smiled at them. She stood up and came around her desk.

"Hey, guys! I'm supposed to take you to Snoopy, but he's so cute, I've decided he's not allowed to leave."

Frankie laughed. "I think you're going to have to fight both of us if that's the case."

Waylon dropped his arm across Frankie's shoulders. "I warn you, Frankie's much fiercer than I am."

Jodie laughed. "I believe it. So, you're in good moods; the hearing must have gone well?"

"It did. Dr. Derek Sloane will not be bothering me."

"Damn straight he won't," a voice called from down the hall past reception. Shane appeared a moment later, accompanied by a woman who had a couple of inches on him. "Frankie, I'd like you to meet Charlie King. She's Watchdog's best bodyguard."

The woman gave her a warm, beautiful smile as she offered her hand for Frankie to shake. "Very pleased to meet you, Frank," Charlie said. "Welcome to the Guy Name Club."

Frankie burst out laughing. "Love it! Please tell me Steve is in it, too."

"*In* it?" Charlie said. "Steve founded it. She informed me this morning when I was there to have a quick swim before work."

"Oh of course she did," Frankie said, pretending to slap her forehead. "Sadly, the Adventure Club is no more."

"Yeah," Charlie said, tilting her head in sympathy. "But Steph—I mean, Steve—is in good spirits. She's not about to let a broken arm slow her down."

"I suppose you're more interested in picking up a certain dog than talking to a couple of humans," Shane said.

"I can multitask," Frankie said as Waylon chuckled beside her. "But yeah, I miss my puppy."

Shane and Charlie turned and Jodie joined them. "He had a

great time with the other dogs," Shane said as they all walked down the hall toward the kennels. "Peetie's adopted him."

"Peetie?"

"Shane's Lab," Charlie said. "I'm not surprised. I call him Peetie the Sweetie."

They walked past the kennels to an outdoor, fenced-in area full of doggie obstacles. Frankie spotted Snoopy in the outdoor play yard, locked in a tug-of-war with a black Lab as Kyle and another man watched. Other dogs darted around them—Malinois, Shepherds, mutts—wrestling, playing fetch. Others were napping in the last warm puddles of sunlight for the day.

"So many dogs," Frankie said. "And they all get along?" She looked at Shane.

"They're a pack," he said with a shrug. "All Watchdog dogs." He lifted his chin toward Snoopy and Peetie. "Looks like Snoopy's been accepted."

Kyle lifted his hand and waved and the other man nodded, then gave a command to the Lab, who immediately let go of the rope and sat. Kyle swept Snoopy up in his arms, along with the rope the puppy refused to drop. As he crossed the courtyard, a gold-and-black Lab got up from one of the sunny patches and trotted alongside him.

"This is Camo," Kyle said as he transferred Snoopy to Frankie's arms then handed her a leash.

"I was just going to ask," Frankie said as she let Snoopy lick her chin. "Gorgeous dog."

"He's a chimera—genetically two dogs in one. And smarter than two humans put together."

"Is he *your* dog?" Frankie joked, remembering what Arden had said in the exam room.

Kyle laughed. "More like Arden and me are his humans. Camo runs the show." Kyle scratched Camo's ears and the dog leaned against him in obvious love and devotion. "So, you're welcome to the shooting range anytime you want. I'll get you set up with an ID badge, which also works as your key."

"What?" Frankie asked, confused at the abrupt change in subject. Kyle looked at Waylon. "You didn't tell her?"

"Sorry, Pix." Waylon dropped his arm around her shoulders. "I didn't get a chance to tell you that I asked Kyle if you could practice here. I know you've got your Glock but I don't know how long it's been since you went shooting."

"Oh." She blinked rapidly, realizing the implications—Waylon wanted to make sure she could defend herself against Derek. "I honestly don't remember. It's been over a year though."

Kyle's gaze strayed to her short hair and quickly darted back to her eyes. "Of course. Well, Charlie's offered to help shake off some of the rust."

Charlie narrowed her eyes at her boss. "Shake off some of the rust? Really?"

Frankie laughed. "It's all right. I get what he means. And thank you." She tipped her head at Charlie and Kyle. "I appreciate what you're doing for me, but the good news is, I have a shiny new restraining order against Derek Sloane."

Shane and Waylon shared a quick look that was easy for her to interpret—they trusted a restraining order about as much as they'd trust driving across a bridge made of balsa wood.

"We'll get out of your hair." Frankie set Snoopy on the ground and snapped his leash to his collar. "Sorry to be a bother. Thank you."

"Negative," Kyle said. "Not a bother at all. With either watching Snoopy or using the range." He looked over his shoulder at the other man, who had rounded up the dog. "Alex is also a fan of the new pup. He's my kennel master. He was having fun teaching Snoopy a few basic commands. He should sit and heel for you now."

"Thank you!" Frankie shouted to Alex, who nodded in return. She straightened up and told Snoopy to sit. The puppy responded immediately. Frankie started walking. "Heel." Snoopy trotted right at her side.

"Cool." Frankie beamed at Kyle.

She turned to see Waylon's reaction and caught Shane handing him a small black bag. She raised her eyebrows in question, but Waylon only smiled back.

It wasn't long after they got to Waylon's apartment that Frankie discovered what that was all about.

"The bag's full of quarters."

Her eyes went wide. "Oh my God. *State* quarters?"

He laughed. "Yeah. All the different states. I've been saving them ever since you told me you were going to leave your next destination up to fate. But I didn't have one of each state, so I asked Shane if he would ask everyone to donate to the cause until we had all fifty states plus D.C., Puerto Rico, Guam, the U.S. Virgin Islands, Samoa, and the Mariana Islands." He shook the bag and the coins inside jingled.

"No way. I can't believe you went to all this trouble."

"Believe it, Pix. Reach in, pick one, and that's where we'll go." He held the bag up just over her head. "Let's do it, gambling woman."

She laughed before she plunged her hand in. The bag was indeed full of quarters. She was tempted to cheat and try to find Hawaii by touch. It was on her list, after all. A moment's flicker of bittersweet pain stabbed her heart.

As Frankie scrounged around in the bag, she noticed something strange. Each coin felt the same—or did they? No, it had to be her fingers, left tingly after chemo.

Unless...

Frankie finally picked one and pulled it out. When she opened her hand, sure enough, there it was resting in her palm—the Hawaii quarter.

Did he...? He couldn't have.

She pretended to be surprised, letting out a delighted laugh. "Hawaii. Yes!" She high-fived him. "I can't believe it!"

But, she'd take the bet that the bag was full of nothing but Hawaii quarters.

"Wow, look at that," Waylon said. "Just where you wanted to go. First, the restraining order came through right away, now this." He swiftly put the bag of quarters away. "I'll just give these back to

Shane to redistribute with the ones I put in there first. Man, that was lucky."

Frankie could tell he wasn't the least bit surprised. He was a terrible liar.

Her lips curved into a smile as she turned and headed for the bedroom. "I'll show you who's lucky..."

The door had barely clicked shut before Waylon was on her.

Frankie backed into the wall, breath catching as he kissed her—slow at first, making sure she still wanted this. Which was almost funny, considering the only thing she wanted more than him at that moment was air, and even that was debatable.

His body pressed into hers, all heat and muscle and safety, and something deep in her belly sparked to life. She grabbed the fabric of his thermal and tugged him closer. She could taste his desire and it wound her up even tighter. He tasted so good, and she wanted more.

"Tell me what you want from me," he murmured. His lips brushed hers, warm and intoxicating.

Frankie reached down and slid her hands under his shirt. Her fingers trailed lightly over his skin and he hissed. "I want everything. I want all of you."

His eyes closed slowly as if he were savoring her words. When they opened again, they were filled with an intensity she'd never seen. "Good," he breathed.

Then he lifted her up. She gasped, instinctively wrapping her legs around his waist as he pinned her gently to the wall. His mouth found the soft curve of her throat. Frankie felt his teeth scrape against her sensitive skin and she moaned as she tipped her head back.

He gripped the hem of her sweater and dragged it upward inch by inch, his thumb grazing over her skin until her toes curled.

"You drive me crazy, Pix," he muttered against her skin.

"In a good way or a bad way?" she teased.

"Right now—good," he growled. "In an hour, God knows with you."

He carried her down the hall to the bedroom. Then they were lying on the bed in a tangle of limbs and laughter and desperate need.

Clothes vanished, flung aside in their haste. She didn't care where they landed. One minute his shirt was there, the next it was somewhere across the room, and her sweater half-covered the lamp. Waylon's hands were everywhere—slow and reverent one moment, demanding the next. She arched into him, helpless not to.

When he finally entered her, Frankie gasped—every nerve ending lit up like someone had thrown a match on dry kindling. He stilled above her, watching her face, letting her feel all of him.

She reached up and touched his cheek. "Don't be gentle. Not tonight."

Something fierce ignited in his eyes, and then he moved.

Every thrust was fire. Every kiss, thunder. Every moan, a prayer.

And when she came apart beneath him at the same moment he called her name in ecstasy, Frankie clung to him like he was the only thing anchoring her to the world—because he was.

Coming down from her high, she thought of how the earbud on the bus had been her anchor to her old BC world, and now Waylon was her anchor in the new one.

She smiled against his throat as he tried to catch his breath. The more she thought about it, the more certain she was that he'd filled the bag with Hawaii quarters to surprise her and give her what she wanted.

In return, she had a surprise for him—for both of them—waiting in her duffel bag.

Or so she hoped.

TWENTY-FIVE

Waylon was still trying to catch his breath when his brain, fogged with post-orgasmic bliss and saturated with the taste of her on his tongue, finally caught up with the weight of what they'd just done.

I didn't put on a condom.

No thought. Just raw instinct and heat.

"Shit," he muttered.

Frankie stirred against his chest. "What's wrong?"

"God, Frankie. I'm so sorry. We didn't use protection." He kept his voice low, apologetic. "I'm clean, I promise. I get regular check-ups and I always use a condom. I didn't even think. I was just...lost in you."

She lifted her head, blinked at him, then gave him a soft smile. "It's okay."

"It's not. Dammit, I should've stopped. That was reckless. Are you...do you use birth control? I don't want you worried about—"

"I'm not worried about anything." She kissed his shoulder, then rested her chin on it. "I haven't had a period since chemo. It just...never came back. They said it wouldn't right away. That it might not ever, actually."

His heart twisted.

"So, you don't have to worry about me getting pregnant," she added gently. "I can't."

Waylon didn't know what hurt more—that she said it so matter-of-factly, or that she was trying to reassure and comfort him.

He cupped her face. "Hey. I don't want you worried about me. I just didn't want you to be upset." He clenched his eyes shut. This was coming out all wrong. "I'm sorry. That must be just...awful."

"If all this has taught me one thing, it's to let go of the things I can't control. Maybe one day I'll get pregnant and have kids, maybe not. Maybe I'll adopt." She gave him a mischievous smile. "Maybe I'll be the cool auntie to a friend's kids and spoil them rotten, then hand them back."

Waylon chuckled. "You are something else." He stroked her face.

"I should have thought about protection, too," she said. "But, I know I can't get pregnant, and as for 'being clean' as you put it." She held his gaze. "I trust you. You'd never hurt me."

God. Her raw, naked trust in him killed Waylon.

She doesn't know who I am. What I can do. What I have done.

Her eyes softened. "We're good. You're good. And I'm not mad. I promise."

For several minutes, they just lay there, skin to skin, hearts beating in sync.

Finally, Waylon whispered, "If it had happened, if you'd gotten pregnant, I'd do the right thing."

Frankie's regular breathing told him she was asleep and hadn't heard him.

But he knew it was true. If she'd told him she was going to be a mother, he wouldn't walk away. And he wouldn't just be a name on a check once a month, or show up only at holidays with awkward smiles and empty promises. He would be there in her life and the life of their child every single day.

As he listened to her breathe and smelled the rosemary in her hair, he realized that if she never had a baby—if that door stayed closed forever—he'd still want to wake up next to her. Still want to hear her laugh. Still want to be the one she came home to.

Every damn day.

WAYLON HAD EXPECTED Derek to make a move by now.

The asshole had been served two weeks ago—by Ben, no less. According to Ben, it took Derek a moment to realize what hit him. He took the papers with a smug little smile, then realized what they were when Ben told him he'd been served. That smug smile had snapped clean off his face. Derek had acted confused. Then pissed.

And now—quiet.

No calls. No texts. No late-night drive-bys or surprise pop-ups. No inappropriate mail.

Nothing.

Waylon's brothers were taking turns keeping an eye on Derek, but he only went to work and back home. Not even a grocery trip, just deliveries. No eating out or seeing anyone, either.

Waylon's guard wasn't completely down, but Frankie had relaxed enough to breathe again. She was still staying with Waylon. They'd been back to her house—together—to pick up some more of her things. His previously empty bathroom looked like a lived-in, his-and-hers now, with fancy shampoo and conditioner in the shower, and face cream and make-up cluttering the counter around the sink.

Which didn't bother him in the least.

They'd fallen into a comfortable routine. Frankie gave him shit every time he gargled and made fun of his cowlick every morning. He dished the teasing right back at her. And then he surprised her with scuba lessons ahead of their trip to Hawaii.

Scuba lessons he'd arranged before she'd pulled out the lucky coin.

When Waylon had held up the bag of quarters, he'd held his

breath, hoping Frankie wouldn't notice. As she dug around, her expression went a little funny.

She knows. She figured it out.

But she went ahead and picked out a coin. Her smile said it all.

"Where are we going?" he'd asked.

"Hawaii. Yes!" She high-fived him. "I can't believe it!"

He could. Because he'd gone to three different banks trading out quarters for the Hawaii coins. He didn't have quite enough to feel like fifty states, so he'd told Shane what he was doing and his brother had come through with the rest.

So, from that point on, they ate together, cleaned the apartment together, slept together, went to scuba lessons together. Things actually felt...normal.

Normal enough that Frankie had gone out with Wren, Rochelle, April, Ellie, and Arden to look for a dress for the dinner Frankie had promised Waylon. It was someplace fancy, that was all he knew, and on Halloween night.

Elias gave him shit about it at work. "Do you have to get a costume?"

"Nope. Just wear something nice, I guess."

"Told you at the last wedding, you shoulda just gone ahead a bought a tux instead of renting. Save you money in the long run."

Waylon only grinned. The first time Elias joked about it, Waylon felt annoyed. But now? The man had a good point, dammit.

Waylon ended up not buying or renting a tux after all. Frankie told him it was fancy but not tux-fancy. He did own a suit or two, and he cleaned up well enough, he thought. Frankie, however, looked drop-dead gorgeous in a cobalt-blue dress and matching heels.

The maître d' met them at the door and walked them down a long, dark hallway that made Waylon feel like he was about to get mugged. He took them to a table toward the back of the tiny dining room, maybe fifteen, twenty tables total. No one was eating yet. The meal would start once everyone had arrived. Family style—if that family's last name was Addams.

When everyone was seated, waiters brought everyone a sheet of paper with the menu on it. Waylon couldn't make heads or tails of the course descriptions, which were written as haikus.

"Uh, Pixie? How are we supposed to eat something called, 'Crimson leaves retreat. A crow laments the twilight. Salt remembers flame'? If they're suggesting I eat crow—"

"Dude. You tried to feed me an MRE."

"It didn't have actual *crow* in it."

"Shhh!" She pointed at a man dressed in chef whites, who'd just stepped out of the kitchen.

"Welcome to Liminal, friends, and happy Halloween. I asked each of you to submit an essay about one thing you feared when you requested a reservation."

Waylon was appalled. "An essay? You did actual homework to get a reservation here?"

"Shush!"

The chef continued. "After reading your essays, I've created a multi-course meal for you tonight. There is a course specifically inspired by each story, answering your fear with hope. It is *my* hope that you enjoy this tasting menu."

Then the chef encouraged everyone to taste the menu itself.

"Wait, what?"

But Frankie had already taken a photo of the menu, and then taken a bite out of it.

"Edible paper," she said, munching happily. "You should try it."

"I'll pass, thanks." He set the menu aside.

"Pfft. No sense of adventure." Frankie rolled her eyes.

The waiter eyed the menu but left it there when he brought two plates to their table. He set the first one down in front of Frankie. Only, it wasn't a plate but some sort of flat stone. It was unlike anything Waylon had ever seen. He got out his phone and started typing.

> Is this the food, or some sort of centerpiece
> for the table?

When Frankie's phone buzzed, she raised an eyebrow at him and read her screen.

The waiter placed the second 'dish' in front of Waylon. He sent he a second message.

> I got a rock.

Frankie's eyes widened at the Charlie Brown Halloween reference and she rolled her lips in to keep from laughing.

Ignoring their antics, the waiter announced, "First course. Ocean's brittle kiss. Ashes of squid, whispers roe—Petals judge your soul. A puffed rice brittle dusted with powdered squid ink, topped with roe and flower petals."

"Thank you, it looks amazing," Frankie said, trying her best to stay composed.

Waylon was already typing.

> Crispy rice cereal in ash, with fish eggs and
> compost. Got it.

She read his text. He didn't think her eyes could get any wider, but nope, they were now defying physics. Also, her face was about the color of the rose petals on their plates. He composed and sent another text.

> Nothing says "fine dining" like squid ash
> and judgmental petals.

Frankie bit her lips so hard, he was afraid she'd draw blood. Her thumbs flew across her screen and his phone buzzed.

> I kind of hate you right now.

I'm not wrong.

Oh there is SO much wrong with you,
mister.

Wait. Is THIS the course he made for YOU?

No. They're supposed to tell you which one
is yours.

Just wait til the next dinner I feed you.

I'm scared.

Nothing should scare you after this.

Just eat.

Waylon looked around to see how everyone else was handling the thing on their plates.

Am I supposed to pick this up and stuff it in
his face like a nacho? Because I got nothing
else.

Frankie simply smiled and folded her hands on the table, the wench. She wasn't about to give him a clue.

"Fine." He picked it up and popped the whole thing into his mouth and chewed.

And dammit, didn't it figure that it tasted good?

Really good.

He couldn't begin to describe the flavor except to say it put him in mind of taking a bite out of a clean ocean wave, one that had a light, crispy texture. Solidified foam, maybe. No, the lightest, crispiest pork rind ever, even though it didn't taste anything like that.

Did you just close your eyes?

Shit.

Maybe.

"Mmm-hmm, you did," she said out loud. "You're enjoying yourself." Then with more grace than should have been humanly possible, she broke off a piece with the side of her fork and popped the bite into her mouth. Her eyes closed. "So good."

"It's okay."

"You are such a liar."

The next course was some sort of paper-thin sliced white root vegetable layered with perfectly round green leaves shingled over some kind of cream-looking sauce with little orange dots of oil in it. He was too busy studying it to catch the waiter's description. By the time he looked up, the guy was walking away.

"What is this?"

"He just told you."

"Sorry, I was too distracted by the dots. What are they made of again?"

"Taste it and see." She dipped her spoon into the cream and captured a few. She brought the spoon to her mouth and sipped. Her expression remained totally neutral.

Not fair.

"Fine." He gave her a tight smile and dunked his spoon in. Flavor burst across his tongue.

"Fuckin' A. This is incredible."

She giggled.

The next course arrived. A single scallop sat dead center on a dark blue slab of slate, surrounded by what looked like tiny orange pearls and micro greens that would've felt right at home in a dollhouse garden. Waylon listened to the waiter's description.

"Lone scallop awaits. Pearls weep, sprouts whisper secrets. Love, plated in fear."

Because nothing says romance like edible existentialism.

Frankie fought back a smile. "You're ruining the vibe. This is art."

He stabbed the thing in the center with his fork, ready to stuff it all in his mouth at once, but Frankie was staring at him as she cut hers in half. He picked up his knife and fork and stuck his pinkie out, which made her snort-laugh. He sliced the scallop in half and popped it into his mouth.

A pause.

Then another.

Frankie stared at him. "Well?"

"I think my tongue just proposed to the edible existentialism."

Frankie snorted louder. The couple at the next table flinched. She covered her mouth with her napkin, shaking with silent laughter. Then she picked up her phone and typed:

You're such a dork.

He smirked and, pinkie extended again, sipped his wine in victory.

It was getting late and the waiter still had not told Frankie one of the courses was hers. She looked anxious, as if she were afraid she'd been left out.

"There's still a couple left, Pix."

Then the waiter approached their table, smiling. "This one is yours."

He set a flat chunk of concrete down. Other pieces of what looked like thin, broken concrete lay on a burst of greens and tiny flowers poking up through the fragments.

"Winter's heart still aches. But beneath the cold concrete. Green dares to return." Then the waiter bowed his head and left.

Frankie silently studied her plate with a bittersweet smile. She looked up at Waylon through her eyelashes.

"It's a sidewalk in spring," she said. "Life returning."

His heart stuttered. "Breaking through, no matter what."

She looked like she was about to say something, but then she picked up a fragment of concrete and bit right into it. She chewed it with a grin. "Meringue. Very delicate, especially for something that's supposed to be tough."

Just like you, Pixie.

After the actual concrete slabs were cleared away, Waylon had no idea what was going on. A half-dozen waiters appeared carrying two balloons each and went around the dining room handing them out to each guest.

Frankie, however, looked on with ecstatic anticipation.

"Wow. If I'd known you liked balloons so much—"

She waved at him, shushing him. "Just wait!"

"The hell?"

A waiter arrived at their table with the last two helium-filled balloons. "If you would be so kind as to wait until the chef has addressed the room, you may then enjoy your dessert."

"Sure, as soon as you bring it out," Waylon said, which earned him a good-natured smirk from the waiter before he turned on his heel and walked away.

Waylon looked at Frankie, who by now was positively dying.

"What?"

She pointed at the balloon. "Beefcake, that's dessert."

Dessert? Waylon frowned as he studied the balloon floating over his head. The string was not cotton, but some sort of...God, he had no idea what the string was made of.

"I'm not eating a latex balloon, Frankie." Then again, he'd just eaten concrete.

"Right. You're not." She gave him a full-toothed smile.

"Dear friends." The chef had returned. The entire wait and kitchen staff flanked him. "It has been our pleasure delighting you tonight. I hope you've experienced the kind of wonder only a young child possesses—"

"Yeah, like wondering how I'm gonna hide an uneaten balloon under the edge of my plate."

Frankie mock-frowned as her eyes danced with joy.

"—so with no further ado, please enjoy being a child again." The chef started making his rounds from one table to the next.

While Waylon looked on, Frankie and every other person in the room pulled their balloons down and bit into them, sucking in the helium.

"Just do it, you big goof," Frankie said, her voice higher than Mickey Mouse's. She broke into squeaky laughter like everyone else in the room. Then she started chewing on the string. "Caramel apple taffy."

"When in Wonderland," Waylon mumbled before he bit into the side of his balloon and inhaled.

"Whoa, it tastes like fruit. And I sound like a munchkin."

Frankie lost it. She bent in half with laughter.

She's the woman from the bus.

He knew it. *Knew* it.

The earbud's in my winter coat pocket.

It had to be. He'd played with it all winter and didn't remember ever taking it out.

Frankie had worn that coat several times now, and never said a thing about it.

Maybe it's not there.

More likely, he was wrong about the bus.

"Frankie, did—"

The chef had made his way to their table. "Frankie, I hope you've enjoyed your meal."

The guy had memorized every guest's name. Classy move.

Frankie smiled while blinking back tears. "Very much. The course you designed for me was perfect. Thank you, Chef."

Those unshed tears told Waylon this must have been one of the adventures she'd thought about while going through chemo. Wondering if she'd get to experience it.

And she'd taken him with her for this moment. His heart felt like bursting.

The chef turned to Waylon. "And you, Dan?" he asked. "Everything to your liking?"

Dan?

Frankie's spine straightened so fast her chair squeaked. Her smile froze and she looked like she'd been stabbed through the heart with an icepick.

Waylon blinked. "It's Waylon."

The chef blinked back. "Ah, my mistake. Apologies."

"It's all right, Chef," Frankie said quickly. "Last minute substitution."

He bowed. "My apologies again, Waylon. Frankie, it was an honor." He lifted her hand and kissed it, then floated off to the next table.

Waylon looked at Frankie as unease creeped into his gut. "So. Dan?"

She was still watching the chef, a look of shock mixed with devastation on her face.

He tried again. "Were you dating?"

Frankie blinked. "Who what now?"

"Were you dating *Dan?*"

Her attention snapped back to him. She scoffed. "No."

"Who's Dan then, if not your boyfriend?"

She shook her head.

"Come on." He gave her his best, boyish smile, the one that had charmed women right off the dance floor and into his truck.

"Waylon. I mean it. I don't want to talk about it."

TWENTY-SIX

She doesn't want to talk about it?

Waylon tried to tamp down the dark feelings rising in his chest, threatening to drag him back into his past.

It's not the same. Frankie's not Camille.

He closed his eyes and the laughter in the room faded. Better that than imagine they were laughing at him for being a fool.

"Waylon?" Frankie's unsure voice cut through the darkness. "I'm sorry. I didn't mean to be a bitch."

He opened his eyes. The sight that greeted him sliced through his chest. His Pixie looked as devastated as before, only now she was calling herself a bitch because of him.

I'm toxic. Dangerous. This is why I don't deserve to be with a woman. Don't deserve to be loved.

"Don't ever apologize to me," he practically growled.

She sat back and folded her arms as her devastation gave way to irritation. "Waylon, that's ridiculous. I shouldn't have—"

He put his hand up. "Stop, Frankie. Not another word. Don't you *ever* call yourself a bitch, you understand? Especially over something that I said or did."

I don't deserve her.

"Waylon, talk to me. Please." She unfolded her arms and laid her hands on the table.

But I want her.

Waylon took a deep breath. He felt calmer but still terrified that he was about to watch her stand up and walk out. "You've made it clear it's none of my business and that you have your own life outside of mine. I said I'd never tell you what to do or try to limit you or anything like that. But I... Look, I've come to really enjoy you."

"Enjoy me?"

"Not like that. Yes, like that." He growled and pulled at his hair. "I enjoy spending time with you. I enjoy seeing you. I enjoy sleeping with you. I know we said just Buddies."

He reached across the table and grabbed her hand.

"Frankie. Pixie. I want more."

Her face gave nothing away. "More?"

"Yeah, Frankie. I want us to be more than Buddies with benefits. I also know you have this standing date thing. So, I guess what I'm asking is, who's Dan? Is he an ex, did he abandon you when you got cancer? *Are* you dating someone else? Is it Dan?"

Anger slowly grew in her eyes.

"You think I had a boyfriend walk out on me when I got sick? Like, he left when he found out he'd have to hold my hair back when I puked after chemo so he freaked out and took off?" She shook her head slowly as she said, "No. No, that's not what happened. My life is not a trope in a romance novel. And you aren't here right now to take the place of some loser dude who abandoned me when the going got tough." She wiped her arm across her eyes. "There was no *dude* holding my hair back."

"Then there should have been, dammit!"

He was vaguely aware the laughter around them had faded so he dropped his voice. "You should have had some guy who held your hair back when you puked and then fed you ice chips until you could keep something substantial down. He should have held your hand while you sat in the chemo chair, and read you stories at night when you couldn't sleep, and been there when you woke after surgery. Fucking been there every damn minute, Frankie. Because that's what you deserve. You deserve a good man."

He let go of her hand. "Not someone like me. So, if you are dating some else, if he's better for you..."

Frankie bit her bottom lip and stared off at some distant, invisible point. "Okay." She nodded. "Okay. You're coming with me right now. To meet my standing date."

"Frankie. I...you don't have to—"

"No, Waylon, I do. I really do."

Frankie stood up and grabbed her purse. "Are you coming?"

She kept her gaze locked on his as he stood until he towered over her. She stood there fiercely staring down a man twice her size. And winning.

"Tell me where to take you," he said.

Frankie nodded. She broke eye contact as she turned away and Waylon felt like she'd loosened a physical grip on him. He followed her and watched as she graciously thanked the chef again, and then their waiter, slipping what looked like two hundred-dollar bills into his hand.

Outside, the temperature had dropped considerably since the sunset. Frankie had only taken a lacy shawl into the restaurant, leaving Waylon's winter coat, which she'd basically stolen from him, on the passenger seat in his Camaro. He'd driven her in the Camaro for the first time that night, speeding through Boulder's streets, showing off. The valet recognized them and brought the car around quickly. Frankie stood shivering and it killed Waylon not to put his arm around her, but every fiber of her being screamed *don't touch me*.

Waylon opened Frankie's door and grabbed his coat off the seat before she got in. He wrapped it around her, and as he did, he carefully slipped his hand into the right-hand pocket where he was positive he'd left the earbud.

Nothing but pocket change.

———

THEY'D SPENT the ride in silence until Frankie said, "Take the next left onto Silverton and park across from the first house. We're here."

They'd been driving from the heart of Boulder to the southern outskirts, into a newer, expensive neighborhood, judging by the large houses to their left. Across the street from the neighborhood was an open space framed by trees and a chain link fence. Waylon slowed down and took a left. He parked across the street from the first house, beside another wide park running the length of the street. Waylon studied the house. He knew real estate—if it went on the market, the place would sell for one-point-one million at least.

Looked like Dan did well for himself.

Waylon killed the engine. The porch light was on and another one upstairs but the house was dark otherwise. A Jack-O-Lantern sat on the steps, its candle extinguished like all the others dotting the neighbors' porches. It was late, well past trick-or-treat time, except maybe for the random older teenager not quite ready to let the tradition go.

"I didn't notice you call or text. Are we expected, or will this be a surprise?"

"Dan always expects me," Frankie answered as she toyed with her purse strap.

Waylon got out of the car and went around to open Frankie's door. He helped her out and shut the door. He started around the car toward the house when Frankie said, "Not that way. This way."

She pointed at the open space across from the neighborhood. Waylon noticed a gate across a gravel turnoff. Was it actually a driveway through someone's huge yard? He didn't see any house lights past the pines and bare cottonwoods.

"Come on. We have a bit of a walk."

"Wait, we're not going here?" He pointed to the house on the corner.

"No." She started walking. He followed her without another word across the street to the chained gate.

And into the cemetery behind it.

They walked in silence, gravel crunching beneath their feet, then dry grass. The moon was full, and the straight lines of headstones cast long shadows. The air was colder here, fitting for Halloween night. Waylon couldn't help but look around, imagining a certain Ace WWI pilot sneaking on his belly toward a Halloween party.

They made their way between the rows until Frankie stopped in front of a headstone with a bench beside it. The granite was simple and the base held a small plaque. Waylon stooped to read it.

Danielle Cruz

Beloved Daughter. Fierce Friend. Pure Chaos.

"Dan," Waylon said. "Of course."

"One more gal for the Guy Name Club." Frankie sat on the bench, pulled out her phone, and tapped the screen. Seconds later, the tinny-sounding intro to Peter Gabriel's "In Your Eyes" crackled through the air, complete with snaps and pops, and hissing as if it were on a cassette tape.

Waylon blinked. "Sounds like it's coming straight out of an old boombox."

"She had a real one that she left me. I still bring it every time. It's in the trunk of my car right now so this'll have to do."

He sat beside her. "You always play this song for her?"

"Are you kidding? I play an entire mixtape. She made me promise I would whenever I visited or else she'd haunt me with glitter and judgment."

Waylon chuckled. Frankie smiled faintly and scooted a little closer to him. "This song is from *Say Anything*. John Cusack, trench coat, boombox over the head. It was our romcom holy grail."

Waylon smiled. "Classic."

"Dan loved eighties movies," Frankie said. "*Say Anything* was her favorite. She used to say if a guy didn't know the boombox scene, he didn't deserve to see her boobs."

Waylon let out a quiet laugh.

"We met on my first day of chemo. I was sitting in that awful chair, scared out of my mind. She was already hooked up next to me. Cracked a joke about how an IV cocktail that bad should at least come with a little paper umbrella."

Waylon laughed again. "She was funny."

"Yeah. The kind of funny that makes you forget you're dying for a while." Frankie looked at Waylon. "Do you think it's weird that I talk to her? And talk about her like she's still alive?"

"Not at all. It's your way of processing your grief, of keeping her alive inside. It's like leaving a light on in a dark room; it doesn't change the loss, but it softens its edges."

"I like that."

"Do you want me to go back to the car and leave you in peace to talk to her?"

"Oh no. Dan would be so upset if I didn't let you stay." Frankie leaned closer to Dan's stone.

"All right, Dan. I was going to visit you tomorrow in the daylight, but here we are. I'm sure wherever you're at, you're absolutely thrilled I'm visiting your grave on Halloween under a full moon."

Waylon grinned.

"*And* as a Halloween treat, I brought a hot guy. Not the fire-fighter you'd hoped for, but he has a nice ass, so I'm pretty sure you'd approve." Frankie leaned back.

"Dan was going through treatment for the third time. Her body was wrecked, but her spirit was... big. Loud. Bright. Made the whole room warmer."

"In Your Eyes" ended and Berlin's "Take My Breath Away" started as the playlist moved on. They sat in silence for a while. Frankie leaned her head on Waylon's shoulder as "Don't You (Forget About Me)" began to play.

"She'd kill me if I didn't mention that every time I hear this song —no matter where I'm at—she wanted me to throw my fist in the air like Judd Nelson crossing the football field at the end of *The Breakfast Club*." She stood up and did it. "There. This playlist is how I keep her with me."

She sat back down and Waylon gently wrapped his arm around her and pulled her closer as the wind rustled through the trees around them.

"Dan made me promise more than just playing her mixtape." Then she whispered, "It still doesn't feel real sometimes. That she's not here. That I'm still here."

Waylon took her hand. "I get why you didn't want to tell me," he said. "This wasn't a secret you were keeping from me. It's...sacred."

Frankie's eyes filled, but her smile was real. "Yeah. I miss her every day."

"I'm sorry I pushed. It was wrong of me."

Frankie shook her head. "It's all right. I wanted to bring you here. I did. But, there was just something about not bringing you that kept her a little more alive. I kept telling myself I'd wait until tomorrow. Then another tomorrow."

He smiled. "I'm honored."

Cyndi Lauper began singing "Time After Time."

"You visit her every week?"

"Every week." Frankie brushed away a tear as she sang the line about a suitcase of memories. They quietly listened to the rest of the song.

"She's the reason for your list, isn't she?" Waylon said softly.

Frankie nodded. "Yeah. We used to talk about all the adventures we'd go on once we were done with 'this cancer bullshit,' as she put it. Have a wild weekend in Vegas. See penguins on an Australian beach. Eat a work of art at Liminal. As Dan got sicker, our plans started getting weirder the worse she got. Swimming with sharks. Paragliding naked. Eating a hot dog in Fiji. She wanted to lick a rainforest frog just to see if she'd hallucinate about a llama named Steve." Frankie laughed—softly but it was genuine.

"Sounds like she would've gotten along with Steph."

Frankie glanced at him. "Yeah. Dan would've loved this whole group."

Kevin Cronin began singing "I Can't Fight This Feeling" as Frankie studied Dan's headstone.

"When Dan realized she wasn't going to make it, she made me promise to live big. Big enough for both our lives, and to squeeze out every drop." Frankie paused. "She told me to have every adventure I could. Even if I had to do it alone."

"You're not alone," Waylon said. He squeezed her hand gently. "Let's keep her with you. Wherever you go. I'll help you check off every adventure. Even the weird ones. Especially the weird ones."

Frankie grinned. "I won't make you lick any frogs."

"I'm not sure I didn't already at Liminal."

Frankie laughed. "True. I might have to mark that one off as done."

Whitney Houston's "How Will I know?" took over from REO Speedwagon.

"What about Hawaii?" Waylon asked.

Frankie tilted her head. "Hawaii? What about it?"

"Was that her adventure or yours, or both?"

"Oh, both. I guess." She paused. "Okay. *Mostly* hers. But I'm excited to go, too," she quickly added.

"You've told me about Dan's adventures. What about yours?" Some instinct kicked Waylon's heart up a notch as he pushed. "You must have some from before you met her."

Frankie gave him an odd look. Instead of answering, she picked up her purse from beside her and put it on her lap. She studied it like it held the secrets of the universe. "Can I ask you something kinda weird?"

"Anything. As long as it doesn't involve licking frogs or a llama named Steve."

Frankie giggled before she grew more serious. "Do you believe in fate?"

"No. We make our own choices and our own way through the world. Or at least I do. Nothing's dictating my destiny."

"Then what about coincidences?"

"They're just that—coincidences."

Frankie nodded thoughtfully as the playlist segued into "Vacation" by the GoGos.

"Maybe meeting Dan was only a coincidence. She was my soulmate except for one thing. I don't mind the cold while she hated it. She called cold weather a personal attack from Mother Nature. That's why most of our adventures were going to be tropical."

"So you set your arctic adventures aside. You weren't about to go anywhere cold with Dan?" Waylon asked.

"No way." Frankie fiddled with the top of her purse. "But I sure want to see puffins someday."

Puffins. Didn't that podcast on the bus mention a boat ride to some sort of puffin island right before it faded out? A strange excitement filled Waylon's chest.

"Puffins, huh?"

"Yup."

"Where?" he asked tentatively.

She side-eyed him. "Someplace I could also see the northern lights. That's at the top of my personal list."

"Yeah?" Waylon's heart skipped. "Puffins and northern lights. Is that all you want to see?"

"Oh, heck no." She grinned. "I need some culture, too. Like a museum."

This can't be happening.

Waylon tapped his chin, pretending he was in deep thought. "So, where can you see puffins and Northern Lights, *and* go to a museum, I wonder?" He looked her straight in the eye. "What kind of a museum? There are all kinds, you know."

Frankie nodded. "Well, I like eighties movie music as much as anyone else, but I'm kind of a fan of punk, too."

Waylon felt almost light-headed. "So, you'd want to go to a *punk* museum?"

God, the way she was looking at him. "Does that sound crazy?" she asked.

"Not crazy at all," he told her. "As a matter of fact, I once heard something about a punk museum somewhere and I thought it sounded pretty cool."

He watched her face light up and it was the most beautiful thing he'd ever seen.

"Did you?" she asked.

"I did. So. Any other kind of museum you'd like to see?"

Instead of answering, Frankie opened her purse and rummaged around inside.

Then, slowly, she pulled out a small earbud case.

Waylon's heart filled with goofy joy.

It's her.

It is her.

She found the earbud in my pocket and didn't tell me.

Frankie flipped open the top. Inside rested two earbuds.

Except they were mismatched.

One looked practically new just like the case but the other was horribly scratched up.

It occurred to him that an earbud could get pretty scuffed if it spent the winter jangling around in a pocket full of change.

Frankie studied the case, then took a deep breath like she was preparing to bungee jump off a cliff.

She doesn't know if they'll work. She hasn't tested them yet.

Then with one swift, decisive move, Frankie took them out of the case. The little red light on each one turned blue and "Vacation" cut out from her phone speaker. At least one earbud had connected to her phone. Frankie hit pause on the playlist.

Chuck, her beefy partner in crime. The apartment felt quieter without him. Less...bouncy.

It's not quite home without Snoopy here.

Home? Is that what this is?

"I don't know about you, but I'm ready for bed," she said, nudging the closet door shut.

"You go on ahead, Pix. I'm not quite ready."

She tilted her head. "Everything okay?"

Waylon leaned in and kissed her lips, soft and sure. "Yeah. Just hungry."

She smirked. "Liminal didn't fill you up?"

"It filled my soul," he said dryly. "My stomach, not so much."

He planted another kiss on her forehead and headed for the kitchen.

Frankie lingered a moment watching him, then padded barefoot down the hall toward the bedroom.

Waylon's old childhood Snoopy was back on the dresser, sitting there like he'd never been demoted to a drawer. Frankie didn't know when Waylon had taken him back out. He hadn't said a word. Neither had she.

She peeled off her dress, hung it up, and slipped into her night-shirt. In the bathroom, she poured rosemary oil into her palm and ran it through her hair, breathing in the grounding scent.

The night had been heavy, cathartic. She'd finally told Waylon about Dan. And instead of feeling like Dan was gone for good, she felt closer to her.

Closer to Waylon.

I'm not in love with him, right?

She picked up her big wooden brush and ran it through her hair. She'd read somewhere that brushing her hair with the rosemary oil would make it come back thicker. Frankie watched her reflection in the mirror, then she studied all the bottles and cotton balls and make-up on the vanity until her eyes fell on Waylon's mouthwash.

I care about him, sure. But I can't possibly love him. I hate the way he gargles. He teases me mercilessly. He's got that funny little cowlick in the morning before he showers and plasters it down. He stays in the bathroom until I finish showering and then hands me a towel. He's got a great laugh. He makes me smile every time I win an argument. He's sexy as hell. He gives the sweetest kisses. He's always got my back when we're hiking. He's the first person I'd call if the cancer came back.

The brush slipped from her hand and clattered loudly against the tile.

"You okay, babe?" Waylon called from the kitchen.

Babe.

"I'm good...babe," she shouted back. "Just clumsy." She waited for him to say something snarky. Nothing. Just the faint sound of something sizzling.

I'd call him first if the cancer came back.

But as she looked at her reflection, at her thin face, her short hair, the outline of the chemo port under her nightshirt, she knew she was lying to herself.

No. He'd be the last person on earth I'd call.

Because I wouldn't put him through that.

Whatever he was cooking, it smelled good. Frankie wandered back out to the kitchen.

The kitchen lights were low, warm and golden. Waylon stood barefoot in front of the stove. His suit was gone--replaced by flannel pajama pants and a dark T-shirt he must have pulled from the pile of laundry. He was flipping something in a pan.

Frankie leaned against the doorway and took a second to drink him in.

"Do I smell... bacon?"

Waylon didn't turn. "Among other things. I got inspired. Liminal activated my inner chef."

Frankie wandered closer, stealing a peek at the cutting board. "You're making a breakfast sandwich?"

"I'm making art," he said, gesturing grandly to the pan. "With real food. No judgy petals and definitely no crow."

She snorted. "Need a sous chef?"

He gave her a sidelong glance, then grinned. "Only if you promise not to critique my knife skills."

"No promises." She grabbed an apron from the hook near the fridge and slipped it over her head. "Tell me what to do, Chef Ramson."

Waylon nodded toward the eggs. "You can crack those into a bowl. Whisk, not beat. Gently. We're making artsy Liminal eggs, not hangover food at a Waffle House."

"You are such a dork." Frankie cracked the first egg.

He flipped the bacon onto a plate with unnecessary flair. "And yet I'm the master chef and you're the sous chef." He put the plate of bacon in the oven to keep it warm.

Frankie whisked the eggs with salt and pepper. The warmth of the kitchen settled deeper into her skin. She handed Waylon the whisked eggs and he poured them into the pan with a hiss. For a while, the only sounds were the gentle sizzle, the clink of utensils, the occasional hum from the fridge.

"I've only ever cooked midnight breakfast for one other person," Waylon said quietly.

Camille, Frankie guessed. But she didn't want to ask. Not yet.

Waylon kept his eyes on the pan as he stirred the eggs. "I need to come clean with you, Frankie. About... things. Considering the bus. The earbuds. The fact that you might be fate."

Frankie's heart skipped. "Okay..."

He glanced at her. "If I believe that—if I believe we were meant to find each other—then I have to be honest with you."

Frankie felt her stomach clench. "About what?"

He took a breath. "About the man I used to be."

And just like that, the air shifted.

"I went straight from high school to boot camp, trying to get my act together. I was wild back then—me and Elias both. Ben knocked some sense into us one night, and we enlisted after graduation."

He stirred the eggs gently, eyes on the pan but clearly seeing something else entirely.

"Being away from home for the first time, I got lonely. Then I met Camille at a club. I followed her around like a lost puppy until she said yes to a dance. After that, we were a thing. Man, I'd get jealous if she even looked at another guy. She was my first." He smiled, a bit sheepish. "Thought she'd be my only. I didn't want to date around—I had Camille. We married way too young."

He gave the eggs one last stir, then turned off the burner and scooped them onto a plate.

"She said she could handle being an Army wife. Bragged about it. Showed me off. And I ate it up. Elias became a Ranger before me, and when he talked about being a medic, I got curious too. Camille loved that. She thought she'd married a future doctor. I got stationed at Hunter Army Airfield in Savannah. She loved it—beach, people, all of it."

Waylon paused to turn the burner back on. He grabbed a clean pan and tossed a few slices of butter into it. As he watched the butter melt, he sighed, voice softer now.

"Those were good days. We were happy. Talked about starting a family. I wasn't ready and told her so. That's when things started to crack."

Waylon reached for a package of English muffins and took two out. He opened them and dropped them into the sizzling butter.

"At first, I blamed it on my new post as a newly-minted Ranger—Joint Base Lewis-McChord, in Washington, about thirty miles south of Seattle."

He leaned on the counter as the muffins browned, not quite ready to turn them yet.

"JBLM was a good post. Not exactly laid back, but command had a sense of humor—maybe to make up for the rain. We got a nice house off-base. I figured everything would keep rolling along. Yeah, it rained a lot, but the place had a strong community. I thought Camille would dive in, make friends, find her people like always."

He finally flipped the muffins, golden now, added more butter, and watched them toast on the other side.

Frankie said softly, "But that didn't happen, did it?"

Waylon took the bacon out of the oven. He slid the toasted muffins onto two plates and layered on the still warm bacon.

"No, it did not," His voice dipped lower, like the weight of memory was pressing against his throat. He reached for the scrambled eggs and spooned them onto the muffins. "Camille got moody. Withdrawn. Snapped at me when I was home, then we'd fight, make up, promise to do better. Same cycle, over and over. I blamed the weather. That year was brutal."

He sprinkled shredded cheese over the eggs as he spoke, not bothering to glance up.

"She said she'd get a job but didn't. The other wives reached out —she pushed them away. Said she couldn't relate. They had kids. She didn't. Because of me, she said. Threw that at me like a knife."

Frankie winced.

"I brought her flowers, candy, anything to keep the peace. Then she started demanding things. Big stuff. Stuff we couldn't afford. And I gave in. I felt guilty that I wasn't giving her what she really wanted."

Waylon paused, finally glancing over at Frankie before continuing.

"I wasn't ready to be a dad. I'd just made Ranger. I didn't want to give that up, but I didn't want to miss my kid's first steps either. She called me selfish. But seeing her after a mission, waiting at the airport —it made everything worth it."

He started to grab the plates and paused, jaw tight.

"Then I'd get home and find closets full of crap she'd bought while I was gone. Unopened. Still in the box. They weren't impulse buys. They were punishment."

Frankie silently reached for the paper towel roll near the sink. She tore off two sheets and handed one to him.

"She got a job. Finally. Started smiling more. Selling off the junk online. I thought, hell yeah, we're on the upswing. I should've known. She wasn't putting the money in our account, and I wasn't seeing anything new come in, either. But I ignored it. I wanted to believe things were better."

He handed Frankie her plate. She accepted it gently.

"Then the fights started again. And this time, she was... gone. Checked out. I had to leave for a mission—six, maybe eight weeks. I knew we weren't good. But what could I do?"

They both moved to the table and sat. Waylon didn't touch his sandwich. His fingers toyed with the edge of the plate as he stared down at it.

"Halfway through, she messaged me. Said she was sorry. That she'd been in her head, but was thinking clearer now. Wanted to talk when I got back. I thought—finally. We're gonna fix this. Save the marriage. I was ready to walk away from the Army for her."

Frankie looked up, eyes wide. He met her gaze, then dropped his to the table.

"I had my speech prepared—I wasn't gonna re-up, we were going to move someplace warm, start our family. Got off that plane, practically ran through security, and scanned for her in the crowd waiting for us."

Frankie's voice was barely a whisper. "She wasn't there, was she?"

Waylon exhaled, short and sharp. "Nope. Sent someone else. To serve me divorce papers."

Frankie covered her mouth. "That was an absolutely shitty thing to do to you. I'm so sorry."

He held up a hand, stopping her. "Don't. She's not the villain in this story."

Frankie blinked. "What? Because you had to move for work? Because you weren't ready to have a kid on her schedule? That makes you normal, not the bad guy."

He shook his head slowly, voice low. "It wasn't any of that. It was what I did after she served me. I didn't believe her. Thought she just wanted to scare me. Punish me a little more."

"Oh my God, Waylon, I still don't see how you're the villain here."

"Let me finish, babe." He pushed his plate away, untouched. "This is the part I've never told anyone."

"Like what you just told me wasn't bad enough?" Frankie whispered.

Waylon leaned forward, forearms on the table, his voice dipping. "I got home. The place was empty. Her stuff gone. The house smelled... still. Like it hadn't been lived in for weeks. I dropped my bag on the floor and went looking. Knocked on neighbors' doors, demanding answers. Went to her work—lost it. Made a scene. They said she was on vacation. Security had to drag me out."

He raked a hand down his face. "That kind of behavior? At JBLM? Career suicide. And I didn't give a damn."

He looked up briefly, then added, quieter still, "That came later."

Frankie froze, sensing the shift.

"I borrowed a buddy's car," Waylon said. "Sat outside her work every morning, watching. For a week. Waiting to see her car. But she got out of someone else's."

Frankie barely breathed. "Waylon..."

He covered his face again. "I followed them. Back to his place. Looked him up. Found out he was her boss. Saw photos—months old. Back when everything started falling apart. I should've let it go. Signed the papers. But I couldn't."

Waylon let his hands drop to the table. He folded them. One thumb rubbed a slow, restless circle over his knuckle.

"I couldn't let her go. I stalked her, Frankie."

Frankie stared at him, her pulse ticking up. "No..."

"Yes. I called her till she blocked me. Took leave so I could follow her around. She saw me. I wanted her to. Wanted her to know she was still mine."

Frankie's stomach twisted.

"She showed up at my place one day with him, only he was her fiancé now. Little guy, not a threat—but he was there to protect her. From me. I'd scared her, Frankie. Bad. She said if I didn't stop, she'd file a restraining order. That would've ended everything. My career. My future. All of it. But this was my final warning."

He looked away, jaw tense. "I almost didn't listen. I was ready to keep going. Then Elias called."

Surprised, Frankie asked, "Elias knew? How?"

"He'd been following *me*. Watching. Making sure I didn't cross another line. He said he didn't know who he'd find if he came inside —so he called first."

She pressed a hand to her chest.

"I let him in. He looked me dead in the eye and said, 'She's not yours. She made that clear. You either stop, or you're not my brother anymore.'" Waylon's voice cracked. "Said that's not who we are."

His hands curled into fists. "And he was right. So I stopped." He exhaled. "I signed the papers. Let her go."

His voice quieted, rawer now. "Over the next year, my brothers checked in on me, one by one. Making sure I didn't spiral. They didn't have to. Elias had already made me face what I'd become. I hated that guy. Swore I'd never be him again."

He looked up, eyes full of fear. "That's why I never let myself see you that way. I care about you too much. I'm terrified I'll screw it up. That I'll scare you. That I'll turn back into that guy."

Frankie paused, studying his face.

Then, softly, "You don't scare me, Waylon."

"I should."

"Stop. Right now."

He opened his mouth, but she cut him off. "You haven't been in a relationship since?"

"No."

"Just hookups?"

He nodded once.

"And you and your brothers—you help women."

His jaw flexed. "Help them get away from men like me."

"No. *Not* like you," she snapped. "Men who never learn. You *learned*."

He shook his head. "That doesn't excuse what I did."

"No one's making excuses. I'm telling you the truth. That guy? The one who scared Camille? He died the second you listened to Elias, did the right thing, and let her go. And you've never let him come back."

Waylon looked down.

"Only because I haven't let myself fall again."

She pushed her plate aside and leaned closer, voice gentler now. "You really believe the only thing keeping you from being a monster is staying alone?"

He didn't answer.

Frankie stood up and came to Waylon's side. "You're lying to yourself. And it kills me. Because I can see the truth. I see a good man. A man who's made mistakes, learned from them, and refuses to stop trying."

He finally looked up at her. She gently took his face in her hands. "What you did is not who you are."

Waylon let that sink in. Then, quietly, "But I didn't stop on my own."

Frankie rolled her eyes. "Of course you didn't! Would you go on a mission alone and expect to win? I mean *all* alone—no HQ, no battle buddy, no, um sergeant? Sorry, I have zilch military knowledge, but you know what I mean, right?"

By now, Waylon was grinning at her. "I know what you mean."

"Almost nobody accomplishes anything hard all on their own. Hell, a lot of people don't accomplish hard things with a whole slew of people behind them. But you did. You saw that you were doing the wrong thing, admitted it, and you *stopped*. You came out better on the other side. I'm not even going to say you changed, because you didn't."

She poked him in the chest. "This is you. This has always been you." Then she smoothed her hand over his heart. "You've shown me who you are, every day. I trust you. Completely. Now, you need to trust *yourself*."

He covered her hand with his. "I love you," he whispered.

"I know," she said as she grinned. "And I love you, too."

TWENTY-EIGHT

Frankie had never seen so many boots by a front door in her life.

On first impression, Kyle and Arden's Victorian ranch house looked like a Cabela's ad exploded—outerwear, hats, and heavy coats, all piled up on a table in the front hall in the kind of chaos that screamed *family*.

The moment Frankie stepped inside, the smell of something rich and buttery hit her nose.

Turkey. Maybe ham. Definitely stuffing. And gravy.

Her stomach turned a little.

Frankie did her best to ignore it. She'd been full of energy the day before and she'd worked out twice as hard. Today she was feeling a little run down, and food smelled strongly again, just like when she'd had—

Nope. Not going to think that way.

"Guess I should take my boots off," she told Waylon.

"Definitely," he murmured back, already tugging his laces loose while hanging onto Snoopy's leash. "Nancy gets testy if you track mud in."

"Nancy?"

"The ghost. You'll meet her." He pointed to a shotgun leaning against the wall next to the door. "That used to belong to her."

"Oh, right. The infamous gun." Frankie smiled and leaned against the wall as she pulled her boots off. Her lower back also reminded her she'd overdone it at the rec center. She wanted to build up her muscles ahead of their upcoming scuba trip to Hawaii. Waylon had surprised her with lessons and they'd been to two already, with Wren and Elias. As soon as she knew Frankie and Waylon were going to be taking lessons, she insisted on joining the class. They had snorkeled on their Hawaii honeymoon and Wren decided she needed to up her game. Not that Waylon or Elias needed lessons. But, they came along as 'moral support' which Wren translated as, 'My husband and your boyfriend want to ogle us in our swimsuits.'

Frankie grinned at the thought. *Boyfriend.* It still felt strange to say, even in her head. But that's what they were. When Arden had invited her to Thanksgiving at her ranch, she told her how happy she was that Waylon wouldn't be coming alone this year. Arden had also asked her if she'd like to invite her mother.

"Sure, you can invite her if you wanna see me have a miserable time. And if you would like every single part of the dinner, your house, and your clothes picked apart."

"Ouch. I'm so sorry about that."

"I am too, but it is what it is. I think it's why I love traveling so much. I spent most of my life trying to get away from her," Frankie added without thinking. "I'm so sorry. That's a terrible thing for me to say. I understand you've lost both your parents."

Sadness touched Arden's eyes, but she smiled. "Thank you. It's alright, I'm not offended. I lost them many years ago. Missing them doesn't go away, but it does get a little easier."

"I agree. I lost my dad in college, too."

Arden hugged her. "Holidays are happier when you have a house full of friends."

Looking at the eight million boots in the foyer, Arden was having a very happy day.

The hallway past the foyer ended at an open kitchen and great room, already buzzing with warmth and conversation. A fire crackled in the huge stone fireplace. Someone had tossed a knit blanket over the back of the leather couch that looked like it had seen a million stories. Camo stretched out in front of the hearth like a sentry on break.

Frankie stepped into the low hum of laughter, the clatter of serving dishes, and the comfort of new friends.

Arden was right. A house full of new friends on Thanksgiving made for a happy day.

Ellie and Rochelle were in the kitchen, both wearing matching aprons that said *Talk turkey to me*. Gabe was carving something that may have once been a turkey, while Bear hovered like he wanted to be helpful but had no actual job.

"Frankie!" Wren called, waving a wine glass in the air. Chuck barreled toward them with Penny hot on his heels, both eager to see Snoopy.

Frankie braced herself for impact. "Oh, God—"

Elias came out of nowhere and caught Chuck by the collar just in time. "As you can see, I've got him well-trained," he joked.

Chuck plopped his butt down on Elias' foot.

Penny, however, looked at Snoopy's leash, barked once in judgment, and stared at Waylon expectantly.

"Okay," Frankie laughed. "*That* one's scary-smart."

"Hopefully, she won't corrupt our puppy," Waylon muttered as he unhooked Snoopy's leash from his collar. The three dogs took off toward Camo. Waylon stood and put his arm around Frankie's waist. She leaned into Waylon and took a deep breath. She still missed Dan, always would, but this felt like the first step toward healing.

"Frankie!" Arden swept toward them, apron dusted with flour and a wooden spoon still in one hand. Her golden curls were pinned up in a twist that was already starting to fall apart.

Frankie was caught in a hug before she could say a word, Arden's arms strong and warm and welcoming.

"I'm so sorry I didn't meet you at the door," Arden said, pulling back to give Waylon a quick hug, too. "It's like a circus in here. I had everything under control until we blew a fuse."

"Are you sure it wasn't Nancy?" Waylon asked with a wink.

"She knows better than that." She looked up. "Then again, she hates when I make green bean casserole with canned soup, and that's what was in the oven at the time."

"Well, Nancy is totally wrong. It smells amazing in here."

"Thanks. I haven't sat down since six this morning, but if I don't hear at least three people moan over the biscuits, I've failed as a hostess. Now—go find a drink, make yourself at home, and keep an eye on your man. Every time he wanders into my kitchen unsupervised, he steals a pie."

Waylon held up a hand. "*One* time."

"Three times," Arden corrected. "But I'm feeling forgiving today. It's Thanksgiving."

She disappeared back into the kitchen, and Frankie barely had time to breathe before Stephanie emerged from the crowd. She wore a flowing red-and-gold tunic, glittery earrings, and a sling decorated with stick-on leaves, one of which had googly eyes glued to it.

"Well, well," she said. "If it isn't my heroes."

Frankie pulled her into a hug. "Hey, Steve."

"I was hoping the arm would heal in time for the holidays," Stephanie said, holding up her slinged arm and wiggling her fingers. "Unfortunately, it's about as useful as a turkey wing. And *someone* won't let me take the cast off early. Speaking of which—"

She turned, scanning the room. "I need to introduce you to Dr. Boyfriend. He's here somewhere, I swear. Unless Nancy ran off with him. Again."

She cupped her good hand around her mouth. "Dr. Boyfriend! Paging Dr. Boyfriend! If you're in the coat closet again, I told you, that is not an appropriate place to practice auscultation!"

With that, she wandered off, still calling his name.

Frankie blinked. "Do we know if Dr. Boyfriend is a real person?"

Waylon shrugged. "Jury's out."

"Oh, you guys, stop it! He's real," Wren said as she breezed over, giving Frankie a warm hug. "They're adorable together. He's just...a little on the quiet side."

"Quiet?" Waylon arched a brow.

"Okay, not quiet," Wren admitted with a grin. "He just can't get a word in edgewise when Steph gets going. But he dotes on her."

"Dotes?" Waylon's lips quirked. "So, what, he follows her around like a lost puppy?"

"More like a very well-trained retriever," Wren said with a wink. "He's smart, loyal, and completely smitten."

"Still doesn't explain why we've never met him," Waylon murmured, his tone playful but laced with curiosity.

"He's around." Wren's grin grew sly. "You know how Steph loves to keep us guessing," she said with a laugh. "But trust me—he's not imaginary. And if Nancy *did* run off with him, she's in for a treat." Wren's smile turned downright wicked. "Steph says he's got very *skilled* hands both inside and outside of the OR."

Waylon groaned. "Didn't need to hear that."

Frankie was laughing when Stephanie's voice floated back toward them from the kitchen.

"Found him!" Steph called triumphantly. "He's out on the back deck. Come meet him before he startles and disappears."

Frankie's eyes widened. "Gee, I wonder why that is," she joked.

Waylon chuckled and put his arm around Frankie as they walked toward the back of the house.

"Finally," he muttered to her under his breath. "The man, the myth, the legend."

BY THE TIME the food was served, the great room had transformed into something out of a cozy fever dream. The long rustic farm table groaned under the weight of every side dish imaginable, and still people were bringing more from the kitchen, squeezing them into every open space like they were playing Thanksgiving Tetris.

Frankie sat with Waylon at the far end, across from Bear and Ellie. Ellie wore a fuzzy burnt orange cardigan over her maternity dress and had tucked her hair back with a leaf-shaped clip that kept slipping free. Frankie had already met her at Steph's book club a week ago and had liked her instantly. Ellie had an easy smile and sparkling eyes that crinkled when she laughed. She'd also met Bear briefly when he'd come to pick Ellie up. Bear—who was aptly named—was a massive man with a beard thick enough to hide an actual bear. He didn't talk much, but when he did, Frankie had quickly learned he was thoughtful and insightful, with a quiet strength that reminded her of Waylon.

"Ellie tells me you grew up on a ranch," Bear said as he passed the mashed potatoes.

Frankie smiled, taking the dish. "I did. Mostly cattle and horses, but we had goats and chickens, too. The foxes kept things interesting with the coops."

Bear's lips twitched. "Yeah. We had that problem when we first put in the chicken coop. Took a bit to figure out how to keep the foxes from thinking it was a KFC."

Frankie laughed hard. She liked Bear. He had that same calm, steady energy that Waylon had when he wasn't giving her a hard time.

"Waylon mentioned you've been doing some work with Wwoofers," Bear said, his gaze warm and genuinely curious.

"Yeah," Frankie said, perking up. "I've been helping write grants to get more Wwoofers out to smaller operations that really need the extra hands. It's been amazing to see how much of a difference it makes."

Bear nodded, clearly interested. "That's good work. Hands-on experience is hard to come by."

"You'd be surprised how many people think they can run livestock just because they watched *Yellowstone* a couple of times," Frankie said.

Bear tilted his head, then laughed low and deep.

Frankie sighed. "Grant writing's fine, but I really miss getting my hands dirty."

Bear nodded. "I would, too."

Ellie beamed, clearly enjoying how easily Bear and Frankie were getting along. "A desk job would kill him. When I inherited the cabin from my uncle, it was a little on the rough side, wasn't it, Bear?" Ellie gazed up at her husband.

He looked adoringly back down at her. "Rough's being generous, honey."

"Bear rebuilt practically all of it by hand." She patted his massive arm. "And the chicken coop. And the goat shed. And the beehives."

Bear shrugged. "You wanted goats."

Ellie beamed at him. "I just wanted chickens. You wanted goats. And bees. And the bison will be coming soon, too."

"I got excited."

"Bison's a smart choice though," Frankie said. "They'll be good for the land. Much better than cattle."

Bear studied her thoughtfully. He started to say something when Kyle stood at the head of the table, glass in hand. The room gradually quieted.

"Alright," he said. "Before we all collapse into a collective food coma, I just want to say—thank you. For being here. For showing up for each other. For helping to make my wife's ranch house into a home filled with loved ones again."

Camo let out a low huff in agreement from under the table.

Kyle's expression softened. "Some of us came here lost and broken. Some of us came here looking for a safe place to hide. And some of us didn't want to come at all—until someone dragged us in kicking and screaming." His gaze flicked meaningfully to Bear, who scowled without fooling anyone—his twinkling eyes gave him away.

"But all of us stayed," Kyle finished. "It's good to be reminded, especially today, that family isn't always blood. Sometimes, you find it. And sometimes it finds you."

He lifted his glass. "To the family we've found, and to the ones still finding their way to us."

Glasses clinked around the table. Waylon leaned in and kissed the top of Frankie's head.

She didn't speak. Couldn't quite trust her voice. But she reached under the table and squeezed his hand.

Dinner was loud after that—jokes flying, laughter booming, dogs roaming beneath the table hoping for contraband.

"You wanna watch our place?" Bear said out of nowhere.

Ellie looked at her husband, wide-eyed. "Really?"

Frankie shared a look with Waylon. He looked just as surprised as she felt.

"Sorry," Ellie said, patting Bear's hairy cheek. "We're flying to Arizona next week to visit my cousin before I get too pregnant to fly."

Bear grunted. "Before I get too stressed to let her."

"Don't let him fool you; he's just as concerned about leaving the chickens and goats, even though Arden said she'd check in on them."

"She's got her own critters to watch," Bear said, jerking his head toward the barn behind the house where Arden boarded horses— along with a small herd of alpacas, a donkey, and countless barn cats. "Frankie knows what she's doing."

Bear nodded.

"So, in that case, would you and Waylon be interested in staying at the cabin?" Ellie asked tentatively. "It's quiet. Private."

"Good for stargazing," Bear added quietly. He and Ellie shared a look.

"And Spot is hibernating," Ellie added.

"Spot? Don't tell me Spot is a bear." Frankie took a bite of cranberry sauce.

"Oh, no, he's our pet skunk."

Frankie almost spat out her food.

"Really?"

"Bear tamed him."

I'm not surprised.

"We've got a wood stove and a big clawfoot tub," Ellie continued. "And Bear built the guest room bed frame to survive an earthquake, so you're good there too."

This time, Waylon choked on his water.

Frankie's mouth twitched. "That sounds... Amazing. Like I said, I've missed ranching and farming." She looked at Waylon, who was still coughing into his napkin.

"We'll take it," he said once he got his breath back.

"Wonderful! Come up Thursday and we'll show you around. Introduce you to all the animals. Oh, and we can invite Gina and Lachlan over on Thursday, too. They only live about three miles away in the new development. Then you can spend the night. Me and Bear have to leave for the airport first thing Friday morning." She turned and hugged her husband. "Great idea, Bear."

Bear winked and returned to his sweet potatoes like he hadn't just offered Frankie and Waylon the best gift in the world.

TWENTY-NINE

The glow from the Scuba & Dive Adventure Center sign reflected off the sheet of ice coating the parking lot. November was being a trickster. The day had been unseasonably warm, then the rainclouds rolled in. Once the sun went down, the night air had enough bite to it that it had frozen the rain slicking the pavement within minutes.

But inside, the heated pool was waiting.

Waylon was supposed to meet her here tonight after his shift, along with Elias and Wren.

Frankie had scanned the parking lot when she drove in, but there was no sign of them. She glanced at her phone. No texts from Waylon yet, or from Wren and Elias. She figured they were running late. Traffic plus icy roads, since evening rush hour actually lasted several hours and there was probably an accident or three. Her car was cooling off so Frankie decided to go in and wait there.

She slid her phone into her coat pocket and carefully stepped out of her car, her gym bag slung over her shoulder. She started duck-walking toward the glass doors, wishing she hadn't worn an old pair of tennis shoes. She didn't realize just how much the tread had worn down. She slipped but caught herself on one of the cars in the crowded parking lot when a low voice off to her side stopped her dead.

"Hey, beautiful."

Her breath caught. She knew that voice.

Slowly, she faced him.

Derek.

The bastard must have been crouching on the other side of the car, waiting for her. The parking lot light one row over cast eerie shadows across his face. He looked...off. Hollowed out, like he hadn't slept in weeks. And his smile—thin, too wide—sent an icy ripple of dread down her spine. He walked around the front of the car, the ice giving him no problem whatsoever.

He's not supposed to be anywhere near me. She hadn't thought about him in weeks. He'd shown no sign of violating his restraining order.

Frankie casually slid her hand into her coat pocket, curling her fingers around her phone. Waylon was the last person she'd texted. If she unlocked her phone and hit call...

She forced herself to keep her voice steady. "Derek. You're violating the restraining order."

He smiled like she'd just made a joke. "You don't have to play this game. He's not here yet. We can talk alone."

Jesus! "No." She pressed her finger against her phone's screen, hoping it was in the right spot to recognize her fingerprint. It vibrated, telling her she'd successfully unlocked it.

Now to call Waylon.

Derek kept talking. "Come on, Francesca," he purred. His voice dropped, like he thought he could coax her. Like she belonged to him. "I know what happened. I know your *friends* forced you to say all those things to the police. They twisted things. Tried to make me the bad guy when you know in your heart I'm not." His grin softened as he tilted his head, giving her his best little-boy-lost look. "I'm a nice guy."

Her pulse pounded. *Oh, my God. He really believes this.*

She kept her stance firm as she slid her finger down the screen and hoped again that she'd pressed dial. "You *are* the bad guy, Derek."

Something snapped in his eyes. The innocent look left his face, replaced by the flattest expression she'd ever seen. He looked around.

"You don't mean that," he continued. "I know you don't. You wouldn't have sent me that message otherwise."

Message?

"What message?"

He reached into his pocket and Frankie flinched. If he pulled out a knife or a gun, she had no chance; she'd go sprawling across the ice if she ran.

Derek pulled out his phone, much to her relief. He cocked his head as he gave her one of his annoying chuckles. "Stop playing with me, silly girl. You know what message. You just sent it half an hour ago. You told me where you were going and that you wanted to see me. That if I showed up, we could talk. Alone."

Frankie's stomach dropped.

She squared her shoulders and spoke loudly in case Waylon had picked up and was listening. "I didn't send you a text, *Derek*. You're delusional. I don't want to talk to you. And if you don't leave me alone in the scuba parking lot right now, I'll—"

"Is he here somewhere? Is he listening to you? Is that why you're acting like this?" Derek's voice had taken on a hysterical tone.

"No, I—"

"Get your hand out of your pocket right now, Francesca. Give me your phone. He's listening on it, isn't he? He's always listening to you. Controlling you." There was a high gleam in Derek's eyes that terrified her. Was he strung out on something?

"That's not true."

"No?" He laughed—high-pitched, unhinged. "He doesn't want us to be together. He's got his thug friends watching me around the clock. He's hacked my phone, too. I'm sure he's read our texts. He knows how much you want me and he's not going to let you go."

Shit. Did Waylon's friends hack Derek's phone? Did Watchdog?

"You're crazy. I don't want you." She took a step backward.

Derek put his hand out. "Give me your phone and it'll be all right. We'll get rid of it. I'll take you where they won't find us."

Frankie tried to run.

Derek charged. He grabbed her wrist. Her gym bag hurtled between cars.

"Derek, let go of me!" Frankie twisted, trying to yank free, but his grip was iron. "Someone help me!" she shouted. She whipped her head in all directions but she and Derek were alone in the parking lot.

"Give me your phone. You don't have to put on this act—"

"*Help!*"

Derek's mouth twisted into a scowl as she kept shouting. "Why are you acting so cold? I'm a nice guy. I've only ever been nice to you, bitch. You owe me a conversation at the very least." He pulled her with him as he started back around the car, which beeped as he unlocked it. Frankie hadn't realized it was his—she'd only ever seen his sports car.

He drove it so I wouldn't recognize him. So he could make a getaway. With me.

"You don't want to fight me right now. Just get in the car, Francesca, and we'll go somewhere safe." he murmured. "God, I want you *so much.*"

She jerked hard, but her feet slipped. Derek pulled her against his chest and wrapped his arm around her, pinning her arms. In his other hand, something gleamed in the dim light.

A syringe.

"No!" She twisted and tried to knee him in the balls but she couldn't get enough traction on the ice.

"It's only a mild sedative, Francesca, just enough to make you relax so we can talk." He kissed her forehead and she winced at the touch of his cold lips.

Headlights flooded the parking lot.

Derek stiffened.

Frankie sucked in a sharp breath as a Dodge Ram roared into the lot, tires screeching as it slid to a stop between the row of cars and the building.

"Waylon!"

He was out of the truck in an instant. His expression was pure fury.

"Get your fucking hands off her." Waylon started toward them. Frankie watched his hands flex, saw the raw anger in his stride.

"She doesn't want you. She wants me. Tell him, Francesca." Derek's grip on her tightened as he brought the syringe to her neck.

Frankie turned her head and bit his hand as hard as she could.

Derek shouted in pain and surprise. His grip loosened just enough for Frankie to slip down and out of his grasp. Her knees hit the pavement with a hard crack and she knew they'd hurt like hell later. For now she just needed to crawl away from Derek as fast as she could.

She registered another set of headlights lighting up the parking lot as Elias's truck rolled in behind Waylon's.

Frankie barely had time to process before Derek grabbed the hood of her coat and started pulling her back up as if she were a rag doll.

And then Waylon was there, towering over Derek. His fist connected with Derek's jaw with a sickening crack. Derek let go of Frankie's hood and stumbled back, dazed. Frankie rolled out of the way just as he snarled and charged. Waylon was ready. Using Derek's own momentum against him, he caught the bastard and turned on the ice, slamming Derek into the hood of the car. His breath left his body in a whoosh.

"Goddamn it," Waylon growled, twisting Derek's arm behind his back. "You fucking touch her again—"

Derek bucked, throwing his weight back. He broke free, staggering upright. "She wanted me to come," he wheezed. "You think you can keep her from me, you and your friends? You're the problem here—"

Waylon drove a fist into his gut.

Derek crumpled forward with a grunt, but he still didn't go down.

Truck doors slammed behind them.

"Hey, Ram, you need a hand?" Elias shouted.

Still on the pavement, Frankie turned her head just in time to see Elias striding forward, eyes locked onto Derek like a lion scenting blood. Behind him, Frankie could make out Wren's silhouette, phone pressed to her ear.

"My friend's been attacked in the parking lot," Wren shouted. "We need the police *now*."

Elias grabbed Derek by the back of his coat. "Man, you just don't take a hint, do you?" he growled. But Derek slipped free of his coat, a knife somehow in his hand. He charged Waylon.

"She's *mine*—"

Waylon leaned back, dodging the knife, and deflected Derek's arm with his forearm. He grabbed Derek's wrist and hand with both of his hands and pivoted to the side. Waylon turned his whole body, taking Derek with him. Frankie heard bones snap, then Derek was on the ground, howling. Wild-eyed, Waylon knelt over him, still gripping Derek's knife hand. Derek dropped the knife.

"My wrist," he blubbered. "You broke my fucking wrist."

"You touched my woman," Waylon snarled. He spotted the knife and Frankie knew exactly what he was about to do.

"Waylon."

He looked at her, eyes full of fire.

"Stop. He's down. I'm safe. Stop."

Waylon blinked the bloodlust away as the sound of sirens filled the air.

Derek's face twisted in pain and disbelief. "No," he rasped. "No, this isn't how this was supposed to happen."

Two squad cars tore into the lot, lights flashing. Four officers rushed out, hands on their weapons, scanning the scene. Elias waved them over.

"That's him," Elias said flatly, jerking his chin toward Derek. "Dr. Derek Sloane. There's already a restraining order against him."

Derek scrambled on the ice trying to get up but Waylon held him until the first cop was on him.

"Stay down," he snapped, grabbing Derek and forcing him onto his stomach. "You, out of the way," he addressed Waylon, who let go of Derek and stood. A second officer yanked Derek's arms behind his back and slapped the cuffs on while Derek bawled about his broken wrist.

"You have the right to remain silent," the first officer started.

Derek, finally grasping the reality of the situation, stopped yelling and went *very* silent.

Waylon turned away. His focus zeroed in on Frankie.

She hadn't moved, still kneeling on the cold pavement, her knees beginning to sting, arms wrapped around herself.

"Aw, Pix," he murmured.

He reached her in two long strides and crouched beside her, gently touching her shoulder. The second she felt his warmth, she felt her whole body sag, like her adrenaline had finally run dry.

"Come here," he whispered.

Waylon pulled her into his arms and cradled her against his chest. He pressed a kiss to the top of her head. "You're safe, Pix," Waylon said, and Frankie wasn't sure if he was trying to reassure her, or if he was grounding himself in the fact that she was safe.

"I had my phone in my pocket," she mumbled against his shoulder. "I think I called you when it started."

Waylon exhaled. "You did and I heard you. Heard him. I couldn't get here fast enough. I'm so, so sorry."

Frankie snuggled into his neck. "Don't apologize. You saved me. He's crazy. He thinks I wanted him. He was going to take me somewhere." She stopped as her voice hitched and she sobbed once.

"Frankie!" Wren dropped down beside her and put her arm around her. "Are you okay?" She looked up at Waylon. "We gotta get her inside."

Frankie reached out and clasped Wren's hand. Waylon scooped her up and started walking toward the scuba center. The door was open and a small group stood watching them.

"I so was stupid. I wore stupid shoes. Stupid, stupid," Frankie babbled.

"Pix, stop it right now," Waylon commanded. "You didn't do a damn thing wrong. He should have never been near you. I'm the idiot, I shouldn't have trusted a restraining order. I shoulda been here."

Still squeezing her hand, Wren shook her head. "You couldn't have known. The only dumbass in this parking lot is Derek." She looked over her shoulder, red and blue light flashing across her face.

They'd reached the door and the small crowd parted, letting them through. The owner of the scuba center directed them into his office. Waylon sat down in a leather office chair and cradled Frankie in his arms.

"Did he hurt you?" Waylon asked, cold steel in his voice.

Frankie shook her head. "No. The needle didn't get me."

"Needle?" Wren gasped. "Holy shit."

"He said it was a 'mild' sedative. I bit him before he could jab me with it."

"Oh my God, we should have you tested for rabies," Wren said. "The guy is seriously messed up."

Frankie's knees started aching now that they were warm. Her pants were stained with grit and melted ice.

"I think my knees are bruised."

The words were barely out of her mouth before Waylon stood, turned, and set her down in the chair. He dropped to his knees and started rucking up one leg of her pants.

"I should have looked you over immediately," he growled to himself.

"I'm fine, I'm fine, I promise." But Waylon was determined to check for himself. Frankie looked over his head at Wren, who had a small smile on her face. She shrugged.

"They do this when you get hurt," Wren told her, like she was talking about a misbehaving dog. "Just let him or he'll drive you crazy for the rest of the night, asking how you are. Actually, he'll do that no matter what." She waved her hand. "Voice of experience here."

Frankie smiled and bit her lower lip against sudden, totally inappropriate laughter.

"Go ahead and laugh," Wren said. "It's a great release. Almost as good as an orga—"

"Don't." Waylon grumbled.

"What? I'm just telling her what you probably have in store for her later. Like I said, voice of exp—"

"*Wren.*"

She rolled her eyes at Waylon, and this time, Frankie couldn't hold back her laughter.

Wren was right. Laughter was a good release, right along with the tears streaming down her cheeks, washing her fear away.

But nowhere near as good as any of the orgasms Waylon gave her later.

THIRTY

The second the apartment door shut behind them, Waylon flipped the deadbolt. Frankie didn't say anything—just bent and scooped up Snoopy, who was wiggling so hard his entire backside wobbled. She buried her face in the puppy's fur and let out a breath that sounded like it'd been stuck in her lungs all night.

Waylon pulled off his boots as he watched her walk to the couch. She curled into the corner with Snoopy on her lap, her eyes half-lidded and unreadable.

He crossed the room and sank down beside her, then draped his arm around her shoulders. Waylon brushed his other hand over Snoopy's fur until the puppy started dozing.

"You warm enough, babe?"

She nodded. "Just tired."

Waylon tucked her closer, but his jaw clenched as his mind circled back to the office at the scuba center. To the questions the detective had thrown at her.

He had been standing right beside Frankie, his hand on her back. She was sitting in the office chair while Detective Carter sat across the desk from her. The fluorescent lights overhead were too bright and the smell of chlorine made his nose sting. All he wanted was to take his Pixie home and comfort her. She looked exhausted, staring at the desk blotter and not meeting the detective's eyes.

"Ms. Whitmore," Detective Carter said. His voice was calm but Waylon could hear the underlying skepticism. "Derek claims you invited him to meet you in the parking lot."

Frankie's head jerked up, her eyes narrowing.

"What?" She looked at the detective, then at Waylon. Her eyes were full of confusion. "I told him not to contact me again. You can look at my phone. Where...?" She looked around wildly and Waylon grabbed her bag off the floor and set it on the desk. "I'll show you," she said as she dug through it. She pulled out her phone and unlocked it. Waylon watched over her shoulder as she scrolled through her texts. When she got to Derek's name, she scrolled to the last text and Waylon read the words, *Derek, the lingerie you sent me was wildly inappropriate. Do not contact me again.* There were no texts after that.

"Here you go." She turned her phone so that Carter could read the screen.

If anything the detective looked more skeptical. "Not texts. He says you sent him messages through an app."

"An app?"

"Yes. It's a friend-finding app called BeMyNeighborCO."

Frankie blinked, then let out a shaky laugh. "Oh my God," she murmured, relaxing slightly. "He's definitely lying. It was my last day of chemo. He must've overheard Bea giving me the name of that app. She insisted that I check it out to make some new friends." She glanced at Waylon. "After Dan..."

He squeezed her shoulder. The look of pain in her eyes nearly undid him.

"So you downloaded and used the app?" Carter asked, his expression unreadable.

"Yeah, but..." Frankie hesitated, her voice trailing off. "I made a profile back in April, then immediately forgot about it. Chemo brain fog." She tapped her forehead.

"Do you remember your username?"

"Yeah. WereWwoofer." Frankie frowned. "I deleted it at the end of September."

"Why?" Carter's gaze sharpened.

Frankie's mouth pressed into a thin line. "Well... I got a match. But the guy sent me..." Her cheeks flushed. "An inappropriate photo. So I reported it and deleted the app."

"Do you still have the photo?"

"No," Frankie said softly, her voice tight and clipped.

"And you didn't reinstall the app and use it to communicate with Dr. Sloane?"

Frankie looked appalled. "No, of course not! Why would I be in contact with him? He's been stalking me. I wanted him out of my life."

Carter paused before speaking. "May I see your phone?"

Waylon squeezed her shoulder again, this time protectively. "Frankie, you aren't the criminal here." He kept his voice low and steady. Now Carter was studying him like *he* was a criminal.

Frankie gave him a small smile and reached for his hand. Her fingers brushed his. "I know." She handed her phone to Carter. "Go ahead. I've got nothing to hide."

Carter scrolled for a moment, his expression neutral, but then his jaw tightened. He tapped the screen, reading intently, and scrolled some more. When he finally looked up, his gaze landed squarely on Waylon.

"Mr. Ramson," Carter said firmly. "Would you mind stepping out for a moment? I need to speak with Ms. Whitmore alone."

"No," Frankie said, her voice firm. "He's not going anywhere."

Carter's voice softened. "Ms. Whitmore... do you feel safe right now with Mr. Ramson in the room?"

"Yes, of course I do. I have no idea what Derek was talking about.

I never told him to meet me or any of the other weird things he said." Frankie frowned. "What... what is it?"

Carter sighed and handed the phone back to her, but his eyes never left Waylon.

Waylon leaned in and glanced at the screen just as Frankie gasped.

"I... I don't understand." Her voice trembled. "This can't be right. I deleted the app. I swear."

But there it was on her phone. Open. Active.

A conversation stared back at them between WereWWoofer and XMarksTheSpot. The last line was from WereWwoofer, saying that she wanted to meet up in the parking lot before Waylon arrived. Frankie scrolled up to the beginning of the chat. Waylon felt sick as he read the messages.

The first one was dated a couple of days after Frankie spent the night at Waylon's, after her alarm failed. As the conversation continued up until that night, WereWwoofer made it clear she was in love with XMarksTheSpot but that her boyfriend, Waylon, was possessive, dangerous when he was jealous. That he made her file a restraining order against her will. She felt helpless and controlled and wanted out.

This can't be real. She wouldn't.

Frankie's hand shook as they read the messages. "This is a setup. Derek set me up." Her wide, panicked eyes darted between Carter and Waylon. "This isn't me."

"It's your username and his. It's on your phone," Carter said grimly. "And the chats match what's on his."

Frankie looked shocked. Then her eyes widened again.

"Wait a minute," she whispered, her eyes narrowing. "*XMarks-TheSpot*..." She blinked rapidly. "That's the guy who sent me the dick pic back in April."

Waylon stiffened beside her. "What?"

"I'm sure of it." Frankie's voice was stronger now. "I told Steph about it."

"Steph?" Carter asked.

"Stephanie West. She works at the rec center. I went in later that day and told her what happened. I knew she'd laugh. She asked to see it, but I told her I'd deleted the app. She wanted to see the picture, but..." Frankie's voice faltered. "That was gone too. I thought I deleted it by accident. But...maybe not." She clenched the phone, waving it at Carter. "He's manipulating my phone," she said. "This is all a sick joke."

She turned to Waylon. The desperation in her eyes gutted him. "It's not real. I don't love him. I'm not afraid of you. I swear."

Waylon touched her cheek.

Carter stood. "Well... either way, Derek's been arrested for attempted kidnapping, violating the restraining order, and assault." He slipped his notepad into his pocket. "If I have any more questions, I'll be in touch."

"I didn't chat with him," Frankie said softly, her voice barely above a whisper.

Carter's eyes flicked to Waylon one last time. "Frankie... once more, are you sure you feel safe?"

"Yes." His Pixie spoke firmly and without a hint of hesitation.

Waylon settled a sharp gaze on Carter. "I believe her. And even if I didn't..." His jaw clenched. "I'd *never* hurt her."

Carter studied him for a moment longer before nodding. "I'm sure I'll be in touch. If you need anything..." His gaze lingered on Waylon as he pointed to his business card on the desk. "Don't hesitate."

As the door closed behind the detective, Frankie stood and Waylon pulled her into his arms.

"You believe me?"

"Babe, of course I do," he murmured, his voice low and fierce. "We're gonna figure this out."

Frankie buried her face in his chest, her body trembling.

"Promise?"

"Promise," Waylon whispered, pressing a kiss to her hair.

NOW, back in their apartment, Waylon was determined to keep that promise. He'd called Shane immediately after the 'interrogation' and his brother was out the door and headed for Watchdog before Waylon had even finished filling him in.

"You and Frankie meet me there. I'm calling our IT guy the second we hang up. He can clone Frankie's phone, dig around in there and figure out what Derek did. In the meantime, I can fill you in on Kathy Rhodes."

"You found her."

"Sure did. And we had an interesting conversation. We'll talk when you get here."

Elias and Wren followed them to Watchdog. While the tech guy, Flint, worked on Frankie's phone, Shane filled them all in.

"Derek had a pattern. Hell, he had a whole playbook."

Kathy Rhodes had been a cancer patient at the Chicago hospital where Derek practiced. She'd filed a restraining order after Derek turned obsessive. She'd told Shane about another woman Derek targeted—also a cancer patient—but she wouldn't give him her name. That woman never filed—too scared.

"He targeted women at their most vulnerable, the bastard," Shane said. "He was the doctor who would save their lives and win their hearts."

"Disgusting," Waylon said.

"Kathy told me he love-bombed them. Played the sensitive-but-awkward card. Softened them up with compliments and flowers. Then when they started to see him for what he was—when they said no? He didn't hear it. Or he didn't care."

He doubled down.

Sent gifts they didn't want. Messages they didn't answer. Accusations. Obsession.

"He never crossed the line far enough to get arrested. Always knew when to back off—just enough. Like it was a game. Like he'd

studied the law and learned how far he could go without consequences."

Kathy's restraining order was the only one on record. It wasn't
enough to tank him—just get his privileges yanked temporarily.
When that happened, he paid Kathy off in return for her not showing
up at the hearing. Her bills had piled up and she was desperate. He
promised he'd leave Chicago and never contact her again. At least
he'd kept his word on that.

Waylon's jaw flexed.

Frankie wasn't his first target. But he would make damn sure
she'd be his last. At least the son of a bitch was in jail now, unable to
mess with Frankie.

When Flint was done with Frankie's phone, Waylon finally
brought her home.

He looked at her now, curled up, pale, trying not to show how
rattled she still was.

She let out a slow breath. "He knew you were watching him,
too."

Waylon had been—along with his brothers. Twenty-four-seven at
first, then less as Derek stayed quiet. Or so they thought.

Mistake.

"Yeah. I don't know how he knew we were watching him. We're
good at what we do. And Watchdog? Hell, they're even better."

But something had tipped him off.

"At least it's over," Frankie said. "And even if the detective
doesn't believe me, it doesn't matter, so long as you do."

"You know I do."

And you believe I'd never hurt you, that I'm not the man I was.
That was all he needed.

Frankie scooped up Snoopy carefully so as not to wake him and
set him down on his doggie bed beside the couch. Waylon pulled her
onto his lap. She kissed him.

"I need a shower," she said.

He picked her up and carried her to the bathroom.

She curled into his chest, her arms around his neck. His Pixie.

Waylon got the water to the temperature she liked. He helped her peel off her clothes slowly like he was unwrapping something precious. He reached around her and undid her bra then eased it down her arms and let it fall. He kissed her scars like they were sacred. The right one first, then the left. His fingers skimmed over her ribs, her hips, down her thighs. Every inch he touched made her shiver.

Frankie stepped into the shower first. Waylon was right behind her, his body pressed to hers. He washed her like it was a ritual—gentle, reverent, unhurried. Gentle hands and warm water, soap trailing over her growing curves. Her back. Her arms. He knelt to wash her legs and looked up at her. He'd never seen anyone more beautiful.

She was quiet at first, letting him tend to her, her breathing slow and steady. But when he stood and pressed a kiss to her neck, her whole body leaned into his.

"Your turn," she whispered.

"Later."

He toweled her off with the same tenderness, then carried her back to bed.

Frankie curled into the pillows as he joined her, her eyes following every movement as he settled beside her. When he touched her again, it wasn't with urgency. It was reverence. Worship.

He kissed her deeply, slowly, his tongue teasing hers as his hand moved over her skin, tracing the lines of her body. She was soft beneath his fingers,

When he slipped between her thighs, she lifted her hips to meet him. She was warm and open. Ready.

Waylon entered her in one slow, deep stroke, groaning as her body welcomed him in. She gasped, her fingers gripping his back, her legs wrapping around his waist as he began to move. He didn't rush. Her hips rocked with his in a slow rhythm. She looked up at him like he was the only man in the world, and he felt it—deep in his chest.

"God, Frankie," he murmured against her jaw. "You feel like heaven."

She whimpered as he thrust deeper, harder. His fingers found her clit and rubbed slow circles that made her tremble beneath him.

She came with a cry, her whole body tightening, her pussy clenching around him like she never wanted to let go.

He followed with a deep groan, burying himself to the hilt as he came inside her, pulsing, his breath catching as he whispered her name.

When it was over, he lowered his head until their foreheads pressed together. He stayed inside her, chest to chest. He brushed his thumb over the curve of her cheek.

"You okay?" he whispered.

Frankie nodded, her eyes shining. "I love you."

"I love you, too." Waylon kissed her gently. "So let's make this real."

"Real?" She looked confused.

"Yeah. Move in with me. For real. I can't stand the idea of coming home to an empty apartment anymore. You made it a home, Pixie." He grinned. "And I'm not talking about the furniture."

She laughed. "Okay. I will."

"Yeah?"

"Yeah."

They lay tangled in the sheets, his hand resting over her heart, his body curled protectively around hers as she drifted to sleep.

And long after she'd gone quiet, he stayed awake, holding her close like he'd never let go of her again.

THIRTY-ONE

Snow fell steadily as Waylon guided the truck to Bear and Ellie's cabin, tires crunching over fresh powder. Beside him, Frankie had kicked off her boots and tucked her feet up beneath her. She looked warm and comfortable as she slept, with Snoopy flopped across her lap like a furry little hot water bottle. The windshield wipers thumped in rhythm to the soft eighties music coming from the mixtape playing on Dan's boombox. Frankie insisted on bringing it and that was more than fine with Waylon.

The road was still new, seeing its second winter. Bear had had it paved over from a gravel forest road—not because he was fond of leaving the cabin, but because Ellie had wanted her friends to have an easier time getting to the cabin and for her to get to town. When it came to Bear, Ellie always won. Waylon had always chuckled at his brother's deference to the tiny woman. He didn't understand the easy power she had over him.

Not until he'd met Frankie.

Long driveways branched off from the road, one of them being Gina and Lachlan's. They'd bought their house last year, and now lived about three miles from Bear and Ellie as the crow flies. The road narrowed down into a lane that ended at a wide apron where a dozen vehicles could park. A short walk through an aspen grove would bring you to the cabin.

Waylon parked his truck in the center of the apron. Bear hadn't gotten around to hiring a crew to build a garage over the apron yet. Waylon knew it was on his never ending honey-do list though and that he would've started on it if he'd known Ellie would become pregnant so soon after they got married.

Frankie stirred and stretched. She'd fallen asleep almost before Waylon had pulled out of the apartment's parking lot and slept the whole way up. Waylon was glad about that. She'd slept fitfully both nights since Derek's attack two days ago and practically sleepwalked all day. It had affected her appetite, too. Waylon hoped she'd relax enough at the cabin that they could forget about Derek, and he could stuff her full of cookies and popcorn and hot chocolate.

"Are we here?" she asked as she yawned.

"Yup. Rise and shine."

She searched through the windshield. "I don't see the cabin."

"It's just through the trees. You'll see."

Frankie opened her door and Snoopy launched himself into the snow with joyful abandon, barking at absolutely nothing and plowing a zigzag path through the powder.

Waylon stepped around the truck, then helped Frankie down carefully. "Easy there, Pix. Might be ice under the snow."

"I'm fine," she said, but leaned into him anyway, her fingers curling into his jacket.

As soon as she was down, he grabbed their bags out of the back seat—just a couple for the weekend, though Frankie had insisted on bringing enough leftover cookies, books, and thick socks to last through an arctic expedition. Waylon whistled and Snoopy came charging back to them dragging his leash behind, his nose white with snow.

They started down the path, Frankie's hand in the crook of his arm to keep herself steady. As the trees opened up ahead, the cabin came into view like a snow globe—tall evergreens, smoke curling from the chimney, soft golden light glowing through the windows. The porch light flicked on as they walked up. The front door opened and Bear stepped out, holding a coffee mug the size of Waylon's head.

He grinned. "You made it."

Ellie appeared behind Bear. "Come in, come in! It's warm inside. And I made cinnamon rolls!"

Waylon's stomach rumbled.

Frankie gave him a look. "You're so easy, Beefcake."

"I'm food motivated. You knew this."

Frankie took one look at the inside of the cabin and said, "This is heaven."

Ellie gave a pleased little hum. "Bear did a great job fixing it up. He restored the old stone fireplace and the original floorboards."

"Old floors creak," Bear rumbled. "Good for hearing people sneak around."

Looking exasperated, Ellie smiled, shaking her head. "Because I drew the line at inside cameras. I grew up being watched like a hawk by my father and my brothers. Even if we used inside cameras only when we're away, they would still feel like eyes on me."

Frankie gripped Ellie's hand. "I don't know *everything* you went through, but you don't need to explain or even think about it."

Ellie gave her a beaming smile. "It's all right. It's over. I have a new life, with an overprotective husband who would tear the world apart to keep me safe. Another reason we don't need inside cameras."

The cabin was as cozy as always, Waylon thought. It was tiny, from the early pioneer days, but Bear had added a full wing to it that tripled the size, with plans to build more. They were standing in the oldest part of the cabin—one room with an open kitchen along the back wall. To the right was the stone fireplace, now fitted with a wood stove, flames flickering behind glass. The cabin's windows were framed by snow-dusted pine boughs, and that same beat-up leather couch Bear had insisted on moving in by himself looked inviting.

As Frankie plopped down on said couch to peel off her outer

layers, Waylon took a second to really look at her again. There were shadows under her eyes. She was smiling, relaxed—but he could still see the tension in her shoulders. Like she hadn't really let herself breathe since the attack.

He exhaled slowly as he sat beside her. *I'll fix that this weekend.*

They'd have this place to themselves. Snow outside, fire inside. Just them.

Ellie went behind the island separating the kitchen from the rest of the room. She started to open the oven door when Bear swooped in with an Ellie-sized oven mitt stretched over his hand. Waylon would never get over how fast his brother could move, considering his size.

"Honey, don't," he told her as he pulled out a baking sheet of cinnamon rolls. "You go sit down with Frankie."

"I'm going to be sitting in a car, then in an airport, then on a plane, then in another car all day tomorrow, Bear. I gotta get all my moving done today." She started to pick up a tray loaded with a stack of small plates and four mugs.

"No." Bear reached past her and picked up the tray with one hand. He still held the baking sheet in the other.

Ellie put her hands on her hips. "So bossy."

"Honey." He jutted his chin toward the couch. Ellie rolled her eyes and went to sit beside Frankie. Bear followed her. Ellie sat down on the couch and gave her small baby bump a pat. Waylon grabbed two mugs off the tray and passed them to the women, then took one for himself. They each took a plate and a cinnamon roll. Bear sat down in a big chair flanking the couch.

Waylon inhaled. "Smells amazing."

"Thank you," Ellie said. "I had to sneak out of bed early to make them." She eyed Bear who was nibbling on the edge of a cinnamon roll. It looked like a mini bun in his massive hand.

Before he could reply, Ellie's eyes went round and she leaned back. "Oh, that was a big kick, little girl."

Bear demonstrated his agility again when he practically materialized on his knees at her feet. He reached out to her belly.

Ellie grinned. "You don't have to act like I'm about to birth her on the couch. I'm only around twenty weeks."

"Just sayin' hi," Bear said, laying his huge hand gently over the fabric of her dress. "She always kicks harder when I talk to her."

Waylon arched a brow. "She's already got your attitude."

Bear ignored him. "Hey there, little star," he said to Ellie's belly. "Be good for mama, now. Let her rest on the flight."

Ellie and Bear both jumped when she kicked again.

Frankie leaned closer, smiling. "Does she always do that when you talk to her?"

"Pretty much," Ellie said. "It's gotten to the point where I can't even watch those nature documentaries he loves—soon as Bear starts narrating, she thinks it's showtime."

"She likes to know I'm nearby," Bear murmured, still focused entirely on Ellie's belly.

The air shifted and Waylon felt something tug in his chest. Not jealousy—Bear had earned this peace. He'd carved it out with his bare hands and his whole heart. But seeing it laid out so plainly—the love, the promise of new life, the kind of future you could build around—Waylon couldn't help but ache for it.

Even if he'd never get to have it that way.

He didn't know if Frankie could carry a child. Hell, she didn't know. The doctors had warned her not to hope, and she hadn't—not in the desperate, holding-her-breath kind of way. She'd said she was okay with however life shook out. If she became someone's auntie, someone's safe place, that would be enough.

She meant it.

But still... Waylon felt that ache anyway. For her. For all she'd lost before she could even choose it.

Frankie caught his gaze and gave him a quiet smile, soft and knowing, like she'd felt that same shift in the air. She reached for his hand and laced their fingers together.

And just like that, the ache in his chest settled.

All he cared about was that Frankie looked like she could breathe again.

He wrapped his arm around her and held her close.

———

GINA, Lachlan, and their dogs arrived a little after four. A chime rang from somewhere and Bear took out his phone. He showed Waylon and Frankie the screen, and they watched as their SUV came to a stop beside the truck.

"Chime means something tripped the sensor across the drive," Bear explained.

"I still need to show you how everything works," Ellie said as she stood up from the couch. "But it's been so nice just sitting here talking."

Bear opened the door before they could knock. Fleur stood at Gina's side, attentive as a sentry. Lachlan held a pie carrier that smelled like apple and cinnamon and a bottle of whisky. Sam was beside him. The older dog's nose twitched as he stared at the pie carrier.

"Just dropping this off in case you run out of food," Gina said.

"As if," Ellie huffed, pretending to be offended. She pulled Gina into a hug.

Frankie laughed as she took the pie from Lachlan. "Arden loaded us up with enough left over cookies and snacks to feed twenty people."

"What about booze?" Lachlan asked in his faint Scottish lilt. "We brought backup." He lifted the bottle.

"I'll take that." Waylon lifted the bottle out of Lach's hand and carried it to the kitchen island. "We'll use it strictly for medicinal purposes."

"In that case, I feel a cold coming on," Lach said. "It goes well in hot cider or with honey and lemon."

"I still have a whole pot full of cider on the stove," Ellie said. "I won't be having any of the medicine with mine, for obvious reasons." She patted her belly.

Waylon picked up the whisky. "Five spiked ciders?"

"Plain for me," Frankie said. "I'm going to keep Ellie company on the wagon,"

"That's sweet, but you don't have to." Ellie patted her arm.

"I'm not really in the mood for alcohol anyway," Frankie said. "I'll go right to sleep."

Waylon fixed their drinks and the five of them settled into the living room. The dogs snoozed in a pile of paws and fur on the rug in front of the fireplace.

Waylon leaned back into the corner of the couch, letting the warmth of his cider sink into his bones while his gaze drifted to Frankie. She was curled up next to him, smiling, holding her cup of cider with both hands as she listened to the others talk. Still too pale. Still too much worry creasing the corners of her eyes.

But looking better every minute.

Gina and Lachlan talked on the couch while Ellie led Frankie and Waylon throughout the cabin, pointing out which light switches controlled what, where the extra blankets were, how to keep the fire going overnight. "If the power goes out, the generator's out back. It kicks on automatically, but if it doesn't, the manual start's on the kitchen wall."

Then it was Bear's turn to take them around outside and introduce them to the animals as he fed and watered them. Snoopy insisted on coming along. The chicken's feathers made him sneeze. He wasn't sure what to make of the goats. But what intrigued him the most was a corner under the porch where Spot was hibernating.

"Oh dear," Frankie said. "We're going to have to keep an eye on him out here."

Back inside, Lach and Gina gave Frankie their phone numbers in case the storm outside worsened, as had been predicted for Friday afternoon and through the weekend. As they left, Gina pulled Frankie into a hug. Her golden eyes locked onto Frankie's.

"You have our numbers. If anything feels off, you call us. No hesitation. We're close by and we have snowmobiles."

"Promise," Frankie said. "Though I'd hate to put you out."

"My lass here is bored," Lach teased as he wrapped his arm around Gina. "She needs something to keep her out of trouble."

"I'm retired," Gina said with a grin.

"Aye, keep telling yourself that." Lach kissed her auburn hair.

Waylon stood on the porch with Frankie, Ellie, and Bear, watching them go. He wrapped his arms around Frankie from behind. She tucked her back against his chest.

The snow picked up again as dusk settled over the cabin.

———

THE FIRE WAS GOING, the room warm and dim with the kind of pinkish glow that only happened right before sunrise. The coffee pot gurgled softly on the counter as steam curled from two mugs on the kitchen island. Outside, snow fell slow and steady, already dusting the porch in white. The animals had been taken care of and it was good to be back inside.

Frankie yawned behind her hand as Ellie rattled off one last set of instructions.

"There's extra TP in the pantry. The fresh eggs on the counter don't need to be refrigerated. But you probably knew that already. Oh, and whatever you do, don't let Spot follow you inside."

Frankie blinked. "Oh, no. Did Snoopy wake him up?"

"Probably not, but he gets curious when new people or animals are around."

A soft *chime* sounded. Bear glanced at his phone. "That's him."

Frankie frowned. "You aren't taking your truck?"

Bear cleared his throat. "No. We have a... hired car."

Waylon nearly choked on his coffee, laughing. "A hired car, huh? Which driver did the family send today—Bernardo or Rupert?"

Bear shot him a look. "Shut up."

Waylon grinned as he grabbed one of the suitcases and followed Bear toward the door. "Yes, *Young Jonathan*," he stage-whispered, loud enough that Frankie could hear. Bear growled back.

A sleek black Mercedes-Benz S-Class idled beside Waylon's truck, snow lightly dusting the roof. A uniformed driver stepped out and opened the rear door.

"Good morning, Ms. Ellie. Young Jonathan." His clipped voice sounded faintly British.

"Mornin', Rupert," Bear said.

Frankie's jaw dropped.

Waylon whispered, "Bear's family is loaded. Old money. Like, *real* old. The cabin renovations? Paid for in cash. Drop in the bucket." He grinned. "Bear is loaded for bear."

Bear gave him a long-suffering sigh as he helped Ellie into the car.

The driver tipped his cap and closed the door. A moment later, the Benz glided down the snowy road and disappeared into the trees.

Frankie stared after it. "That was worth getting up for." She grinned at Waylon. "But I'm going back to bed."

"I'll tuck you in." He winked.

They walked back to the cabin hand in hand. A faint, rosy glow tinged the clouds to the east before the sun disappeared into them.

"Red sky at morning..." Frankie said.

Waylon wrapped his arm around her. "Sailors take warning."

Yep. Snow was coming. A lot of it.

THIRTY-TWO

The storm wasn't declared a blizzard until two in the afternoon.

Ellie and Bear were already in Arizona by then, which was lucky for them because the storm was shutting down airports all along the Front Range and delaying flights everywhere else. As for Waylon and Frankie, they couldn't have been more snug. Plenty of food, plenty of firewood, isolation, and quiet. Peace.

After she'd crawled back into bed, Frankie had slept until noon. Waylon was glad to see her sleep for a solid six hours. She'd been so stressed by Derek, but the cabin was like a balm to her soul.

Waylon, in the meantime, took full advantage of his morning alone by calling Ben.

"Brother," Ben answered on the first ring. "Everything all right?"

"Never been better."

"Good to hear. So, how can I help you?" Waylon could hear the smile in the big man's voice.

"Who says I'm calling looking for your help? Can't an old friend just call to talk?"

"Yes," Ben said slowly, drawing the word out. "But while you're an old friend, you're not just calling to talk."

"How do you know that?" Waylon asked, giving Ben shit.

"Well, let's do some analysis here. I saw you and Frankie at Thanksgiving."

"You did."

"And I overheard that you two are watching Bear and Ellie's place this weekend."

"We are."

"Then she must be sound asleep right now, or you wouldn't have me on the phone. You'd be off enjoying your time with your soon-to-be fiancée."

Waylon's grin stretched ear to ear. "What makes you say she's my soon-to-be fiancée?"

"More rational reasoning. First point, Thanksgiving; it was impossible to miss how much you two adore each other, ergo, you are on your way to becoming engaged."

"True."

"Second point, she's still not your fiancée because you haven't proposed."

"How do you know I didn't propose to her this morning?"

"I know because you don't have a ring. And I know you don't have a ring because I haven't made one for you yet."

"I could have picked one up from that chain jewelry store off of Arapahoe Road and—"

"I'm hanging up now. Have a nice life."

Waylon hoped he didn't wake Frankie with his laughter. "You know I'd never do that, Moose."

"I know. So." Waylon could hear the faint sound of metal clinking and imagined Ben setting the tools he used to make jewelry off to the side while he got comfortable at his table. "We didn't get a chance to talk at Thanksgiving. Tell me about you and Frankie so I know what I'm putting on your rings. Start at the beginning."

An hour later, Ben told Waylon he'd heard everything he needed to know.

"I'll have it finished for you before Christmas."

"Wait. You didn't tell me what's on it."

"You don't need to know. Only I do. It's perfect."

Ben disconnected.

Damn. Waylon looked at his phone. He was about to text Elias and ask him if Ben had pulled the same Mr. Mysterio bullshit with him, when he heard Snoopy's toenails clicking on the wooden floorboards followed by soft steps.

"Hey, Buddy," Waylon said as Frankie emerged from the hall connecting the old cabin to the new additions. She was wearing her big, fluffy robe. "Thought you were gonna sleep all day."

"Tempting," she said as she yawned and stretched an arm over her head. "But we have quite the busy day."

"We do?"

She nodded, eyes half-lidded. "Snowball fight."

"You're not dressed for it so you'd better—"

Splat! Cold softness hit the side of his face.

"What the hell?" He looked down to confirm that she had indeed thrown a snowball at him in the house.

As he was looking down, Frankie took advantage and another snowball hit the top of his head.

"Wench! Where'd you get these?" Waylon scrambled off the bar stool in front of the island but Frankie was already throwing her robe to the side. She was fully dressed underneath.

"Easy. I scraped the snow off the bedroom windowsill."

She made a dash for the front door as Waylon tried to grab her. Waylon's hand closed on air and Frankie was gone.

"Dude, she left us both behind," Waylon told Snoopy, who looked forlornly at the closed door.

A minute later, they were both outside sending snowballs flying through the snowy air. Snoopy tried to catch each one.

Including the one that flew under the porch.

"Snoopy, no!"

Too late. Snoopy disappeared into the darkness under the porch.

Then tore back out like his ass was on fire. The smell hit them a moment later.

"Welp, I know what we're doing for the next couple hours," Frankie said as she grabbed Snoopy. She made a disgusted face. "Good thing Ellie showed me where she stocks the extra cans of tomato juice, just in case."

———

"BIG, EARTH-SHATTERING QUESTION FOR YOU."

"Yeah, what's that?" Frankie asked Waylon.

It was hours later. They'd spent a good chunk of the afternoon bathing Snoopy in so much tomato juice his coat was pink. And it hadn't worked, not entirely. So, he was confined to his crate in a separate guest room where he wouldn't lie on the furniture or rugs and smell them up. The poor little guy was tuckered out and fell right to sleep after his dinner. The blizzard was going full force, there was at least a foot and a half of snow on the ground with zero visibility. The wind howled and shook the cabin. Waylon and Frankie were settling in for the evening after making sure the chickens, goats, and yes, even Spot the skunk, were all warm and safe.

"*Die Hard*. Christmas movie or not a Christmas movie?"

Frankie looked skeptical. "Duh. Of course it's a Christmas movie."

"And this is why I love you."

"We're still starting with Charlie Brown Christmas though, right?"

"Whatever you want, babe."

She grinned until her eyes squinted. "I'll make the popcorn."

With the wood stove blazing, a huge bowl of popcorn, hot chocolate, and a platter of cookies from their Arden Thanksgiving stash, Waylon and Frankie curled up together on the couch to cheer on Charlie Brown and his sad little Christmas tree, then listen to Linus' moving speech about the true meaning of Christmas. Frankie lay against Waylon's chest, her feet up on the couch, his arm around her, both of them wrapped in one of a half-dozen giant blankets Ellie kept folded and draped over the back of the couch.

Waylon played with Frankie's hair, loving how the short, silky curls wrapped around his fingers. It still astounded him, how many coincidences lined up so that he could have this little pixie he'd first fallen head over heels in love with on a bus—yeah, he was done pretending it wasn't love at first sight—wrapped in his arms, safe and warm.

His.

He could think that word without fearing he was some sort of possessive monster. She'd taught him to forgive himself. And as much as she told him she was grateful he loved her as she was, scars and all, he felt ten times the gratitude she ever could, that she somehow saw a man worth loving in spite of his past mistakes. If she'd turned away, even for an instant while he told her about his behavior toward his ex, he wouldn't be here, happy and warm and satisfied. He'd be off somewhere getting drunk and hoping someone could make him forget his loneliness for a night. And he'd turn around and do the same thing the next night, and the next.

I'm going to marry her.

The power went out.

One minute, Hans Gruber discovered McClane had a machine gun, *ho, ho—*

And the next the TV went dark. So did the light over the stove in the kitchen.

The wind howled outside.

The generator kicked on.

—ho. And Hans went back to being coldly evil while McClane took notes as he hid in the elevator shaft above him.

"Thank goodness the generator kicked on," Frankie said. "I'd hate to miss the end of a movie I've seen a thousand times."

"Tragedy averted. Can't leave John McClane hanging."

"I think it's Hans who was left hanging."

Waylon chuckled as he glanced toward the kitchen island. His phone was sitting face down where he'd left it. "I'm gonna check in with Gina and Lach. Make sure their power's on." He hit pause, and Frankie groaned.

"Right when it's getting good?" she teased.

"Just for a sec, Pix." He pressed a kiss to her forehead then stood, stretched and went to the island. Waylon picked up his phone to make the call when it buzzed in his hand.

"Speak of the devil." He swiped to answer. "Gina, you're on speaker."

"Power's off here," her voice crackled through the line. "You two okay over there?"

"Snug as bugs," Waylon said, glancing at Frankie. "Power's off here, too, but we've got the genny."

"Same," Gina replied, but there was an edge to her voice. "I tried calling and texting Frankie first, but I couldn't get through."

Waylon's brow furrowed. "That's weird."

"Frankie?" Gina's voice sharpened. "Is everything okay with your phone?"

Frankie sat up, suddenly more alert. She reached into the side pocket of the couch where she'd stashed her phone earlier. When she pressed the button, nothing happened.

"Battery's dead," she murmured, frowning. "I noticed it was low earlier. Meant to put it on the charger, but..." She sighed and shook her head, brushing it off with a light laugh. "Guess I got too into the movie. Rookie mistake." She stood and crossed to the kitchen island, then plugged it into the charger.

Waylon's eyes tracked her, and for a split second, he saw it. That flicker of concern she tried to hide behind her smile. Now that he thought about it, she'd been losing track of things lately. He chalked it up to stress—except it had started before Derek's attack.

His gut twisted.

Is forgetfulness a sign of brain cancer?

No. He shut the thought down hard. *Not that. She's fine.*

"In that case, Waylon, call if you need anything," Gina said, her tone softening. "Make sure yours stays charged, Frankie."

"I will," Frankie said lightly, but Waylon saw a flash of worry on her face.

"Thanks for checking in," Waylon said. "We're all good."

"Good," Gina said. "This storm's a nasty one. We've got at least two feet of snow over here. Four- to six-foot drifts."

Waylon looked out the window. The snow was blowing almost sideways. "I can't even see far enough out the window to tell how much we've got. Ellie and Bear might be staying in Arizona longer than they expected."

They ended the call, and Waylon set his phone back down on the island. They returned to the couch, Frankie's smile back in place, but Waylon wasn't fooled.

"You okay?" he asked, gently playing with her curls.

"Yeah," she said, snuggling close. "Just... tired, I guess."

She'd know, wouldn't she? And she'd tell me. "You sure that's all?"

"Absolutely." She hit him with one of her killer smiles. "Let's see if Hans gets what's coming to him. Again."

Waylon hit play, and they sank back into the movie. For about five minutes.

Then the generator died.

The TV and all the lights went dark. The wood stove still glowed, casting flickering shadows across the walls, but the sudden quiet was deafening.

Frankie sat up. "Uh... I thought generators were supposed to stay on longer than that."

"They are," Waylon said, already standing. He went back to the control panel. He flicked the switches, but nothing happened.

Waylon rubbed the back of his neck. "I'll check the exhaust vent. If it's blocked by snow, the generator shuts down as a safety measure."

"Want me to help?"

He shook his head, pressing a kiss to her forehead. "It's a five-minute job, Pix. Just stay warm."

"Okay." She found a box of matches and set it next to a row of candles in jars on the island. Then she pulled one of the heavy-duty flashlights from the kitchen drawer and flicked it on. "I'll hold down the fort. I hope all these scented candles smell okay mixed together." She picked two up and sniffed them. "Lemon cake, and... something that smells kinda like a hippie?" She wrinkled her nose. "Maybe I'll skip that one."

"It'll smell better than Snoopy," Waylon said with a grin, pulling on his coat.

"True." Frankie lit the lemon cake and vanilla candles, then settled onto the couch, flashlight in hand. "I'll give you three minutes to come back in, Beefcake, and I promise to warm you up."

Waylon chuckled. "Ten minutes."

"Five and I'll throw in a foot rub."

"Ha! Deal."

OUTSIDE WAS BRUTAL. The wind howled like a banshee, whipping the snow into a swirling whiteout. Waylon pulled his hood tighter around his face, bowing his head as he followed the house's exterior by feel more than sight. His boots crunched through at least two feet of snow.

"Wish we'd gone to Arizona with them," he muttered, squinting against the wind.

The generator was around the side of the cabin. He crouched and checked the vents. Some snow had blown in, but it wasn't packed tight. Didn't look like enough to trigger the auto-shutoff.

Still, he started to clear it, brushing away snow with gloved hands. He leaned in to check again—

Crack.

Something slammed across his upper back. Pain tore through his spine.

Waylon pitched forward with a grunt, the breath knocked out of him. He braced himself against the genny, twisting to look behind him. A figure came at him through the blizzard—heavy coat, knit cap, face masked in a balaclava.

It's Derek. How?

A second blow caught him hard in the ribs.

Shovel.

Waylon rolled and kicked out blindly. His boot connected with Derek but not hard enough. Waylon tried to get to his feet, ignoring the pain. He had to protect Frankie.

Something looped tightly around his throat. Waylon tried to get his fingers under the fabric. It bit into his neck as Derek pulled hard from behind, Waylon's fingers scrabbled at the loop, slipping on the snow-wet scarf.

His pulse roared in his ears as his vision dimmed at the edges. He twisted, trying to drive an elbow back, but the bastard had the angle on him—using Waylon's own momentum to tighten the choke.

Frankie.

He thought of her inside, warm and safe.

Gotta fight. Protect her.

Waylon tried to grab Derek from behind but the world was fuzzing out.

His knees buckled. The world tilted.

White. Then black. Then nothing.

THIRTY-THREE

The TV and lights came back on. Frankie turned off her flashlight and set it next to her on the couch. A minute later, she heard Waylon coming up the porch steps. He paused, probably knocking snow off his boots and shaking it off his hat and coat. Then he opened the door and stepped inside.

Frankie turned to give him grief. "That was definitely more than five minutes, Beefcake. You forfeit—" She stopped.

The man standing in the doorway with a balaclava in his hand was not Waylon. He shut the door behind him with a soft click, as if they were about to enjoy a cozy evening together.

Between one breath and the next, her brain tried to make sense of the situation. What was *he* doing here? A crazy coincidence, and in the middle of a blizzard? Impossible.

And where's Waylon?

"Why are you here?" she asked the man who had repaired her alarm system twice. Frankie scrambled to remember the name on his shirt. "Leon?"

The man laughed—a soft, almost delighted sound. But when his eyes met hers again, they were flat and shining like black ice.

"I know so much about you and here you are, not even sure about my name. That breaks my heart, Frankie."

Her body went cold, colder than the wind outside. Her hand slid beneath the blanket, fingers curling around the heavy flashlight. It was warm from sitting against her leg. She gripped it tighter.

"What do you mean you know me? You've been to my house twice."

"Oh, no, you're wrong about that. We met before I ever set foot in your house."

Leon walked around the cabin, brushing his hand along the back of the couch, across the top of the table, lightly gripping the back of a chair. His eyes never left Frankie's as his hand claimed everything he touched.

His stare said he didn't need to touch Frankie to claim her. She was already his.

God, please, where is Waylon?

"I'm sad that you don't remember me," he said, almost wistful. Leon's expression broke into a smile. Then it resumed being as cold as the storm outside. "You laughed at me. That was unkind, Frankie, when all I was doing was reaching out to you."

"What? When?"

He paced faster. "I watched you. I learned you. You were raw. Alone. Sad. I was patient. So patient." He tilted his head. "I thought maybe you were different. Until you laughed. And then," He wagged his finger at her, scolding her with an indulgent smile. "You tried to get rid of me. That wasn't nice either. *WereWwoofer.*"

Realization hit like a slap.

"You sent the dick pic. I reported you. How do you know I laughed—"

"Because I built BeMyNeighborCO," he said proudly, like unveiling a masterpiece. "It's mine. It's how I find lonely women like you, Frankie, and sneak into your pocket. It doesn't matter that you deleted the app. I'm still there. It's how I learn who you are. Every message. Every photo. Every contact. Through your mic and camera, I saw everything. I heard everything."

His smile faltered. "It wasn't funny."

"You stalked me because I laughed at your pathetic dick?" Her voice sharpened, disbelief overriding fear for one fleeting moment.

Leon's expression twisted. "I watched over you but you dismissed me. You thought you were too good. You threw away what I offered. You threw away *me*."

He was unraveling now, pacing faster, eyes gleaming as he warmed to his own twisted story.

"I've been in your pocket for months," he murmured, stepping closer. "Before I ever rang your doorbell. I watched you cry alone in that tiny rental. I saw your loneliness. I offered you connection. You *laughed*."

Her skin prickled. She kept her grip on the flashlight, her knuckles aching from the pressure.

"The times my battery drained. That was you."

"It was. Takes juice to keep the camera and mic running. And tonight, well, I couldn't let you call anyone for help."

"And you used Derek," she said.

Leon's grin split wider. "God, he was perfect. Derek was even more pathetic than you. You should've seen how fast he downloaded the app after I faked a message from you. I was going to make sure Waylon saw you talking to Derek and then I'd listen to you try to defend yourself when he saw the conversation on your phone, telling Derek to send you lingerie, telling him you didn't trust Waylon, thought he was dangerous. I wanted to hear him beat the shit out of you, Frankie. Think about it—decorated veteran, emotional issues, rocky past with his ex. Then he gets obsessed with you, you try to leave, he snaps. Kills you. I would've laughed and laughed and laughed."

"He would never hurt me."

Leon stopped moving. "You're right. Waylon *believed* you. He'd never hurt you. And Derek, that fucking idiot, got himself arrested.

So you were never going to be punished." The tight little smile he gave her was pure evil. "I had to do something about that."

God, please, don't let Waylon be dead.

"Where's Waylon? What did you do to him?"

Please. Please. I'll do anything. I can't lose him.

Leon's shoulder lifted and dropped nonchalantly. "How would you feel if I told you he's lying dead in the snow outside, hmm?"

The world stopped. Every snowflake in the sky hung suspended. The wind cut off, the trees stopped shaking. Frankie saw Waylon's blood staining the snow. He lay with his arm outstretched, reaching for the cabin, for her inside.

She blinked away the horrible image in her head. He couldn't be dead.

"You're lying," she breathed.

"I had to remove a threat. That's what predators do when they want to claim their prize."

Frankie blinked hard, trying not to cry. Tears wouldn't help Waylon and they would get her killed. She needed to be as cold as Leon and at the same time hold onto the hope that Waylon was only injured.

She clenched the Maglite tighter as she kept him in her peripheral vision, watching the way he started circling the room again, watching her like she was just another piece he'd moved into place.

"What are you going to do now? Kill me right here?"

"And leave evidence that will get me arrested? No, you're going to come with me. And no one will ever find you. Not your friends, not Waylon, no one."

"So he's alive?"

"Only as long as you cooperate." Leon stopped by a window, peering out into the whiteout. "If you don't come with me, he'll die out there. If you do, I'll call 911 once we get where we're going, and he'll have a fighting chance." Leon turned to her. "So what will it be?"

"Do you promise?" She kept her voice as frightened and weak-sounding as she could, to mask the rage inside her.

"Of course I do, Frankie. Now come here. We need to go."

She nodded and rose from the couch, still wrapped in the blanket. The Maglite stayed hidden in her hand. She walked toward him, biting her lip, pretending to hold back a sob.

"That's my girl." He turned toward the door.

Now or never.

Frankie rushed him and swung.

The Maglite cracked against the back of Leon's head with a dull *thud*. He stumbled with a grunt of pain. His hand went to his head, blood streaking his glove.

"You—little—bitch—" he spat.

She bolted into the hallway. Her lungs burned, her heart hammered. The blanket she'd worn dropped somewhere behind her. She slipped on the floorboards and almost crashed into the wall, catching herself just in time to veer into the bedroom. She slammed the door behind her but didn't have time to turn the lock. Didn't have time for anything. Her duffel bag sat on the dresser across the room. She yanked the zipper wide and dug past jeans, a hoodie, and a sweater. She found the gun case and had it halfway unzipped when the door flew open behind her.

"Don't!" she shouted, spinning around with the gun.

But she didn't get the chance to raise it.

He crashed into her. She hit the dresser, the edge biting into her spine, but she didn't let go of the gun. Leon grabbed her wrist, tried to twist the weapon away. They shoved, elbowed, fought for leverage. Her muscles screamed. The gun was between them, both their hands on it, slipping, shifting.

"Let go," Leon snarled.

"Go to hell."

Their feet slipped on the rug as they wrestled for control. Frankie's shoulder slammed into the wall, pain sparking down her arm. She wouldn't let go. She couldn't.

The gun went off.

THIRTY-FOUR

"Waylon."

No.

"Waylon, wake up."

Can't. Hurts.

"Frankie's gone."

That did it.

Waylon's eyes snapped open, pain screaming through his skull. His throat felt raw. The sky above him was a swirling blur of gray and white, snow biting into his face. He sucked in a breath and winced.

Hands were on him—steady, strong. A face swam into view. Lachlan's. Gina was by his side.

"Easy, man," Lachlan said over the wind. "You with me? We thought you were dead."

"Lach." Waylon's voice sounded rusty. He coughed. "What the hell—" He tried to get up. He needed to get to Frankie. She was in the cabin with Derek—

No. She's gone.

"Frankie."

"We need to get you up and out of the snow," Gina said. She gave Lachlan a look and he nodded. "We'll help you into the cabin."

"No!" Waylon coughed again. "We need to get Frankie." Waylon tried to get to his feet. Lachlan helped him up. Gina stood on one side of him while Lachlan was on the other as they walked him toward the porch. The world tilted. His head was killing him. But it didn't matter. "Derek jumped me. Strangled me."

"It wasn't Derek," Gina said.

Not Derek?

He blinked hard, forcing the world into focus. "Who? Sitrep."

"Shane called us twenty minutes after we talked to you. BeMy-NeighborCO isn't just some friend-finder bullshit. Flint did a deep dive on Frankie's phone. He found a backdoor script embedded in the app's code. Whoever it was built himself an admin panel. He could access the mic, camera, everything. He stalked Frankie through her own damn phone."

Waylon's stomach turned. That would explain the battery draining all the time.

"Jesus," he muttered.

"Shane tried calling you and you didn't answer. He called us next. We'd talked to you about twenty minutes before. We stayed on the line while he called Bear and we suited up to come over. Bear checked the camera footage around the cabin. He rewound and saw the whole thing—a man disabling the generator, then attacking you when you came out to check it. We didn't know if you were alive or dead."

They'd reached the porch. The door was standing wide open. Waylon's blood ran cold.

Fuck!

"After you went down, the attacker went inside and came back out ten minutes later carrying Frankie. They disappeared into the woods. We don't know her condition."

The world tilted. Waylon reached out, caught himself on Gina's shoulder.

"I'm good," he gritted. "How long ago?"

"They've got a fifteen-minute head start. We'll get you inside then Lach and I will pursue."

"The fuck you're without me."

"Waylon, you're injured—"

He shook her hand off his arm. Adrenaline cleared his head. "I need my gun." Waylon stormed into the cabin.

Drops of blood ran from the door all the way down the hall.

Waylon broke into a run, Lach and Gina right behind him. He stumbled over a blanket lying in the middle of the hall.

More blood in the bedroom.

No. She's alive.

Frankie's gun case lay empty on the floor, her Glock nowhere in sight.

"Fuck! He's got her gun."

Gina was right behind him. She and Lach were already suited up —black tactical vests molded tight to their frames, built for mobility but solid as hell. Lachlan was talking to someone, presumably Shane via earbud.

Waylon ignored them. He opened the bedside drawer. Thank fuck his Beretta was still there. He took it, then turned toward the closet and yanked the door open. Bear's vest hung just inside, next to a rack of outerwear. It was heavy-duty SAR issue, fitted with Kevlar panels and reinforced shoulder seams. Not regulation military, but damn close—and more than enough to keep a bullet from ending him today.

He shrugged it on and zipped it up over his hoodie.

That's when he heard the whimpering in the other room.

"Oh, fuck. Snoopy."

Waylon dashed into the other guestroom, bracing for what he might see. He clicked on the light.

And saw Snoopy safe in his crate. The puppy scratched at the door, crying to be let out.

"Bud, I'm sorry." He opened the crate door, but left Snoopy in the room. "I'll bring her back home, I promise," he said as he closed the door. Gina was in the hall.

"Snoopy's fine. Let's go."

"Waylon—"

"*Now*! Or I will take Bear's snowmobile and go without you. You'd do the same if it was Lach, and he would for you."

Gina's golden eyes flashed. "Fine." She turned to Lach who nodded.

Waylon took his phone out of his pocket. "Loop me in."

"Elk, call Ram," Lach said. "Yeah, the devil himself won't stop him."

Waylon's phone buzzed. He reached into his other pocket and pulled out an earbud case.

The earbud case.

She's riding with me.

Waylon put the earbuds in and answered his phone. The three of them raced back outside to Bear's shed where he kept the snow-mobiles.

"Ram, you okay, brother?" Shane said.

"I will be once we get Pixie back and I put this motherfucker in the ground."

"Acknowledged," Ben said.

"Moose?"

"Yeah, brother. I'm joining the hunt."

"They're heading his way." That was Bear. "Camera six picked them up in the woods on a snowmobile."

"There's an old shack five miles north," Ben said. "That's gotta be where he's taking her. There's nothing else out there. I'm joining from the west in the Cat. I'll meet you halfway."

"All units tracking via GPS," Shane said, voice clear in their ears. "Lion and Timberwolf are live."

"En route to Moose's position with medevac capability," Elias confirmed.

"Godspeed, team," Gabe said. "Over."

They'd reached the shed and opened it. Waylon grabbed Bear's helmet off the seat, put it on, and started Bear's snowmobile. Lach and Gina took off for theirs, which they'd left just inside the edge of the woods.

The forest behind the cabin offered enough cover for the narrow trail they followed, the fresh snowmobile tracks just visible in the fresh powder under the trees.

They rode fast, the storm throwing everything it had at them. Branches iced and heavy with snow hung low over the trail, and the sleds bucked against the drifts. But the tracks stayed visible. Headed northwest.

Waylon leaned harder into the snowmobile throttle. The trail narrowed, trees pressing close on either side. The snow was deeper here, the path rough. His arms ached from the strain, and his ribs throbbed with every bump. But he didn't let up.

Frankie was ahead. Bleeding. Terrified.

And his Adventure Buddy, his Pixie, the fated love of his life, was still fighting. He knew it in his soul.

"I've got your back, Pixie," he muttered, barely loud enough to hear over the engine and the storm.

After nearly twenty minutes, Shane's voice came through Waylon's earbud.

"Spooky, you should see Moose in three."

"Copy," Gina said.

Waylon didn't say a word. He couldn't. His jaw was locked so tight it hurt. Every bump sent fresh pain through his body, his head was on fire, but he kept riding. Frankie was out there.

She's counting on you. Get to her. Bring her home.

Then he caught sight of a dark shape ahead—Ben's snowcat, its lights off. They stopped on the other side of a ridge from the old cabin. Even with the storm still howling, they didn't want to risk Leon hearing them.

Ben emerged from the trees, tall and silent, a shadow with a rifle strapped to his back.

"Cabin's about a quarter mile ahead, other side of the ridge," Ben said. The snowmobile trail led straight to it.

They *had* to be there.

"I'll take point," Gina said. Glock out, her movements were smooth and silent. Waylon followed, then Lach, with Ben bringing up the rear. They moved through the snow like ghosts, no one speaking. The storm was abating, the howling wind dropping. Waylon knew that could work for or against them. If the walls were thin there was a chance they could hear what was happening inside. But if they made a sound, they'd tip off the psycho holding Frankie, and God knew what he'd do.

The side of the old cabin came into view through the trees—a squat, weather-worn building tucked between the pines. Light flickered through a dirty window. They crept closer.

A sound cut through the wind.

Thump.

Gina raised a fist, signaling halt. They stopped cold, listening.

Another sound—softer this time. A muffled cry.

Frankie!

Waylon's heart hammered in his ears. He took four deep breaths to steady himself. He reached for his weapon, hands steady despite the rage curling tightly in his chest.

Gina motioned—two entries. She and Waylon would go for the front. Lach and Ben would take the back.

Gina met Waylon's eyes.

Count of three.

One.

Two.

Three.

They moved fast—but not loud. Not reckless.

Gina ghosted forward like she was born from shadow, low and

smooth, her Glock raised and ready. Waylon followed tight on her six. Ben and Lachlan split off silently to flank the rear.

They weren't charging in half-cocked. They were trained. Coordinated. And deadly.

Waylon's breath steamed against the cold. His heartbeat thudded in his ears. He felt every bruise, every ache—but he kept his focus tight. Bear's vest rode heavy on his chest. It didn't matter. He'd have come without it.

Because Frankie was in there.

Gina signaled halt again near the front door. She signaled for Waylon to breach while she covered.

He nodded once.

Gina held her weapon high, her back to the wall. Waylon reached out, wrapped his gloved fingers around the icy doorknob. He tested it.

Unlocked.

He gave Gina the signal, then eased the door open with the practice of a man who'd done it on enemy soil countless times.

Inside, the old shack was dimly lit. A single propane lamp glowed near the hearth, casting shadows that moved when nothing else did.

Waylon swept his gun left, then right. The place was one open room with a tiny hallway leading off it. Graffiti covered the walls and beer cans littered the floor.

And Frankie curled up on a ratty couch.

Blood soaked her thigh. Her shirt was streaked with dirt and sweat.

Then she looked up.

Their eyes met. She jerked her head back, the gesture telling him *He's behind the couch.*

Waylon and Gina dove aside as a man sprang up, aiming Frankie's Glock at Waylon.

"Stay down!" Waylon shouted, not sure if he meant Frankie or Gina or himself.

Frankie dropped to the floor and cried out in agony.

Bam! Bam! Bam! Plaster exploded in dust clouds behind Waylon and Gina. A bullet thudded into Waylon's chest.

Bear's vest kept him alive.

A flash of movement—Gina flanked left, taking a hard angle toward the back of the room. Waylon mirrored, closing the gap from the other side. The man jumped up again, uncertain which target to choose.

He chose Frankie.

Waylon watched it happen in slow motion—the man leaning over the couch, his finger tightening on the trigger—

Waylon fired twice.

The man collapsed, his body hanging over the couch.

Silence.

Waylon kept his Beretta trained on the man's body, ready to fire again if he so much as twitched.

But he didn't.

"Clear!" Gina called from the rear. "Soup, you have eyes?"

"Back room clear," Lach replied.

Ben appeared a second later, ducking inside, rifle up, scanning. "We're good. No one else out here."

Waylon was already across the room. He dropped to his knees beside Frankie.

"Pixie. Where are you hurt?"

She was pale but her eyes were bright with tears, and she was breathing.

"He shot you."

"I'm fine. He shoot your thigh? Anywhere else?"

She shook her head. "What's wrong with your voice? It's hoarse." She reached up and pulled his collar back. "You're bruised. Did he strangle you?"

"I'm *fine*, Pix. Now, are you—"

"I'm so sorry. I fought him," she whispered. "I tried. I hit him with the flashlight. Got to the gun, but he was faster. God, he shot you with my gun—"

"Shh. You did everything right." He pressed his forehead to hers for a heartbeat, then got to work. "Gunshot wound to the thigh," he said over his shoulder. "High, but not femoral. She's losing blood. We need to move."

"I brought a med kit. I've got her," Ben said, moving to help. He handed Waylon a combat gauze pack and pressed a trauma pad into his palm.

Waylon's hands were steady as he worked. Frankie winced but didn't cry out.

"You're okay, Pixie. You're safe now."

"I knew you'd come," she breathed.

That crushed his heart.

Ben met his eyes. "If you've got her, I'll get the Cat."

"Go."

Ben disappeared.

Around him, Waylon heard Gina talking to the sheriff's department, relaying coordinates.

Waylon held Frankie's hand and whispered to her.

"You saved yourself," he said softly. "You fought him off, Frankie. You kept fighting, even after he—God, Pixie, you're the bravest woman I've ever known."

"You've got my back," she whispered.

"Always." He pressed a kiss to her forehead. "I'm not leaving your side."

Lachlan pulled the man's head back by the hair.

"Recognize him?" He asked Waylon.

Waylon finally got a clear look at his face.

The guy from the alarm company.

The one who came to Frankie's house twice.

"You son of a bitch," Waylon muttered.

"His name's Leon," Frankie said. "He owns the app. He's been spying on me."

Waylon heard the snowcat pull up, Waylon scooped her up, ignoring the pain in his ribs. Frankie whimpered, clinging to him.

"I've got you," he murmured again. "You're safe. I've got you."

He carried her outside, trying his best to shield her from the falling snow. Lach opened the rear hatch. Waylon climbed into the cab, settled onto the bench, and wrapped himself around her as the door shut and the snowcat began to move.

Frankie trembled. He held her tighter.

"You're going to be okay," he promised. "Then we're going home."

THE RIDE back to Ben's house was a blurred haze of exhaustion and adrenaline. The snowcat plowed through the storm like a beast, heaters blasting. Waylon didn't loosen his hold on Frankie once. As he continued to apply pressure to her thigh, he felt the tremble in her limbs, the tension she was trying so damn hard to hide. Her breath came in shallow, uneven gasps as her head lay against his chest.

"I've got you," he kept whispering. "I'm not going anywhere."

They were all still on the group call. "Give me a report on Frankie," Elias said.

Waylon shifted his weight slightly to keep Frankie steady in his lap. "GSW, upper thigh, right side. Entry wound only, bleeding, but not arterial. I packed it with combat gauze, wrapped it, been holding pressure since we got her clear."

"Vitals?"

"Pulse is one-ten, thready but steady. Resp's elevated, about twenty-four, and shallow. Skin's pale but not clammy. Pain's eight out of ten. She's alert. And absolutely beautiful."

Frankie gave him an exhausted smile.

"What about you?" Elias asked.

"I'm fine."

"Bullshit, Ram. What happened?"

Waylon knew Elias wouldn't let it go. "Got clocked from behind with a shovel. Might've cracked a rib, definitely got knocked out."

"Jesus, brother. Should've brought a second rig just for you."

"I can ride. I'll be in the back with her."

"Ram."

"I'm not leaving her."

Another pause, then Elias said quietly, "Didn't think you would. But only if you're stable. And you better as hell not conk out on me."

"Wouldn't dream of it."

Waylon closed his eyes, just for a second, holding Frankie closer as the snowcat surged forward.

They rolled into Ben's long drive. Emergency lights cut through the falling snow; the ambulance was already waiting, Elias climbed out before they even stopped moving. Tim and Andy followed close behind. They moved with practiced speed, transferring Frankie to a stretcher, checking vitals, assessing blood loss.

"She's stable," Elias confirmed. "Let's roll."

Gina was already climbing into the Cat. Lachlan was on his way back to Bear's cabin to get Snoopy. Ben fired the Cat back up, clearing a path for the ambulance.

Waylon settled in beside Frankie in the back of the rig, holding her hand while Elias moved into full medic mode, confirming vitals, updating charts, and prepping for intake.

THE STORM WAS FINALLY BREAKING, but the world still felt like it was spinning.

They pulled into the ER thirty minutes later. As soon as they wheeled Frankie through the doors, two trauma nurses and a doctor met them in the bay.

Elias gave report. The ER doc nodded, eyes on Frankie. "Any history we need to know about? Allergies, medications, major illnesses?"

Frankie looked dazed, her lips pale, but she answered. "No allergies. I had breast cancer. I... I think it's back now."

The doctor's pen paused mid-air.

Waylon's chest cracked in half. He turned to her, stunned. "Frankie..."

Frankie hesitated. Then she blurted, "I've been exhausted and nauseated and forgetful. My lower back hurts. I think it's the cancer. I think it's back and spreading."

It hadn't been his imagination. He'd chalked it up to Derek, but she'd been tired before that. He was in denial.

Frankie looked up at Waylon, eyes filled with fear and apology.

Before he could speak, they were moving Frankie again.

"We'll get a CT of your leg and a chest scan," the doctor said. "Blood panel, trauma imaging, and we'll consult with oncology tonight. Right now, We're taking you in for imaging and wound assessment. You'll be admitted upstairs for observation."

A nurse turned to Waylon and looked him over—really looked at him. "You're coming with me. I need to get you checked out."

Waylon shook his head. "I'm not leaving her."

"You won't be far," she said gently. "Let us take care of both of you."

He watched as they wheeled her toward the OR. She looked back once—just once—and the fear in her eyes hollowed him out.

He didn't even notice Elias until he pressed a hand on his shoulder. "She's in good hands, Ram. Let them do their work. We'll be in the waiting room."

Waylon nodded, silent, and followed the nurse.

After everything they'd just been through—the attack, the blizzard, the rescue. After wondering whether she was going to make it through the night—

This.

The one thing Frankie feared most. And now it might be happening again.

Unfair. Absolutely un-fucking-fair.

The worst part was that there wasn't a damn thing he could do about it. He couldn't punch cancer. He couldn't shoot cancer. He couldn't tackle it, stop it in its tracks. It was inside of her. Inside his

Pixie. To anyone who didn't know her, her body hardly seemed like it could fight anything.

But after everything they'd been through, Waylon knew differently. Frankie was strong and brave. She met every challenge life presented her and asked for more.

But this? This was devastating.

He clenched his fists and ground his teeth. Well, if he couldn't fight it directly, he would do everything he could to help her fight it. He'd fix her whatever kind of medicinal tea or aloe juice or God knew what to help her fight it off. He'd make sure she was fed, that she was warm, that she was comfortable and out of pain.

But most of all, he would make sure that she was never alone. Not his Frankie, not his Pixie. Not anymore.

He'd never leave her.

They checked him over—concussion, bruised ribs, bruising around his neck where that asshole tried to strangle him. They patched him up, cleared him for now, but told him to rest.

Like hell.

He asked about Frankie and was told to wait. Waylon headed for the waiting room. Elias was there. So were Ben, Gina, Wren, Gabe, and Rochelle.

By the looks on their faces, Elias had already shared the news.

"Waylon—" Wren started, but he held up his hand. He couldn't take sympathy right now.

"They're going to admit her and run some tests. She'll be here all night."

"So will we, brother," Elias said. "Shane, Charlie, Kyle, and Arden are on their way, and Lach'll be here after he gets Snoopy settled at the house."

"I appreciate it. She will, too."

Waylon took a seat, pulled out his phone, and immediately started reading up on cancer on treatments. On anything that reduced pain and made patients more comfortable. But throughout his researching, other articles popped up like a red thread through a white cloth. Articles about caretaker burnout. About coping when your loved one had cancer. How your life was tied to the patient. And how it was okay to grieve when your loved one passed away.

At that point, he slammed his phone facedown. He didn't need that shit. Frankie was gonna make it. She made it once before; she'd do it again. And he'd do anything to support her in any way he could.

All their friends would be there for her, too.

THIRTY-FIVE

They'd taken Frankie straight from the ER bay to imaging—X-rays, CT scans, and bloodwork. The gunshot wound hurt like hell, but what hurt worse was being alone. After the adrenaline faded, she'd started shivering uncontrollably, teeth chattering as techs moved around her like she was made of glass.

The bullet hadn't gone clean through. After examining the X-rays, the doctor decided it was best to remove the bullet. They'd taken her into the OR and numbed her up. She'd felt the pressure, the tug of careful movements as they removed the slug from her thigh and cleaned the wound. Not major surgery, they'd said. Nothing to worry about. After that, everything was a blur of voices, beeping machines, and the low buzz of fear beneath the painkillers. Not just from the attack—but from what the cancer might be doing inside her.

Now, she was finally in a hospital bed, an IV in her arm, her thigh bandaged and throbbing beneath the blanket. It was the middle of the night, the absolute worst time to be awake in a hospital bed.

Waylon knew the cancer might be back. She'd blurted it right out in front of him. She hoped he'd gotten treated, then gone home.

I'm not about to drag him through this. No way.

Someone knocked on the door. Then it cracked open, slowly and carefully. Waylon stepped inside. He looked wrecked.

"They just told me you were settled," he said quietly. "Said it was okay to come in."

Waylon was here. He'd stayed.

Her heart lifted, but she felt very fragile.

"Hey, Buddy." She reached out her hand.

Waylon's expression softened as he quickly crossed the room and pulled up a chair to her bedside. He kissed her softly before settling into it.

"Just so you don't worry, Gina's handling the police. Shane had all the evidence they need to see that Leon Musgrave was a psychopath. He used the app to stalk other women, too. You're the first one he went after, as far as Shane can tell. Watchdog may or may not have hacked into his servers." Waylon smiled ruefully. "The police are still going to want to interview you. I already talked to them downstairs."

Frankie blinked, surprised. "Are they coming up to talk to me now?"

Waylon stroked her hair. "Not tonight. Gina said they'll check in with you tomorrow afternoon. She'll talk to you before the interview and she'll be with you the whole time. I will, too. Are you all right," he tapped his forehead, "up here?"

"Yeah, I am." She was surprised but she realized it was true. "He violated my entire life. He spied on me. He thought he deserved me just because he wanted me. Then he wanted me dead because I laughed at him. He tried to kill you." She met Waylon's eyes. "So yeah. I'm fine that he's dead. Maybe I'll feel differently once the shock's worn off." She gave him a small smile. "And the drugs."

Then her eyes widened as she remembered. "Oh my God, Snoopy—"

"Is fine," Waylon reassured her. "Lachlan went back to the cabin and got him. He's staying with them until we get home."

She closed her eyes as she blew out a relieved breath for her sweet little puppy.

We. Home.

I can't be that selfish.

"You shouldn't be here. You should go home," she told him.

"Don't be ridiculous, Pix. This is where I belong. I'm not leaving you alone."

God, he was breaking her heart.

"Oh, I'm not alone." She tried to keep the bitterness out of her voice. "I'm never alone. It's always me and the Divine. Ninety-five percent of my prayers consist of, thank you, thank you, thank you, thank you. Four percent are, please. But it's that one percent that's probably going to send me straight to hell—I love you, God. I love you, but I am so damn mad at you right now."

"Pix."

"You should go, Waylon. Really, staying here with me will only bore you to tears." She wiped her cheek. "See? *I'm* already bored to tears—"

He cut her words off with a kiss. Not just any kiss, but one that felt desperate, possessive, all-consuming. It was a kiss that said *I'll never leave you.*

She wanted to fight that kiss, didn't want to tie him to her. He'd get overwhelmed by her disease just like everyone else, even the friends who said they'd stay, the ones who couldn't be bothered to even call to find out if she'd made it through her surgery.

She'd made her peace with those friends, but she'd never be at peace with Waylon leaving her first.

Yet her body betrayed her and she returned his kiss with the same passion. She reached up and held the nape of his neck, pulling him closer. He wrapped his arm around her and kissed her harder.

When he finally pulled away, he looked deeply into her eyes. "I know what you're doing. You're trying to push me away before I have the chance to leave you."

She tried to look away but he wouldn't let her. "Even right now, looking away, you're pushing me away. And I'm telling you; I'm not leaving. I get why you're doing this. I know what happened the first time. I know it must have left you feeling totally unloved and alone. I don't blame you for feeling scared that it's going to happen again."

She shook her head almost violently. "You know what? We should go back to just being Adventure Buddies," she said, the words hurting even as she said them. "Nothing serious, just fun. It's what you wanted." She placed her fingers on his lips as he started to protest. "And that's all right. That's what I wanted, too."

He gripped her hand and gently pulled her fingers away. "You know that's not how it is anymore. I love you. I'm never going to deny that. I love you more than any other woman I've ever met. I can't even imagine having another adventure without you at my side, and by adventure I mean life. The exciting parts and the hard parts, like right now. I'm going to be right here cheering you on. Holding out my hand when you need it to pull you up. I'm going to be here through every single night and I want to be the first person you see in the morning. I'm not leaving you alone. Not now, not ever. Understand what that means?"

Tears were coursing down her cheeks. She was afraid to trust his words, and yet he'd never lied to her. Their relationship was based on trust; it was how they'd kept each other safe through every challenge. It was how their bodies were in such harmony when they made love. This wasn't any different.

She finally understood, all the way down to her bones. Waylon would stay, he would keep his promise and stay.

Not now, not ever. He was asking to be in the rest of her life—no matter how long or how short that might be.

Frankie swallowed the lump in her throat and nodded.

His eyes softened. "You understand?" he repeated.

"I do," she whispered.

A knock at the door drew their attention. A doctor walked in, but Waylon didn't let go of her and pull back the way she'd expected him to, as if they'd been caught doing something wrong. Instead, he gave her a squeeze and took her hand while they waited for the doctor to speak.

"Hi, Francesca, I'm Dr. Benson. I'm the hospitalist on call tonight."

"Hi, Doctor. Please, call me Frankie."

Dr. Benson nodded and looked at Waylon, then at her. "I take it I have your permission to share anything with him as well?"

They both nodded, and she couldn't help but smile. Waylon really did have her back, and it would be so much easier hearing bad news if she wasn't alone. He could help her ask any questions or for clarification. A tremendous weight lifted off her heart.

"I understand you're concerned that your cancer may have returned," Dr. Benson said, glancing at the chart in his hand. "We've run a full blood panel, and your imaging—X-ray and CT—look good so far. No obvious signs of metastasis on the scans."

Frankie released a breath.

"So that's good news," Waylon said, squeezing her hand. "Clear CT and X-ray means nothing's lit up in your bones or lungs, right?" He glanced at Dr. Benson. "What about the CA 15-3?"

Dr. Benson gave a small, surprised nod. "Yes. That's right."

Frankie blinked at him. "How do you know that?"

He shrugged one shoulder. "Might've done some late-night Googling in the waiting room."

She stared at him, the corners of her eyes stinging. "You looked up tumor markers?"

"I looked up everything I could," he said softly.

"That said," Dr. Benson continued, "we're still waiting on some of the lab work. Your blood panel's nearly complete, but the lab is a little backed up tonight—storm-related staffing issues. We should have the rest of the results, including your tumor markers, by late morning or early afternoon. Since it's a weekend, I want to prepare you that things tend to move a little slower, and discharges can take longer. I'd like to keep you at least one more night for observation."

She nodded, fighting back tears. "I appreciate your honesty," she told him.

He gave her a quick, terse smile, but not a cold one. She wondered how hard it must be to deliver bad news as a hospitalist. Though the news wasn't always bad. Her news was good so far. She needed to hang on to that.

"I'll leave you two alone," Dr. Benson said. "If you need anything, the nurses here are wonderful. I'll check back during rounds tomorrow and hopefully have more concrete updates."

"Thank you, Doctor," she said.

When he left, she looked at Waylon. "I love you, too. I love you so much."

He kissed her again. This one was sweeter but no less passionate.

"Is it okay if I give everyone downstairs a status report? They didn't want to come up and overwhelm you."

That confused her. "Everyone downstairs?"

"Yeah, babe. Oh, and what do you want for breakfast tomorrow?" Waylon continued as if he weren't fazed at all. "Hospital food sucks, so I'll tell them what you want and someone can go pick it up. Or maybe Steph can on her way in—"

"Wait. Who's everyone?"

"Let's see. Gina, Ben, Elias, Wren, Gabe, Rochelle." Waylon checked his phone. "Looks like Shane, Charlie, Arden, and Kyle got here while I was in the elevator coming up. Lach's at home with the pups but demands we keep him in the loop, just like Bear and Ellie. Steph will be here tomorrow morning when Dr. Boyfriend picks her up on his way in."

Frankie covered her mouth, her shock growing as the list of names got longer. They were all here? In an uncomfortable waiting room in the middle of the night? During a blizzard?

For me?

"Right now?" She pointed toward the floor. "They're all down there?"

Waylon looked confused. "Yeah, babe. Where else would they be?"

"Home in bed, where they belong. I didn't mean to trouble anyone."

Waylon actually laughed. "Babe, it's no trouble when it's family."

Her lip quivered and she found herself holding back fresh tears. "Family," she whispered.

"That's right. You're part of the family now, and family's no trouble. What else do you need? Anything you want. Sounds like we might be here all weekend. You want someone to stop by our place and pick up pajamas? Or, wait, I bet they have some down in the gift shop. You want me to buy you some new ones tomorrow?"

"You don't need to do that—"

"There is need and there is want, and I want to do anything and everything that's going to make this easier and you happier." He grinned. "Get used to it, Buddy."

She beamed a smile back at him. "I'll do my best."

"Yeah you will. You're gonna do your best like you always do." He brushed his hand over her hair. "So. Breakfast. Might as well give me your lunch and dinner choices, too. And what else? Tell me anything else you want in the entire world and it's yours."

Frankie laughed softly. "Honestly?"

"Yeah. Honestly."

"What about something I don't want?"

"Intriguing. What is that?"

"I...don't want to go to Hawaii."

Waylon raised his eyebrows.

"Don't get me wrong. Hawaii is beautiful, and I've loved the scuba lessons."

Waylon grinned. "But? Wait, let me guess. That was more Dan's adventure than yours."

She nodded sheepishly. "I still want to swim with sharks, and go paragliding naked, because who wouldn't? Besides, Wren would kill me if we didn't."

"Yeah, she might."

They both laughed softly.

"So, Pix. What do *you* want to do instead?" He grabbed her hand and ran his thumb across her knuckles.

"As if you can't guess, Buddy."

Waylon nodded. "The northern lights. Iceland."

"Ding ding ding. Give the man a stuffed puffin." She squeezed his hand. "If I only have a little time left—"

"Nope. You're not doing this. You're not going to think this way."

She nodded. "Okay."

Frankie drifted off to sleep, holding hands with her Buddy.

THE STORM HAD FINALLY BROKEN.

Snow glittered against the hospital window in the early morning light. The sky was pale and blue, waiting for the sunrise.

The door opened and the smiling CNA who'd taken care of Frankie all night stepped inside with her rolling vitals cart. She was a little younger than Frankie.

"Hi, Patty. How was the rest of your night?" Frankie asked on a yawn.

"Good morning, sweetheart. It was nice and quiet. Just gonna check your vitals again real quick, okay?"

Frankie nodded and held out her arm. She looked to her side.

Waylon was slumped in the chair beside her bed, his arm draped across the mattress, fingers still tangled with hers. He'd dragged the chair up as close as it would go, and sometime during the night, his head had dropped beside her hip. Patty had draped an extra blanket over his shoulders on her last visit.

He stirred when Patty clipped the pulse ox to Frankie's finger.

"Mm—what time is it?" he rasped, blinking up at them.

"Just after six," Patty said quietly, not missing a beat. "You can stay right there, handsome. I'm not disturbing a thing."

Waylon stretched, his back popping as he sat up straighter. "Nah, you're fine. Just checking on my girl." He took his phone out of his pocket.

Frankie gave him a sleepy smile, her heart aching with tenderness. She'd never felt so cared for.

"You're a lucky one," Patty told her with a wink as she patted her arm. "Vitals look good. I'll let your nurse know. You can order breakfast anytime you want."

"Actually," Waylon said, rising and putting his phone away, "Steph's here with breakfast. I'll go grab it before someone else eats your cinnamon rolls."

"You're not serious."

"Oh, I'm very serious," he said, kissing her temple. "Back in five."

Patty opened the door for him, smiling as he passed. "That's a good one you've got there."

"I know," Frankie whispered.

The moment the door closed, Frankie exhaled slowly. A little ache pulled at her chest. It was getting harder to pretend she wasn't afraid.

Another knock. The nurse was already here to check on her.

"Come in."

The door opened, and a familiar figure stepped inside—a petite woman in blue scrubs under her white coat.

"Hey, Frankie."

Frankie blinked in surprise. "Dr. Tremblay?"

"I heard you were here," she said warmly, pulling the stethoscope from around her neck. "I checked your blood tests and I had to come see you myself."

Frankie's heart froze over. Dr. Tremblay was part of Frankie's oncology team. Of course she'd be checking for markers, checking for signs the cancer had metastasized.

Waylon wasn't in the room with her to hear whatever was coming next. She realized it was a small mercy. She didn't want to be alone, but she also didn't think she could take seeing his expression. Her stomach burned.

Except I'll have to be the one to tell him.

She swallowed hard and tried to sit up a little straighter.

Dr. Tremblay gave her a kind smile. "Frankie, I wanted to see you myself before rounds started. The full tumor marker panel hasn't come back yet but I've reviewed everything else they've run so far."

The doctor reached for her hand, gave it a quick squeeze as she gave her the results.

When she finished, Frankie nodded, numb. Dr. Tremblay might as well have dropped a bomb on her head.

"I know it's a lot," Dr. Tremblay said. "But the good news is, it's early and you're holding steady. No fevers, nothing immediately concerning so far. We just have to wait for the rest of the tests and then look at your options. I know this is the hardest part—the waiting."

Frankie bit her lower lip, her eyes hot. "Yeah," she whispered. "It is."

"I'll check in again later today, all right?"

Frankie managed a nod.

When the door closed, Frankie stared straight ahead at the wall.

She had no idea how she was going to tell Waylon.

Whatever happened next... it would change everything.

———

THE DOOR OPENED a few minutes later. Frankie wiped her cheeks fast. Waylon came in balancing two takeaway coffees and a plastic container.

"As promised, cinnamon rolls from Steph, still hot and fresh. She said to tell you she's eager to see you." He set the bag and coffees on the bed tray and leaned in to kiss her forehead. "They all are, whenever you're ready."

He paused, reading her expression. "What is it?" He sat down and grabbed her hand. "Pixie..."

"My oncologist came to see me. Dr. Tremblay."

His face fell. "Whatever she said, baby. I'm here for you. I love you."

"I hope so," Frankie whispered, her voice trembling. "I really do."

And then the tears came. She couldn't stop them.

"I'm going to have a baby."

Waylon blinked. "A...baby?"

Frankie nodded, laughing and crying all at once. "Dr. Tremblay heard I was here and looked through my chart. They did a pregnancy test. It's standard when they admit women, I guess. It was positive. She couldn't believe no one had told me yet. Waylon—she thinks my symptoms are from being pregnant. Not cancer."

Frankie choked on a breath. "We won't know for sure until this afternoon, but—"

She couldn't get another word out.

Because Waylon was kissing her.

His hands cradled her face, gentle and sure, and the second his lips met hers, the world stopped spinning out of control.

She kissed him back through tears and laughter, through fear and stunned joy, through every ache in her body and every last prayer of thanksgiving in her soul.

When they finally pulled apart, he rested his forehead against hers.

"We're having a baby," he said, wonder in his voice.

She smiled through the tears. "Yeah, Buddy. We're having a baby."

Fresh tears streaked down her cheeks. But this time, they were tears of something sweeter. Something lighter.

Hope.

THIRTY-SIX

The cancer wasn't back.

She'd waited for the news with her heart in her throat, but she hadn't waited alone. Her friends came upstairs in quiet waves—two or three at a time—trading off chairs, bringing jokes, fuzzy socks, and tasty snacks. Somehow, none of them got kicked out. She suspected Stephanie had a quiet word with someone on the nursing staff.

When the doctor came in with the final report, it was just her, Waylon, and Steph. She would never forget the way Waylon sagged in his chair and covered his face, or how Steph pressed a hand to her chest and whispered, "Thank you, thank you, thank you."

That night, Frankie lay in bed—sore, exhausted, and happier than she ever remembered being. She was still in remission. She was pregnant. And she was finally brave enough to believe both.

They didn't want tell anyone right away. A post-chemo pregnancy was risky. But it had been over six months since her last treatment, and her doctors—after some thorough and repeated testing—were cautiously optimistic that everything was fine.

Right before Christmas, with the baby still a secret, they threw a housewarming party—more accurately, a penthouse-warming.

They'd moved to the top-floor unit of Waylon's building. Three bedrooms, floor-to-ceiling windows, and a balcony that overlooked the mountains beyond. The walls were still bare in places, but the furniture was warm and cozy, and the kitchen had already become the heart of the space.

Everyone came. Gina brought champagne. Elias brought ribs. Ellie sat with her feet up while Bear passed out her homemade fudge. The living room glowed in late-afternoon sunlight, laughter and warmth filling every corner. Frankie stood by the window, one hand resting on her still-flat stomach. Her heart thumped loud enough to drown out the voices around her. They were about to tell everyone the news.

Waylon came up beside her, his expression soft. "You ready?"

She nodded.

"Okay. But before you do that—I've got something to say."

Her brow furrowed. "Oh?"

He turned toward the room. "Hey! Can I get everyone's attention for a second?"

Conversations quieted. Heads turned.

Frankie felt a wave of heat sweep through her, nerves lighting up.

"Frankie and I have something to share," Waylon said, his voice clear and steady. "But before we do... I need to take care of something first."

And then—he dropped to one knee.

Her eyes welled with tears before he even said a word.

Waylon looked up at her, his voice thick. "You're my Adventure Buddy, my Pixie, my home. I don't know what's coming next, but I want to face every adventure with you."

Frankie's heart slammed against her ribs.

Ben stepped forward and handed Waylon a small black box. Frankie heard Wren, Ellie, and Rochelle gasp when they saw it. Frankie knew exactly why—Ben had created their wedding rings, and they were stunning. Waylon thanked Ben, who only nodded and stepped back.

Waylon opened the box. Inside, two rings lay on black velvet.

Frankie gasped as she looked closely. One was carved with anchors, the other with tiny earbuds. From the expression on Waylon's face, she knew it was the first time he'd seen the rings, too.

"So, will you marry me?"

"Yes. Of course, *yes*." Frankie dropped to her knees, laughing through her tears as she threw her arms around him.

The living room erupted with cheers. Someone popped a cork. Waylon slipped the earbud ring onto her finger and pressed his forehead to hers.

"I'm all yours, Buddy," she whispered.

"I'll always have your back, Buddy," he said.

She laughed again, kissed him hard, and then stood with him. Waylon lifted his hand and their friends quieted again. He looked down at Frankie and nodded.

"There's one more thing," she said, unable to stop grinning. "We're going to have a baby."

A beat of stunned silence.

Then the room exploded.

Laughter. Tears. Shouts of congratulations.

And in the center of it all, Waylon wrapped his arms around Frankie and held her like she was the most precious thing in the world. Frankie looked around the sunlit room—their friends, their family, their new home—and felt joy settle deep in her chest. They'd trusted fate, weathered storms, survived dark days.

Now came the light.

CHAPTER 37 APRIL TAYLOR

April Taylor, Age 18

The bus station bench was hard and cold through the back of her thrift-store sundress, and the lights buzzed overhead with a flicker that got on her last frayed nerve. April Taylor crossed and uncrossed her legs as she twisted the strap of her duffel bag around one wrist like a tourniquet.

Shane was late. But he was coming. He had to be.

She glanced at the giant clock above the ticket counter. Twenty minutes.

He said he'd meet her here. They were supposed to be on the bus to California, kissing this shitty little town and every bitter memory behind. He was going to defy his family and join the Navy, become a SEAL. She was going to work for one of the tech start-ups and build something amazing, then retire as a multi-millionaire at twenty-five. Shane had told her if that didn't work out, she was gorgeous enough to be an actress or a model.

He'd also told her he loved her. That he'd marry her once they were settled.

That was the plan. *Their* plan.

She blinked hard, eyes burning.

All throughout the graduation ceremony yesterday, April kept telling herself it was the last time she'd see any of those assholes from high school again. Especially Leslie Trent. It wasn't good enough that Leslie and Shane were the king and the queen of Homecoming, and the Snow Ball, and the prom, while April stayed home pretending she didn't care about a stupid dance. Leslie Trent had booted April right out of being valedictorian with that smirky smile and her lies about April cheating on her mid-term exams. Those lies had cost April a full-ride scholarship to Stanford. Leslie Trent had ruined April's life out of jealousy over Shane.

April clenched her jaw. She'd done everything she could to prove her innocence, but the principal stared right through her while she laid out her case, then told April she was lucky she wasn't getting expelled.

She should've known the system would never let a girl like her win. Not when she came from a family of drug dealers and black sheep. Not when everyone in town was just waiting for her to screw up and prove they were right about the Taylors—every last one was a criminal and a loser.

But Shane hadn't cared about any of that.

Had he?

She glanced toward the door again. Seven minutes.

Still no Shane.

April never thought she'd be the girl to catch Shane Foti's eye. Not in a million years.

Shane was the kind of guy who'd been born with a spotlight already shining on him. Rich, handsome, athletic—destined for prom king before he'd even gotten to high school. The kind of boy who never had to try too hard because the world just... tilted in his direction. Teachers smiled at him. Girls practically melted into their lockers when he walked by. And the guys? They could have been jealous but most of them liked him anyway. Shane Foti had swagger.

Everybody wanted to be his best friend but he'd kept the friends he'd made as a kid. There was Elias, the charming disaster. Waylon, quieter but just as dangerous. Gabe, the golden retriever of the group, all kindness and decency. Badger, who was exactly as obnoxious as his nickname. Sean Volker, who threw a baseball like God's favorite pitcher and whose last name spoke of generations of successful Coloradans. Teachers and old-timers nodded approvingly at everything he and his little sister did.

And then there were the two big guys—Jon Behr, but no one dared call him anything but Bear. And Ben. Sweet, stammering Ben who people whispered about like he was slow, which just showed how little they paid attention. April had shared honors classes with him. Ben always sat in the back, quiet as a shadow. Teachers forgot to call on him half the time. Students barely noticed him at all. But April did. And she knew the truth. Ben wasn't dumb. He was a goddamn genius who just didn't like taking up space or making noise.

Maybe that's why Shane had paid attention to her. If he had a smart, quiet friend like Ben, then he could see beyond the pretty, popular girls always vying for his attention. See *her*—smart, hard-working, determined to make a better life for herself.

Friends, sure, especially since she was constantly helping him out. However, April never expected Shane Foti to fall for her. Fall hard enough to share his dreams with her and to take hers seriously. Just not seriously enough to be open about their relationship. She told herself she understood—he was protecting her in his own way, from bullies like Leslie who would openly attack her. From his parents who would never understand or accept her and could not only make life hard for April, but for her whole family if they wanted to.

April looked at the clock again. Ten minutes. The speaker overhead crackled to life and announced departures. If Shane didn't hurry, they'd miss the bus and have to wait until the next day for the next bus to California. Her parents would read her letter and know where she'd gone. They'd come and get her, and that would be—

The top of a head of dark hair caught her eye.

Shane! Thank God.

April stood up and smoothed out the cotton skirt of her sundress. She bent to pick up her suitcase handle and her backpack. They'd have to sprint to catch the bus but they could do it.

He came around the divider and his familiar face caught her by surprise.

Not Shane's. Ben's.

Ben knew about them? Had Shane told him and he was here to stop them? *Or...* Joy sparked in her heart. Maybe Shane had told all his friends he loved her and they had come to see them off.

She tried to look past Ben. Heaven knew half a dozen guys could get swallowed up in his shadow.

But, no. No other friends following the big guy.

And no Shane.

Ben spotted April. He looked at her sadly.

April shook her head in denial as Ben ambled toward her.

"What happened?" she asked. "Where is he? Is...is he all right?" The sudden, horribly welcome thought that he'd been in a car accident popped into her head. She'd rush to his bedside, stay there without being afraid of getting chased away. She'd rather face that than believe he'd abandoned her like this.

"Sh-Shane's not c-c-c-oming," Ben said. He was upset enough that the stutter he fought hard to control and hide was on full display.

April's heart broke right there and then. Ice-cold fury filled its place.

"He couldn't even show his face? He couldn't come and tell me himself that he changed his mind? That he didn't care enough..."

Enough about me.

"...Enough about what he wants versus what his parents want to at least come and tell me that I'm on my own?"

Ben shook his head sadly. "It isn't right, what he's d-doing to you."

"To *me*? I don't care about him," she lied. "This is just convenient for us to go together, that's all."

Ben's eyes told her he could see right through her lies. He reached into his pocket and pulled out his wallet and an envelope.

"What are you doing?" She took a step back.

"He sent a n-note and the money he'd planned on using for both tickets and your f-first s-six months' rent. I told him he should turn over his entire bank account to you." Ben pulled a stack of bills from his wallet. "He said he was." Ben held out the cash and the envelope.

He didn't even buy the tickets. How long did he know he was going to leave me here?

"I don't want that," April said. "I don't need it. I don't need anything from him. Ever."

"April, just t-take the money. You c-can toss the letter. I w-would."

"No." She crossed her arms, wishing to God she wasn't so stubborn. If she had no job nibbles whatsoever, that money plus hers could keep her afloat for eight or nine months—ten if she stretched her budget until it broke. Without it, she'd better hope someone hired her right away.

Just take it the quiet, practical voice in her head told her. *You've earned it.*

That last thought made her stomach heave. *Earned it. Right.*

"April. California is expensive," Ben said. "T-take the money."

She reached out—and curled Ben's fingers closed over the money.

"I don't care if you give it back to him or keep it for yourself, Ben. I'm not taking it."

Ben finally nodded. "Al-all right then."

"I'm going to be fine," April said, smiling harder than she felt.

Ben studied her. "Yes. You will be. You're amazing, April." With that he turned and left.

April watched the bus to California pull away.

I can't go home. I left a letter saying I was leaving.

April went back to the ticket counter and studied the day's bus schedule. She mentally counted up her money to see how far she could get without starving once she got there.

It looks like I'm heading to Las Vegas.

Read about April and Shane in *Thunder on the Mountain, Watchdog Mountain Division Book 5*
    My Book

AFTERWORD

While I wrote this, I realized that it was a continuation not just of the series but of things I talked about at the end of Bear on the Mountain. About my Lyle-Lovett-loving friend I lost to cancer. But also about my other friends, the ones who get me through some of the hardest points in my life, whether they know it or not (I tend to downplay things, to get quiet and tuck into the nearest cave I can find when the going gets tough, often to my detriment.).

If you don't mind, let me take a minute here before you go on to the next book in your stack or queue to tell you a little bit about my best friend, my oldest friendship now, the woman I call my sister.

I met Mish sophomore year of high school after a rough freshman year. First class on the first day, she sat at the bench in front of me in biology. The bell hadn't rung yet when she tipped her head all the way back until she was looking at me upside down.

"Hi. I'm Michelle. Who the hell are you?"

As I looked into her upside down eyes, a voice in my head told me *She's going to be your best friend or your worst enemy. Choose which one you want. Right. Now.*

I chose best friend. No—sister. And through all our ups and downs from then until now, I have never once regretted that decision.

We listened to the same weird music (Kate Bush, Bauhaus, all the punk that's fit to print) and that old time rock and roll when it was still a thing. We were in every art, English, and creative writing class together. We were the co-editors-in-chief of the school newspaper. I was going to be a war correspondent and she was going to pick up where Georgia O'Keeffe left off in the art world.

We had adventures.

College came. She went to one, I went to another.

Didn't matter. Still had adventures in a big city on a big lake, often involving getting lost on public transportation, dancing in punk and goth clubs, and severe lapses in judgment.

Eh. We made it home alive.

After college, I got married and moved to Colorado. She moved out here not long after. We continued our adventures. Now they were in the mountains and involved doing things like identifying wildflowers on hikes. Also, tracking bears and mountain lions to their dens and other lapses in judgment.

Eh. We still made it home alive.

Then, we almost didn't make it home alive.

Not through any adventures. We're pros at those. But through the shit life likes to throw at you while you're having fun.

Cancer sucks.

She's had hers. I've had mine.

We're okay now, but we had some real "Wind Beneath My Wings" moments there, let me tell you, taking turns being the one in the hospital bed and the one sitting bedside.

When it was my turn in the bed, she was there after my surgery when I was missing an internal organ and on a post-op ketamine high. And you know what she did? She brushed my disgusting, tangled, post-op hair and read me "The Snow Queen" as I went in and out of consciousness. But I heard every word. Hell, thanks to the ketamine, I *saw* that story unfold in my head.

And so I was not scared. Not one bit. Because of her. She had my back.

So, that's why this book is dedicated to my adventure buddy, Mish. You and me, punk rock girl.

Other friends have disappeared from my life, like they did from Frankie's. It's sad and disappointing and really hurt for a long time. But, I've come to find that they did me a favor, leaving space for new friends to fill. I think you might be familiar with some of them, probably have a book or two of theirs in that stack sitting next to you or on your e-reader right now. I'll let you go read them—in a minute, in a minute, I'm not done yet. Because I also want to tell you how amazing they are.

This is a lonely business at times. It can be mean. It can be downright cutthroat. But I found women who make sure it isn't. Trinity was the first and best friend I made in the wild and crazy world of romance authors. She's wicked funny (and sometimes just wicked) and I could not do this without her. Her constant message of *Are you done writing my next favorite book yet?* makes sure that I do. Plus, she and I have had the best adventures—through cities, up mountains, and across lakes, all powdered by chocolate and cheese. And lemons. Lemons are key.

Then along came Caitlyn O'Leary who opened the doors wide after I'd been banging my head on them for so, so, sooo long. She also called me the night before my surgery initially to brainstorm a story (my favorite thing to do in the world) and ended up talking me down from a scary place. And you know, she *still* does that for me from time to time, as I hope I do for her, too. Thank you, Caitlyn.

She also introduced me to Riley Edwards. Not sure what I'd do without my Tiki. I can always call her for a laugh or a cry, and sometimes both. We have been through a lot in a short time, to the point where I feel like I've known her forever and wish we'd met sooner.

Riley in turn, introduced me to Bella Stone—my Irish sister from another mister. There are times when I think I made Bella up, because she's so incredibly interesting and she matches everything I ever wanted my imaginary friend to be—smart, funny as hell, a bigger dog-lover than I am, tough as nails, and ready to pass the hat for bail money. Seriously, she's a superhero who saves everyone's bacon and I love her to pieces. Also, Taytos.

Kris Michaels actually ran across a crowded room to hug me the second time we met to congratulate me on launching my author career. That hug meant the world and still does. Now we do writing sprints together. When I don't think I can write another word, she's there encouraging me, and I'm there kicking her butt right back. Time. Ready. Go. Rinse and repeat. That's how books get made, thirty minutes at a time.

And so many, many more amazing authors I'm happy and proud to call friends. Y'all know who you are and what you did and I have the receipts.

Eh. We made it home alive.

FOLLOW OLIVIA

Follow me to catch my latest releases at:

Newsletter:
https://oliviamichaelsromance.com/

Amazon:
https://www.amazon.com/author/oliviamichaelsromance

BookBub:
https://www.bookbub.com/authors/olivia-michaels

Facebook:
https://www.facebook.com/oliviamichaelsauthor

Instagram:
https://www.instagram.com/oliviamichaelsromance/

Want more? Come be one of Olivia's Lovelies on Facebook. I can always use another ARC reader or two...

https://www.facebook.com/groups/639545290309740/

ALSO BY OLIVIA MICHAELS

Watchdog Security Series

More Than Love

More Than Family

More Than Puppy Love: A Christmas Novella

More Than Paradise

More Than Thrills

More Than Words Can Say

More Than Beauty

More Than Rumors

More Than Secrets

Watchdog Security Series Box Set, Books 1-3

Watchdog Security Series Box Set, Books 4-6

Watchdog Security Series Box Set, Books 7-9

Watchdog Protectors

In Susan Stoker's Special Forces Operation Alpha

Protecting Harper

Protecting Brianna

Protecting Sylvie

Watchdog Mountain Division

Bear On The Mountain

Timberwolf On The Mountain

Lion on the Mountain

Blizzard on the Mountain

Thunder on the Mountain

Avalanche on the Mountain

Free Mountain Division Short Story

Tell it to the Bees – A Bear and Ellie Short Story

ABOUT THE AUTHOR

Olivia Michaels is a life-long reader, dog-lover, gardener, and a certified beachaholic. When she's not throwing a Frisbee for her fur-baby, harvesting tomatoes, or writing, you can find her playing in the surf, kayaking, or kicking back on the sand and cracking open a romantic beach read.